FOUL
MATTER

Richard Jury Novels

The Man with a Load of Mischief
The Old Fox Deceived
The Anodyne Necklace
The Dirty Duck
Jerusalem Inn
Help the Poor Struggler
The Deer Leap
I Am the Only Running Footman
The Five Bells and Bladebone
The Old Silent
The Old Contemptibles
The Horse You Came in On
Rainbow's End
The Case Has Altered
The Stargazey
The Lamorna Wink
The Blue Last
The Grave Maurice

Other Works by Martha Grimes

The End of the Pier
Hotel Paradise
Biting the Moon
A Train Now Departing
Cold Flat Junction

Poetry

Send Bygraves

MARTHA GRIMES

FOUL MATTER

VIKING

VIKING

Published by the Penguin Group
Penguin Group (USA) Inc., 375 Hudson Street,
New York, New York 10014, U.S.A.
Penguin Books Ltd, 80 Strand,
London WC2R 0RL, England
Penguin Books Australia Ltd, 250 Camberwell Road, Camberwell,
Victoria 3124, Australia
Penguin Books Canada Ltd, 10 Alcorn Avenue,
Toronto, Ontario, Canada M4V 3B2
Penguin Books India (P) Ltd, 11 Community Centre, Panchsheel Park,
New Delhi–110 017, India
Penguin Books (N.Z.) Ltd, Cnr Rosedale and Airborne Roads, Albany,
Auckland, New Zealand
Penguin Books (South Africa) (Pty) Ltd, 24 Sturdee Avenue,
Rosebank, Johannesburg 2196, South Africa

Penguin Books Ltd, Registered Offices:
80 Strand, London WC2R 0RL, England

First published in 2003 by Viking Penguin,
a member of Penguin Group (USA) Inc.

Grimes, Martha.
Foul matter / Martha Grimes.
ISBN 0-670-03259-X

Printed in the United States of America

To Kent,

who's been there,
but didn't do that.
(Bless him.)

No dark and evil story of the dead
Would leave you less pernicious or less fair—
Not even Lilith, with her famous hair;
And Lilith was the devil, I have read.

I cannot hate you, for I loved you then.
The woods were golden then. There was a road
Through beeches; and I said their smooth feet showed
Like yours. Truth must have heard me from afar,
For I shall never have to learn again
That yours are cloven as no beech's are.

—Edwin Arlington Robinson, "Another Dark Lady"

When I see birches bend to left and right
Across the line of straighter darker trees,
I like to think some boy's been swinging them.

—Robert Frost, "Birches"

"Have no attachments. Allow nothing to be in your life
that you cannot walk out on in thirty seconds flat
if you spot the heat around the corner."

—Robert De Niro, *Heat*

A FRIEND
OF LONG
STANDING

ONE

Paul Giverney aimed a paper airplane at the window of his small office ("off. bdrm 3" in the rental ad) and watched it nose-dive to the floor. The Giverneys' apartment was in the East Village, not quite as trendy as the Village itself. The rent was unbelievable, the agent a scam artist, but they loved the apartment, especially (for him) the "off. bdrm 3," which was the perfect size for bookshelves, desk, and computer, a couple of chairs, and with a window that looked out on leafy branches. Hannah was seven and loved the park. Molly was thirty-six and loved the Dean & DeLuca on the other side of it. Paul loved the hungover, brassy scene of the East Village foot soldiers who always appeared to be walking off a morning after, bits of metallic conversations stabbing backward as they passed in the cold air. People couldn't understand it about the Giverneys; they were extremely rich and yet chose to live in a rental in the East Village. Why didn't Central Park West beckon to them? Why didn't they succumb to the siren song of Sutton Place or the Dakota? Why? Because they didn't. Paul gave a lot of his money to charity, a good third of it. Another third to Dean & DeLuca, but they still managed on the million or two left.

The paper airplane was one of his lists of publishers, one he had stricken several names from. Publishers on the left side of the page, writers on the right side. The airplane he had fashioned was the long list. Now the lists before him were the short ones—five writers, four publishers. He struck one of the publishers off, two of the writers. Three publishers, three writers. What he was doing was matching them up.

"Are you still fooling with that list?" asked Molly, standing in the door and wearing an apron. She might be the only wife in Manhattan who wore aprons to cook. "Dinner's ready. Anyway, what's the problem? You know you don't like any of them, the publishers, except FSG, and you keep saying they wouldn't publish you. So you might as well keep on with your old one." She stood there with a wooden spoon in her hand, looking very much the cook. He always liked the props—and preps—apron and spoon—when she was only microwaving Dean and DeLuca.

He said, "Process of elimination."

"Of what? I mean elimination down to what?"

Well, she didn't know what he was doing, did she? All Molly thought was that Paul was trying to decide on his next publisher. If Molly knew, she'd give him one of those and-I-thought-I-knew-you looks. Paul shrugged, not knowing exactly how to answer.

She said, "You always say there's no difference, that there's not room enough to swing a cat in."

"Swing a cat in? I never used that metaphor. It doesn't even make sense, not in this instance. Maybe 'shake a stick at,' but not 'swing a cat in.' Surely."

"Just tack that list"—she pointed with the spoon—"up on the wall and throw darts. Come on. Hannah's famished."

Hannah was always 'famished.' It was her current favorite word.

"Just ten more minutes," he said.

"The food will be a ruin."

"Then I'll go to Dean and DeLuca and get us another ruin. Please."

"Okay. But I'll have to feed Hannah."

But Hannah was right behind her. Hannah said, "Just another minute, pul-*eze*" in such a copy of her father's tone, Paul wanted to laugh.

Molly sighed. "You, too?" She left.

Hannah produced another chapter of her book. She would ask him to read it before officially including it in the book. "Would you please read this?" she asked, solemnly. It was a grave request.

"Of course," said Paul, with a frown to match hers as he took the single page. This was chapter 99. Hannah had been writing this book for a year, ever since, at the age of six, she had gotten wind of her father's astonishing success. Now she was seven and even more determined to be nominated for an award. ("Either that National Book contest one or one of those others, I don't care which.")

Her book was titled *The Hunted Gardens*. Originally, Paul thought it must have been the "haunted" gardens and Hannah had simply made a spelling error. But she did refer to the gardens as "hunted" and he didn't know what she meant. Also, he pointed out to her that the gardens were oddly bereft of flowers. Why were there no flowers? That had given her pause for a moment. But only a moment. "It's winter," she'd smoothly said.

And there seemed to be a lot of dragons lately in this book, hunted by a curious person, the Dragonnier. (Perhaps the gardens were, then, really "hunted" rather than "haunted," but he still thought it was a Hannah error.) Now, all of this potential slaying was causing her anxiety. But more anxiety came from being afraid "somebody" might steal the idea. More than once she had probed her father about this, whether he ever thought of writing a book about dragons.

Solemnly, Hannah waited while Paul read the chapter. All the chapters were short. Even though this was chapter 99, the book itself was still only eighty-some pages long. Paul read that the Dragonnier "gave the dragon a good thrashing." Paul told her it was very good, but suggested that she supply a few more details about the "thrashing." You know, how the Dragonnier does it, for didn't she want her reader to actually see it in his mind?

Hannah lay her hand across her brow, thought for a moment, and said, "Okay, I've got it. He 'gave the dragon a good thrashing back and forth.'" Pleased with this, she turned and left.

She vanished from the doorway. Oh, for fuck's sake, he told himself, not everything has to be a life-or-death matter. He sighed and with one finger coaxed a book forward. It was the new book, the one that, along with its cover blowup, crowded Barnes & Noble's window. Another best-seller, another two plus mil. *Don't Go There,* the book was called. Despite the fact that its protagonist was not the mild-mannered, brilliant detective Paul had used before, and despite there being no murder, no gunplay, the book would still be stashed with the mysteries or thrillers. He studied the jacket. It was the jacket he had insisted upon in spite of the art department's hemorrhaging all sorts of objections, the main one being that its moody jacket—shades of gray edging into black, one retreating gray figure—couldn't be seen across a room. The chains didn't much like it, either. Barnes & Noble tried to shoot it down and would have done if his sales weren't stratospheric.

Paul's present and soon-to-be-past publisher, Queeg and Hyde, wasn't on the list because there were no writers there who would do in the situation Paul had dreamed up. He looked at the two lists on which he'd matched up four publishers with five writers. The publisher he really was dying to choose was Mackenzie-Haack because of its snob appeal (unwarranted) and its venal, underhanded president, Bobby Mackenzie. What Paul was looking for in a publisher was one who would stop at nothing and if there was anyone who'd do whatever it took to get whatever he wanted, it was Bobby Mackenzie.

Two of the writers on the shortlist were published by Mackenzie-Haack: Barbara Breedlove and Ned Isaly. He crossed out one of the listed writers—Saul Prouil, who was no longer under contract to Colan Meilly, so the plan wouldn't work. Also, Saul Prouil was rich; family money, certainly not from royalties. He was just a superb writer who'd won the National Book Award, the Pen/ Faulkner, the Critics' Circle, and several smaller ones.

Back to his other two writers: Breedlove and Isaly. Paul had met both at a Mackenzie-Haack cocktail party to launch a first book— "debut novel" (a phrase that made Paul want to retch)—by a twenty-year-old writer named Mory or Murray-somebody. Paul did not go to publication parties, but he did to this one, following the inception of his little plan. Barbara Breedlove was a good writer, though not as good as she thought she was. She was also too full of herself, too much a networking writer, too much a summer conference person, turning up at Bread Loaf or one of the others, too much a scene player and much too much a snob about genre fiction. A conversation with her had been like sitting on the down side of a child's slide. She was the one up in the air.

He needed a writer of a certain kind, one who didn't really think about the arena of publishing. Not that this writer didn't want to be published, but that he didn't *think* about it. Ned Isaly had been short-listed for the Pen/Faulkner for his last book and therefore had a certain amount of cachet. Power. But not nearly the power of Paul Giverney. Paul knew that Isaly was a much better writer than he himself, but the quality of writing had little to do with the plan.

What Paul needed was hard to find: a pure writer.

* * * * *

"How long have you been with Mackenzie-Haack?"

This conversation had taken place at the Mackenzie-Haack cocktail party for Mory or Murray. Both he and Ned Isaly had stranded themselves like a couple of frogs on a lily pad (Ned's metaphor) while the social scene swam around them.

Ned frowned slightly at the question, as if he really had to dredge up the answer. "Two books ago, so I guess seven, eight years." He was carrying a brown leather case, which he shifted from one arm to another as he looked for a place to put his empty glass.

"A book every three or four years?"

"That's about right. I'm pretty slow."

"Slow? Flaubert was slow—if that's even a meaningful word."

"By comparison—"

"You don't want to make that comparison," said Paul. Ned smiled. Paul went on: "So, what do you think of Mackenzie-Haack?"

"Oh. I guess they're all right."

"Do you think they publish your books well?"

Ned frowned again, mining for answers. "To tell the truth, I don't pay much attention to that end of things."

"Your agent takes care of that?"

Ned shook his head. "I don't have one, actually. I don't much care for agents."

"I couldn't agree more. But you must have someone to intercede, somebody who yells when they want to print your book backward or make it a pop-up. Things like that."

Ned laughed. "Well there's my editor."

Paul feigned astonishment. "You mean you've got an editor who actually looks out for you?"

"Tom Kidd."

Paul felt a stirring of envy that he hadn't felt since fifteen years ago when a friend had landed a publisher while Paul's own first book was still hanging out in the slush of unsolicited manuscripts. Christ, he thought, just try that today. "The fabled Tom Kidd." One of a few—a very few—who actually edited and would turn a script over to a copy editor only after he and the writer had decided it was all right. "The bane of all copy editors. I've heard he even does line editing."

"He does."

A waiter passed with more flutes of champagne. They exchanged their empty glasses for fresh ones.

"Do you think Mackenzie-Haack is better than, say, oh, I don't know, Delacroix?" This was a small house known for literature of the highest standard. But it was in the process of being taken over by a Dutch conglomerate.

"I don't know," said Ned. "I haven't really had much experience with different publishers. My first book was with Downtown. Then I went to Mackenzie."

Downtown had tried too damned hard to be elitist and had folded barely a year after it had opened. They'd hardly had time to get Ned Isaly's book through production. But it had gotten a lot of good critical attention and that, in turn, had brought several publishers to his doorstep.

"Twelve years ago, that was published." Ned moved the leather case again, from one side to another, where he clamped it under his arm.

"You know, even twelve years ago it was possible to send in an unsolicited manuscript. Try that today and you might as well try to fly a pig over the transom. What's in that case you're guarding?"

"Oh, this? Part of a manuscript."

"You've brought it here to shop around? You've sure got enough book people here to make it worth your while."

Ned smiled. "No. Not likely." He didn't explain. He said, "The only time I think about publishing is in wondering what it must have been like fifty, sixty years ago. But, then"—he shrugged—"I like to imagine what *everything* was like sixty years ago."

"You don't really—"

"Don't what?"

Paul hesitated. *Care,* he'd been going to say, but that was the wrong word. "I was going to say—if you were to find yourself minus a publisher, how would that affect your writing?"

Ned frowned. "Should it?"

Should it? Jesus Christ, *here* was a writer to give one pause. "If that book"—Paul tipped his glass toward the leather case—"wasn't to be published, how would you feel about it?"

"This book?" Ned looked down at the case.

"Yes. Would you keep on with it?"

Ned appeared genuinely puzzled. It made Paul smile inwardly, the way Ned was regarding him, as if he, Paul, were a man of stunted intellectual power and limited imagination. "Of course. Wouldn't you? Anyway, publishers come and go."

Paul thought Ned Isaly didn't give a damn. It was as if he were turning up occasionally in life—as he'd turned up at this party—just to be polite.

*　*　*　*　*

Paul sat in his office now looking down at the shortlists and remembering that conversation. He crossed the other publishers and the other two writers off the lists. He was left with *Ned Isaly. Mackenzie-Haack.*

Over the sushi, Molly asked, "Did you ever decide on a publisher?"

"Yep. Mackenzie-Haack."

"That's the best one?"

"No. It's the worst." Paul grinned and went on eating his sushi.

T W O

There was a small park not far from Saul's house, nearly always empty of people except for a tramp and his dog, a soulful-looking pair to whom Saul always gave something (a surprisingly large something), which probably accounted for their not going farther afield. The dog (an old golden retriever that looked purebred) always sat up and pounded his tail against the grass when he saw Saul coming.

Saul liked this park, the sheer emptiness of it, as if he and his friends (and the tramp and dog) were the only ones who knew it was here. It was unaccountable, for in Manhattan, any green space was immediately overrun by people. Yet the only others he saw here were Ned and Sally. Ned's apartment building and Ned's apartment faced it, and occasionally, Saul could look up from his bench and see Ned waving. The three of them—if he counted the tramp, the four of them—sometimes used this park as a meeting place.

The tramp had little to say, but what he did say he said cogently: "I'm a tramp, not one of your 'homeless.'" He seemed almost proud of this calling a spade a spade. He also seemed proud to be one of a dying breed and not this yuppie-invented one. But, ordinarily, the tramp said not a word, just nodded his thanks to Saul. The dog did more talking with his tail than his owner did with his mouth.

When the three of them were here—that is, Saul, Ned, and Sally—the tramp would move closer, listening but never speaking, never interrupting. He was keeping what seemed to be a "respectful distance," with his head down and his hands working a section of rope, taking in the conversation. The dog would listen, too. He'd lie down and put his head on his paws and watch them carefully in case they might say something about him. At least, Saul liked to think of the dog that way.

He stopped on one of the gravel paths that crisscrossed the park and put his hand against the bark of an oak. Every so often, he felt compelled to carve tiny initials in the trees. He did not understand this. There were tiny *SP*s all over Chelsea. He walked around this tree trunk, looking it over for other initials, not wanting the oak to take too heavy a hit.

Every year, he sent the park service an anonymous contribution of two or three thousand to make restitution for the trees. He hoped the trees could take it. If they had the constitution of writers, they could.

It wasn't as if Saul were giving them bad reviews.

THREE

Clive Esterhaus drew the back of his tie through the knot, pulled it down, pushed the knot up, and straightened it. He looked at himself, still with chin lifted and turned slightly to the right to check on the tautness of the neck. He gave the flesh under the chin a few quick pats. He considered himself in the mirror: gray-on-gray silk tie, subtly striped gray worsted suit that had cost him fifteen hundred, white shirt (always the best choice). Everything muted and bespeaking a senior editor who pulls the strings quietly behind the scenes.

He was sure he was on his way to being associate publisher or vice president. Bobby Mackenzie had said as much. Bobby had been on his third whiskey when he'd said it, of course, but Bobby didn't forget. Bobby *never* forgot; his memory for conversations, incidents, names, places, all of these details was legendary. What Clive had to worry about was whether Bobby would keep his word. Sometimes he did, sometimes he didn't. He'd just look at the person confronting him with past promises and say, levelly, *I changed my mind, didn't I?* or he'd simply give the person one of his cold looks, freeze him where he stood.

In this case, though, Clive thought it was a promise Bobby would keep because there was no reason not to. The titles meant little but looked good, and the hike in salary made up for the impotence of the new title. Not that Clive was plagued by feelings of impotence, not today, certainly. Especially not today. He had invited two people to lunch, two counterparts from other houses. He had told them Mackenzie-Haack (modestly deferring to the house itself, though he was the one responsible) was celebrating signing up a new author. He had not told them who; they would have at least some reason to believe it was Paul Giverney, since he was the author all of them were trying to snare. Clive's fantasy delighted in their insincere smiles dissolving and hardening into something quite different.

What if he were precipitate, though? There was still Giverney's mysterious "condition" that had to be met before he'd sign. What it could be, Clive had no idea. Certainly not more money; they were offering him $7.5 million for two books. This was easily as big an advance as they'd paid out to Dwight Staines (the leading execrable horror writer in the country). Both of them, Staines and Giverney, sold in the millions. The house wouldn't earn it all back, but what Mackenzie-Haack was buying was the cachet of publishing Giverney. That in itself was money in the bank. Giverney was one of the few best-selling authors who could actually write ("an oxymoron" Tom Kidd called it).

Paul Giverney had cut loose from Queeg and Hyde (his present publisher) and had been in a state of what the sports world called "free agency." Every publisher in New York was trying to get him under contract, but Giverney's agent was playing his cards close to his vest. He'd passed the word around that Paul was "taking a breather" and didn't really want to discuss business.

The hell he didn't. Giverney was simply waiting for the publishers to raise the ante. Which publisher Giverney would go with was the one offering the most money and a lot of sweeteners. But Clive was too smart merely to wait, hands folded on his desk. He began to turn up at places Giverney frequented, which, actually, were few. The man always seemed to be in Dean & DeLuca or a kid's store just off Fifth. Still, it had paid off, or something had. It had happened almost overnight. Mortimer Durban (the agent) had called Bobby Mackenzie to tell him Paul was ready to sign a two-book contract with Mackenzie-Haack.

And Clive assumed he would be Giverney's editor. An easy assignment since Giverney didn't need much editing. That was fortunate, since Clive had pretty much forgotten how.

His intercom buzzed with its irritating fly-diving sound and his assistant, Amy, said, "Mr. Giverney is here to see you."

Clive rose and extended his hand to Paul Giverney. He smiled warmly, imagining this writer's stroll past offices with open doors and through the honeycomb of assistants' cubicles. He'd already have created a stir. It wouldn't take the people who recognized him long to get the word out. Or perhaps they all recognized him from his book jackets or the *Times* art section or even television. The publicity and promotion departments adored him. It meant that they could spend money hand over fist because Bobby Mackenzie would want it that way. It was one of publishing's mysteries: those writers who didn't need publicity or promotion would get it in awesome quantities; those poor stand-alone books that could hardly survive without a little promotion had to do without.

Giverney took his hand and Clive was a little surprised by the hardness of the handshake, as if the writer were only just resisting splintering the small bones. He was also surprised by the suit—definitely off the rack and not a top-of-the-line rack, either, such as Façonnable's or Ferragamo's.

"Delighted to see you, Paul." Clive waved him into a chair.

"Save your delight." The smile didn't leave Giverney's mouth, but something distinctly unsmiling had crept into his voice.

Clive straightened the knot of his tie, silently cursed himself, lowered his hand, said, "I can't imagine any condition you'd set that we'd be unwilling to meet. More money? Different scale of pay-outs? *Both* of Barnes and Noble's windows?" He leaned back in his swivel chair as Giverney returned a smile, but not Clive's smile; the smile was returned to the ether. Writers like Paul Giverney commanded huge advances and had a good deal of power. These were the writers whom foreign conglomerates understood. The men at the top didn't know books, but they did know money, and money drove publishing just as it did everything else. Literary quality had little to do with it.

"I'm not worried about B and N's window or front-of-store placement. I'm sure your guys in promotion will take care of that."

Was there, wondered Clive, a tinge of irony there? Was he being a little tongue in cheek? The "guys in promotion" at Mackenzie-Haack were notorious for fuckups, such as getting writers on wrong trains, switching tour stops, and so forth. "I really wanted Anne Law to be here—she's head of promotion, you know—"

"Oh, please."

Clive raised his eyebrows. "I'm sorry?"

"I know Anne Law. She couldn't promote a case of Macallan to Bobby Mackenzie."

Clive had no rejoinder to this; he thought Anne Law was incompetent, too. Why was Giverney fixing him with that unswerving stare?

"You want to know the condition."

"Yes, of course, we—"

"You publish Ned Isaly, right?"

Clive was baffled. What in hell did Ned Isaly have to do with it? He asked the question aloud, or started to: "What's Ned Isaly—?"

Giverney stepped on the question. "Everything. Did you think I chose Mackenzie-Haack because it's the best 'home' for my books? Hardly. We'd probably get along because you're as arrogant as I am." His smile said no one but a fool could believe Mackenzie-Haack the best publisher. Then he said, "It's because you publish Ned Isaly. Isn't Tom Kidd his editor?"

Clive was extremely confused. Why on earth would Giverney—one of the most commercial writers around—why would he want to align himself with Isaly, one of the best writers, the least commercial, to say nothing of Tom Kidd, whose writers were as literary as writers could get. "I just don't see—"

"What I'm driving at? No reason you should. My condition is that you drop Ned Isaly." Giverney leaned forward, feigning the utterance of a confidence. "Then I'll sign a *three*-book contract instead of two. Come on, don't look so speechless."

Clive had opened and closed his mouth a couple of times. He tried an abrupt laugh and a head shake, stalling. Was Giverney kidding? Or was he crazy? Yet he sat there on the other side of the desk looking quite sane. "Paul, I'm sorry, but I don't understand all of this—"

"You don't have to. Just drop him, dump him, whatever. Mind if I smoke?" He had his cigarettes out, a pack of Marlboro Lights, offered the pack to Clive.

Clive almost took one. He didn't even smoke. "You're serious?"

Giverney didn't seem to think that warranted an answer. He lit his cigarette, sat smoking awhile.

"Assuming, just *assuming* we *would* do this, I don't see how we *could*. The man's under contract for his next book. We can't just tear it up."

"Why are you hiding behind the legality of a contract? Because it suits you; it suits you now. When I walk out the door, it won't suit you. There are ways, there are means. This isn't Chrysler we're talking about; this isn't Microsoft. This is publishing. You guys can always find ways and means."

"Such as?"

"Well, Christ's sake, try not to be completely stupid. You and Bobby can come up with the ways and means. Just find something in the contract. They're all written to favor the publisher, not the author. And what I heard is Ned Isaly doesn't even have an agent."

"He doesn't, no. He doesn't need one, he says."

Giverney laughed. "Nobody really *needs* one. It's like being mobbed up; it's like paying protection money." Giverney leaned forward. "Listen to me: if Mackenzie-Haack wanted to drop a writer, you'd find a way."

"May I ask why you want to see Ned dropped?"

"No."

As he had done several times during this encounter, Clive ran his hand through his hair, shook his head. "Honestly, Paul, I just don't think I can do that."

Paul Giverney held up both hands, palms out. "Okay, I'll take the books to some other house." He rose, smiled. "But I think you're being a little precipitate about refusing without even giving the deal any thought. Do you know what Ned Isaly's sales figures are?"

Clive could feel the flush burning his face. "Of course I do."

"And mine? Of course you do. To say nothing about your own career—right? Getting me to Mackenzie-Haack would hardly be a blemish on it."

Dumbly, Clive nodded. He simply could not let Giverney slip from his grasp; signing Paul Giverney meant too much for his career. He said, as if this might save him, or at least buy him time: "Tom Kidd wouldn't stand for it; he's Ned's editor and he'd probably resign." Probably? To a certainty. Clive knew what Tom was like.

Paul pursed his mouth, reflecting. "*That* would be bad. He's one of the three editors in town who know what editing means—"

Clive wondered who the other two were.

"—and I want him for my books."

"*Yours?*" Oh, Christ, thought Clive. It gets worse and worse. Anyway, he shouldn't sound so astonished by the notion of Tom Kidd's editing Giverney's books. "I assumed I was going to edit—"

It was Paul who laughed. "You? Oh, come on, Clive. You're an acquisitions guy. I'll bet you haven't edited anything in years."

"You don't really need a line editor, Paul." What good was this flattery doing? Even if they could dump Ned Isaly, Kidd would scream the house down. He loved Ned Isaly's stuff. Clive tried to regain a little ground. He leaned forward, gave Paul his best smile. "Look, Paul, we've got no clause we can invoke to break this contract, which is, incidentally, for only one more book." Clive was sure he was on the right track now. "One book. *Then* of course we don't have to offer another contract. Tom Kidd wouldn't like that, either, but we'd have a dozen reasons for refusing to sign Ned again. I know Bobby would be perfectly okay with that, and—"

"You're not hearing me, Clive. I'm not asking what Bobby would be okay with. I'm not negotiating."

Christ. Clive took it from another angle. "Ned would find another publisher with no problem—"

Paul shrugged. "Not if you did it right."

"Right? What on earth do you mean? Are we also supposed to see he gets blackballed by every other publisher in New York?" Clive fell back in his chair.

Paul shrugged again, smiled. "Well, that part of it we'll see when we get there." He stood up, checked his watch. "I'm doing lunch with my agent. He's all in favor of the move, thinks he'll get another sack of gold. Frankly, I don't really care about the money. There'll be no quarrel about that, though I'm sure Mort will haggle to get you to throw in the Chrysler Building. Let me know and you'd better not moon over this for a year. I don't sign the contract until you drop Ned Isaly, that's all. But I'm reasonable, I'll give you guys enough time, you being a publisher and publishers having such a weird view of time." Giverney sketched a salute and made for the door.

Clive was on his feet. "Paul—"

Paul was gone.

FOUR

Ned set the coffee on the flat part of the drawing table and lit another cigarette, looking at it, at the burning tip of it. He'd stopped smoking, hadn't he? Why was there a lighted cigarette in his hand? He stubbed it out in the small metal tray he used for paper clips. He had tossed out all of the ashtrays. A bottle of ink, two sharpened pencils, two fountain pens, notebook. Every morning he arranged this little hoard and every afternoon filled the pen and resharpened the pencils. He always wrote first with a pen; ink could make weaknesses stare you down that a cursor barely glanced at.

Paris. The Jardin des Plantes. Nathalie spent nearly all of her time either here or in the Luxembourg Gardens; she favored gardens. She had a lot of time on her hands, and she seemed to spend most of it in waiting. A cloud of birds lifted from the fountain in the center of the Jardin des Plantes, blown away by the morning breeze.

Nathalie—

Like the flighting birds, Ned's thoughts lifted from the gardens and darted everywhere but the Jardin des Plantes: to Sally and her acrobatic lunge one day to capture his blown-away manuscript page; to Tom Kidd—what was he doing right now? Sitting at his desk, behind his towers of books, editing a manuscript?

He could go to the kitchen—it was only four steps away, for God's sakes—and make a cup of coffee. No. He could make the coffee after he'd figured out what was happening to Nathalie at this moment, while she sat on a bench by herself in the dusty and somewhat decrepit gardens. (There was a tiny ragged zoo there. Nothing terribly interesting, an afterthought of a zoo. She had wandered around it sometimes.)

No to the coffee. The bigger time increments—what writing he had to do before lunch or by dinnertime—were peppered with tinier ones, such as *in twenty more minutes* or *after the scene in the Jardin des Plantes*. Only in this way could he get through the day's writing, by making small bargains with himself. It made surprisingly little difference that he was at the end of the book, rather than at the beginning. Every writing day was like the beginning; it was as if he'd never written a word in his life until that moment and didn't know how the hell to go about it.

In the Jardin des Plantes, Nathalie—

She could walk around to the zoo, but that didn't seem to fit her mood. Mood? Nathalie was always the victim of mood, of time, of place. Ned inspected his two pencils to see if the points were sharp. He used the pencils for making changes, for adding words above lines or in the margins. Was his pen running out of ink? He'd hardly written a dozen words, how could it be out?

In the Jardin des Plantes, Nathalie's face—no—Nathalie's pale face lifted to the birds . . .

Yes, he liked that phrase as he wrote it; he was pleased with it. That was before he recognized it was W. H. Auden's: ". . . pale, no— *child's* hands lifted to the birds." He had always liked that poem, the sadness of it. ". . . of hands across the tablecloth . . ." Lines like that never failed to knife him in the gut. Auden's poem was heavy with nostalgia.

Nathalie. *There would be, there would be—*

He put his head in his hands. How had he ever written his other two books? Of this one he had written 402 pages and still found himself in that same state of nervous suspension as he'd been in when he'd started. Why would anyone in his right mind choose this as his work when there were hundreds of people out there who were better at it? Saul, to name just one. There were thousands who were worse, of course, but that was no consolation.

Nathalie sat on a little iron bench in the Jardin des Plantes. If it had them. If there were little iron benches in the Jardin des Plantes. Would that detail be in a guidebook? He doubted it. Here he'd been writing about Nathalie in the Jardin des Plantes as if there were no tomorrow and now it was tomorrow. Would he have to go to Paris? He hated to travel.

He looked at the neatly stacked pages. The pages reproached him. Each one had burning eyes that watched him sink into his talentless bog of uncertainty and not one page would lift a finger. Not one.

Not one single page. Just like them, he thought, *just like a bunch of already written pages, thinking they had nothing else to do but relax and sit there. This was after all the care, all the trouble . . .*

From her black iron bench in the gardens, Nathalie watched the wrens wheel above the fountain, thinking, There is no telling, no telling at all.

Ned got up and went the four steps to the kitchen counter to make a pot of coffee. While he was measuring grains into the filter, he thought of Hemingway in the Brasserie Lipp on the Boulevard St.-Germain, which was not far from the Luxembourg Gardens. Nathalie spent some of her time in the Boulevard St.-Germain. He must stop being flippant about Nathalie's plight. He was really concerned about her. It would all end badly; it had to, given the direction in which she was going. These affairs always did. He thought about this as he poured water into the well of the coffeemaker. He measured out coffee.

Nathalie looked across the wide gravel path at the little metal tables where old men sometimes sat and played chess but where now a tall man was sitting, writing. She wondered what he was writing, sitting with his elbow on his knee, his head propped in his hand, and a pipe in his mouth. A letter? A book?

Ned stared out of the window above the small kitchen counter, scarcely aware that it was dusk and the magnificent crown of the Chrysler Building was lighting up. Wispy layers of pink and blue and a bottom of molten gold. What he was making of this mise-en-scène was the little park below his window turned into the Jardin des Plantes or the Luxembourg Gardens (depending on which one Nathalie was sitting in). He remembered them from twenty years ago, the colors in the borders of flowers melting into one another, fusing with the grass and the walks. Sixty years ago, Hemingway was here, and Joyce and Gertrude Stein, whose lives Nathalie's own would never touch, and yet be touched by, as if the air she breathed had drifted toward her from the places inhabited by these wondrous writers. He saw Nathalie below in the park, sitting on one of the benches. She was as still as a statue, thinking.

Across the path, a man, real or imagined, rose from one of the benches.

Patric's other life. They did not talk about it; she was afraid to know about it, yet also afraid not to. Not knowing canceled out that part of his life; if she knew about his separate world she would be able to imagine it—his wife, his children and what they were like. It would expose that other side of his world that was now left safely in darkness, like one of those lamps with a turning cylinder one sometimes sees in a child's bedroom that illuminates cut-out figures in the turning shade. Now, the cylinder didn't turn and the other side of the shade lay in darkness.

And it was, of course, much more than half his life, for she saw him only on Thursday afternoons and sometimes Tuesdays as well. Looked at one way she felt grateful, for there was regularity in their meetings. She could depend on Thursdays. But then it was difficult to ignore the weekend that followed. She reminded herself that it could be much worse; it could be a constant shuttling around among days and times so that she couldn't enjoy the exhilaration of a day or even two preceding Patric's arrival in the gardens—the Jardin des Plantes or the Tuileries or the Luxembourg Gardens—places where she spent much of her time even when he was not with her because in these places she could think of his sitting or walking beside her—

And the cafés—

Ned stopped writing. The cafés. He took up his pen again.

Most of the ones they liked were on the Boulevard St.-Germain (the Brasserie Lipp, the Café de Flore) but sometimes they visited the Right Bank cafés when they'd been in the Tuileries. They would walk up the Rue de la Paix to the café of that name to look at Americans who had found this street that they'd heard of in that old wartime song about Mimi, Mimi on the Rue de la Paix. Patric liked Americans more than other foreigners because they were so much brighter, so much more enthusiastic, and, in Patric's words, "starry eyed."

Ned listened to the water hiccup, hiss, and burp its way through the Braun system. "Starry eyed." Was that too much of a cliché, even for Patric? No, he was like that.

Paris, sixty years ago.

Here it came again, that revenant, that sack of shadows, the past, lighting up like the tops of Manhattan's skyscrapers, cascades of lights and colors, deceptive as a tinhorn fair. The past—there was hardly anything it wasn't, or couldn't be. It could aim straight as an arrow, or walk like a drunken lout, cavort, dissemble, deceive, seduce: anything to be let in. It could find him anytime, for he was always thinking about it in trying not to.

The man across the path had gone; the sky eased from dusk into darkness. The huge hulk of the past lumbered on.

Nathalie sat alone in the Jardin des Plantes.

He left her there, he felt, at his peril.

FIVE

That's his condition," said Clive. "That's it." He seemed to be trying to convince himself even more than he was trying to convince Bobby Mackenzie.

Bobby's office was not a reflection of Bobby himself; it had an almost cabin coziness brought on by the big, soft sofa against one wall, the upholstered chairs, a couple of Audubon-like paintings of birds in flight, a very good and very worn Karastan carpet, and a zillion books. But the thing that separated publishers from assistant editors in the pecking order was a view of Central Park that could be better seen only by one of those flighting birds.

Bobby snorted. "That's crazy."

Clive nodded. He usually did when he was talking to Bobby. So did everyone. "I said as much."

Bobby's eyebrows danced upward. "You told Giverney he was crazy? Good career move." Bobby wheeled his swivel chair over to the liquor cabinet, which was nearly within arm's reach. He grabbed up the bourbon and a couple of glasses and wheeled back again.

Now Clive snorted. "Not in so many words, of course not." Christ, he wished Bobby would stop connecting everything Clive did to the furtherance of or the setback to his "career." It was like blackmail. Why was he surprised? "I simply pointed out what would happen."

Bobby unscrewed the bottle with the finesse of a sleight-of-hand artist (which in many ways he was), raised one of the glasses in question to Clive, who nodded, and then poured a couple of fingers of bourbon into each glass. He sat back, rolled the glass between his hands across his chest as if to warm a frostbitten heart, and said, "Of *course* Tom would leave. Of *course* Ned would find another publisher. This is what would happen: Ned gets the heave-ho, Tom resigns, Ned waits to see what house Tom goes to, and then goes there himself. Giverney gains nothing—at least as far as we can see, Giverney being not only crazy but an egomaniac—and . . ." Bobby drank and shrugged. "Beats me."

"At least we'd get Giverney."

"Believe me, I intend to. But Isaly and Kidd, that's not all we'd lose. Tom Kidd has the four best writers in this house. You know what would happen; they'd all follow Tom. Tom would get his own imprint, deservedly so, no matter where he went, and in that imprint would be included four of the perhaps dozen honest-to-God writers we or anyone else has."

Clive sighed. He hadn't thought that far. Of course, Bobby was right. He usually was. Clive took another sip of the velvet bourbon and remembered he had a lunch date. He looked at his watch; he could still make it, but what on earth was the reason for it now? "To say nothing of there not being anything in that contract which would let us slide out smoothly."

Bobby was staring at some point over Clive's shoulder, deep in thought. He shook himself and said, "Oh, that's the least of it."

Least of it?

"Isn't the date for the delivery of his new book nearly up? He's got another couple weeks, from what I remember."

How in hell did Bobby remember all of these details? "I think you're right, yes. But, good God, we've never invoked that clause in the case of a writer as important as Ned."

"No, but we could. Or demand to see part of it and reject it. Though that wouldn't go down well either with Tom. There are a lot of ways I can get out of a contract, but none of them private and none of them without repercussions."

Clive thought for a moment. "And we haven't even mentioned the acrimony it would stir up in the publishing community."

"'Acrimony'? I don't think so. More like laughter. More like Mackenzie's loss of face, a lot worse. We're famous for publishing good books, literary books, not Giverney-style books. In the wake of getting him, we lose not one but four"—Bobby held up four fingers as if Clive couldn't count—"writers. To say nothing of the best editor we or anybody else has." Bobby shook his head and held out the palms of his hands as if to forestall an unbelievably evil image. "No, no."

"Then I'll tell him it's no dice. After all, we just signed Dwight Staines."

"Don't remind me." Bobby slugged back his drink.

Bobby hated that science fiction-horror writing genre, except for Stephen King. Oddly enough, though, Bobby wasn't a book snob; he'd read anything. And Dwight Staines, phenomenally popular, would have sales high enough to offset any triviality such as artistry.

Clive was considerably disappointed in throwing the Giverney contract to the winds. He wanted to be the editor who signed him up. What was he going to tell his luncheon companions now? "I'll tell Paul it's a nonstarter, then."

"A nonstarter? Did I say that?" Bobby unscrewed the bottle again.

"I certainly infer that's what you're saying; signing Paul Giverney wouldn't be worth losing Kidd, Isaly, Eric Gruber—" He stopped.

Bobby sat there, eyes closed, shaking his head. "No, Clive, what I said was breaking the contract wouldn't do it."

"I must be dense."

Bobby leaned way back in his ergonomically designed chair. "Think about it, Clive."

Clive frowned. He felt the onset of a migraine. "I don't—"

Bobby sighed. "You remember that Bransoni snitch? We did his book—probably got his dog to write it—a couple years ago."

"Sure. Danny Zito. Actually, he did write it himself."

Bobby tossed back the rest of his bourbon. "Believe that, you'll believe anything."

Clive smiled. "No, I'm telling you. *Fallguy.* It sold much better than we thought it would. Why?"

"Well, you could look him up."

" 'Look him up?' " Clive gave a laugh that turned into a choke. "Zito's been in the witness protection program ever since the trial. You know the way they do that. Change of name, change of home, change of everything; buried so deep he couldn't find his own ass." So what in hell was Bobby doing, bringing up Danny Zito?

"Come on, all you have to do is put it out that we want another book from Zito. You can find anybody that way. If you were lost in an African jungle and said, 'I've got a book contract here,' half a dozen people would pop out of the bush to sign it. Wiesenthal should have come to us when he wanted to find Himmler. Make it known a publisher wants a book out of someone and suddenly"— Bobby rat-tat-tatted on his desk with his hands—"you've got them on the phone or the doorstep. Magic."

Clive rose, walked around the desk to peer out of the window, down at Central Park. Yellow cabs beetled along so slowly it was hard to believe these were the same death traps he took every morning and evening. He turned, brows knotted. Magic maybe, but why? "Are you suggesting what I think you're suggesting?"

"And what would that be?"

Clive stared at the ceiling, doing a sort of little half-turn dance step as if this might shake off what could only be a bad dream.

SIX

The only thing Clive could do at lunch was to be mysterious. He had made the foolhardy gesture of insisting the meal be "on him" and "on him" at one of the more expensive restaurants in Manhattan. He had wanted so much to enjoy the sheer delight he could take in gloating. Now, of course, he had nothing to gloat about. Lunch would be a trial.

His two companions were well-established editors at two other publishing houses. Nancy Otis was at Grunge. She was almost unfailingly right in the projects she signed on, purely on the basis of a skimpy outline, but more often nothing but the naked and unembellished "idea." ("For God's sakes, if you've got Tom Cruise saving the lives of an entire Nepalese village, do you have to see a fucking manuscript?") Rarely, rarely was she wrong. But there had been those rare occasions, and Clive had basked in one or two of them.

Bill Mnemic's success was in getting his nose in other publishers' bags of oats and then leading off their prize horses in what he called "a moonlight flit." Bill was British; he was at DreckSneed

(Sneed having been the once venerable British publishing house, now part of American Dreck, Inc.).

Both of them (especially Bill, for raiding another house's writers was his specialty) had put everything on hold when they'd heard about Paul Giverney's wanting to make a move away from Queeg and Hyde, his publisher for the last decade. It started out as gossip and, as was generally the case in publishing, had not risen into verifiable fact, probably wouldn't, until the deed was done. Folks in publishing rather preferred it that way; it led to much more interesting huddles over lunch. The three of them had, in a sense, "grown up" together in publishing. Nancy had been in the publicity department of Hathaway and Walker, long since embalmed and raised to life again by the Dracula of foreign conglomerates, Bludenraven; Bill had started out in marketing, at which he was brilliant; Clive had always been in editorial, had started out as an editor's assistant. That was twenty-five years ago and the three of them had risen on the corporate ladder almost nose to nose. A competitive spirit was hard to avoid, then, and it had been at first a friendly one. But as the stakes got bigger and publishers were shelling out higher and higher advances to less and less deserving writers (nonwriters, most of them), the spirit had changed. Changed slowly, but changed. It became harder to conceal (and it had to be concealed) spite, rancor, enmity. But these three were good at such concealment.

There were times when his memory turned to the lunches of twenty years ago, then held in whatever deli was nearby, and he felt threatened by sadness, a great wave coming over him that he barely managed to outrun before it crashed on an empty shore. Feelings like that were bothersome, and he didn't really understand them.

The waiter had come and taken their order for wine and food. All three of them always ate the same thing. Today, Nancy came down hard on the grilled swordfish, and, after wading around through the monkfish baked with ginger and the steak and shiitake mushrooms, both Clive and Bill had said, yes, they'd have the swordfish, too. They did not do this because they were so closely bound in temperament that they were bound in taste; no, each was afraid that a dish would be brought which was obviously superior to the ones the others had ordered. It was simpler to get the same thing.

"Come on, Clive," said Nancy, leaning toward him until her bosom nearly flattened on the table. "What?"

Over the years the three of them had grown as cagey and mono-syllabic as illegal aliens.

Bill gave him a razor smile and said, "Yeah. What've you got?"

Well, Clive hadn't got anything, had he?

Both Bill and Nancy had X-ray vision and mirror eyes good enough for a *Village of the Damned* remake. Because of that, Clive might have believed they could see straight through him had he not known their vision was clouded by their own predilection for sham and subterfuge. So, having nothing at all, he resorted to a wide-eyed innocence designed to pique their curiosity even more about the coup they thought he must have brought off.

His shrug was elaborate. "I haven't got anything."

Nancy put on her disbelieving face, turned sideways in her chair, and shook her head at this witless attempt to convince her.

"Yeah, right," Bill said.

The three of them had never actually discussed Paul Giverney. Had never so much as mentioned it over the telephone, because none of them had wanted the others to think he or she was working ropes and pulleys like holy hell behind the claptrap scenes of their dusty stages, trying to grab Giverney's agent's ear, hurling more and more outlandish offers. Clive knew he was right in assuming their offers had been intoxicating. But Bobby Mackenzie's had been so far off the charts Giverney's agent could easily retire on the commission. Never have to return another call in his life, he wouldn't. It was just the sort of advance that would bring the publishing industry to its knees, eventually. Monster advances of the kind being offered would never be earned out.

This, too, thought Clive, was sad. But, again, he wasn't wearing this fifteen-hundred-dollar silk suit by virtue of adhering to the Tom Kidd publishing virtues.

"Lunch, for God's sakes," answered Clive, affecting a laugh insincere enough to prove it must be otherwise. "We haven't had lunch since—" He bethought himself.

Nancy answered: "Since I signed Tasha Gorky for a one-mil advance on spec."

That was walking right into a trap she should have foreseen, being Nancy. She must be desperate.

Clive smiled. "As I recall, Nancy, the spec turned out to be one purely ghosted outline with the ghost departing into the ether."

Tasha didn't have any ideas, much less could she write. Tasha's writing expertise extended to autographing tennis balls.

Nancy's preeminent trait was her ability to stonewall anybody. "Yes, why're you surprised? It was obvious I was taking a big chance. But like I always say, no pain, no gain." (The only thing she got out of her occasional bouts with AA were the aphorisms.)

Of course, she was managing to turn things around to make her editorial errors look like brave risks. They were off the subject of the reason for the lunch. But Clive knew well enough they'd be right back on it at any second. They were too sharp to be taken in by his we-haven't-seen-one-another-lately gambit. Too sharp and too envious. Too much like him, in other words.

Did he dare? He cut off a bite of swordfish with surgical precision. Given Bobby Mackenzie's determination to sign Giverney, wasn't it already a foregone conclusion that they'd get him? If by some chance they didn't, surely he'd be able to cover himself. So he dropped it right in the middle of talk about Tasha: "We're signing Paul Giverney for two books. That's what we're celebrating."

They seemed to turn to stone right before his eyes. He thought about Lot's wife . . . but, no, that was a pillar of salt, wasn't it? Their mouths looked as thin as fissures in rock. He wanted to chortle out loud, but constrained himself. He had bested them, no doubt of it—grabbed the gold ring, kicked the ball into the end zone, gone for broke, and hit the jackpot.

But it was rather a thin payoff. They both recouped, stone turning back to flesh, and congratulated him and began the process of pretending they hadn't lusted after the same writer.

"Naturally," said Bill, "we considered Giverney—"

Didn't you just! Clive wanted to yell.

"—but his agent—what's his name?"

As if he didn't have it carved in blood on his wrist!

"Mort Durban." Apoplectic Mortimer, the agent's agent.

"Ah, yes. Anyway, he was demanding so much we knew the advance would never earn out. We'd lose a helluva lot. But Bobby Mackenzie can probably afford to carry the loss. He's got millions to throw around." Bill flashed a smile.

As if, of course, Bobby was some spoiled kid who had no idea how to run a publishing house. Raging inwardly, Clive kept on smiling. "Lose? I guess our people must be using different figures. We're planning a one-million first printing."

Bill laughed. "With a fifty, sixty percent return?"

"Giverney's books never have that kind of return. Twenty-five at the most."

"Come on, Clive. Half those books'll come back, they always do. It gets worse every year; publishers just can't afford these humongous advances anymore—"

Oh, Christ! Bill was turning this to his advantage. Bill pontificating about publishing excess? The very man who'd tried to lure Rita Aristedes away from Mackenzie-Haack by brokering a Tuscan villa? (Rita was mad for everything Italian except their love of the earth and each other.) Clive just sat, swordfish forgotten, arms folded, featherweight smile on his face.

Nancy's turn: "Thing is, Mackenzie-Haack always had this absolutely fabulous list—I don't mind admitting I envy you (a supercilious smile meant to belie that envy)—until lately."

Clive had to respond to that, he couldn't help himself. " 'Lately'? Mackenzie's still got the best list of anybody in town."

"Better than Fritz Pearls?"

Fritz Pearls was the most literary of all of them. "Of course not." Clive grimaced as if surely it was clear F.P. outshone all of them. "Mackenzie's size, I mean."

Nancy went on: "You just signed on Dwight Staines. So you've got him, Rita Aristedes, and now Paul Giverney. I'd say"—she slugged back her half glass of wine—"you're getting as commercial as Disney." She smiled widely, showing her platform teeth.

Clive managed a hearty, false laugh. "Not much chance of that, Nancy girl. Not when we have writers like Eric Gruber or Ned Isaly. In addition to a dozen others."

Bill strode in again. "Yeah, but they're all midlist writers, except maybe Isaly. And he only turns one out every four, five years. You haven't got a Mailer or an Updike. You haven't got any literary heavy hitters."

"Saul Prouil." This was a lie, but Clive was getting used to it.

"What? Come on. You haven't got Prouil under contract. Hell, Saul Prouil hasn't published a book in a decade."

"No. But what he's working on is brilliant."

"Like, what's he working on?"

Clive laughed. "You know Saul. He doesn't like anyone talking about work in progress." God, why had he brought Saul Prouil up? He hadn't as much as said hello and good-bye to him in nine years. And he had never been the man's editor.

"Yeah? Maybe that's because he's not making any." Nancy was helping herself to the last of the wine.

This whole lunch was not going the way it was supposed to, damn it. They were supposed to cut open a vein and bleed jealousy all over the gardenia-white cloth. They were supposed to be humbled, supposed to see that in the long run, Clive was the most successful of the three of them, better, the best.

"Shit," said Bill, pulling himself sideways in his chair, blowing smoke from the cigarette he wasn't supposed to be smoking there. "You know what we are? Pimps, that's all." He inhaled again, his brows rammed together, looking angry.

This pretense of self-denigration might have fooled an outsider, but not Clive. Anyway, the denigrating was all for Clive, so that Bill could push Clive into pimpdom. One could hardly do that without generously including oneself. Clive slumped. He felt he had put himself in jeopardy for nothing. Hadn't he known that their face-saving techniques were every bit as good as his? He couldn't impress them; they were all unimpressible. It was rather a shock to think that.

And there was still the unsigned Giverney contract. Hell.

Without a care in the world for an expense account (as it wasn't theirs), Nancy and Bill ordered up a couple of Remys.

"Make it doubles," Bill called to the waiter's departing back. "Anyway, congrats, Clive. Good job. I'm glad I'm not going to have to take the heat, though, when Giverney doesn't earn out."

Clive mumbled a response.

"You know what one of Giverney's demands is going to be, don't you? He's going to want Tom Kidd as editor. You know that, don't you?"

Clive stared at him. How in hell did Bill know that? Well, he wasn't going to tell him he was right. "What makes you think that?"

Bill shrugged. "Makes sense, doesn't it? Giverney'd want the best. He's such an arrogant bastard." He had that stupid smile pasted back in place. "I'm only glad I don't have to be the one to tell Tom Kidd." He swiped at his knee with his hand, laughing. "I'm just glad I don't."

Nancy said, straight faced, at least at first, "Tom will just take out a gun and shoot you. Fancy that. Poor Clivey."

When Clive returned to his office after lunch, feeling deflated, he found a book lying in the center of his desk blotter. It was one that Mackenzie-Haack had published two years previously, *Fallguy*. This was the book Bobby had mentioned, the one by Danny Zito, who took a lot of heat for it, but would have taken more, and worse, had he not gone into the witness protection program right before the book had come out.

It had been one of Clive's books, though he'd told Bobby Mackenzie another editor, someone like Peter Genero, would do a much better job (meaning, the book was beneath Clive) and that Peter would get on a lot better with Danny Zito.

"Why? Because he's Italian? You mean, it takes one to know one?"

That had been Bobby's response. He'd told Clive that the book needed some toning up, some class, however superficial, and Clive was just the one to supply it.

Danny Zito had turned out to be a very down-to-earth (well, sure), entertaining guy. He was a hell of a conversationalist over pricey lunches (though Clive was always watching his back) and the book had done somewhat better than expected.

Clive sat down then with the book in his hands.

Why?

He got up and went to the door. His assistant, Amy Waters, was working on some copy. "Amy, where did this come from?" He held the book up. It had quite a handsome black-and-white jacket with an embossed silver title.

Amy squinted as if she couldn't see the four-inch-high *Fallguy* from a couple of feet away. "Maybe Bobby left it?" She went back to her copy.

"You put that as a question, Amy. The question is what I'm *asking* you, for God's sakes." Why did he bother saying that? Amy always put statements in the form of questions.

"Oh. What I mean is: Bobby was in your office before."

"But what did he say?"

"Nothing. Just walked in and walked out. He said, 'Hi, Amy,' but I wasn't paying much attention; I'm trying to get this copy ready for the catalog?"

Clive grunted and walked back into his office with the book, sat down, and stared at it.

Danny Zito?

SEVEN

Clive was still looking at *Fallguy,* thumbing through the book, about to pick up the phone—no, to go to Bobby's office to ask him what in the hell he'd left the book for. He was thinking this when Tom Kidd materialized in Clive's open doorway. "Materialized" was the right word for Tom had found a patch of darkness and it was difficult to make out his features, except for the tonsure of pale hair that, lit from behind, foamed around his head.

Tom was not one for telephone chat or a "Hey, got a minute?" approaches. Clive rarely saw him, and when he did it was usually in a sudden appearance, such as this. Rarely did he have an opportunity to talk with Tom; Clive certainly never made one. Tom was not one to stop by for an editorial chat; he fairly lived in his office, small but with a view that was magnificent, even by New York City standards. The view was meant to keep Tom happy. It was wasted on him; views of Manhattan didn't interest him, since he doubted the place changed much from day to day (he'd said). Tom had merely found the New York scenery a good backdrop for stacks and stacks of books.

Clive imagined that even when Tom's head came up from reading one of his manuscripts, he didn't really see, as on a winter's night, the lighting up of Fifth Avenue, all of the lamps in front of the Plaza pressing through amber fog, nor did he see the dark drapery of trees at this end of Central Park. He saw words. Tom would still be seeing the words of the manuscript in his mind—this sentence, this image, this transparent page superimposed upon the Plaza and the park— whose sentence? Whose image? Isaly's? Gruber's? Grace Packard's? describing the scene down there with such precision that the words seemed to melt into the fog and the trees and the snow and become it.

That, thought Clive, was what editors like Kidd saw. There weren't many of them. Thank God. Kidd always made Clive feel inadequate; he did this without even trying. All he had to do was appear in the damned doorway.

Clive would have to rally. "Tom!" he said, rising from his chair.

"Clive." Tom was lighting up one of his big cigars. They were quite vile. All of the flack on smoking seemed to have sailed right over Tom Kidd's head. "I just saw Tootsie Malone."

Agent for Clive's one good writer, Jennifer Schiffler. "Was she coming to see me? What'd she say?"

"I don't know. I couldn't read the balloon above her head."

Tom hated agents of all stripes and kidney except for Jimmy McKinney, one of Mort Durban's agents.

"I understand you're signing Paul Giverney."

Clive tried for hearty self-denigration, laughed, and said, "Trying like hell to."

"Why?" Tom had taken a step into the room and smoke billowed out behind him as he exhaled.

"Why?"

Tom nodded. "Why do we need another commercial writer? A new one seems to pop up every day. Now it's Giverney."

"Come on, now, Tom. You know every house in Manhattan is trying to get him."

Tom shrugged. "Again I ask, why?"

"Look, sit down, will you?"

"No, I've got to finish going over Mary's contract."

This was Mary Mackey. Clive saw an opportunity to get off the subject of Paul Giverney. "Mackey's such a good writer. I'm glad you got her an extra twenty thousand." He could have bit out his tongue; he was leading right into the subject of advances. Mary Mackey had originally been offered fifty thousand, but Tom had shoved it up to seventy. Still, it was mere change compared with someone like Dwight Staines or Paul Giverney. If Mackenzie-Haack took just 15 or 20 percent of the money it was paying writers like Staines or Rita Aristedes, it would be enough to keep really good writers out of trouble for years. Clive certainly wasn't going to say this, or Tom would come back with one of his "forgotten world" speeches. Back there, in the mists of the forgotten world of publishing, it used to be that money would be paid to keep new writers afloat, even though there wouldn't be a return on their books for years. The "forgotten world of publishing." Back there with the dinosaur bones.

This made Clive recall a recent sales conference during which Tom had presented a new novel by Eric Gruber. He took pains to point out that in this novel one character was a dinosaur. "Please keep in mind, when you go into the bookstores, that Eric Gruber is a fabulist, that he's really not Stephen King or Michael Crichton. If you need a buzz term, call it magical realism, that's as good as any— unfortunately."

Tom hated buzz words.

Leo Brand, who headed up sales, told Tom he always talked as if the whole publishing machine–including sales–was a damned thorn in the writer's side, as if the house were some obstacle course that Tom's writers had to run, and Leo wished Tom would keep in mind that without Mackenzie-Haack, Tom's fucking writers wouldn't even be in print.

"What's so great about print–" Tom had asked, unfazed "–if you've got a pencil and a piece of paper?"

He made other editors–God knows he made Clive–feel as if they'd all come up short. Well, they had, hadn't they? Tom's writers took all of the literary prizes: a dozen National Book awards, several Pulitzers, scads of notable book citations, a number of New York Critics' Circle awards, and the same number of foreign prizes. This was, admittedly, over a couple of decades. But decades had not turned up a rash of prizes such as these for any other editor, indeed, not for all of the editors put together. There had been a sprinkling of awards to other editors' books, but that's all.

Of course there wasn't a publisher in New York who hadn't gone fishing to get Tom away from Mackenzie-Haack. The biggest lure they had tossed out was the offer of his own imprint, which was Queeg and Hyde's offer. All of this was very hush-hush, of course, but there being no secrets in politics and publishing, the word had drifted around to Bobby Mackenzie, who had, naturally (and uninventively), offered Tom the same thing: his own imprint. This would mean Tom would have a small segment of Mackenzie-Haack all to himself. His name would appear right beneath the publisher's own on the spine of the book and on the title page. A very prestigious thing, one's own imprint. Clive had been trying to get one for years. "A Clive Esterhaus Book." He loved the look of it when he typed it on a piece of paper. But it was a look that hadn't materialized.

Tom Kidd had (to no one's surprise, really) turned down Queeg and Hyde and the imprint. "Why?" he had asked Bobby, when Bobby had offered him the same thing, "Why would I want that?"

"Why?" was generally Tom's answer to the underhanded, back-biting, envious maneuvers that went on at Mack and Haack. When Bobby had once offered him the position of editor in chief, assuring him he wouldn't be doing anything more than he was already doing, that had been Tom's response. "Why?"

Now Clive had to answer the "Why?" with respect to the proposed contract for Paul Giverney. "Because he's the hottest thing around these days. Because we want him on board. Of course."

Tom didn't fall for the "of course" (implying Tom would be a fool not to agree). He merely puffed at his cigar, looked at the lighted end to make sure it was, and said, "So what? He'll never earn back that advance. It'd take sales in the millions to get it back. You'd be losing money."

Clive laughed. "Tom, you're such a literalist."

"So's money. Well, you might get him 'on board' as you say, but if the ship goes down you can bet Giverney will be batting the rest of you generous folks out of the way to get to the lifeboat first."

Clive frowned. "Is that just a general statement about all millionaire authors or particular to Paul?"

Tom checked out the end of his cigar again. He didn't answer the question except to say, "Well, never mind. As long as you're his editor and not me."

That gave Clive a little chill. Tom emptied the doorway of shadows when he walked away.

Clive picked up the Danny Zito book again, opened it to where the bookmark had been (and presumed Bobby must have put it there), and read.

This wasn't one of your regular hits. People don't realize killing is easy, I mean gets easier and easier, like the more you practice. Like roller-blading. Like the piano. I play, you know.

Now, I write.

I wouldn't go so far as to say that, Danny, old boy. The prose was torturous but Danny had insisted he be the one to write this book; he didn't want it ghosted or "told to" some hack writer. Clive had tried to dissuade him, telling him writing a book was not fun—

"Then why the hell they do it, these guys?" He waved his arm to take in a display of books by Mackenzie-Haack writers.

A good question, really. Clive sighed and went back to reading:

Write. Here's something I never thought I'd do. I hope I live to do another one. It does something to you; I mean, your name on a jacket, your words printed on a page. Who could resist, right?

Clive shut the book, stared at the air for a moment, wondered if Bobby was really suggesting just that—that Danny write another book. It was true that this one had actually sold more copies than they ever thought it would. And it seemed to have developed some sort of cult following. But—

He picked up the phone, put it down, and picked up the book. As he walked by Amy's desk, he told her he'd be in Bobby's office.

"I'm finished with this?" She held up the pages of copy for the catalog.

Clive gave her a prissy little smile. "I don't know, sweetheart. Are you?"

"Is he in?" Clive asked one of Bobby's assistants, who was chattering on the telephone. What was her name, Polly? Dolly? Why weren't these girls called secretaries, which was more or less their work? Probably because publishing houses had to pay secretaries whatever secretaries were worth. Editorial assistants, on the other hand, worked for a pittance and the glamour of it (some glamour!). And the hope of winding up as editors themselves (fat chance). They loved to talk shop. There was enough gossip floating around Mackenzie-Haack to keep them busy all day long. That's probably what Polly was doing on the phone right now. She hung up and looked at him as if she wouldn't lower herself.

"I asked you, is he in? Polly?"

"Dolly. No." She pushed back a great wad of hair that looked as if it had been brushed by a steamroller. Then she pointed a silver-sequin-decorated nail in some direction. "He's down the hall. In Peter's office." Dolly turned away.

"Peter Genero's?"

Dolly's smile was just this side of a sneer. "He's the only Peter we have, isn't he?"

All of Bobby's assistants were big on attitude, just like Bobby; they were working for the great man himself, and who were you?

Clive walked into Bobby's office. He liked looking at the floor-to-ceiling bookshelves that lined three walls (the fourth being the glass-covered view). The shelves were full, with the newish books displayed upright, spread like a whore's legs. As usual all the really good ones (meaning the beautifully written ones) were from Tom Kidd's writers. There was a Grace Packard, an Eric Gruber. The other editors (himself included) had, of course, a literary writer here and there, but rarely more than one, and that one none of the editors Clive knew (again, himself included) would have the guts to edit.

Clive's literary plum was Jennifer Schiffler. She was close to being on a par with Gruber and Packard and Isaly. Rarely did Clive see her, and when he did, he wasn't sure he was "seeing" her. She was one of those writer-wraiths who gave the impression she was merely engaged in a corporeal visitation that could end at any second. Once he had taken Jennifer to lunch, expecting her merely to pick at her food, and ended up wondering how she had managed to consume all of her blini without seeming to chew or even swallow.

Looking at all of these books, Clive sighed, feeling a pang of guilt for Jennifer and writers like her, knowing he had come a long way from books such as hers and by back, not main, streets.

"Clive!"

Clive jumped at the sound of Bobby's voice. Bobby came in and sailed around his lakelike desk, then settled into his leather swivel chair, feet on desk as if he were wearing jeans and a T-shirt. He wasn't. Bobby had his own tailor who had made him a dozen suits (at two or three thousand per), all of them the same design in different wools and silks, but the colors were so muted it looked as if Bobby always wore the same suit.

"What've you got?"

"This?" Clive was afraid he was beginning to put every statement in the form of a question, like Amy.

Bobby sat back, smiling in a way that was meant to be mysterious but ended up being merely cocksure. He laced his hands behind his head and rocked back toward the huge window and beyond it, into space. "You found it."

"Were you trying to hide it? In the center of my desk?"

"What do you think?"

"About what?" He decided that if Bobby wanted another Mafia exposé, he'd have to bring it up himself. Clive wasn't helping him.

"Didn't you read the page I marked?"

"Yes, I read the page you marked. He—Danny—carried on about the writing life. Danny, more than anyone, would know, of course."

Turning his chair back and forth like a kid, Bobby smiled. "That and other stuff."

Clive frowned. "'Other stuff'?"

Bobby stopped turning and leaned forward, lowering his voice. "Don't you remember what we were talking about this morning? Have you forgotten already?"

"Of course, I remember. It was about Paul Giverney, mainly."

"Didn't you just love that bit about killing getting easier with practice, like roller-blading?" Bobby grimaced. "I was thinking maybe you should look up Danny Zito."

Clive gave a choking laugh. "Zito's gone into the great beyond of witness protection. You talked about it yourself. The man doesn't want to be found."

Bobby pulled over his Rolodex, fingers spilling over it like a card shark, plucked out one of the little punched cards, and shoved it across to Clive. "Here's his unlisted number." Bobby rat-tat-tatted on his desk with his hands. "He doesn't want to be found by his old buddies, or by his wife, or by his girlfriend. Who would? But by his publisher? Come on." Bobby made a blubbery sound with his lips. "You might lose track of your bookie or your fence, but your publisher? No way."

Clive rose, walked around the desk to peer out of the window, down at Madison Avenue. He turned, brows knotted. "Bobby, why in hell would we want another book from Danny Zito?"

"We don't. But he probably does."

"So?"

"So he knows people." Bobby folded his arms hard against his chest and waited.

"'Knows people.'" Clive was trying to resist the same unpleasant knowledge he had tried to resist that morning. He sucked in breath, felt it tighten in his chest. He wasn't so young anymore that he couldn't have a coronary. "You want me to get some information from Zito about taking care of this little problem Paul Giverney has set?"

Bobby gave him one of those exaggerated who-me? shrugs.

Then Clive said, "How in hell do you think we could trust Danny Zito, anyway? He's obviously the biggest snitch around. If he'd take on the Bransoni family, why do you think he'd keep quiet over a deal with us?"

Bobby slowly shook his head. "Bransoni didn't promise him a book contract. Only the other kind." Bobby found this a real howl. When he'd finished laughing, he said, "Come on, Clivey. Just do it."

Clive left Bobby's office, wishing people would stop fucking calling him that.

EIGHT

Clive was back at his desk again, looking (again) at the Zito book.

Fallguy. Clive remembered the book proposal: one page, outline form.

It had been Danny's contention that the best way to introduce the reader to the life of a Mafia hit man was to use the format of a twelve-step program.

Admit to being helpless in the face of the Bransoni family.

Bobby had (and no wonder) thought Danny Zito was kidding and gulped back laughter all the way down the page until he got hiccups.

Clive wasn't so sure. Danny Zito could be as inscrutable as the Las Vegas Luxor. He had a poker face that could clean out the casino at Caesars Palace. Danny had said he couldn't figure out the approach his book should take: should it be the twelve-step program offered in the bloody garb of the Bransoni family? Or the Bransoni family reported upon in the guise of the twelve steps?

Danny and Bobby had stayed closeted for two hours in Bobby's office discussing this.

The book was insane, but wait a minute—no one, reviewer or critic, had been able to work out whether this was true or whether it was a hell of a send-up both of the Bransonis, all of the twelve-step programs that had wound their way into everything people did, and, therefore, satire. Clive personally thought it more evidence of Danny's ego, total lack of talent, and ignorance of everything except what he did best: kill people.

But most of the celebrity books put out there you could say the same thing about, the worst of them often becoming instant bestsellers. Some of these success stories Bobby had given the go-ahead to. And one or two he'd told to get lost; ones that had appeared at first to be surefire hits had, in the end, gotten lost.

Clive sat staring at the jacket. By all that was right and holy, Peter Genero should have been the editor to handle this book. Genero was the celebrity maven, "celebrity" here including hit men, political assassins, tennis players, serial rapists, anyone who'd ever lived in L.A., leaders of coups, offshore banking, anybody with a scam or a dirty story to tell. These author manqués were the ones who thought they were already wonderful enough and didn't need to write their own books.

This was right up Peter Genero's street, this job. But Genero was probably busy shoveling lunches into the mouths of his celebrity "projects," people who, having become recently famous, assumed what they should do is write a book about it. About their recent fame.

Clive detested Genero. It was not in the same way that he hated Tom Kidd. Even though he wished Tom would just vanish, he had a lot of respect for him, envied him for still keeping alive the old fire of publishing. Kidd was in his book-tiered office every day, sometimes on weekends, early morning until darkness settled. Peter, on the other hand, was hardly ever in. He conducted his editorial commitments—his projects—from an Upper East Side apartment or a spread in Great Neck. He clearly felt he was too prime time to be handcuffed to a desk, to inhabit anything that smacked of a nine-to-five working world.

He shared his luxury real estate with a brace of wolfhounds that he enjoyed dragging around Central Park and into his office when he did come in, and sometimes to Petrossian, where he liked to lunch when he had a "project" to manipulate.

Clive used to wonder how Genero had pulled the wool over Bobby's eyes. Then one day he realized Peter hadn't. Bobby had him doing exactly what Peter was good at, what he was fabulously good at (Clive had to admit), and that was to curry and nurture these instant celebrities until they swelled up like balloons to float over Central Park. They would then do what Peter Genero wanted them to do: not get drunk as a skunk before appearing on the Larry King show; not hire PR people and trumpet their books before Mackenzie-Haack had set its own show in motion; and most important, not attempt to write their own books.

There wasn't one amongst them who wasn't convinced he could write *War and Peace* over the weekend. When Peter was working on selling his celebrity-writers on how much Mackenzie-Haack valued them, how absolutely great it considered them, he was very careful never to say that their greatness encompassed any kind of talent for writing. "What we want from you is your story. You had to live it, why should you have to write it? Leave the writing to the hacks! (Toss back that third martini, baby.) It's all they're good for!"

Almost always, this worked. When it didn't, another of Genero's gambits—reserved for those hard-core budding Thomas Manns that he couldn't convince before dessert—was to go along with them: absolutely! If you want to write the book yourself, that's great! Let me have a chapter by Monday because, you know, we're bound by this ridiculous production schedule. By Monday, the

Thomas Manns would call up and tell him he was right and to get one of the hacks to do the actual shit work; they had more important things to do.

Because there was no doubt about it. Writing was shit work.

Yes, Peter Genero was good at what he did.

Clive had stared at the dust jacket long enough to commit it to memory for all time. What he should have done was walk into Bobby's office and tender his resignation.

What he did do was look at the Rolodex card and pick up the phone.

NINE

Swill's was an ordinary bar that had achieved café status (if such is an achievement) by the positioning of three or four metal tables outside that, in summer, were sometimes occupied by tourists who thought they were in the Village. The regulars in Swill's disdained, even complained about the tables as being at odds with the ambience inside. They especially detested the espresso machine, brought into play largely for the customers sitting outside. As for ambience, the owner (named Jimmy Longjeans) said he no longer believed that less is more, having had to deal with the regulars all of these years, where less was indeed less.

Swill's was a stripped-down, workingman's bar whose decor consisted of a blaze of beer ads like ships' insignia over the long mirror behind the bar. The bar itself had a copper top and was both beautiful and unusual. There was nothing else that garnered comment, the rest of the room being filled with ordinary wooden booths and tables and mismatched chairs that had never intended to match and were consequently thought to be chic.

This was Chelsea, not the Village. But then Ned thought Greenwich Village wasn't even the Village anymore. Thirty, forty years ago you could have drowned in a sea of writing talk in the old Greenwich Village. MacDougal Street. Greene. Houston. Swill's was patronized by a number of novelists and poets, a few painters, and the unknown person who played "A Garden in the Rain." Swill's still had a fifties-style jukebox, containing a wealth of forties- and fifties-style singers. Johnnie Ray was the star performer here, at least to the writer who played "Cry" over and over again.

Swill's had its regulars, but so does any bar that keeps its doors open for five minutes every day. It had nothing to do with loyalty, only with habit. Still, the ones who had been coming there for years liked to complain about the ones who hadn't. Lately, or over the past year or so, men wearing suits and carrying briefcases had drifted in after five o'clock, sometimes alone, sometimes accompanied by women wearing suits and carrying briefcases. The regulars didn't know who they were or why they were there, as if the place were off-limits unless you had a personal invitation from Jimmy Longjeans, who didn't care anyway as long as you had the money up front.

Somehow, word had gotten around that Saul Prouil had won all of these awards for one book and was possibly the only writer who ever lived to do so. This was why the table in the window at the front was known as Saul's table, and, by virtue of being both a writer and his friend, Ned's table, and by further extension, Sally's. Sally worked at Mackenzie-Haack, assistant to Ned's editor. But they had not met there, oddly. Saul and Ned and Sally had met in the little park when a page of Ned's manuscript had kited away in a stiff wind, and Sally, walking toward them, had made the most acrobatic jump they'd ever witnessed and caught it.

Every once in a while someone would shamble up to the table

with a copy of the nine-year-old book and a request that Saul sign it. Most of these people had never gotten through an entire book in their lives and for the most part, such intellectualism was looked upon with deep suspicion. But having this award-winning writer in their bar, one in whom they had a proprietary interest, well, that was different. Saul had thus achieved a kind of Swillian celebrity.

There were the other writers, but none of them well known and most of them as yet unpublished, at least in book form. Three of these were poets: b. w. brill (who disdained a capitalized name, in the fashion of e. e. cummings, whom he resembled not at all), Alison Andersen, and John Laughlin. b. w. brill had actually published a book of his own and won a lesser known award. Before the prize he had been a pack-a-day Camel smoker. Now he smoked a pipe and wore corduroy jackets with leather elbows. The other two, Andersen and Laughlin, had thus far published only in little magazines and anthologies. It was therefore left to b. w. brill to steer the poetry table in the right direction. They flocked together in the back like pigeons to annoy one another. They talked about Stanford and Iowa and Bread Loaf and Yaddo.

Ned was thinking of this when he saw b.w. waving his pipe in the air either by way of saying hello or gesturing for him to come to the poets' table. Ned preferred to interpret it as the first and waved back.

"Were you ever at Yaddo?" Ned asked the others.

"Me? No," said Saul.

Ned shrugged. "Neither was I. What's that other one?"

Sally said, "You mean Bread Loaf. That's in Vermont, isn't it?"

"It's not Bread Loaf; that's one of the writers' conferences. You can buy your way into those. I'm talking about the retreats, where you have to be invited. You have to apply. Depending on the circumstances, you could stay for one month or six. Yaddo is one."

"The MacDowell Colony," said Saul.

"That's it."

"I hate those places."

"Why?" asked Sally.

"Because we love to complain about not having enough time, or that we lack a proper writing environment. We don't want any more time, and any environment will do, if we're honest. Writing's just damn hard. It can be torturous. I don't want to torture myself any more than is absolutely required. Besides, can you imagine having to sit down to dinner with thirty or forty other writers?"

"Is that what they do?" asked Sally.

"You're in your room all day until dinner. Your lunch is delivered to your door," said Ned. "It sounds like a great deal for someone who's broke. Room and board and quiet."

"Until dinner," said Saul.

"But you guys are always complaining about distractions and not having enough time," Sally said.

"Then we guys are lying. It's what I just said. Writers always lie about things like that. I mean, really, look at me; I live alone. I have plenty of time and a five-bedroom house and no one to tell me what to do—"

"Five bedrooms. Hell, start another retreat," said Ned.

"I probably have the ideal environment; so does Ned. So if we talk about distractions and too little time, we're just lying. Anyway, as to these retreats—so called, I mean—I can't see many writers getting much out of them. Writing is an antisocial act. Dinner with thirty is not it."

"You probably don't have to go to dinner."

"You do, if you want to eat. Anyway, I leave those places to brill back there."

Jamie Flynn, disheveled and staring eyed, as if she'd just got up in a place she had no claim on and was trying to discover where she was, made more money than all of them put together—and this was a poor comparison, since all of them put together were not even within shooting distance of Jamie's royalties. Jamie wrote genre fiction, every kind of genre—mystery, science fiction, horror—but, naturally, used a pseudonym from her treasure trove of pseudonyms. She always published two or three books a year, and one year had done four.

What staggered Jamie was that Saul could write and write and then shove the manuscripts all in a drawer instead of shoving them across an editor's desk. Any publisher would grab a new book by Saul. And here he was, not making money at it (except for the royalties—meager, but still coming for *The End of It*) after ten years.

Saul had said, "I haven't finished one of those books, Jamie."

She snorted. "Put a period."

Saul had laughed and told her that was the best advice he'd ever been given. But he was sick, neurotic, decrepit, and he couldn't do this.

Jamie couldn't understand it. "You don't think an editor would notice, do you? Besides, who in hell would ever actually have the almighty gall to 'edit' one of your books? What, you think a reviewer would figure out you never finished it? Don't make me laugh."

Jamie's view of writing was completely outer directed, reader directed. She never entertained the notion that writing had nothing to do with money. Ned had said this once and Jamie had gazed at him, eyes wide with shock. How could he say that? Was he nuts?

"Look at Saul."

"Saul has money."

"Whether he's got money or not," Ned had gone on, "do you

think money would motivate him? Saul? And what about b. w. brill and the others?"

"They're poets, for God's sakes! Everyone knows you can't make money writing poetry. Unless you're famous for something else, unless you're a celebrity-poet, and how many of those are there? The only famous poet's mostly a dead poet."

"We're not talking about fame; we're talking about money."

"Funny how the two of them go together. 'Rich and famous,' it's a lock." Jamie drank her boilermaker. That's what she did these days, tossed back the whiskey in one gulp, then went for the beer.

Ned wondered: when was the last time he'd ever heard of boilermakers? Had he ever seen anyone drink one except for Jamie? For all of her money talk, for all of her disdaining the past, Ned thought Jamie was mired in it. In old times. He suspected Jamie's considerable output masked a considerable loss, one she could no longer sustain. He often wondered what it was. The death of someone, of course. Father? Mother? It was hard to get Jamie to talk about her past.

It was always coming at you, thought Ned, forcing you down paths you would never otherwise have gone.

She went on: "And all of that 'writing-is-torture' stuff, Saul. I'm amazed you'd stoop that low."

Saul raised his beer in a sort of salute. "Jamie, I wish I had half your confidence."

She dropped her head in her hands, shook it. "Christ, this from a man who's won the Pen/Faulkner, the National Book Award, the New York Critics' Award, and blah blah blah." She lifted her head and looked at him. "Do you really expect me to believe you need my confidence?"

"No."

"Haven't you ever had writer's block?" Ned asked. "Even when you were starting out?"

"Why should I? Why should anybody? You can't be blocked if you just keep on writing words. Any words. People who get 'blocked' make the mistake of thinking they have to write *good* words. I look at words the way whoever wrote *Field of Dreams* looked at that damned baseball field. 'Write it, and they will come.'"

Ned said, "You don't seem to think there's anything hard about writing."

"Oh, I sure do," Jamie said, picking at the label of her beer bottle. "Page numbering, that's the hardest thing to do: number the fucking pages. This one I'm doing now. I wound up with two 198s. I'm just lucky the first 198 is the end of a chapter and there are only two lines on it. That means all I have to do is excise the two lines."

Saul had laughed. "For God's sakes, Jamie. If you put in the two lines in the first place, I'd think you'd consider them a little necessary."

"Oh, pul-*eze*. Don't pull that pompous every-word's-set-in-stone writing crap with me. The only two lines I think are necessary are the first two lines of 'Cry.'"

And she'd trotted off to Swill's jukebox to play it again.

TEN

Ned was sitting that morning on the flaking green bench, always the same bench, in the little park, watching people going off to their jobs in other parts of the city, hurrying down subway stairs, rushing to catch buses just pulling away, stopping at newsstands, hailing cabs, lurching in and out of delicatessens and Krispy Kreme with paper cups and sacks and cartons. He liked to watch all of this. There was so much preparation for something other than jobs, something to take up the slack between desk and work, something filling—newsprint, doughnuts. There had to be something to move a person from the fecund mysteries of sleep, through the harried showering and shaving and dressing, to the harsh elliptical light above the desk. Something had to cushion the blow of a job.

Especially on a Monday, and especially one that promised to be oppressive, the sky cold and gray. He was happy to sit in isolation here (sometimes wondering why the park got so little foot traffic) and watch all of this. He felt lucky not be to be part of it. Yet he understood the need for that buffer between waking and settling into work. He had his own cup of coffee, cooling beside him on the bench, and watching all of this early-morning hurry was itself a kind of shield between him and his writing.

Ned picked up the part of the manuscript he'd been carrying, got out a pencil, clicked the lead into place. He enjoyed that *click* of a lead pencil or pen; it sounded so obedient, granting him control.

Which of course he didn't have, for the *click* was all there was.

Instead of Paris and Nathalie's dilemma, he was thinking of Pittsburgh. Ned was born in Pittsburgh. He remembered so little about it, and this haunted him. How can a person live in a place for seventeen years and not remember it?

After half an hour of this, of thinking about Pittsburgh instead of proofreading his manuscript, he decided to go to Saul's house.

*   *   *   *   *

Saul came to the door wearing slippers (calfskin), a cardigan (cashmere), and smoking a cigar (Cuban). No matter what time of day, whenever Ned saw him, Saul always looked dressed for something—some expensive, exclusive place no one else knew about. It was as if he had a men's club in his mind. But Ned knew Saul never strove for effects; this was simply the way he'd been brought up.

"How about some coffee?" said Saul. "Go on into the living room; I'll bring it in."

His great-grandfather had been rich; his grandfather had taken that and made the family richer; his father had reshuffled the money and made himself the richest yet. Ned did not know how much money Saul had, but he knew it was plenty. Lawyers, accountants, money managers—they handled things. Ned doubted that Saul even knew what he was worth. In any event, all of that entrepreneurial magic had ended with Saul. He spoke of himself as the end of it. He spoke of this so often that he'd finally used the phrase as his book title.

Ned had not sat down yet. He liked moving about the room, looking around. The house was so beautiful, the rooms so tactile with their moss-brown velvets and rain-washed silks, and the history so abundant—Ned could touch it and taste it, like the smooth ripe fruit in the porcelain bowl on the marble-topped commode. He stood looking at the portraits that hung above the fireplace and to the right of the mahogany butler's desk at which Saul sometimes sat and wrote, liking its position near one of the long windows that opened over the street and whose thin curtains were buffeted by summer winds. He could sit and look out, he said.

The portraits were of his grandfather and great-grandfather; a third portrait of his father, the smile he wore in the picture that hung between the windows was particularly chilly, only barely a smile. All of them looked equally serious, as if a scowl were the only way to get the job done.

On the other side of the window, though, were two small oval frames of some rich and seemingly pliant wood. One was a sepia print and the other a charcoal drawing of the same woman, who was Saul's grandmother. Her beauty was almost unnerving, for one had to wonder how in God's name she could manage ever to coexist with the no-nonsense menfolk in this abstemious household. Even though neither picture was in color, Ned could still see it from Saul's description: reddish gold hair and eyes of the dark blue of lapis lazuli.

Saul's grandfather and great-grandfather were men of so grim an aspect that they looked as if they embodied every homily on thrift and the curative powers of work imaginable. They would probably be scandalized to find they would live out their days in these opulent gilt frames overseeing their descendant who sat around *writing*.

But they were also powerful paintings that looked as if the artist had sucked out the soul of his subjects and returned them to the canvas, reconstituted. That was how alive they looked.

"Don't look at him too long; he'll burn your cornea," said Saul, coming in through the dining room carrying a whole coffee service on a heavy silver tray. He poured out coffee for both of them into thin, nearly transparent cups. He handed one to Ned, then he retrieved his cigar from a heavy glass ashtray that the sun, striking it suddenly, turned to a swirl of blue. Saul had to light the cigar again to get it going.

Both of them remained standing, looking at the inhospitable trio on the wall. Saul said, "The irony is, of course, that the life I lead is far more austere and rigorous than anything they could ever have devised, much more than were their own lives. I don't do anything. Their ghosts probably move about, watching me in the exciting act of holding a pen. My grandfather was a legendary ladies' man; and old Noah, there"—he nodded toward the portrait near the butler's desk—"was addicted to both gambling and booze. How boring I must seem in comparison. No, they wouldn't be able to stand me, you know. Too dull, a dull life, nothing in it but writing and reading. For them, it was all action, and most of the action was aimed at making money. That was probably their recreation, too, together with slipping at night across the back porch of the lady of the moment. How in hell did I descend from such people? Maybe I'm a changeling. More coffee?" Saul raised the silver coffeepot.

Ned held out his cup. "That was your father's side, but what about your mother?"

"I remember my mother only as an unobtrusive woman, silent, but never quite still, always moving, like a fleeting shadow. But I always remember myself as stationary. That window seat there—I spent my childhood in it, reading. That gold cord that holds back the drape? I can remember pulling at it or working the threads apart as I sat there. I'm surprised it held up at all. My reading drove them all crazy; I don't think they read a book through, in spite of the library back there." He nodded toward a room behind him. "Reading was what I did. Funny, but I think that was my way of rebelling, instead of dope or fast cars or fucking. Reading. It was only a small step to writing, I guess. My past seems to be a series of flickering images, like an old silent movie." Saul laughed. "I've never done one damn thing, except in my head. How would they like that?" He poured himself a cup of coffee and sat down on the moss-brown sofa.

Ned sat down then in the leather wing chair he always favored, positioned to take in most of the objects in the room. He could not imagine the things here as fleeting. In firelight and lamplight they looked crusted over, sealed against the looting of time.

"You know more about the past than I do. You've cracked its code. I don't even recognize these people sometimes." Saul prodded the air with his cigar.

" 'Cracked its code'? Don't I wish. Yesterday I couldn't write at all. Literally, I didn't set down a word for three hours. The story's set in Paris, yet I keep thinking of Pittsburgh."

"Pittsburgh, I've always thought it a mysterious sort of city."

Ned laughed. "That's the last thing I'd think. Why?"

"Oh, it's reinventing itself. Becoming beautiful after having been so ugly. At least, that's what I've read."

"Maybe so. Anyway, it stalled my writing well enough. What do you do when you can't write? I sharpen pencils into spears. They're lethal by the time I get through with them."

"According to Jamie, we can always write. How the hell she

does it, all of those books, all of those different genres, I don't know. I wander around and pick up things—silver bowls, pieces of porcelain—and look on the bottom to see whether the stamp's there and looks authentic." Saul blew a smoke ring and pierced it with his finger.

Ned got up to look at the pictures again, the two small ones of Saul's grandmother. Saul, like his grandmother, was a softer rendering of the sharp-eyed, imperious male ancestors. She had been alive through his childhood. Saul felt himself lucky; he was fifteen before she died, and even then she was young, only in her late fifties. She had been quite young when Saul's mother had been born—the unobtrusive mother. Her death (Saul had said) had leveled the house and everyone in it.

It had not occurred to Ned before that "everyone" was not really Saul's grandfather (he of the mutton whiskers) or Saul's father (of the chilly, painted smile), but Saul himself. It rattled Ned to think this; it shook him, only because he'd pictured Saul as another, altogether different sort of adolescent—distinct and distant, a writer even then who didn't trust anyone or anything not of his mind's own making. Because his mother and father had pretty much cast him adrift, Ned had assumed everyone else had, too. Or at least that Saul felt they had. But this was not so.

He turned from the two oval pictures and asked, "Do you think about her much, your grandmother?"

Saul took the cigar from his mouth and studied the coal end in the way of those strange lunar moths that beat their wings slowly before fire in an unquenchable need of light. "All the time," he said.

Ned looked at him, surprised again; he would not have thought Saul to be stuck in the past. Then he wondered why, why had he not thought this? *The End of It* dealt precisely with an overwhelming loss suffered by the austere and exacting narrator. Indeed, how could anyone have written this book other than a person who had never recovered from the loss of someone—or something, even—and never would. *The End of It*. Ned foundered here, wondering if there was some clue in this that would explain why Saul couldn't finish the novel he'd been working on.

"They called her Ossie; her name was Oceana. She was the dose of good humor that the others had to take daily. Though you could see," Saul said, "it lay on their tongues like lead." Saul looked at him. "What are you thinking?"

Ned just shrugged; he did not want to say what he had been thinking because he hadn't thought it over enough. Neither of them was given to talking off the top of his head. Neither was given to epiphanies in their writing, either. Any page or paragraph that seemed prompted by "revelation" they each saw as suspect.

Saul stood up. "Listen: let's go to Swill's. Early yet, but I want to get out of the house. At least, go to the park or for a walk."

Then Ned wondered if he'd been wrong, too, about the house. Perhaps it wasn't a refuge, a "safe house."

ELEVEN

Clive was still in his office, where he'd been waiting for Amy to go home since 5:30. He still heard papers rustling, the printer stuttering out pages, drawers opening and shutting with a jarring clatter. What in hell was she doing? At times he found Amy's devotion to her job irritating as hell. But it wasn't really "devotion"; it was merely its semblance, imitation "devotion," which she hoped would carry her up the ladder to editor. There were enough titles sailing through the windy corridors of most publishing houses that Amy should have been able to snatch one out of the air. And a lot of them meant the same thing: executive editor, editor in chief, managing editor; then there were publisher, president, vice president. And God knows what else.

He would have to tell her to go home. He did not want to be overheard when he made this telephone call.

Just as he was getting up, Amy stopped in the doorway, wearing her coat, and said, "Well, good night?"

As if it were a question. "Yes, good night, Amy. Did you finish that copy?" Stupid of him not to leave it at "Good night."

"I told you before?" It was close to a whine. "I finished it, yes."

"Good, good. Well . . ." He nodded. She didn't move. Would there be any closure here at all? He picked a rubber band from a little jar and started snapping it.

Then "Bye!" she said, as breathless as if she'd been running past the door and the sight of him had taken her by surprise.

With her gone, he had no further reason for procrastinating. What he needed was a drink, a bracer, a snort of cocaine, an anesthetic. He kept a bottle of Bombay gin in his bottom desk drawer (homage to Sam Spade and the others), but decided against the gin, which would, at this point, have traveled to his brain like a cruise missile. Bobby had Scotch, which would warm him without putting his mind out of commission.

Clive rose, pocketed the Rolodex card (afraid that it might be discovered by someone), and walked out of his office, through the open-office pen, and down the corridor to Bobby's office. He walked through the outer to the inner office, where he opened the little doors of the burled mahogany cabinet, took out the Scotch, and poured a couple of fingers into one of Bobby's Venetian glass tumblers. Bobby didn't mind anyone helping himself to his private stock. Bobby was, in things like this, quite generous. Then he sat down on the old soft sofa and stretched out his legs.

Yes, Bobby would've been a great guy to work for if only he could stay the same guy for three days running. Some of this erratic behavior could be explained by the man's being a kind of publishing genius. But, really: wasn't all of this business about Paul Giverney pretty childish? He finished off the first drink, got up, and poured himself a second. He felt a little looser, more relaxed, composed, in charge of the matter, and decided to make the call from Bobby's office. Lie on the couch and call. The image pleased him. This whole half-baked plan was so crazy he might as well relax.

One of the telephone extensions was sitting on an end table by the arm of the couch. He took out the card, dialed the number. It surprised him that it was a 212 exchange; he would have thought Danny Zito would have gotten as far from New York as he could.

He coiled the phone cord and listened through six rings and was about to hang up (with thanks to God) before he heard the receiver's being lifted. He wondered how big this apartment was the bureau had found for Danny.

"Yeah." The voice wasn't surly, just bored.

"Dan—sorry. Jimmy Bradshaw, is he there?"

Silence. "Who wants him?" More interested now, perhaps a little tense.

Clive wondered if there was a sort of password Bobby had neglected to give him. "Tell him (why not string out the game?) that Clive Esterhaus would like to talk to him. See, I know Jimmy."

"Clive!" All pretense of Jimmy Bradshaw and taking a message dropped through the floor. "Hey, man, long time, no see."

"An interesting comment coming from someone in the witness protection program."

Danny was easily amused. He laughed.

Clive said, "I thought you'd be living somewhere like Bozeman, Montana, Dan—ah, Jimmy. I'm surprised you're still in New York."

"Couldn't live nowhere else, Clive-O."

"But—isn't it dangerous?"

"Nobody's found me yet, pal. Nice to hear from my publisher. Book's doin' great, ain't it? But what happened to my Barnes and Noble win-doooowww?" He sang the two syllables, trilled them up and down.

Clive shut his eyes tightly and tapped his forehead with the cold black receiver. Give me a fucking break! Every damned fool who put pen to paper thought he deserved a shot at a bookstore window.

"Sorry about that, ah, Jimmy" (and if Danny Zito insisted on mouthing off about his book, what the hell difference did it make what Clive called him? Jimmy or Danny or semiretired Snitch, who'd brought the Bransoni family to its knees, got "Papa B"—as they fondly called him—a stretch in jail, together with two of his sons, but left plenty more relatives who were looking for Danny).

Come to think of it, Clive decided it was not such a hot idea to be belting his own name and the publisher's around, either. "We did try to get it for you (a lie), but DreckSneed beat us to it with that Dwight Staines book—"

"Shit. Genre stuff. No class at all. So what's up?"

"Well, Bobby's talking a sequel."

"No problem."

No problem? Christ, the writer's ego. At least he supposed he had to give Danny credit for actually writing *Fallguy*. It had taken several bouts of heavy editing but it had, in the end, been readable. So here he was, revving up for book number two. Almost taking for granted there would be a number two. "What I'd really like is to talk to you in person. Can you manage that?" He wondered if Danny ever went out.

"Me? Hell, yes. I just take a little extra care, is all. Gotta watch my back. You know."

Which gave Clive the uncomfortable feeling that he soon might have to be watching his. "You should work in publishing for a day. Listen: there's something you can do for us. It's a, uh, another kind of contract. We figure you'd have the connections."

"Connections? To what?"

"Maybe you could give me the name of a, uh, an agent? A representative. A middleman. Someone like that?"

Danny seemed to have gone away from the telephone for something. Clive heard him laughing in the background. Probably went to get his drink. Clive checked his own Scotch. Then Danny was back. "Yeah, I'm sure."

"So just pick any place you like. I'll meet you wherever."

"You mean now? Tonight?"

"Why not? In a couple of hours. If you're not otherwise engaged."

"Nah, I ain't got nothin' on. As you can guess, my popularity's suffered some. Okay, so let's say the Chelsea Piers. Say, Pier Sixty-one?"

"All right. Around seven thirty, eight?"

"Great. Should we exchange contracts?"

Hysterical laughter. Clive hung up.

He lay on the leather couch with the phone on his chest. He checked his watch. Two hours. The Chelsea Piers, then afterward he could go to that restaurant on Ninth that was getting a lot of play. Would Danny want to go with him to dinner? He hoped not. Clive sighed and replaced the telephone receiver.

The Chelsea Piers, for God's sakes, for someone in the witness protection program.

TWELVE

The Chelsea Piers.

It was not a mise-en-scène Clive had often feasted his eyes upon. Rarely did he venture below Thirty-eighth Street, either West or East, and never had he done it in the last decade. His mental map of this far downtown was covered with fuzz and dust. Yet many years ago, he had gone all the way down to Greene Street to talk to one of Mackenzie's young hopefuls, sitting outside some coffee bar at a table on the pavement. The funny thing was, he forgot the writer, the book, what either of them had said, but the little wedge of Greenwich Village, shaped like the Flatiron Building, had stayed in his mind, had never dislodged.

Clive wondered why. And why he hadn't gone back.

Bobby Mackenzie, never reality's groomsman, had finally come across a scheme, a marriage of greed and inventiveness that truly merited the Mackenzie-Haack imprint. It made kicking out André Schiffrin seem small potatoes. It made HarperCollins's reneging on a hundred contracts hardly worth the postage it took to send the manuscripts back.

So why hadn't Bobby just done that? Found some flea-bitten clause in Ned Isaly's contract, or some unacceptable thing in Isaly's manuscript when it came in that would "forbid" publishing the book.

Well, he'd already said it, hadn't he? This scheme had the Mackenzie-Haack logo all over it.

So here he stood on Chelsea Pier 61, waiting in a dim, dim light. Ever since Clive had been a small boy he'd been in love with fog. Fog was the gray area between black and white; it was the medium of deceiving and forgetting. You could hide in it; you could walk out of it, mysteriously.

It was in this broody state of mind that Clive (still clutching his collar) saw a black shape bearing down on him like a small ship plowing through the pier mist. He shook himself.

Danny Zito stood there dressed head to toe in total and unforgiving black, looking as if he'd invented the witness protection program single-handed.

"Clive-O," Danny stuck an affectionate *O* on the end of names, including (Clive imagined) those of most of the men he'd murdered. He put out a hand to slap into a handshake.

Clive put out his own, almost felt tiny bones shatter in Danny's sudden grip, like a bat cracking against a ball. "Dan—" Clive caught himself. "Jimmy. Sorry."

"Hey, forget it. Nobody's listenin'. Nobody probably ever was."

Clive frowned. Danny had a way of making these inscrutable pronouncements.

Slowly, Danny chewed his gum. "You bring it?"

In the furtive way a pusher might bring out a Ziploc bag filled with white powder, Clive pulled the contract from his pocket. It had been written up and signed in record time. Usually, it took months, but with no agent involved, minutes sufficed.

Danny shook it open; in the dark it glimmered, a magical thing; a book contract from a reputable New York publisher, the Great White Hope and aphrodisiac of every writers' workshop, colony, conference, convention. Of course it was worth killing for.

"Only one copy?" Danny quickly thumbed through the eleven or twelve pages.

"We're sending the others."

Danny brought out a pen flashlight. (During one frantic second of which movement Clive was afraid he was going to burn the contract, toss it flaming into the Hudson, and pull out a gun.) "Lemme just check it out. Same terms? I'd like a better paperback split, say fifty-five/forty-five?"

Christ, these writers. Clive wanted to hit him. With what restraint he could muster, he said, "I imagine we can manage that."

It obviously hadn't occurred to Danny they couldn't. He was already on to another clause. "Jacket approval, too." He turned a page, traced it with his light beam.

"Danny, what the hell do you know about jacket art? Come on—"

"Yeah? I know as much as that stogie-smoking dyke you pay no doubt a handsome salary to. Did you see that last jacket?" He turned another page of the document.

"Obviously. I was your editor."

"My own mother didn't even want to read it with that jacket. She saw the mock-up, she says—"

"Danny—"

"—says 'what kinda cover's this, Danny? Black, white, silver, no picture, no girls? Go beat some sense into them.'"

"Danny—"

"Jacket approval." Danny rolled up the document and took a few friendly swipes at Clive's chin.

"Could we get to our problem?"

"You mean, can I handle somethin' personal? I'm in—"

"No, no, not you yourself. Just recommend somebody. Put us in touch with someone. I know you're supposed to be in"—he'd almost said "hiding," then thought Danny wouldn't like that, so he changed it—"visible these days. You're keeping a very low profile. You might be out of touch—"

"Outta touch? Hell, no. It ain't safe to be outta touch."

Clive thought it didn't look all that safe to be *in* touch.

"I know some guys might do me a favor. Me a favor: you, you pay, right? Ones I'm thinking of, it might take a few days. They make themselves hard to get ahold of."

They? "We only need one."

Danny shook his head. "Ones I'm thinking of work absolutely together. They're the best, don't leave no trail, nothing. Only they're particular. Well, that's what you want, ain't it? Wet work may be wet, but it don't have to leave a puddle. I guess I'm not surprised; I guess it was only a matter of time before they got in."

Clive frowned. What was he talking about?

Danny took a long drag of his cigarette, flipped it, and watched it arc out over the river. "Hell, if they're into spas these days, no reason they're not into publishing. Makes sense, just look at the way publishing's going. Big conglomerates taking over, big fish sucking up the little fish—"

Clive was still back on spas. Spas?

"—it was only a matter of time. I guess the mob don't miss nothin', right?"

"You mean, you think this is a mob thing?"

"Ain't it?"

"Not exactly. It's a, ah, publishing thing."

"Same difference. Meet me back here in a coupla hours. No, let's say midnight. Back here at midnight."

"Come on, Danny, can't you simply give me a call?"

Danny just looked at him. "Better to do it in person. These guys, they don't like their names bandied about over a cell phone. Back here."

Clive sighed.

The dinner at Pastis had done something to restore Clive's flagging spirits, which were quickly dissipating again as he stood on the pier, beating his gloved hands against the cold.

Danny appeared again, fog bound. From somewhere came the deep, hollow growl of a boat.

"Candy and Karl. They'll meet you and Bobby Mackenzie two o'clock Friday at the RTR. They don't wanna do lunch, necessarily, but they'll have coffee, drinks, whatever. Get a banquette in the rear. They said."

"That's the Russian Tea Room, Danny. It's closed."

Danny's eyes widened; he stopped chewing his gum. "Get outta here!"

"No, it's true. It shut down."

"Jesus. You can't depend on nothin' anymore. Okay, Michael's, then. Only make sure Bobby gets a table near the front. Michael's is a swell restaurant only I remember me and Jerry Bransoni went in there once—that's when we were still talking—and they stuck us in the back room. I mean around the *corner*. As far back as you can get. The whole fucking Giancarlo family could have walked into

Michael's and me and Jerry none the wiser. You'd think, my God, they'd be more careful, that maître d' and all. The place coulda gone up in smoke."

"I don't think Michael's gets all that many drive-bys, Danny."

"Yeah, well all the same. Don't get the idea of meeting in some crumby coffee shop on Lex."

"There are no crumby coffee shops in New York."

Danny's gum traveled from one side of his mouth to the other. "Just remember, these two, they're the crème de la crème."

Pronounced, Clive noted, with a long *e*.

"Make 'em sit around the corner and I can't answer for what could happen."

Oh, for God's sakes. Clive sighed and said, "Look. Bobby won't get a table back there. He's too damned important."

"In the window, maybe?" Danny was recklessly chewing his gum.

In another minute, Clive swore to himself he'd kick this guy into the Hudson and not look back. "Maybe, maybe. But wouldn't it make more sense to meet somewhere private?"

"Like, you mean, here? Maybe in some dark alley? You see too many gangsta movies." Danny twitched his shoulders to better settle his black cashmere coat. "You're afraid they'll show up wearin' porkpie hats and yellow shoes?"

"Of course not." Clive's laugh was stagy.

"In case you want to know for future reference, they get all their stuff at Armani or Façonnable." He reached out and plucked a bit of fluff from Clive's lapel. "As do I." He pulled on his own lapel. "Armani, this is. He makes good wpp clothes—grays and blacks, deconstructed—hell, you could carry a Uzi." Danny still had the contract and stuck it in an inside pocket. "I never stopped, you know."

What? Killing people? Clive took an involuntary step back.

Danny, though, was looking out across the river. "I got maybe ten chapters going on this"—he patted his pocket—"so it's not like I'm going at it, you know, cold turkey."

"Good. Look, I hope coming out here tonight hasn't, you know, compromised your, uh, safety." What did these witness protection people do for God's sakes?

"You kidding? I go out all the time."

"But isn't that dangerous? You've got a lot of people looking for you, surely. I mean, I would have thought remaining in New York pretty dangerous."

Danny laughed, shook his head at, it would seem, Clive's ingenuousness. "People see what they expect to see. Papa B, he expects to see me run like hell. The Bransonis are looking for me all over the map—except in Manhattan. I live here, you know." There was an inclination of his head toward the streets behind them.

"You live in *Chelsea*?"

"Hub of the art scene, Chelsea. SoHo's moved out, moved here. You should see the installation over at White Columns. You know this scene?"

Clive said no. "Look, uh, Danny, about—"

"You gotta see this stuff. There's one installation of ephemeral art that'd blow you fucking away."

"Ephemeral? Look—"

"Yeah. Ephemeral art, it's hot—"

"Danny—"

"—see, it wears itself out, I mean, like some of it disappears like hours after it's put in. Some of it in just minutes. Like the cut flowers wilt, like ice in the trays of ice cubes melts. Funny nobody ever thought of it before."

"Somebody did. Frigidaire. I'll just continue creaking around the Metropolitan and MOMA, thanks. Now, about these two—"

"Listen, I got nothing against that stuff in the Met. I just don't happen to think Monet and that bunch speak to a lot of people right now."

"They speak to me. You've got your contract. Tell me about these men, how I can get hold of them if I need to."

"I told you. Michael's. Two o'clock, Friday." Danny reached up his hand almost daintily to adjust his tinted glasses and walked back into the fog.

THIRTEEN

Bobby Mackenzie's assistant—he had four—Melissa was retooling her face in front of a mirror propped against a small pillar of what had turned out to be Jordan Strutts's nonbest-seller, a book that Bobby and Peter Genero had championed the past June: "championed" meaning talked about, gotten the buzz out on rather than actually "stood behind." "Stood behind" would have been a real commitment, one for which Bobby could get the entire roller coaster of promotion, publicity, and sales fired up to launch a book like a rocket. Strutts's book hadn't been so blessed.

As Sally passed by the outer office, Melissa rose quickly, rushed to the door into the corridor of plush carpeting, and called to her to come back.

"I've got to go to Bloomie's for a final fitting and it sounds like they'll be in there"—she bucked her head back toward the inner office—"like, forever. Are you busy?"

Sally sighed. She was always busy. It's what came with the good fortune of being the right arm of an editor who more than did his job. Tom Kidd took on more books than he could comfortably manage within the limits of the ordinary working day, so he changed the limits. Right now he had four books on the spring list, and there were endless tasks to perform in the publication of just one, much less four. If you were Tom Kidd, there were.

"You want me to sit at your desk. Okay, but not, believe me, 'forever.' If I see forever coming, I'm out of here. What fitting?"

"My dress. My wedding dress, for God's sakes. I *am* getting married."

Married. Did people still do that sort of thing around here? Did Bloomingdale's have a bridal department? Fat lot Sally'd know about it. So Sally smiled at Melissa, hoping it was a smile worthy enough for a woman about to marry. "I forgot, sorry. Yes, of course I'll answer your telephone. And whatever." She could hear the voices in the inner office. Loud laughter, then laughter pitched low.

Melissa was shrugging into a black cloth coat, pulling her long taffy-colored hair out from the imprisoning collar. "There's not really much 'whatever.' Bobby's been energy deprived the last few days. That, or what he's doing doesn't involve anything I do. 'Bye."

Sally sat down in Melissa's typist's chair, which was just like Melissa: pert and small. How a chair could be "pert" she didn't know, but this one, with its little curved back and ergonomic seat like a sealed buttock, managed to be, as if it might spring into action at Melissa's slightest touch. Melissa wheeled everywhere—to the filing cabinets, to the Xerox machine—with the momentum of a veteran paraplegic racing down a ramp. There should be contests. Sally felt what little energy she had brought into the office was being sapped by the chair.

She closed her eyes, heard the drone of voices, heard a few words that sounded like "over my dead body" (Bobby talking), and felt weary, weary and old. She was thirty-two and, although she really loved her job (and how many could say that?), she still felt wasted. For Sally really wanted to write, too. It would be almost impossible to have so much exposure to good writing and the thrill (writers mightn't admit it, but that's what it was: thrilling) of seeing one's words in print, more than "in print," published by a prestigious publisher who's willing to pay for it. Well, she had tried to write, but—and she supposed that this was the difference between writers and nonwriters—had grown horribly frustrated in the mere attempt to set down one single sentence. It was as if she were staring at nonreflecting glass, the words congealing in her mind, coagulating into a full stop. It was simply transferring the words in one's mind to the page, wasn't it? Then how was it the words seemed ungraspable? She had attempted this time after time and the same thing happened. It brought her to tears.

Without giving her own poor attempts away, she had asked Tom Kidd, who had told her, after mulling the question over (one of the reasons she liked him), that writers just kept on staring at nothing until they wrote something. Might be two minutes or two weeks. Maybe it was something ordinary mortals couldn't do. Not write (Tom said), but wait.

"You make it sound as if they're more holy or more noble." She had been irrationally irritated by his answer.

And Tom mulled that over, too. "Holy, maybe; noble, no."

They talked a lot about things like this, sometimes eating their lunch in Tom's office, Sally bringing in her insulated bag with the colored cats on the cover; Tom getting out his brown bag that always held his white meat of chicken sandwich. On white bread, Wonder Bread. This same sandwich his wife had been making for him over the years and he said every lunchtime that it was the best chicken sandwich in the world. Sally had once accepted a quarter of his sandwich to see if this was true, expecting that she'd be sampling stars or the silver dust of a comet's tail, and being disappointed when it turned out to be plain old chicken. Just chicken, butter, Wonder Bread. But she'd made an *ummm* sound and told him that yes, he was right.

After perhaps a hundred failed fiction-writing attempts, Sally hit on possibly writing nonfiction. That might be her forte. She didn't believe this, but one day she did ask Tom, from the other side of the piles of books on his desk and her chin nearly grazing the garish jacket on top, whether anyone had recently written a book about the sheer hell of writing.

Tom had said he didn't know it was sheer hell, at least if what she meant was incredibly hard work, which he could only demonstrate by citing four of his own writers, and the rest—and God only knew the rest of the house's—made it look like a day at the beach. Anyway, no, he didn't know about any nonfiction books about a writer's turmoil (though he could list off the top of his head a dozen fictional accounts of turmoil). There were, however, a lot of how-to books, which were relatively worthless. Would-be writers read them for company, not direction.

He must know, of course, why Sally was asking these questions, but he didn't come out with it. He was too much of a gentleman to embarrass her.

She thought about Ned and Saul and holiness. What did Tom mean by "holy," anyway? It had been a word she'd tossed out like a sneer that he had taken at least semiseriously. Was it like dedication? No, it had to be more than that, or something other than.

The telephone rang again just as the fax machine started spitting out pages. She told the caller Bobby was at a sales conference and the caller rang off. The fax machine stopped. She paid no attention.

Concentration, what about that? Was that some kind of "holy" thing? Being centered? Focused? They—Ned and Saul—certainly shared the capacity for all of these things. It was almost transcendent, the way they kept their writing selves intact and nearly untouchable. She wondered if the more that ability was used, the more the centered and transcendent part grew until one day it was all of them, it was the whole self. They became their writing; they were their characters. She thought: how incredible, no longer having to drag around as if you had a dead body shackled to your ankle, that part of the self that wept over publishers' indifference, that wailed at bad reviews, and, once landing on the *TBR* list in fourth place, raging against the three guys who had bested you at first, second, and third.

The egos of writers were really that hard to satisfy, that insatiable. Yet who could blame them? Having poured a quart of blood into even the shoddiest offering, why blame a really good writer who had poured out the whole four quarts? It was his life's blood in that book, don't you forget it! But Saul and Ned—

"... Ned Isaly ..."

Sally jumped slightly in her chair. For a second, she thought the name had been spoken in her head. It came, of course, from Bobby's office and it wasn't until then that she realized the door was open a crack—just a sliver, enough to let through light and sound. The voices rose and fell like the tide coming in and going out.

"... Isaly's contract ..."

One of them said it again ...

Inside the office, Clive was pacing. His steps took him nearer to the door and farther from it. "Bobby. For Christ's sake—!"

"You said it yourself; you used the argument yourself. If we break Isaly's contract, we'll have to contend with Tom Kidd."

Bobby had his feet on his desk and was leaning back, sans coat, holding a dust jacket up to the light splashing in through his window. Central Park glittered in the light. "This jacket sucks, Clive." He tossed it across the desk. "As long as Ned Isaly delivers a manuscript, we can't touch him. I mean, it would be pretty foolish to pretend it was unacceptable. That's even without the complication of Kidd's walking out if we did it. So what else did Zito say?"

Clive made no move to pick up the cover mock-up, appalled that Bobby could take this whole business so calmly. "That's all. Just that these two always work together."

Sally sensed, if she didn't actually hear, someone moving toward the door. She zipped the typist's chair over to the Xerox machine and punched it on. She had nothing to copy but a page from a book lying there, but it made no difference as her back was to the door and she was on the other side of the room. She slapped the open book down and pushed the button.

"Where's Melissa?"

It was Clive. She removed the book and turned to face him, trying to look really dumb, her mouth slack, eyes wide. "Oh. Melissa had to leave for a while. It was a kind of emergency about her wedding."

Clive wasn't interested in the wedding; he was looking at her for a long moment, obviously trying to assess what, if anything, she'd heard. He wouldn't have worried about Melissa; she was too self-absorbed to let any talk intrude that hadn't to do with her wedding. But Sally, that was cause for concern. Sally was known to be smart, quick, and intuitive.

Sally turned back to the machine as if she couldn't care less what they got up to in there.

"What're you doing out here?"

Over her shoulder she said, "Copying some pages. Why? Did you want something?" Still wide eyed, she was all candor.

"What? No. Yes. Make some coffee, will you?"

She nodded. She could tell he had determined she was harmless and had heard nothing.

The door would not stay shut, that's what it was. Even after Clive had made a point of pulling it to, it was clear (to her, not to him) that the catch was worn or dislodged.

She wheeled to the coffeemaker and dumped several spoonsful of Blue Mountain into the grinder (God, but this man was spoiled!), which she then transferred to the cone holder of Bobby's space-shuttlelike-looking coffeemaker (designed, she noted, by Porsche); she added water, turned it on, then wheeled back to the desk. The desk was as close to the door as it was possible to get, short of putting her ear up to it, and she daren't get that close.

At first, Clive's voice was considerably lower, and he'd stopped pacing, so that she heard nothing but a mumble. But it wasn't long before the voice returned to normal levels and he had resumed his movements again. She would make sure her hands were on the computer keyboard if one of them suddenly appeared again.

Ned. They were still talking about Ned and Ned's contract. Why? This meeting seemed to be taking place for that sole purpose . . .

Clive was out of his chair and pacing again.

"So who are they?" Bobby wasn't about to let him get back on the subject of Ned-if-Ned-publishes.

"Candy and Karl," said Clive. "Those are the names he gave me."

"Two. We don't want two. That's just one more person to know about the, ah, project."

Clive took a weird delight in being able to tell Bobby for once he had no choice. No Bobby choice—this included no rewriting of the Constitution, no reimagining the universe, no reinventing the world. The World as Bobby Mackenzie Sees It. Fuck you, Bobby. "Whether you want two or not, you've got two . . ."

"Whether you want to or not, you've got to . . ." Sally couldn't understand why Clive seemed to be telling Bobby what to do. "Got to" *what*?

Clive moved closer to Bobby's big desk. "They work together." Jesus, were they really talking about this? Clive had known Bobby was a megalomaniac, a virtual Attila the Hun, but this . . . ? And Clive himself—he was afraid to think about what he thought about himself.

"Huh." What came from Bobby was a kind of exploded sigh. He picked up another colorful, shiny jacket and held it at arm's length. "Where in hell was Mamie Fussel when this got done?"

"It was Mamie who did it." She was the art director, a rough-cut woman Clive didn't particularly care for.

"I'd rather be back in the days of tits and ass."

"These *are* the days of tits and ass," said Clive. "Could we focus here? Could we just stay on the point here?"

Bobby dropped this jacket on the other one. "Another thing is, Isaly's going to be giving Tom a new manuscript soon. It's due this month."

They always talked about manuscripts like long-overdue babies. Tired, Clive had finally dropped onto the sofa. "Why in hell does that make a difference?"

"Why? Because I don't think Paul Giverney would relish a new

Isaly coming out, even after this little reversal of fortune Ned's going to have. And God knows not with all of the attendant publicity around the publication of Isaly's new property. Right?"

Clive could only stare.

Bobby picked up the phone, then thought better of it, plucked up the two jacket mock-ups, and went to the door.

"Where the hell's Melissa?"

"Small emergency," said Sally as she raised her fingers from the keyboard. "Coffee's just about ready."

"Uh. Call Tom Kidd and ask him what's the progress on the Ned Isaly book. Then tell Mamie Fussel I want to see her asap. These are fucking terrible." He tossed the jackets on Melissa's desk.

"I can–" She stopped. At Bobby's raised-eyebrow inquiry, she mumbled, "Nothing." She could have, too. Told him about the progress of Ned's book. But that might eclipse Tom's own reaction to all of this. Tom wouldn't stand for their giving Ned any trouble.

Bobby disappeared from the door and, as Clive had done, pulled it shut.

Sally felt a chill descend and rubbed her arms against it. She thought she knew what the theme of this conversation between the two of them was about. If Ned reneged on the delivery date of his book, Mackenzie-Haack would drop him. She could not work out what Paul Giverney had to do with it.

Tears came to her eyes. What in God's name could Bobby (or Clive) have against Ned? How could they even consider such a thing?

Sally stared at the gaudy jackets Bobby had dropped on the desk. They were not inspired, no, but neither were they awful.

And to Bobby it was all the same—the end of Ned Isaly at Mackenzie-Haack and two dead-in-the-water dust jackets.

*   *   *   *   *

"She was nothing like my mother," said Saul, still talking about his grandmother.

They were sitting in the park, on this now-luminous November day, such a rarity in New York that all one wants to do is sit and look at it, at the light that lay like a transparent crust across the cold grass beyond them. It was so clear, Ned's head was spinning a little with the dazzle and clarity of it all, as if he were drunk on air.

Saul had stopped talking and sat smoking a fresh cigar. Then his talk resumed: "I could never understand how my mother and my uncle Swann could be her children. I got it in my head there was a mix-up in the hospital. You know."

"Maybe you believed that; kids do, don't they? It's a way of explaining discomfort and pain to themselves." Ned was leaning forward, his elbows on his knees, and now looked up at Saul, waiting for him to go on, but he'd stopped. Ned was surprised he'd talked this much about himself. About anything, really.

"Isn't that Sally?"

Ned followed the direction of Saul's gaze. It was Sally and she seemed in a dreadful hurry, walking so fast she might at any moment break into a run. Getting up, smiling, he regretted there was no wind to snatch up a page of his manuscript and send it flying, just to see her, once again, make that leap and pluck it out of the air.

"Hey! Hey!" she called, as if in standing they meant to run away from her.

By the time she reached their bench, she was out of breath. "I was going—" She stopped, breathed deeply.

"What is it?" Saul asked.

She didn't look at Saul, but at Ned. Without preamble, she said, "They're trying to get rid of you."

Ned gave a little half laugh. "What're you talking about? Who?"

"Clive and Bobby. I heard them talking. I just took over for Melissa for an hour or so, and the door was open an inch but they didn't know—" Then she shook her head, as if with growing impatience at herself for bothering with details, even for being breathless. "It was open an inch and I wasn't even conscious of their voices until one of them spoke your name. I didn't think too much of that, there was no reason they shouldn't, but then it was 'Ned Isaly' several times over." And here Sally turned a stricken face upward to Ned. "They said 'Isaly' and 'contract' several times. So it wasn't a casual mention of your name. The meeting was about you—"

Ned interrupted. "Was Tom there?"

It annoyed her immensely that Ned would look for some benign reason for this meeting. "No, of course he wasn't! Wouldn't I have said? That's part of it, that he *wasn't* there, that they were making decisions about you without him. Clive was upset, too. I could tell from his tone. And to upset Clive—he's such a selfish creep—would take a lot. Listen: it sounded as if they were going to try to break your contract." Her voice rose steadily, anxiety squeezing it out.

Saul laughed. "Oh, come on, Sally. Why the hell are you so worried? This is Oz you're talking about. So you pulled back the curtain and found some damned fool was pulling the strings—"

Sally flashed at him. "Shut up, shut up!"

Saul did a little dance backward, a boxer's step, threw up his hands.

Ned only shrugged and said, "How can they? It's a contract for two more books, isn't it?"

"How *can* they? This is publishing, Ned! They can do whatever freak things they want. You know what it's like—" Then she shook her head in a kind of hopeless way. "No, you don't. You never pay any attention to them."

"Hear, hear," said Saul.

Ned only laughed. "Well, there's a limit to even what they can do."

Sally, much shorter than Ned, who was over six feet, tried to shove her face into his by standing on her toes. "Didn't I just *say*? This is publishing and there *are* no limits. They can do whatever the hell they want to."

"I doubt it," said Saul, puffing on his cigar. "Come on, let's go to Swill's. Take the afternoon off."

"I can't. I have to work for a living," said Sally.

Saul put his arm around her shoulders. "You call that 'living,' girl?"

FOURTEEN

Bobby Mackenzie sat at a table not in, but near the front window of Michael's, with Giverney's new book on the table beside him. Michael's was packed as usual at lunchtime. Bobby delighted in seeing Damon Rich, publisher of Queeg and Hyde, sitting a dozen tables behind him, in the back room. He delighted even more in seeing Nancy Otis, high-powered editor, who had left Queeg and Hyde for Grunge, sitting at a table just barely visible around the corner of the back room, which was where they put the real nonstarters.

When Clive had come up to the table an hour ago, Bobby had been eating bread sticks delicate as bird's legs and was now rolling one of them across the back of his hand. He reminded Clive of a drum major sometimes; he moved through the corridors of Mackenzie-Haack as if he had a whistle in his mouth and was pointing the parade in the proper direction.

Bobby kept craning his neck to see who was coming through Michael's double doors. "Where are these guys?"

Clive touched a napkin to the corner of his mouth. "They'll be here." He loved it that Bobby was kept waiting.

"You told them two o'clock, right?"

"No, they told *me*. They'll be here, Bobby. It's only a little past."

They wouldn't want lunch, Danny Zito had said. A drink, maybe. Coffee and dessert, maybe? Bobby and Clive had already ordered and eaten. The remains of Bobby's risotto lay on a big plate. Clive had ordered his usual salad. If he ate like Bobby, he'd be a blimp. Bobby's metabolism hammered every calorie to its knees.

"These them?" Bobby gestured toward the front.

Clive nodded, sighed. *These them.* If Bobby's articulation had leaned ever so slightly closer to gangland, it would have come out "Dese dem?" How could anyone who talked like that be president of one of the most prestigious literary publishers in New York?

The two men at the front of the restaurant, quite decently dressed except for the Ray-Bans on the taller one, were pointed in the right direction by the maître d'. They made their way—carved their way, rather—through the flotilla of white-linen tables, every table taken, making no allowance for the strained space between. Elbows got jostled, scarves fluttered away, silk-lined furs slid halfway to the floor. Women gaped; men glared.

Clive cringed.

Could the two coming toward him care less?

Bobby smiled. He loved any "fuck-you" attitude as long as it wasn't directed at him.

They arrived at the table. Odd the way they occupied space without seeming to be fully there. Or perhaps Clive was trying to divorce himself from the whole transaction. He wished Bobby had stayed at home. But, no, Bobby had to be in on everything, have a finger in every single pie. If Bobby's kinetic energy was to travel down his arm to the hand he now extended, these two would fry where they stood.

Clive was doing the introductions while the three shook hands, Bobby more enthusiastically than his guests. "Mr. Candy . . . Mr. Karl . . . (were these first names? last names?) Bobby Mackenzie of Mackenzie-Haack."

Whatever was going on in the minds of these two, Clive couldn't say. Their faces were twinned, both expressionless as store-window mannequins. They looked amazingly alike despite their obvious differences: one tall, the other short; one stocky, the other angular and thin. They sat down.

Bobby's enthusiasm was pumping. Clive couldn't believe it, not in these circumstances. But Bobby got excited over anything rich and new: new writer, new failure of another publishing house, new lawsuit, new hit men.

Karl's head swiveled around, looking for a waiter, saw one, crooked his finger. The waiter came. "One Scotch rocks, one bourbon rocks, double."

"Doubles, sir?"

"Doubles."

"Toil and trouble," said Clive, smiling. They all looked at Clive, including Bobby, as if Bobby had come in with them. They might have been measuring Clive for a side of beef, one eye on the cold locker. Clive was annoyed, largely with himself. It was, after all, his show. He shot his cuffs, fiddled one of the gold links. He spent so much time in Façonnable and the menswear section of Bergdorf's reinventing himself that he had become especially attuned to designers' garments, masterly at identifying them. The suits these two wore, with their strange shades of browns and grays like remembered soft autumns: Armani, clearly. Did they all wear them, then, the men in Danny's line of work, for the jackets' roominess? Still, for some reason, their taste in clothes relieved him, gave him some confidence.

The waiter set the drinks before the two men. Bobby looked at them, ordered another for himself. He'd blitzed the first and second. "Scotch. No rocks."

He had to be different while being the same. Clive sighed. "Gentlemen—"

Candy looked behind him as if Clive were addressing someone as yet unseen. Then Candy said, "Nice restaurant you got here. Classy. Where's this place stand in *Zagat*'s?"

"This place *is Zagat*'s," said Bobby, with his usual passion for hyperbole.

"Yeah. Look at the paintings. It's like a whole fucking gallery."

"Contemporary art. Jasper Johns, Jim Dine—"

Danny Zito, thought Clive.

Bobby went on nodding around the room: "—Robert Graham—"

Candy swelled the list, saying, "You got your David Honkey, your—"

"Hockney," said Clive. He really had to.

"Huh?"

"David Hockney."

"Right. You like him, too? The place is a lot bigger than it looks. We oughtta come here more, right K?"

"Food good?" asked Karl.

"Excellent," said Bobby. He pointed at his plate. "The Cobb salad is a knockout. Best in New York."

Karl looked at him, singularly unimpressed.

Clive said, "Shall we get down to business?" When no one said not to, he went on: "The, uh, deposition of this man—"

Now Karl did interrupt. "'Deposition'? Interesting choice of word. As in 'depose'? Does that fit, though? You got to be more careful of your word choices; words can do a lot of things. That old rhyme we used to say as kiddies—'Sticks and stones can break my bones but words can never hurt me'? What a bunch of suckers we were back then, right?" Karl skidded the heel of his palm off his temple in some larking "Oy" gesture.

Probably a neo-Nazi, Clive thought, removing a photograph from the pocket of his Burberry. It was a glossy four by six. "This man." He slid it beneath his hand across the table.

Without touching it, Candy and Karl looked down.

"Waiter's coming," said Bobby, with a curt warning nod, as if he were already hip to the ways of gangland.

Candy flipped the photo over as the waiter set Bobby's drink before him. Behind the waiter, Mortimer Durban was sitting down at the next table where two women Clive didn't know were seated. Apparently finished working his own table, Mort had come to work somebody else's. Mort Durban gave them a nod, checked out the two strangers in a wondering way. He was a powerful agent. You had to nod back. Clive did. You hardly had time to eat in Michael's, you were so busy checking things out.

After he'd gulped down some wine, Clive asked, "What . . . advance are you looking for?" He liked putting it this way. If anyone overheard (and the other diners were all too busy with checking out the room front and rear to focus for more than three seconds), it would be thought just the old familiar publishing argot.

"You mean total?" asked Candy.

Bobby nodded.

"A mil."

"That's a steep advance," said Bobby.

Steep? wondered Clive. After a three-million advance to that eminent true crime writer Barry Shooter, who, despite his name (not to mention his speciality), couldn't tell a gun from a corncob?

Karl gave a tiny shrug. Take-it-or-leave-it.

Bobby said, "Okay, but is that the actual *advance* money or is it half on signing, half on completion?" Bobby grinned.

"Divvied up, right. Only, fellas—" Karl chuckled "—Candy and me. We don't sign nothing, surprise, surprise."

Bobby took another gulp of his Scotch. He was loving this. In another moment he'd be chewing a chair. "Okay, a handshake's good as a signature."

Clive hoped Mort Durban didn't hear that, for God's sakes. But Mort was too deep in studying the cleavage of the women on either side of him.

"So when can we expect, you know, the first installment?" Bobby asked.

"That depends," said Karl, "on whether we, ah, undertake the project. You know, whether we go for the idea." He was rolling an expensive cigar in his mouth, as yet unlit.

Clive wondered how Karl would respond if the waiter told him about the no-smoking rule. Clive was glad he wasn't the waiter.

Bobby was confused. His brow furrowed into rows you could plant beans in. "'Take on the project'? But that's why we're talking in the first place. I mean, I assumed you'd already decided—"

Closing his eyes as if against the blatherings of a child, Karl said, "Depends on this." Eyes open again, he tapped the upside-down photo of Ned Isaly. "We have to find out more about—" He tapped the photo again. "We have to research it; otherwise we'd be, you know, writing this project blind." He gave them a scimitar smile.

What was this contract killer talking about, for God's sakes? Clive asked, "Are you saying you have to get *close* to the subject? You're saying you want to get to *know* the subject?"

Candy, who'd been busy sussing out the room, waded into the conversation. "We have rules: one is we never, I mean *never,* take on anything without we get to know the, uh, subject."

Bobby and Clive looked at each other, for once equally at a loss. They shook their heads. "Mackenzie-Haack," said Bobby, "pays out half a million on *spec*? That's what you're saying?"

"So what'd'ya want, Bobby? An ear?" Candy's laugh was like a rasping cough.

Karl's was more of a snort.

Bobby looked quickly around, shoving his palms down on air, motioning them to keep their voices down. "Then what about the advance?" Bobby asked. "I mean if you decide not to, uh, you know, write it?"

"Return it, obviously." Karl rolled the cigar. "Why do you want this thing done, anyway?" he asked.

Crossing his arms in front of his chest, sealing himself in, as it were, Bobby shook his head gravely, as if what he knew would never pass his lips; it was too solemn to be disclosed. He said, "Can't help you there. Can't talk about it." Bobby was boss again; Bobby was in control of the situation.

Karl and Candy looked at each other as if someone at the table were crazy and it wasn't them. Karl turned to Bobby. "Well, if you can't help us here, I guess we can't help you there. Ready C?"

"Yeah, we're outta here." They got up.

"Just a minute!" said Bobby. "Come on, sit down." They did. He said, "It's a very volatile subject, see." Bobby slid *Don't Go There* carefully across the table, the photo on the back face up. "It's him, he's the reason."

Clive had been getting increasingly more nervous and now was utterly astounded. Surely, he wasn't going to tell them . . . "Bobby, let's just drop it. The whole thing."

The look Bobby thought twice about turning on Karl and Candy he didn't even think once about turning on Clive.

Clive threw up his hands. "Okay, *okay!*"

Bobby continued, with relish, leaning across the table, across the smiling face of Paul Giverney, and keeping his voice to a whisper so that the two men had to lean toward him, too.

Clive looked at the three of them, heads nearly touching. The Three Stooge Conspirators. He shook his head and looked away.

Bobby said, "It's this guy, this writer. We can't sign him unless we get rid of Isaly. *His* idea"—Bobby tapped the dust jacket—"his, not mine."

"So," said Candy, "he told you to cap the guy."

Clive watched, disbelievingly, as Bobby made a movement of his hand and head that would have been completely ambiguous if anyone in this business knew what ambiguity was. "Bobby—"

This earned Clive a kick beneath the table. "So you see the problem," Bobby said, leaning back with a satisfied air.

Candy and Karl both stared at him. Karl said, "Yeah, yeah, we see the problem. This is one shitty business you guys are in."

Candy asked, "You all like this? I mean is all publishing this fucked up?"

The face of Paul Giverney seemed to grin up at them. *"No,"* it would have said, *"it's even more fucked up."*

Bobby said, smiling. "Listen: have you two ever thought of writing a memoir? It'd be big. I guarantee it."

Until now, Clive had never realized just how much Bobby (the son of a bitch) was in the right business.

FIFTEEN

What's the deal on this guy?" Candy inclined his head toward the plate glass of Barnes & Noble, which today was full—swamped, really—with *Don't Go There*.

Karl considered. "Giverney's really hot. The way those two acted—" Karl motioned vaguely back downtown in the direction of Michael's. "You'd think he was the only waiter around. You never read one of his books?"

"Not to my knowledge."

His eyes still on the window, Karl shook his head. "You read a book and don't remember?"

"Well, have you? I see you with books sometimes. Me, I ain't got the time."

Karl extracted a fresh slice of gum from his Doublemint gum packet, then put the packet away and considered the Barnes & Noble window as he folded the fresh piece into his mouth. "He sells almost as much as Stephen King. He doesn't write straight horror though, I don't think. Maybe psychological horror."

"With a display like that, I bet he's number one on the list."

"The what?" Karl was surprised.

"*New York Times* best-sellers. They call it 'the list.' I been doing my homework. After all, we don't want to be completely clueless about this game, do we?"

"We *are* clueless. I mean, one big clue is you never heard of Paul Giverney." Karl nodded toward the window. "I think maybe we better stop in, look around."

Candy looked indecisive. "I dunno. We might not even decide to take this job. This Ned Isaly might be someone we don't much want to whack. Then we'll have wasted the look around."

Karl stepped up to the door, motioned to Candy. "Come on."

For a few moments, they simply stood, looking around at the stacks and shelves of books, books on tables, on counters, and stretching along the walls, back as far as they could see.

"Jesus," said Candy. "What did we let ourselves in for?"

"You don't have to fucking read them all."

"Yeah, I know; all the same, it's like another world in here, and it ain't ours."

Karl ignored this. "Here's what I think we ought to do—you listening?"

Candy nodded, his eyes narrowed as if he were caught in a white water of books, swirling around in his vulnerable little kayak.

"We buy these two books. I'll look for Isaly's—"

"And me, I get this Givenchy's, right?" Candy was on top of it.

"Right, except it's Giverney, not Givenchy." There was a stack right in front of them and another stack on the counter. This in addition to the book's having been given another key place in the store, a separate display across one entire section of the wall. Karl gave a low whistle. "Wow. This guy gets a lot of play." He turned to Candy. "You okay with this idea, C?"

Worriedly, Candy said, "Yeah, only the book looks thick as hell." He reached down to the stack that was still high enough to topple. He took up the book and straightened the stack a little. *Don't Go There* had a murky jacket, gray and black and kind of watery, as if it had been left out in the rain. Candy didn't like the jacket and said, "This bodes ill."

Karl rolled his eyes. Candy loved this expression, had picked it up from a cretinous screenwriter in L.A. who said it with his back against the wall, looking at two gun muzzles. *"This bodes ill"* he'd said just before they shot him. It boded ill, all right. But Candy had been full of a rather grudging admiration for the screenwriter. He'd said so.

"He's a *screenwriter,* for fuck's sake," Karl had said. "We should have shot him for that alone. What did you expect him to say? 'Don't'? That strike you as a Hollywood ending? 'Oh, please, don't'?"

Karl thought if he ignored the "bodes ill," Candy would give it up sooner. "It's not a bad jacket. It's atmospheric."

"It's raining. I don't like books like that."

"You just got through saying you didn't have time to read them, so what the fuck do you mean?"

A woman bumped into him, vision obscured by the stack of books she was carrying. "Sorry," she said. "Can you find what you're looking for?"

Karl smiled. "Depends if you're talking about books. Yeah, I'm looking for one by a writer named Isaly."

She frowned a bit, mouthing the name *Isaly, Isaly* to herself. She brightened. *"Ned* Isaly, you mean? Yes, I can—"

The pile of books teetered and Karl clamped his hand on the top one. "Where're you headed? I can take these for you."

Round eyed (green eyed) she said, "Well . . . well thanks. If you take them over there to the counter, you see, where the line is and just leave them, I can get your book for you."

"Right."

She took off, weaving through customers and shelves, and Karl balanced the stack of books. "Come on, C. Over there to the counter. You can get in line."

"The damn counter's a mile long. Look at the line."

The place was crowded. It was hard getting through it with a pile of books. Must have been a lot harder for her because she was small. Karl made two stacks of the books on the end of the counter, then joined Candy in the line.

Candy wondered what *Don't Go There* was about. A lot of things he didn't care if he ever knew, probably. He looked to see how many pages, and it was as he'd feared—nearly five hundred. Four hundred eighty pages. He wouldn't have to read it all, though. Then it occurred to him—why did he have to read any of it? Why did they have to have either book? Which is what he said to Karl.

Karl's face showed impatience. "We'll have to know this guy Isaly. When we run into him strictly by accident do you want to stand there with your teeth in your mouth saying, like "Yo, you say you're a writer? I never heard of you."

"I'm not that unclassy, K."

"We got to see what makes these writers tick, right?" They had already moved up a half dozen places in line. Karl saw the saleslady coming toward them.

"Thanks," he said, taking Isaly's book. *Solace.* "Do you know anything about this?"

"Of course. It's wonderful. I just wish he'd write quicker. And thank you for depositing all of those books—" Her head nodded toward the counter. "Well, 'bye."

Karl wondered how old she was. She was very pretty. "Yeah, see you."

Candy fanned the pages of *Don't Go There* and wondered where "there" was. Well, that was the idea, he supposed. To keep you guessing and make you buy it and read umpteen million pages. A good plan. He looked around again, still astounded. "Did you ever think how a book was competing for fucking space? Look at all of them. You'd have to be shit crazy to try to break into this. You'd have to have solid gold balls to do it."

"Either that or get an agent that already has them."

Candy shook his head again. "So what's yours called?"

Karl held it up. *"Solace."*

Candy studied the title for a moment. "It's only one word."

"Yeah. Why? What's wrong with that?"

"The title's only one word and there ain't no picture on the jacket. I think your jacket sucks, if truth be known. It's white. I mean, if the publisher didn't like it enough to put a picture on—" Candy shrugged.

"Yeah? Well, apparently this guy Isaly can write, really write. It won some award." Karl frowned. "New York Critics,' it says back here." He had turned the book over and was reading the blurbs on the back of the jacket.

"So how d'ya know mine *can't* write? I mean, you don't have to get awards to prove it. Look at Russell Crowe." Candy moved his shoulders to sit his jacket better across his shoulders.

Karl just looked at him. "The fuck's Russell Crowe got to do with it?"

"He never won the Academy Award for playing that nutty code breaker. Doesn't mean he can't act."

Karl let Russell Crowe go, saying, "I think Giverney must not write all that well because the guy's spread all over the fucking store, C."

Candy didn't understand this reasoning. "Which means he's popular, popular big time. Which means he's good."

"No, it doesn't, C. If everybody's reading this fucking book, do you suppose this Giverney's been wasting much time on how good his writing is? Consider: if everybody and his old gran's reading it, how good could it be? I don't know about your gran but mine's so fucking stupid she gets the news of the day from cereal boxes. I bet she eats this stuff up." Karl punched a finger toward the book in Candy's hands.

"Well, we'll see. You read yours and I read mine and we'll just see."

JARDIN
DES
PLANTES

SIXTEEN

Nathalie sat alone on a dark green bench in the Jardin des Plantes. At first she had been sitting in sunshine but now sat in the gathering shadows, waiting. Nathalie closed her eyes as she had often done, feeling as if she were drifting in and out of consciousness. When she opened her eyes the garden colors seemed too diffuse, melting into one another. She could not seem to grasp them—the blue (or was it green?) of the peonies; the etiolated, pale yellow (or perhaps white?) of the lilies.

She waited for Patric; she had been waiting all day. A weariness settled over her like the shadows in which she sat. She had strolled around the old-fashioned zoo and along the paths of the alpine garden, taking in little of it.

Had he forgotten? Had he gone to L'Hérault to be with his wife and children? Michel, Leon, Angelique. She knew their names. They lived in Roquebrun all summer long in the country house. Villerosalie. It was a beautiful word. Was Rosalie the name of someone in the family or had the name been inherited with the house?

Nathalie wished she had paid more attention to details, had stored up flourishes and embellishments against such a time as this when Patric didn't come. But of course she hadn't foreseen this, had she? She had been understandably careless in not committing things to memory. In not staring at them until the little pansies along the rail of the Café Dumas burned into her brain—the exact shade of purple, the velvet texture of the petals, or the white glare of the waiter's apron.

There had been so much to choose from for memory's sake, such as the rim of lavender anemones against the dark green hedge over there; or the lighted lamps along the Champs-Elysées; coffee and brioche sitting outside in the chilly last days of October along the Boulevard St.-Germain; the Americans so well dressed, heavy with gold jewelry in the Rue de Rivoli; Patric's arm around her waist as they walked, as if he could never get close enough.

The shadows were turning into night. She tried to see her future; it was full of blank pages. They fluttered away like the pages of a calendar in a film, dated but empty.

I t was too close to the end now, thought Ned, as he read over these pages. Perhaps it *was* the end. He might have condemned Nathalie to sitting on the green bench forever. It hardly seemed fair. Ned got up and moved to the window. He looked down and saw Saul sitting in the little park. There were two men he'd never seen before sitting on a bench farther along the path. Seldom did anyone cut across the park, even more rarely did anyone sit in it. He wondered who they were for a moment and then went back to his story, wanting to rescue Nathalie. But there was nothing to hold her to the gardens or the page.

*   *   *   *   *

After Candy and Karl had purchased the books they had taken the A train to Chelsea and had a cup of coffee in a café there and marveled that this was what people did. This is how they spent their time. Now they sat on a bench near a flower bed, mostly planted with zinnias, in a little triangular park in Chelsea and compared books. Candy decided he liked Giverney's flap copy better; Karl liked Isaly's face more than Giverney's.

"Your guy looks too fucking pretty and rich," said Karl. "Look at that chin, that coat—cashmere, it looks like." But Karl had to admit his jacket copy sounded a little slow going: the two main characters, the man and the woman, keep almost meeting yet never do. So where's the solace in that? Karl frowned.

"I don't like the sad stuff," said Candy. "I mean, you read a book, you want to escape the sad stuff, right?"

Karl grunted. "Maybe. Maybe not."

"This Giverney writes genre books."

Karl frowned. "You sure you're pronouncing that accurately?"

" 'Books'?"

" '*Genre*,' asshole." Karl swatted Candy on the shoulder with *Solace*.

Candy shoved Karl's hand away, settled his jacket on his shoulders. "Go easy on this suit. Fucker cost me three grand."

"This guy"—Karl was looking at the author's photo on the back of the book—"he could use a decent suit. I wonder what kind of money's in this racket. I mean for guys like Isaly. Now your guy Giverney's obviously rolling in it, but my guess is only a few get that kind of money," he said, knowledgeably. He took out his cigar case.

Candy waved *Don't Go There* back and forth. "Three or four mil, that's what the girl at the counter told me."

"What? Jesus Christ, that's more than the both of us make in a couple fucking years."

Candy put the book down. "We do all right, listen. And we're particular, remember."

"Half a million we got for the last job. That's only a quarter apiece. And this joker gets that kind of money for a damned novel? A *mystery* at that? It isn't even one of your *literary* type books. At least my guy's literary."

"But ain't that what you were saying in the bookstore?" said Candy. "If everybody including your old gran was reading this guy, then how good can he be? Anyway, it ain't as much as writers like Tom Clancy and who's-it get. That's more like fourteen, fifteen million."

"Who's 'who's-it'?"

"You know, that horror guy, one you were talking about. He wrote that book where Jack Nicholson goes berserk with a hatchet?" This was one of their favorite movies.

Karl lit his cigar (Cuban) and waved his platinum lighter into a couple of figure eights like fireflies homing in on Peter Pan. "Stephen King."

"This clerk was talking about what this publisher, Queeg and Hyde"—Candy held the spine out—"pays that authoress that writes the chick-jep books."

"What's that? Hebrew?"

"Nah. It means girl in a jam. Jeopardy."

Karl shrugged. "I don't get it."

"Me, neither. Fuck, you could waste your entire life doing this shit." He held up his book.

"Yeah, but at three or four mil a crack, that's not exactly wasting, Candy."

"Money ain't everything, Karl."

"Since when?" said Karl.

*　　*　　*　　*　　*

He was right at the point in the manuscript where any other writer would, in a few more pages, a chapter at most, have reached The End, and, as Saul knew he'd do, he aborted, called it quits, deep-sixed it.

Saul was sitting on his usual bench in the park, regarding the cold-looking but intrepid zinnias, still blooming along the path. On the other side of the zinnia bed sat two men who looked oddly alike, in spite of their different builds. Maybe it was the clothes. Saul knew expensive clothes. They had books, unusual enough for a couple of businessmen, but these two actually appeared to be discussing them.

He slid down on the bench, thought of going to Swill's, wondered what in hell was his problem. He did not understand himself; he never had. Perhaps if writing was his livelihood he could see this manuscript through to a close. Saul could finish nothing—not a book, not a meal, not sex. There were several women who could attest to that last bit. What was behind it? His mother's sudden death? His father's following shortly after? It was as if they couldn't live without one another, but both could live without Saul. A double shock such as that could derail anyone, but why a derailment so voluptuously self-destructive as a writer's finding himself, after having successfully published one book, incapable not of writing another, but of ending another?

Perhaps it was simply fear (if fear is ever simple) of not being able to write a book as well received as that first one. One cannot imagine coming even close to this kind of success. Saul did not think this was the reason because "success" had never meant that much to him. He certainly wanted readers, all writers did.

The hell with it. He leaned back, stretched his arms along the back of the bench, and looked again at the two men on the other side of the path. They were still talking about these books they held, one even taking a swing at the other. All in good fun, apparently.

Saul became so curious about these two men with their books

that he couldn't help himself; he saw a story. The little scene was complete within itself. That's it, isn't it? The linear world stops. The temporal world fades.

Watching them, he was cheered. There were men in the world in suits who still read books.

*   *   *   *   *

Sally sat at her desk in Mackenzie-Haack arranging and rearranging a vase full of deep blue delphinium. She was trying to work up the courage (if that's what she needed) to tell Tom Kidd there was some sort of plan that would harm Ned Isaly. She hated to say "plot" against him. And maybe she was reading too much into what she'd heard.

Tom Kidd was talking on the phone. He could be talking right now to Ned, the way he sounded. Sally could usually work out who he was talking to even if she couldn't hear the words. It was a contented mood she heard; it was a mood he fell into only when talking to certain people, all writers, such as Ned or Grace Packard or two or three others. Any other telephone "vampires" (Tom's word, which included people like Kikki Cross, agent; Jani Gat, publisher of a trendy little house that was trying to make it on looks and couldn't; or the would-be writers who managed to glom his phone number and pitch the books they hadn't written and never would).

Sally lifted her head and listened. Yes, it was Ned, or about Ned, for Tom had said his name. She went around her desk to lean toward his open door, but Tom's voice rose and fell, rose and fell, as gently as if he were lullabying a baby.

So it wasn't Ned for he never needed the poor-baby treatment. Ned wasn't a baby about his writing. Either Chris Llewelyn or Henry Suma, both wonderful writers, both babies about it. Chris would "go off" a novel in the middle and start whining about writer's block. Tom Kidd couldn't stand it when they started in on writer's block, since Tom didn't believe in it.

"You're bored, that's all (Tom's pep talk began). *Imagine being confined with a bunch of people who can't think right, act right, and, worst of all, speak right. Mouths full of marbles, that's them, and you have to keep watching what they're doing and listening to them for months, for years. So just to be bored by this is a miracle. I'm surprised you don't go off and shoot yourself."*

It was rare for him to deliver that message (since his empathy with writers was boundless), but when he did, it was delivered in Tom's lullaby tone to counteract any sting they might feel. Such a message didn't sound consoling, but it did seem to be to such a writer as Chris Llewelyn. All Tom wanted to do was talk them down from the high ledge of the Writer's Block Building.

But with Ned, Tom never had to use any of his little tricks. He talked to Ned as if Ned were an adult—a writer-adult, that is—not a full-blown actual adult, that is, not from Sally's point of view. Ned often gave the impression of zoning out on her the way teenagers do with their parents. They only pretend to be paying attention to the other guy; they were actually paying attention to whatever was going on in their self-centered, bookish little world—! and she was getting madder by the moment that Ned wasn't taking this whole Bobby-Clive plot more seriously.

* * * * *

"What's up with you?" Tom Kidd was standing by her desk.

"What? Me? Nothing."

"You were gnashing your teeth."

"No, I wasn't. People don't really do that." She swung around to her computer screen and started hitting the keys. Gibberish.

Tom Kidd stood there. "That was Eric. He says he won't meet the deadline because he's going to burn the manuscript."

Seeing he'd dropped her teeth gnashing, Sally swung back to face him. "That *would* interfere with the publishing schedule. Except Eric always makes fifteen copies, so I'm sure he'd put one aside. How much longer does he need?"

"Couple extra weeks. Can you imagine? Making yourself crazy just because you'll be two weeks late?"

"Production will break out in hives if a book's two *days* late. You know them."

"Oh, them."

"Yes, well, oh-them got on his case a couple of years ago because he didn't get galleys back on time. I can think of a few other scripts Mackenzie-Haack might want to throw on the pyre."

Tom smiled and leaned against the doorjamb. "Inform me."

"Well, there's Dwight Staines's massive new book. Then—" There was nothing to do but tell him, though she felt the passing on of information gleaned from listening outside somebody's door would work against her in the end. "I've got to tell you something. It's—" Sally stopped.

Tom had lit a cigarette and was blowing the smoke away from her.

Why didn't she say it? I think they're trying to ruin Ned Isaly. What was that bird with the tongue of fire that, after delivering its burden of knowledge, fell to Earth with the flames extinguished? The thing that kept it soaring was what it knew.

*　　*　　*　　*　　*

Ned was trying to call Tom Kidd. The line was intractably busy. Even the busy signal sounded like one of those roadwork drills.

He turned to look out of the window, down at the park. A fringe of branches hid most of it; he couldn't see the zinnia bed. A restless wind whipped the branches apart.

Was that Saul down there? The wind moved his line of vision and he saw that old cat that hung out walking on the path. They had never known where it came from, and it was never around when the tramp and his dog were. The cat looked well fed.

He'd leave in a moment. For now, Ned leaned his forehead on the cold glass and watched the wind tearing at the leaves and looked at the sky, thinking how dusk looked like dawn, and then thought of Pittsburgh's smoggy dawns. City snow. He could see himself at the end of that bridge (what bridge was it?) ornamented by four panthers, two on each end. The bridge spanned Panther Hollow. He had stood looking at the statues, licking an ice cream cone with three scoops of ice cream. Chocolate. Strawberry. Vanilla. Well, he couldn't be sure of that, could he? Was he even certain there'd been a bridge spanning Panther Hollow? Was he even sure about Panther Hollow?

Stupefied, as if he'd just come awake, he took down his windbreaker, realizing he'd drifted a long way from the Jardin des Plantes.

*　*　*　*　*

If she didn't tell him, Ned would have no ally with the power of Tom Kidd. He stood there, a slightly built man with milkweed hair and almost colorless eyes, the best editor in New York, one who knew what an editor was supposed to be. Tom was quixotic, a champion of the lost causes of literature.

Times she had been in Tom's office on one or another pretext—reshelving books, picking up copy, looking terribly urgent, and pretending not to listen when Ned had been there—Ned or Chris Llewelyn or one of the other good Mackenzie-Haack writers—and she'd never heard a word said about sales, promotion, publicity, or the damned list. It was all writing and not necessarily their writing. Writing was everything.

All of this went through Sally's mind in the time it took her to say, "Nothing. It's not important."

He waited (since it was obviously "important") but did not prompt her. He said, "That's a pretty bunch of flowers, Sal. You should always have blue flowers around."

Tom walked away and she felt she had flunked some rigorous test. She covered her face and in a minute felt tears leaking through her fingers. Coward. She reached out and pulled the book she was reading over. Wiping her eyes on her blue sleeve, she opened the book, at the same time pulling open her desk drawer and getting out a Hostess cupcake.

It was Henry Suma's new book, but it could have been any of a number of books. She read and ate and was calm once again.

*   *   *   *   *

Saul watched the old tomcat sit down in front of the two suits. He smiled. Story: here's the cat; here's the tension: the cat becomes the still point. Saul couldn't help himself with a layout like this; what writer could? That was arrogant, he thought, maybe a lot could, wouldn't think it worth thinking about.

Yet maybe that was it: we think like dreams. We throw all kinds of junk into the stew pot because we believe it will all go together, will cohere no matter how unlikely the match is. As fluid as a dream yet as fixed as the moon.

Focus: cat or zinnia bed, or books or suits. One or the other. As suits, he meant. The men inside them? They meant nothing. They were no problem.

Saul looked up at the sky at dusk. It was mottled, the faintest blotchy colors—yellow, blue, brown. He thought it was a New York sky. Only in New York would you see a sky like a bruise, darkening up. He checked his watch. Time for Swill's.

* * * * *

"Throw something."

"Yeah, like what? I ain't got nothin' to throw. You?"

Karl yawned. So did the cat. That irritated him to pieces. "It's mocking us."

Candy made a noise in his throat. "Nuts."

"I hate cats. I think I've got that phobia."

"Christ's sake, a phobia yet." Candy didn't like the way the cat was looking at him, but he wouldn't say so. "A big-ass phobia."

Karl ignored the sarcasm.

"Kick it, you feel that way," said Candy, ready to go for the damn cat himself. It just fucking sat there, as if it owned the park.

"No way. It'd be just like one of those animal-rights protesters to pop out of the trees and go for us."

"Jesus, but you got some imagination, Karl. Come on, let's find a drink." Candy yawned.

Karl thought the yawn was just like the cat's and was made even more nervous. "Yeah, a drink sounds good."

They got up with their books. They didn't like it that the cat might be thinking he'd forced them out of his place.

"That cat," said Karl, "that cat's made his bones."

* * * * *

Patric had left her. He had gone, thought Nathalie. He had gone to the place with the beautiful name: Villerosalie, the summer home.

He had given up on her. He had left her with nothing to hold but blank pages.

Nathalie had managed to get up from her bench and walk to the little zoo, much beloved of children, but a rather scruffy place.

She looked at the tiger. It was awfully small for a tiger. But what did she know about tigers? The tiger returned her gaze. No menace. No menace at all.

Perhaps like her, it was left with only a blank page.

Ned thought, how can I leave her there? Is this, then, the last page? It's too indefinite. But what, really, was indefinite about it? Patric had gone.

As far as Nathalie was concerned, yes, it was the last page.

Ned capped his pen and sat back and stared at nothing.

Nathalie sat alone in the Jardin des Plantes.

SEVENTEEN

Those two hoods, thought Clive (wondering if that appellation was still in use). What had Bobby Mackenzie set in motion? Rather, what had Clive set in motion, going to Danny Zito? If the police ever came into this, you can bet Bobby would fade the heat, play the innocent: *"Did what, officer?"* And point the finger at Clive. That's all Clive was, one of Bobby's goons. No, he was *main* goon, *capo* goon.

He had just gotten off the phone with Paul Giverney, who'd called to see if they were making any progress. *Yes, absolutely,* Clive had told him. They had a couple of very good men on the job.

"Like who?"

"No one you know, I'm sure. Trust us."

That, of course, had been the wrong thing to say to Paul Giverney, who had told him to hang on for a second while he laughed himself into oblivion. "That's very good, Clive. So I ask you again, who's this 'on the job'?"

Clive had told him about Candy and Karl, explaining that these men were consultants who occasionally did specialized work for Bobby Mackenzie. Clive immediately regretted having told Paul their names when he remembered Paul had written a novel about that Mafia killer, which was only a thinly veiled portrait of the guy. Clive couldn't recall who, but this meant that Paul actually had sources.

"What does that mean? Consulting?"

Clive sighed.

Wondering why in hell *he* had to think of everything, and why didn't Bobby do it, it was *his* idea, Clive slid out the bottom drawer in his desk—a big handsome desk, a goon gift, Bobby buying him off for little and big things over the years—and brought out a fifth of Bombay gin.

"All right, Paul. I'll be frank with you." No he wouldn't. "They're following Ned Isaly."

"Why?"

"To see if they can find out anything, you know, that Ned might not want made public."

"What? Are you saying you're looking to blackmail the man? You mean you've got to go to those lengths—?"

Oh, ho. Clive wished those were the only lengths to which Bobby Mackenzie *would* go. "You're the one who wants him out of the way, Paul."

"Oh, for God's sakes! Just tear up his contract. You've got a raft of lawyers! What the hell else are they good for if they can't fuck with a contract?"

"Paul, that's all I can say at the moment." There was a longish silence. "Paul—?"

"I want to know Ned Isaly's movements. Since he's being followed, that shouldn't be a problem."

The "since he's being followed" held a definite smack of sarcasm.

"Well, that wouldn't be easy; they made it quite clear this is a 'don't-you-call-us' deal. They report when they're done. We can't really control them." This admission made Clive extremely uneasy.

"Why not? You're paying them."

Clive toyed with the image of trying to get the hoods to report in every hour. Fat chance. "I'll do my best."

But what Clive would do was between him and his Bombay gin, since Paul Giverney had hung up. Clive broke the seal, twirled the cap off with his palm, tilted it, and drank straight from the bottle. Ah. *Ahhhhhh.* He recapped the bottle, shoved it back in the drawer, and closed the drawer.

He turned and looked out of his window at the silver flowering of the Manhattan skyline, the Chrysler Building, the Empire State, the Metropolitan Life Building, this juggernaut of light and thought, this rush of night and stars. He thought of the condo in his own prewar building and the view from there, the same skyscrapers on view from the other side. This office, that condo, these views. Clive couldn't imagine being anywhere else; there *was* nowhere else. Losing them did not bear thinking about.

Why was he sitting here fooling with the Dwight Staines manuscript when what he should be doing was trying to figure out what in the hell was going on with Paul Giverney? Giverney had sat right there (Clive even nodded toward the chair as if he were recapping the story for some gossipmonger or journalist. Or the police, if he wanted a chilling example). He told himself Karl and Candy at the very worst would only "rough up" Ned Isaly, just enough to "persuade" him to leave town and take his new novel with him. If that was all, then why did he keep trying to bury that phrase "wet work" that Danny had used almost in passing?

But how did he know? They were weird, those two. Imagine wanting to know more about Isaly before they took the job. Those two were fucking weird, as far as he could see across the table in Michael's. What hit man wants to know the kind of person he's going after? What sort won't even commit himself until he does? What sort wants to meet at Michael's, for God's sakes?

And this Giverney-Isaly thing. Maybe he could talk to Ned Isaly himself. . . . No, not a chance. Bobby would think Clive was warning Ned and get rid of him along with Ned. Clive, unlike Tom Kidd, was thoroughly expendable. Talk to Tom Kidd maybe? Tom Kidd knew Ned through and through, but it's unlikely he'd want to share that knowledge with Clive. No, it would be impossible to get anything out of Kidd.

Giverney's agent. Agents usually knew what their clients ate for breakfast, what they slept in, and with whom. Who they hated and why. Clive grabbed his Rolodex, thumbed through the names of agents (under "A," cross-referenced with their clients), and came up with Mortimer Durban. Christ, but he hated Mort Durban, the insufferable egotist, the Donald Trump of agents, interested only in the deal, the deal, the deal. Not the writer, The Deal. He was one of the most powerful agents in the business. Mort Durban negotiated a book contract as if he were orchestrating the Normandy invasion. He thought he was fucking MacArthur. He was also agent for a couple of high rollers on Clive's list. All Clive wanted to say to him when Durban started turning a contract into a fretwork of arcane bits and pieces, clauses of clauses nobody ever paid any mind to or gave a damn about, some nobody seemed ever to have heard of except Mort Durban—all Clive wanted to say to him was, Here's a pile of money, asshole. Now give me the goddamned book!

Mort Durban wanted you to believe that he believed that agen-

try was a mission and he a missionary spreading the gospel and pre-
pared to be buried in an anthill for the good of his client, about
whom he really cared nothing. This bloated belief in his abilities
had him demanding totally inappropriate advance moneys for his
authors, meaning, of course, for his own commission. To give him
credit (if you could call it credit), he was motivated not as much by
the money he himself would collect as he was by the stars in his
crown, the rush of the deal.

Clive regarded the bottom desk drawer but decided not to. He
started chewing at the bit of dry cuticle on the side of his thumb,
thinking. The Giverney thing must have to do with something in
the past, some unsettled dispute, some unforgiven slur or slight. Irritated, he hit the intercom button.

Amy answered with a tentative "Yes?"

"Get me stuff on Paul Giverney. Facts."

"He's not one of our authors? I don't understand."

Clive squinched his eyes shut. *I know you don't understand,
you simpleton.* Then he said, "He's *somebody's* author, isn't he?"

Silence. A deduction to be made here, but it was too much for
Amy. "Amy, what I'm trying to hint at is that Queeg and Hyde,
Giverney's publisher, would have information like that."

"Oh. Well, I'm not sure how to get it?"

"Ask your friend Stacey (talk about the blind leading; Amy was
Diogenes compared to Stacey) to messenger over a copy of their
fact sheet on Paul Giverney. You know what that is; we have them,
too. They're no big secret; they're just a source for publicity and
promotion who might need a few salient facts for print, interviews,
that sort of thing."

"They do?"

"Amy, I'm not asking you to exhume Elvis's body or excavate

Graceland for unrecorded tunes. I only want to know stuff like where he went to school and his mother's maiden name, and so forth."

"I could call him up? He was just in here a couple days ago."

Where in the bloody *hell* had Bobby found this girl? He bet she was recycled from Bobby's outer office. "No, Amy. Listen. Are you having lunch with Stacey this week?"

Amy's voice brightened. "Oh, yes, tomorrow? We're thinking of going to that new place on Fifty-fifth? I–"

Clive cut her off before she really got into either hers or Stacey's eating habits. "Tell you what: I'll treat the two of you to lunch at Michael's Restaurant. Just have Stacey bring the fact sheet with her."

She was thrilled. She probably *would* exhume Elvis's body for a lunch at Michael's.

"Now, get me Mort Durban."

"You want him to come here?"

"On the tel–" Oh, what's the use? "I'll do it myself."

Flick off intercom, resort to telephone.

A voice far more confident and cold than Amy's would ever be answered, "Durban Agency."

How did the woman manage to get so much swagger into two words?

Clive didn't give an inch. "Let me talk to Mortimer Durban."

"May I ask who's calling?" An iceberg calving.

"The I.R.S. It's personal, if you don't mind."

No response, but Mort Durban came on, very cautious with his "Yes?"

"Mort! Long time no see! It's Clive here."

Mort expelled the breath he'd been holding. "What the hell's the idea, Clive?"

"Had to say something to get past that subzero receptionist you've got. She was with Scott of the Antarctic?" Amy's habit of sticking on a question mark rubbed off on him sometimes.

Mortimer Durban seemed to be considering this description for some reason. He didn't reply.

"Look, I thought maybe we could do lunch tomorrow or some-time?"

"Let me check my bookings."

Bookings? Clive could hear the half-baked British accent click-ing into place. Mort spent a lot of time in London, a lot of loud time in that fey Soho club cleverly called Groucho's that was so popular with the publishing crowd.

"Sorry, Clive, old man. I'm booked up for a month."

"Okay, how about dinner?"

"Dinner?"

His emphasis suggested dinner was foreign to an agent's experi-ence. How about breakfast, then, you overbooked asshole? Clive said, "I was thinking of the Old Hotel." Now Clive was delighted, snickering with his hand over the mouthpiece.

Oh! What a plum!

The Old Hotel was legendary; it was famous for turning people away. Not because the tables were all taken but because they didn't like you, or at least didn't like some of you, though how the maître d' or the various persons who took reservations *knew* they didn't like you was beyond Clive's ken, as it was beyond everybody's ken.

There were edicts handed down by the owner, a man rumored to be all sorts of things with all sorts of connections, but no one Clive knew could tell him which, if any, of these rumors were true. The owner's name was Duff and no one could say whether that was a first name or a last. "Duff" was all they knew. It was said that Duff kept a long list of suppliants who were not welcome. But for the ones who *were* welcome, hell, it was like getting on the fast track for Lourdes. No one knew the rationale for this list. The names were not always persons; the name could be an area, so that anyone living, say, on the Upper East Side between Sixtieth and Eighty-fourth needn't bother getting dressed for dinner at the Old Hotel.

What, exactly, *were* the criteria? No one knew. But the standards (if such they were) had been implemented and stringently upheld to the point where Clive had witnessed the eviction of a party of four one evening around nine P.M. Standing before the maître d's narrow lectern, one of the four (a loutish-looking man) had raised a hue and cry, shouting that he was a writer of such renown that they damned well better let him in. For all Clive knew, one item on the "no admittance" list could have been "writers of renown." It was all extremely peculiar. But since there was such cachet in getting into the place, in being one of the chosen, none of them was about to put down this system; indeed, they fully approved and made much of it over cocktails at a less particular club or restaurant. There was no end of pleasure in knowing people, including your own acquaintances, who couldn't get into the place. And what a plum of a question to put to people and watch them react. Have you dined lately at the Old Hotel? It had a blackball list worthy of the McCarthy hearings, except in this case one didn't know what in hell the hearings were about.

It was Kafka-like. Clive had often wanted this Duff to write a book for Mackenzie-Haack. He sounded like a real stunner. So would the book be. People were more atwitter over the Old Hotel than a gaggle of college freshmen during rush week. Clive would have to include himself in the rushees, to be honest. And whether he would have entertained the book idea had his name been on the "no" list—well, he was quite sure he would not.

So, for reasons he would prefer not to speculate on, Clive was among the anointed. He bet Mort Durban wasn't. Heh, heh.

"You'll never get a table, are you kidding? They're booked until Christmas."

That told Clive all he needed to know. *"Sorry, sir, we're booked solid until Christmas"* (or Easter, or Doomsday) was the canned Old Hotel reply if you were on the forbidden list.

"Oh, I'll get us in."

It must've been killing Durban to hear this. He said, "Into the Lobby, maybe, but not up there on the rail."

He was referring to the bar on the first floor and the dining room on the mezzanine. It was an unusual feature for a restaurant, a balconylike upper level. But it was simply part of the architecture of the glorious house it once had been; had it not been in Manhattan, had it been in some "fiddle-dee-dee" city like Savannah, it would have been described as antebellum. A marble staircase swept up to the mezzanine. It was quite long, and the tables set by the copper fretwork of the rail that went around on four sides were choice. A table up there allowed the diner to look down at the bar area and see what lesser lights (although still a hundred watt, compared to the unanointed) were sussing things out. This meant that the viewers were on view themselves. There was always a great deal of rubbernecking.

The Old Hotel was not quite so strict about its downstairs bar—"the Lobby"—which took up the entire first floor with its huge bar and all of its tables and admitted people it might not permit in the upstairs balcony dining room. But that didn't mean just any old stiff could get through the door. A less demanding set of criteria operated for the downstairs, but there were still criteria. Since no one knew what the criteria were, the only way to find out was to walk in. Or try to. And there was the other rule: that one of the unanointed could get in *if* he or she was a guest of the anointed. So Durban could walk in if he were, so to speak, on the arm of Clive.

Durban grumbled. "All right, what time?"

"Whatever suits you."

"You mean whatever suits the Old Hotel." He hung up.

EIGHTEEN

So, what do you think?" asked Candy.

"Not much." Karl put a toothpick in his book, saving his place. He had just hit a passage in the story he really liked and knew Candy was referring not to the book but to the bar and its customers. They were in Swill's, observing Ned Isaly and the people around him. "Except you should take off the shades and turn that baseball cap around."

Candy shrugged. "I think I look like I belong."

"Yeah, but to what?"

Karl was interested in Ned Isaly, and his interest grew the more he read this book, *Solace*. It was a strange book, not much actually happening with the two main characters—and they were nearly the only ones—leading separate lives. It was funny: they seemed to be meant to be together yet they never got together.

Candy, now, was different. He wasn't much of a reader, well, he wasn't *any* kind of a reader except a little science fiction, and Karl kind of admired the fact Candy would take on this book of Paul

Giverney's. What excited Candy was new people, new places. It was a good job for that. They traveled a lot. Candy was all for living in Vegas. They'd had an assignment there, taking out a casino owner and his doll-faced partner. Karl really hated poofs. Guy could be black, white, red, or rainbow colored. African American, Asian American, Native American, American American, Karl didn't give a holy damn. But poofs? No, thank you. In here, the first three guys his glance lighted on he knew were gay. That's why he said, "Not much," in answer to Candy's question. Not to mention dykes. There was one over there leaning against the bar with slicked-back dark hair, a stubby figure, stubby fingers firmly closed around a bottle of Bud. That's not enough, she was smoking a cigar. She was talking to a tall guy with long, unwashed hair.

Swill's was crowded; Karl thought at first this was an after-work office crowd stopping in for a drink. The men and women who formed chic little cliques looked as if they bought their suits and briefcases from the same place. Swill's must have been one of the last places in the city that paid little attention to the city's edicts about smoking.

The suits Karl had noticed first. But most of the other customers in here looked as if they hadn't done an honest day's work in their lives. What was it these days that had so many unemployed, ones who were obviously fit to work? They were all fucked-up, lazy kids expecting to be taken care of. Christ, he himself had worked his way, all of his way, through a small college in upstate New York, had come that close to graduating, then done a fine-tuned job on one of the college deans behind the Sigma Kappa fraternity house. It sure wasn't his fault if things had gotten out of hand. There was no way he could have known two of the dean's sycophants—the chair of the phys ed department and the dean of students—would be packing heat, for God's sakes. Of course the fraternity took it all as a reason to party. They were all drunk; that's what they did. Their parents paid for all of this and the kids got stoned and shot birds off telephone poles.

And because of the whole fracas, he himself had had to get out of town just a month before graduation. His class in the contemporary novel hadn't finished, so he'd gotten an incomplete; well, that's the way it went. But he didn't flaunt his college education; that could be taken wrong by some people who might claim he was overeducated for this kind of work.

"Maybe," said Candy, "we should be going after *this* prick." He flicked his thumbnail against the jacket photo of Paul Giverney.

It amused Karl that the present contract was put out on a writer, someone in the literary scene, something Karl thought he knew a little about. It was a milieu with which he wasn't totally unfamiliar. There'd been places like Swill's at college; he'd had many an argument about Hemingway standing at the bar in Loser's—Hemingway and Ayn Rand (talk about your butch writers!).

Karl had paired up with Candy for a host of reasons that went beyond Candy's wanting to operate independently of the Fabriconi family (for whom he'd worked for several years). He, too, didn't like being told to take out this guy or that guy, no questions asked or answered, just do it.

"Shit," Candy had said back then. "It's like the guy's already walking around dead meat and don't know it. I mean I'd know more about his stupid Irish setter than I would about Conrad Gravely."

Karl raised his eyebrows. "That was *your* hit?"

Candy nodded.

"That was classy, that was an A job, man. You picked that poor bastard off without so much as touching a hair on the guys with him. I always wondered who did that hit."

Modestly, Candy rocked his hand in a *comme ci, comme ça* gesture. "But then they find out the vic—Connie Gravely—wasn't the one turned on them after all. It was some other guy." Candy blew on his coffee. "What a bummer."

"Not your fault. You shouldn't take the heat for that. You were doing what you got paid to do, that's all."

"So when that happened, I walked into Gio's office (this was Giovanni Fabriconi) and told him I was finished, to get another button man."

Karl laughed. "I bet he liked that."

"Oh, yeah, only not enough to let me live. More than one goon came after me."

"You reduced his staff considerably's what I'm thinking."

Candy snorted. "Considerably's right. Thing is, if they'd let me follow Gravely around for a few days—hell, even twenty-four hours—I'd've known. I got this instinct, see."

And *this instinct, see* was the other reason Karl had teamed up with him: Candy had an uncanny ability to intuit whether the mark had done what he was accused of or, on a broader spectrum, whether he deserved to die, accusations aside.

"But these guys, the ones like Gio, all they see is getting theirs back. They ain't really too particular about the truth, you know?"

Karl knew. And it was the only time he'd ever heard anyone else voice his own concern. Once he had questioned the guilt of the guy he was supposed to relieve of his life, and said so, and got no thanks for his concern.

"Fuck you care?" one of the other guys had said, in real nervous agitation, shoving the slide back on his own .9 mm.

Truth. That was a pretty heady word for a couple of hit men to be tossing around. So those were the reasons, aside from Karl's just plain liking Candy. Karl knew he was good at sizing up a man, but in a more superficial way, like fitting him for a suit. It could be all that education he'd had (whereas Candy hadn't made it past the first year of high school) that had muddied the waters of his perception. Too much Hemingway. Everybody was guilty to Hemingway.

Now in Swill's, Karl knew that Candy was only half serious about going after Giverney. They weren't interested in pro bono work. And, of course, they knew nothing about Paul Giverney other than his being a sensationally popular writer.

Karl answered, "Yeah, well, we don't know what Ned ever did to Giverney. Maybe he screwed around with his wife."

Candy turned to the back flap copy. "His wife's name is Molly."

"What? You think you'll find it in the bio? Her telling Giverney Ned Isaly tried to screw her?" Karl reached over and turned the book around. "I still think it's a shitty jacket."

Candy's forehead creased in deep perplexity, as if being called upon to authenticate a painting at the Met. "You know, it kind of fits the book, though."

"How come? Is it gray and rainy and everybody's sunk in anomie?"

"In fucking *what*?"

"Anomie. I like that word."

"Ho, ho, well, fuck your college education. Remember, you never graduated, same as me." Candy snatched back the book and pretended to read.

Karl could have pointed out where they never graduated *from*, but he didn't. "So what's it about?"

"I've only got around fifty pages read. It's way out weird. It sounds like science fiction."

"Philip K. Dick?" Karl asked. This was the one writer Candy knew about. For some reason he was crazy about Philip K. Dick.

"No, no, no. It ain't nothin' like his stuff. No, in Giverney's book it's like everything around this person, this woman, has sort of collapsed. Everything we see around her has changed."

"Anomie." *Sunk in anomie.* He should get a medal.

"Whatever. Near the beginning she goes into this drugstore—well, that's not the right word for it now because it's all changed. Now it's one of them old-fashioned pharmacies. She parks her car and when she gets out she sees the other cars in line are old models. So she's got this new Lexus and the others look like they're straight from the 1940s and '50s, like a two-toned Chevy Belair. When she goes inside what used to be this familiar drugstore—"

At this point a scrawny girl—or woman—holding two beer bottles by their necks paused at their table and looked at Candy's turned-around baseball cap and shades. "That is *so* yesterday." She walked on, swinging the beers.

Karl laughed. "Told you."

Candy looked back and forth from the girl to Karl. "If she only knew. Her life in her hands."

"Go on."

"Okay, so she goes in, into the pharmacy, and everything's changed. Instead of all glass shelves and chrome there's dark wood paneling and those colored bottles these pharmacies used to have along the rear counter, beakers, they're called. And this guy, the pharmacist, that's where it gets even more hairy. The guy is still the same one she knew, same name, same person except he's dressed different, you know, more old-timey. And he knows her, calls her by her name—it's Laura—asks about her kid. He's like nothing ever happened—"

"And it's not like Philip K. Dick?"

"No! I told you, it's not like him. It's more like—what's that guy, that program that used to have a lot of episodes about people turning up in the old hometown and finding it changed?"

"Rod Serling. Rod Serling—what was the name of the show . . . ? Never mind, go on."

"Then she goes to this boutique next door.

"In the windows were dresses on headless and armless mannequins, dresses that might have been stylish back in the thirties or forties. A pleated skirt, the polka-dot one with small capped sleeves—"

"Jesus," Karl said. "Is this supposed to be scary or is it set on Seventh Avenue?" Karl twirled his toothpick to the other side of his mouth. "Though come to think of it, I guess Seventh Avenue *is* scary, I mean if you have to deliver shit there."

"He's just setting the *scene*, Chrissakes. So she looks in and sees this woman, Miss Fleming, who owns the joint:

"Miss Fleming looked as she always did. No, not quite. Her hair was done differently, in a coil at the nape of her neck—"

Karl slid down in his seat. "Come on, C, get to the scary part."

"Well, but this *is* scary, you think about it. To have everything changed just a *little*, just enough to make you think maybe it's *her* that's changed." Candy sat back, pleased with this analysis. "Okay, I'll leave out the beauty shop business—"

"Please do."

"She starts walking.

"Telling herself, Don't hurry, don't hurry. She forced herself to look at the houses she passed, relieved they all looked familiar. Except this house, with its Moorish architecture, the recessed door under an arching stucco roof—"

"What in fuck's Moorish architecture? I have a hard enough time with modern and Victorian and that crap."

The writer at the next table was looking their way. Karl was about to say something emphatic—like "Fuck off!"—until he realized the fellow wasn't really looking at them but through them. He was in his own head. Karl liked that.

"Okay," said Candy, "I'll just capsize some of the description; suffice it to say, there's a *little* something wrong with each place she passes. So she walks along

"—in dread of her own house. Then she thought she knew what all of this was: a dream, one of those lucid dreams where one inhabits his own dream, knowing that he's dreaming—"

"*Whoa!* That went right past me. You know you're dreaming in your own dream?"

"Yeah."

Karl shifted the toothpick back. "It's a tautology."

"A *what?*"

"Tautology. A kind of contradicting yourself. Like that."

"Like what? Where're you going with this, K?"

Karl shrugged.

"Well, don't go there," said Candy. Then he laughed; this book was really getting to him. He looked over at the writer. "Look there, guy's still writing away. Only time he's stopped is to drink his beer."

"Maybe he's like that writer in that King story, the Jack Nicholson one. Remember when his wife finds a whole stack of pages beside his typewriter with only one thing typed on them, one line: 'All work and no play,' et cetera? Remember that?"

Candy nodded. Swill's was filling up even more. A little group with punk hair shades—electric blue, eggplant purple—were moving like a small squadron through the room. The girls seemed to be dressed in scarves, no hemlines or sleeves discernible, just a lot of material, bunched here and there or flowing behind. This squadron—three girls, two boys—sported enough body jewelry to open a branch of Robert Lee Morris. They stopped at the table where the writer sat. It was a table for four and the spokesman, a skinny guy with a rhinestone in his eyebrow and a fade haircut, was telling the writer to sit somewhere else because it was a table for four.

"Fuck they think they are?" Candy was incensed.

There were five of them, so they still needed another chair and quickly homed in on the extra one at Candy and Karl's table. Candy immediately clamped his feet on the seat. Without a word, the skinny guy wrapped his hand around the third chair, the one that Candy had just stashed his feet on, and pulled. Candy's feet stopped him in midpull.

"We need this, man," said the skinny guy.

"Ever think of asking?"

The kid yanked and Candy's feet hit the floor. Candy stood up. He was a head shorter than the kid, but that made no difference to the armlock Candy got him in. And twisted. The kid yelped like a puppy. Candy repeated it: "I *said*, ever think of asking?"

The kid blurted out a "Please" tacked on to an apology.

Candy let him go. "Punk." He sat down again, scarcely noticing the attention he'd attracted.

*   *   *   *   *

Swill's was packed for this hour in the evening when Saul sat down at the table in the window. It pleased them that most of the other regulars had accepted that this window table was Ned's and Saul's.

Most of them, but not all. Whenever he had the chance, b. w. brill would flop there, take out a roll of foolscap, a pen, and his pipe. He would be joined occasionally by Freida Jurkowski, another poet, and they would try to top each other with their most recent recitals. b. w. brill was all over the Village coffeehouses where he made as much impact as the background music.

There was a pecking order in here, but it had nothing to do with Ned or Saul; no one could come anywhere within pecking distance of them. But b.w. and Freida liked to make it appear they could because they'd been published. True. Only there were certain terms of publication that didn't impress even the unpublished (that is, nearly everyone in Swill's). Paperback original was one (although more publishers were turning to it) and especially paperback original *romance*. The only thing worse was vanity publishing, Vanguard Press, one of those the writer had to pay to get his stuff published. Insofar as anyone knew, none of the Swill's regulars had ever opted for it. Or if they had, certainly wouldn't want to admit it, which pretty much undercut the whole idea of (modestly) flashing your book around. Then there were the "little poetry" reviews that weren't of the *Sewanee, Kenyon, Prairie Schooner* caliber. The ones Freida could count as hers were chapbooks and ones with stapled pages. b.w. had published nothing since his book, five years ago, except a poem in a small review called *Unguentine Press. UP* had since folded, and b. w. brill had found no new home for his "verses," which is what he liked to call them, as if self-deprecation would summon up admiration in his listeners, which, of course, it didn't since everyone (except Freida and a couple of other poets) knew he was a horse's ass whom it was impossible to deprecate too much.

Swill's clientele all gave the impression they weren't aware of anything but their own projects—novels, short stories, poetry, screen and TV treatments, or pilots for new sitcoms, written on spec. But they *were* aware, maddeningly and jealously, of success.

So when Ned and Saul walked in, Freida and b.w.–although they tried to make a leisurely job of leaving–made sure to vamoose. They could be ostracized. To be ostracized in Swill's was a novel experience since (as stated) no one wanted to be thought to care what the other guy was doing. The novelty arose from the low-key fashion in which the ostracizing was carried out. You could hardly put your finger on it; indeed you *couldn't* put your finger on it if you were not the object of it. There would be that ever so slight push or a back turning at the bar, that hard to be seen curl of the lip, that minutest raising of the eyebrow or flicker of the lid.

So Freida and b.w. hopped it and Saul and Ned sat down.

Saul looked the room over and saw the same two men he'd seen in the park, now without the suits. The suits had been swapped for jeans and leather jackets. They were still carrying the books. While he was watching them, Ned came in.

*   *   *   *   *

Ned Isaly they recognized from both the photo in Michael's Restaurant and the dust jacket. He was at a table in the window now backlit by the blue and green top of the Chrysler Building. He was sitting with the fellow Karl thought he remembered from the park. There was also a tall dark-haired girl standing by the table, looking as grim as a process server, the one who'd been putting the coins into the jukebox, playing that ear-splitting song again and again.

"Look at him," said Candy, nodding in the direction of a nearby table. "Fuckin' everybody in here's writing a goddamned book, it looks like." This one was a man probably in his early thirties seated with several notebooks spread out across the table, writing in one.

"Novelist wannabe?" said Karl. He lifted his shot of whiskey, said, "Cheers."

"Likewise," said Candy, lifting his beer, watching the moisture condense on the glass.

Karl said, "I wonder what it's like to write a book."

Candy was quiet for a moment, thinking this over. "Well, look, it can't be that hard if everybody in here's doing it. I mean the ones that aren't into art, you know, painting. Hard thing about writing a book is you'd have to think up something to write about. Enough it'd take up a whole book, couple hundred pages. That's a pretty tall order."

"Couple hundred? You must be joking. This"—he tapped Ned's book—"is three hundred eighty-four pages. And Giverney's must be over a hundred more. Nearly five hundred. That's a hell of a lot of pages to fill."

"Well, yeah, if you're talkin' novels. These are novels. Made-up fiction."

"I know what fiction is, C. I'm talking nonfiction."

"If it's only facts you got to report, then that'd be a lot shorter. You wouldn't have to put in all this description and the, you know, insights. Still, it'd be hard, looking up all that shit . . ." Candy took another pull at his beer. Then he leaned back, chair tilted, and watched the ceiling fans creaking circles.

"Even so, you'd still have to put in the small stuff," Karl said.

"What small stuff?"

"Like the fly up there," said Karl. "Two flies. You'd have to put them in."

"You wouldn't have to put the flies in."

"Yes, you would. It's how you describe something like this room so people would see it. They ain't gonna see it if you don't put in the flies. No way." Karl grabbed the Giverney book, leafed through it, scanned a page, and read:

"It was an old-fashioned pharmacy, the sort she might have gone to as a kid and had a strawberry shake or chocolate soda or cherry phosphate. Before drugstores, big, impersonal, crowded with goods. The different glasses that lined the shelves behind the counter— ribbed glasses for shakes and sodas—

"Or here:

"The window was stuck; she could open it only a few inches. The air that entered was as warm as the air inside. It felt heavy, exhausted. She would have shut the window but thought, 'Why bother?' She thought, one enters and one leaves. Between these two events, nothing happens. Outside, in the still tree sat a bird, an ordinary wren or—"

Candy thought about these passages. "I don't see any small stuff in it."

Karl said, "Well, what about the bird in the tree? Or the ribbed glasses and so forth?"

In his annoyance and impatience, Candy pushed back his chair. It collided with one behind him. A woman in big horn-rimmed glasses looked over her shoulder.

"Hey! Watch it!"

Candy had to smile. People just didn't know that a *Watch it!* to either of them could get you a choice site in a cemetery. Oh, well, when in Rome. He mumbled an apology, repositioned his chair. "All I'm saying is, who'd want to read about some dame going *mano a mano* with a fucking bird?"

"That's not *mano a mano,* for Christ's sake; that means a face-off, one-to-one's what it means."

"So, yeah." Seeing his glass was empty, Candy lost interest in the bird. "You want another one?"

"Yeah." Karl picked up *Solace.* While Candy was at the bar, Karl checked on Ned's table, where the jukebox-playing, the "Cry"-playing woman was sitting down. She had dark hair done in that crazy curly way that was popular. Or maybe that was just the way it came. Christ, but her hair was black; it shone black as licorice. She wore designer jeans and a white silk shirt and a lot of jewelry. He couldn't tell what color her eyes were; he could only see her profile. Her hands were clasped on the table, fingers heavy with rings. He would recognize her now anywhere, just as he would Ned Isaly and the other guy. If one of them turned up off a tramp steamer in Port Said, he'd know him.

"That guy over there," said Saul, "three tables back, the one staring at you—no, don't look. Wait . . . *now* you can look; he's reading."

Jamie looked. "Yeah, he's kind of cute."

"He and his buddy over there at the bar were in the park a few hours ago, sitting on that bench under the maple."

"So?"

Ned said, "I saw them, too. You"—he nodded at Saul—"were sitting across the walk from them."

Jamie said it again. *"So?"* She dragged out the syllable to register impatience.

"For God's sakes, Jamie, don't you have any imagination?" asked Saul.

"No," said this writer of sinister sci-fi, this hacker of violent mysteries and hot romances.

Saul said, "Go over and talk to them. Make up some excuse."

"*You* go over; you're the one who thinks they're so weird."

"I didn't say weird. Out of place, maybe."

Jamie said, "That's only because you've never seen them in here before. And don't trouble yourselves. I'll get my own beer." Her tone was testy as she rose.

Ned always tried to be at least half a gentleman. "I'll get—"

Jamie waved him down and went to the bar.

Saul said, his eyes still on the familiar duo, several tables away, "The thing is, I don't think they're a couple. Do they look Chelsea to you?"

Ned shook his head. "No. That's almost the *last* thing they look."

Eyes not moving, Saul drank his beer. "What's the first thing?"

"Mob," said Ned, leafing through his pages.

"Oh, come *on*. Mob guys don't frequent this place. Maybe they're terrorists." Saul frowned. "They could be terrorists."

"Sure. A couple of Italian terrorists in black leather."

"But they're reading fucking *books*."

"You don't think any made guys can read?"

"How do you know they're made?"

"I don't. It was just something to say."

"Like 'mob.'"

"No, I meant that. 'Made' was something *else* to say."

"Jamie's walking by their table."

"Good for her. Are they announcing the jihad on Swill's?"

"Ha, very funny."

Jamie appeared at the table again. "Here's something you might find interesting about these two. The tall guy's reading *your* book." She smirked, for no discernible reason, at Ned, as if she'd won a bet.

Ned looked over at them, narrowed his eyes, but couldn't see enough through the fretwork of Swillians who kept moving like sea grasses, back and forth, rising up from tables, sinking down into chairs. The cover of *Solace* was easy to make out since it was white, totally white except for the word in black and his name in smaller black letters. (Tom Kidd had said, "It's crap, but what else would we expect from Mamie Fussel?")

"Tell him," said Saul, "to come over and Ned'll sign it."

"They're looking this way," said Jamie. "Maybe they've figured that out for themselves."

"I don't wanna be pushy," said Karl.

"Christ's *sakes,* K, that's one of the reasons for coming in here with the *book,* to get him to sign, so we can talk to him."

Candy got up, then Karl did. They shouldered their way through the crowded room, stopping at Ned's table, which was in a nice window position. Beyond the window, it was raining. A Mayflower moving van was parked across the street, the two moving men unhappy with the rain.

"You're Ned Isaly, aren't you?" Karl opened the book to the inside back jacket and the small square picture of Ned that Ned still couldn't remember ever having been taken.

Ned smiled. "That's right. And you're—"

"Larry Blank. Pleased to meet you. This is—"

"Uh, Paulie Givinchy."

Karl glared at Candy, who went on to say, "Almost like this guy, Giverney?" He held up the book he was carrying. "Only, I can't write worth a double damn." Candy laughed.

They smiled. Jamie said, "I don't think I've seen you in here before. You live around here?" She pushed out the two empty chairs. "Come on, sit down."

Karl and Candy sat. "We live over on Houston," said Karl. This, actually, was the truth. The two had gone together and purchased an old warehouse in the Village and taken on an extra assignment or two to pay the extravagant sum needed for the remodeling. (Candy was fond of saying that Tony Giovanni and Fats Webber had died for that window treatment and that arrangement of Japanese screens.)

"How do you know?" said Ned.

"What? That we're over on Houston?"

"No. That you can't write."

Surprised and, for some reason, pleased, Candy modestly waved away this suggestion. "Oh, please."

"You don't know unless you try."

Karl and Candy looked at each other. "You're sayin' anyone tries can do it?"

"No. I'm just saying you don't know whether or not you can."

To get them off the subject of Candy's potential as a writer, Karl went back to *Solace.* "This is a pretty sad story, you know? These two just don't get the breaks, do they?"

"I guess not," said Ned.

"Me," said Candy. "I'm reading this. It's a best-seller, right?" He held up the book, front out.

"The new Giverney book," said Saul. "It's a best-seller, all right; all of his books are."

"It's number three on the list. I saw it in Barnes and Noble," said Candy. "And it's only just been published. Now, *that's* impressive. How many books'd you say are sold any given day? Thousands?"

"More like hundreds of thousands," said Ned.

"To be three from the top. Makes me wonder what the first two are, all right."

Saul said, "The Bible, Shakespeare. Giverney's a little melodramatic for my tastes."

"No kiddin'?" said Candy. Feeling slightly abashed, as if it were personal, he looked down at his book. "To me, it's got a lot of suspense in it."

Ned said, "He's a much better writer than he gets credit for being."

Already, Candy liked him. He moved his chair a little closer.

Saul laughed. "Come on, Ned."

"He is. He's been locked into the thriller genre—"

"Because he writes fucking thrillers, that's why," Saul said. He relit his cigar. Swill's lax smoking policy favored just about everybody except those whose tastes leaned toward crystal meth.

"I've read the first half of this," Ned said, nodding toward *Don't Go There*. "It's not a thriller."

Candy's forehead crinkled like a fan. "It ain't? It's this woman lost her memory, no, more her memory, it's not telling her what it should. So nothing looks familiar to her, not even her house. I mean, it's creepy stuff. That says thriller to me."

Ned shook his head. "It's something else. It's way outside genre."

Karl said, "You know him, Giverney?"

"I've talked to him a couple of times at publishing parties. But I wouldn't say I know him."

"Oh, well, look," Candy opened the back flap to the biographical note. "He's from Pittsburgh. It says so here."

"So are you," said Karl. Then, realizing his tone might be slightly accusatory, he smiled and added, "Some coincidence, I guess. So we thought maybe you guys might have known each other like in high school or something."

"Nope. At least not as far as I remember. I suppose I could have run into him and not remembered."

"Huh," said Candy, not knowing how far he could take this. He looked at Karl, who nodded. Candy didn't know why. "Man, when I think back . . ."

All the while Candy had been talking, Karl had watched Ned. He was searching out some reason the world would be better off without him. Arrogance? Isaly had plenty of reason to be, being a published writer who'd won prizes and all. But he didn't seem to be arrogant.

Well, it was too early to tell, wasn't it? Through the window, he watched as the movers dropped what looked like a valuable piece of furniture, a small, delicate table. He saw at least one leg snap off. Fuckheads. Karl disrespected anyone who couldn't do his job 100 percent.

"What do you two do? What line of work are you in?"

Candy and Karl were so taken aback by the question that Candy almost slipped and told him. "Uh–"

Karl's eye flicked to the movers across the street. "We're in re-movals." Candy smiled. Karl wished he wouldn't. "You know, like so–" He nodded toward the window. "Sort of like them."

Ned and Saul turned to look. Saul said, "Moving furniture." He turned back. "Funny, but you don't seem the type."

Karl laughed. "There *is* one? A type that moves things around?"

Saul said, "Not exactly. Or maybe you have your own company."

"We're strictly independent," said Candy. "We don't work with nobody else. Then they can't get in the way."

"They also," Karl said, eyes still on the moving van, "can't drop stuff. They also can't leave evidence–see that table leg?" (He caught himself.) "Lying all over the bloody street."

Saul said after he'd sucked in on his cigar again, "Evidence. In-teresting way of putting it." He smiled.

Karl cut a look toward Saul. He wondered if maybe that asshole

Mackenzie was interested in putting out a contract on this guy, too. Here was arrogance. Saul got right up Karl's nose.

"So you pretty much work for yourselves?" Ned said.

"That's it," said Karl, who looked at the tablet under Ned's arm. "You could say—though I don't want to sound too arrogant"—he sent a quick look Saul's way—"our job is kind of like yours." He held up both hands, palms out, as if staving off potential criticism. "I mean because we work alone."

"Yeah, we've had enough weird experiences to write a book. Right?" Candy shoved his fist into Karl's shoulder.

Karl nodded. "It's a thought."

NINETEEN

Jimmy McKinney sat at his desk in the Durban Agency eating a cheese sandwich (how anachronistic could a person be?) and wondering (for the gazillionth time) why he kept on working for Mort Durban, a man who was a complete prick, not to mention a bandit. Most of his writers didn't earn back their advances half the time, and that meant they were in danger of having their publishers drop them; but Mort still went on insisting on big advances because it was such a coup to be able to get a quarter-million advance for a debut (God! but Jimmy hated that word!) novel from a writer who had never, until now, tested the publishing waters. The undertow took a number of them down, leaving Mort himself splashing in the shallows. Mort managed never to endanger himself.

What Jimmy had done before he married and had a kid was write poetry—good poetry, too, though there wasn't much of it: one book he'd published ten years before; he hadn't turned out enough good poems since then to make up another collection. He was still managing to place a poem here and there in the quarterlies, though.

But how many times had Lilith—*"with her famous hair"*—(Jimmy couldn't help it; lines of poetry—Frost, Robinson, Dickinson—were always popping into his mind, one to fit nearly every thought he had)—said, *"We can't live on air"*?

"No," Jimmy had said, *"not if the air is being funneled in from Barneys and Bergdorf Goodman's."*

That had earned him an abrasive look. Most things did, coming from Lilith (*"not even Lilith, with her famous hair . . ."*).

He found the lines comforting. He always found poetry comforting. And prose, too, words, even. Jimmy supposed it was one of the reasons he'd taken this job—just to be around words.

As he ruminated on this, finishing up his sandwich, the outer door opened and Paul Giverney walked by Jimmy's office, tossing him a wink and a salute.

Mort was always saying what an "arrogant bastard" Paul Giverney was. As Jimmy couldn't imagine anyone more arrogant than Mort himself, he could only question this assessment. Mort was the least self-aware person Jimmy had ever encountered. Publishers hated him because he gouged them for such huge advances, but Jimmy had no sympathy for the publishers, not a scrap; if Random House (and all its little Randomettes) were willing to pay these over-the-moon advances to get a writer they wanted, or else engage in an auction—a pissing contest to see who had the biggest set of brass ones—then why blame Mort for going around with a mask and a gun?

Paul Giverney could afford being as much of a bastard as he liked because he was on the top tier of authors who breathed the rarefied air of seven-digit advances. Giverney's last two-book contract had been for $6.2 million. His current contract with Mackenzie-Haack, for $8 million, was as yet unsigned and would remain so "until certain conditions were met."

"What the hell conditions?" Mort had asked Paul awhile back.

"You don't need to know, Mort," Paul had said.

"What? I'm your agent *for God's sakes."*

"All the more reason."

This enigmatic estimate of Mort's worth was followed by Paul's thumbs-up, not to Mort but to Jimmy, who'd brought in the promotion plans for Paul's new book, *Don't Go There.*

It was this book that Jimmy was reading now at his desk. It had taken him completely by surprise. He had always thought Paul Giverney was better than he was given credit for being, but with this last book the writer had hit the ball way, way out of the genre ballpark. Yes, it was still a page-turner, a sinfully readable book, even more so than the others, at least the two Mort Durban had been agent for. Something was going on in this new book that certainly bore thinking about, something ineffably sad. It was more than anxiety (and why not fright? If familiar surroundings had turned foreign, why wasn't this woman scared as hell? She seemed merely confused and questioning).

Jimmy loved the book. If he had been Paul's agent, he would have swept aside the extra million advance and forced its publisher, Queeg and Hyde, to produce a promotional campaign that would take the book to another level. People should realize just how good Paul was.

* * * * *

"How come you have this rep?" Jimmy asked. "For being, well . . ."

"A son of a bitch?" Paul grinned. "Because that's what I want people to think, some of them. You'd be surprised how it cuts through the crap, publishing being a particularly crap-filled occupation. Or maybe you don't agree."

This conversation had taken place a few days ago when Paul

had suggested coffee. They'd gone to the coffee shop just outside the entrance to the massive building where Mort Durban had his suite of offices.

"I agree." Jimmy poured another ounce of sugar in his coffee. "In the five years I've been doing this, I can count on one hand the people who didn't make me want to head for the shower."

"Why do you stay, then? You're too good for this life; you're too good to be working for a scumbag like Mort."

"The money."

Paul shook his head. "Uh-uh. Not you. You must be in hock to someone for something. Wife? Kids? Private schools? Barney's? Mob? Tony Soprano?"

Jimmy laughed. "All those things except the mob and Tony. I guess it would be hard on the family to get along on a lot less."

"Why would it? That's what you've been getting along on."

Jimmy was astonished that anyone, much less Paul Giverney, could see into him so well. He was silent, turning this over. Then he said, "I write poetry."

"I know." Paul pulled a narrow book out of the inside pocket of his mac. "My wife wants your autograph. Molly, that's her name." He slid the book across the table.

Jimmy was stunned. He opened the book and looked down at the title page, seeing it as if for the first time. He remembered that time, ten years ago, his spirit soaring when he'd opened the package that held the ten copies sent from the publisher. It's why he could understand how important publication was to writers. It wasn't money, or at least it didn't start out to be. It was seeing your words in print. He took the pen Paul reached toward him.

"Molly loves poetry; she reads most of the quarterlies, the little magazines. She especially likes yours. A book of poetry published by FSG—that's no small matter."

"It seems small to me." No, it didn't, not really. Small only by comparison with novelists like Paul. He handed back the pen.

"It shouldn't. You're just too used to book publishing."

"Where did she find the book, though? It's been out of print for years."

"From your publisher. She has a friend there. It's one of the two or three really good publishers."

"Why don't you go there? Why Mackenzie-Haack?"

"FSG would never publish me. Too commercial."

"FSG publishes commercial stuff. Best-sellers. Don't they publish Scott Turow?"

"He's not that kind of commercial. I'm more the John Grisham kind of commercial." Arms folded on the dull Formica top, he leaned toward Jimmy. "What you should do, Jimmy, is go to a place like Yaddo or the MacDowell Colony. You really should."

Jimmy's shrug suggested the uselessness of this. "I wish I could."

"You can. MacDowell's stints go for as short a time as a month. Imagine not having anybody bother you—no claims on your time, you can write all day, no Mort, no wife, no one breathing down your neck. You can't get away for one fucking month?"

"Somehow the bills have got to be paid."

Again, Paul leaned toward him. "Listen to me: I have a wife and a seven-year-old daughter, both of whom I really love. But if I was trapped in a system that didn't allow me to write, I'd leave. There's a great line Robert De Niro got off in a movie a few years ago: 'Allow nothing to be in your life that you cannot walk out on in thirty seconds flat if you spot the heat around the corner.' That's good advice, Jimmy."

Jimmy stared. "*Hell* it is. You're telling me you could leave your family in thirty seconds?" He shook his head. "No, you wouldn't."

"I would." Paul nodded.

"That's pretty damned ruthless."

"I know. Could you understand it any better if I were, say, Salinger or Thomas Pynchon? Some writer we consider truly valuable?"

Jimmy thought about this. "I see your point. But I'm pretty sure I couldn't do it. I don't mean from some high moral plane, just that I'd have a failure of nerve."

"Okay. But right now, there's no heat"—Paul tipped his head backward—"around the corner. You still owe it to yourself."

"Those places—you have to apply far in advance . . ."

"So apply. You can do that without ever leaving."

There was a silence. Jimmy said, "Could we talk about your book? I think it's enigmatic, to say the least."

"Isn't that what you'd expect of a thriller, for lack of a better genre?"

"No. I don't mean in that sense. Maybe I should say 'ambiguous.' My question is: Is her environment—like the pharmacy and the garden—unreal, or is she?"

Paul laughed. "That's very good, Jimmy."

Jimmy opened the book to the point he'd stopped reading it.

"Even along the moonlit paths of the maze there were striking differences: the white iron bench should have been sitting not at this turning but at another, though she would have been hard put to say exactly where.

"Ambiguous, at least. I was going along with her until I came to this garden business. So is it she or the world around?"

Paul shrugged. "Are those the only alternatives?" At Jimmy's frown, he went on: "They could both be."

"Unreal, you mean?"

"Or, possibly, real."

"Real? Come on, Paul." Jimmy smiled, realizing he was no longer intimidated by Paul Giverney's fame and fortune and felt thankful for it. "It can't be both. How can it? In the beginning section, when she goes into what she had last seen as the drugstore and now finds is an old-fashioned pharmacy—it must be one or the other, mustn't it?"

"Maybe. Maybe not. Read the rest of the book. It's way too early to wonder about the nature of reality." He leaned across the table. "You don't want to be an agent; that's obvious. I hate agents; they're working both sides of the street. They want to retain the publishers' goodwill, so they're not working a hundred percent for their writers. It really makes me mad, that does. At least with real estate agents, if one advertises himself as a 'buyer's' agent, he isn't around sucking up to the seller the way agents keep sucking up to publishers. They should be acting as guides through this swamp; they should be monks, not pimps." Paul stopped and took a sip of coffee. He held up the signed book, *Lapses*. "This is what you should be doing, Jimmy."

"My wife—"

Paul was shaking his head the moment the excuse started out of Jimmy's mouth. "It's not down to her; you know it isn't. Or your six kids. Or keeping your dog in Kibbles."

"Yeah, well, that's easy for you to say—"

"Oh, *come* on, Jimmy. Not that old dodge, that poor man, rich man shit. Imagine how you'd feel if I were, say, an oncologist telling you you had only a couple of months to live. You'd be shocked out of your mind not just by death but by the realization you'd squandered a big part of your life. Think about that. It's my theory that none of us really believes he's going to die. We think we believe it, given all the evidence, but we really don't. Freud said a man can't imagine his own death. Probably, we think there's something more due us and maybe that's the reason immortality is such a popular idea. What we really want is another chance, and we think we're going to get it—the chance to straighten out everything, to get it right."

"What about you? Wouldn't you have any regrets? Such as being sorry you squandered your talent for so many years?" His voice was rising along with his anxiety at being found out, at having what he feared was his cowardice exposed.

This charge surprised Paul. "Have I?"

"Well, look at *Don't Go There*. You know you're one hell of a good writer. Why do you do this genre stuff?"

"You like this new book?"

"Hell, *yes*, I like it! It infuriates me that it's going to be lumped with writers like Dwight Staines."

Paul laughed. "Doesn't make me very happy, either."

"I'm not saying I don't like your other books. But this one"—he held up the new book—"this one is beyond good—"

Paul interrupted. "Why aren't you my agent?"

Jimmy, poised to continue his rant, fell back in the booth as if Paul had whipped out a gun and shot him. "Me?" He stared at Paul wide eyed, and then he laughed. "*Ha!* Mort would never let that happen."

"He wouldn't have any choice, would he?"

"He could make my life miserable."

"Oh, really? You mean more miserable than you're making it all by yourself?"

Jimmy reddened and smiled. Then he said, "He could just make up some excuse to fire me."

"Good. Then you could go to Yaddo and write poetry. Or wait a minute: I just remembered there's a writers' retreat upstate that'll let people go there for a weekend to see how they like it. Now, don't tell me you couldn't get away for one weekend."

"I suppose I could. What's it called?"

"Birches." Paul was writing down the address.

Jimmy smiled. "Birches. I like that. '*When I see birches bend to left and right—*'"

Paul looked up. "'*. . . I like to think some boy's been swinging them.*'"

"You like Robert Frost?"

"Of course I do; who doesn't? Do this, Jimmy. One weekend. If you hate the setup, that's that. Tell you what—be my agent for a year, rake in enough money to quit for at least two years. I'll tell Mort it's only temporary, make up some reason as to why I'm doing it."

"There is a reason: altruism."

Paul snorted as he motioned to the waitress. He said, "No. I doubt I've ever done anything for that reason—at least not wholly, maybe not even largely. No. I want to see something."

The waitress put down the check.

"I want to see how far you go."

Jimmy regarded Paul quizzically. "How far I go?"

Paul nodded, putting a bill down for the check. "That's right. How far you go."

TWENTY

Paul Giverney didn't like the sound of it. He didn't like the sound of it at all. He slapped his cell phone shut and slouched in one of the cheap molded-plastic chairs that were kept on the roof for tenants in case they wanted to party up there.

Sitting in his overcoat, Paul had been flinging darts at the dartboard he moved from living room to study to roof whenever the dart mood came over him. Darts were as good as any alcoholic's booze: to celebrate success, to shore up failure, to be a live wire at a party, to be isolated on a beach, to—

In other words, anyplace, anytime. In a write-up in one of the newspapers or magazines—there were so many of them—the journalist had suggested darts might permit him to tap into his creative power and solve writing problems. Paul had told him that all darts did was keep your mind on the fucking board.

The dartboard was leaning against the roof's balustrade and every time he got up to collect the darts he would treat himself to a view of Manhattan against the black sky. For Paul, it was always a treat; he was besotted with love of the MetLife and the Chrysler buildings. He couldn't write if he didn't have this knock-out view of Manhattan always at his bidding. It was especially strange since he had never set one of his books here. People, fans, were always asking him where he did most of his writing and he would answer (with a kind of pride) "right here in New York." They thumbed this unexciting news through the book of places in their heads and came up disappointed. That wouldn't inspire anybody. They wanted a destination more exotic to take away with the book he'd just signed (not to forget standing in line for an hour to get it). Yes, New York as an answer saddened them, saddened the smiles on their faces, so that he leaned closer across the little table, engaged their eyes, and told them the truth: "It's the only place I can write." But this clear admission of a New York neurosis didn't get the smile back. The fan only took this metaphorically—the writer is New York—when he'd meant it literally.

He had even been forced to go to a psychiatrist whom a friend of Paul's had recommended who wasn't in any better mental shape after seeing this doctor for three years. He was still the way he'd been all of his preceding forty years. Paul's friend swore by Dr. Nutley (despite the name), said he was downtown and down to earth. A great guy.

Nutley was downtown, all right (Twenty-second Street), but as for the "down to earth" bit, Paul could only wonder, what earth? And Paul would never have been able to describe him as a "guy." Nutley, with his tweeds and his beard, his casual erudition, his quoting of learned books and articles, his determination that the transference must get under way tout de suite or what were they all here for? The good doctor was not one of the guys. Insofar as Paul's

problem was concerned, Dr. Nutley made no suggestions, no diag-
noses, gave no advice. You could say that Nutley was the most perfect example of noninvolvement with another human being that
you were ever likely to find this side of Transylvania. Paul went
along with this for some months. Hell, he could afford it. He could
probably afford making his own psychiatrist: putting some young
swab through Johns Hopkins Medical School, then a four-year tour
of duty in the psychoanalytical arena, then get him a duplex in the
Upper Eighties, Eighty-seven, Eighty-eight, near the Metropolitan
Museum—which Paul had often found very therapeutic, even if you
couldn't tell a Vuillard from a Monet. Get him established and then
go to him for problems such as the inability to write outside of
Manhattan.

For even though Paul would say "right here in New York," his
writing geography was bound by this even smaller playing field:
Manhattan. His childhood had not been contained here; he was
from the Midwest. He had lived in Manhattan for only fifteen years
and now he knew he could never live anywhere else. Paul considered himself lucky; he had found what people mean by "home."

*   *   *   *   *

Paul had met Ned Isaly only twice, the first time at one of those
drunken brawls publishers like to throw for books and writers
whom the publishers think deserve them, meaning, of course, the
best-selling, *TBR* list writers. The moneyed elite, the Hamptons of
writers, the Great Neck, the Back Bay, the Aspen, the Colorado
Springs of writers, the Tahoe, the Vail, the Santa Fe of writers; any
of the chic and pricey in places—take your pick—*those* writers. Paul
was high on the list of the Flashy Few, this despite his living in
nothing more than a two-bedroom-plus-study rental on the edge of

Greenwich Village. But then the publishing world didn't know how he lived because it never got invited up.

Paul liked to schmooze at these parties, mostly to see the new arrivals to the list. Whose "debut" novel would be buzzed onto the *TBR* list? What "genre" novel would be touted as having shot the mystery/thriller/sci-fi genre up to the stratosphere? What commercial book would break the literary glass ceiling? And what literary novel would push through the commercial floor? That, of course, was the big prayer answered, to publish a book that would pay back millions, and also be reviewed in *The New Yorker* by John Updike.

Ned Isaly fit none of these categories.

It had been, he supposed, a wretched thing to do and Paul knew he would probably fry in hell, but he couldn't get rid of the idea. Actually, it had come out of that long conversation with Ned Isaly at one of these cocktail parties.

He could have simply made it all up, but Paul was certain that his own imagination, which had served him so well for years of deadpan genre-noir thrillers—that even he could think of nothing so outrageous as what appeared to be happening. The blackmail angle hadn't really surprised him. Trust Bobby Mackenzie to think of that.

But even Paul, for whom nothing was too shocking, shameful, twisted, harrowing, whatever—even Paul had not considered they would set a couple of hired killers on the man, and he still thought he must be wrong to think it. He'd expected them to break the contract, to get around the problem of Tom Kidd somehow. Of course, Tom would threaten to leave and take Isaly (not to mention Kidd's other writers) with him. He'd thought of other things they might do, such as framing Isaly for plagiarism. Any damage to Ned's reputation Paul would counteract by exposing Bobby Mackenzie.

Well, how to deal with the Isaly dilemma had been their problem. Except it had become his problem with this news about the "consultant" team of Candy and Karl. Jesus Christ. What had he set in motion? He'd put in a call to Sammy Giancarlo, a mob "consultant" about whom Paul had written (wearing his noir hat) a fairly moving novel. Sammy had been pleased as punch and only hoped it had been thinly enough veiled so his momma and the rest of his extended family would know it was Sammy Giancarlo.

*   *   *   *   *

"Two guys named Karl and Candy. I don't know if it's first or last names. Do you know them?" This was the phone call he'd made earlier.

Sammy said, "I'm not personally acquainted with them, but you know the way they work."

Paul made his forefinger and thumb into a gun and aimed it at the telephone. Why did Sammy always assume Paul knew everyone in Giancarlo's world and "the way they work"? Just because Paul had met a few in researching his books? "No, Sammy, I do not know. Else I wouldn't be calling you. Tell me, how do they work that's any different from your standard hit man?"

"Because they get to know the mark. You can't get them just to aim and fire like the rest of the palookas."

Sammy's argot was strongly reminiscent of the 1940s or even the 1930s. Paul got a real kick out of it sometimes. "Yeah. What in hell do you mean, 'get to know' the person? That sounds like it's breaking some criminal code."

"Those guys want to know exactly what kind of person they're taking out, never mind you wouldn't think they'd want to know. I wouldn't want to, you wouldn't want to. Hell, no. I mean what if it turned out you really liked the guy? What then? It's like surgeons,

166

ain't it? I mean if you had a kid needed a kidney you wouldn't want your wife doing the surgery, would you? If your wife was a surgeon. Anyway, these two, I know once they hung around for nearly six months and still didn't whack this guy. And those two, I'm surprised they're even on the road, they hardly ever take a job anymore. Never mind, they don't need the money. These two are top of the line. They are prime time, believe me. Now, you need somebody put on a bus to nowhere. I can help you. What—"

Paul had started yelling. "Hold it! Don't send anybody—"

"No no no no. This guy could voice your concerns is all. Or do you want me to do it personal? Never mind, for you I'd do it. Listen, we're all waiting for the—what'd'ya call it? Prequel? Like maybe *Giancarlo: Learning a Trade.* You know, when I was a snot-nosed kid. Pretty good, eh?"

"Yeah. Wonderful, Sammy." Paul loved that "voice your concerns is all." "Now this guy you're talking about—"

"It'll cost you; you better be ready with fifty large—I mean up front, with another fifty later. But this guy's absolutely top of the line."

"Sounds pretty much like they're all top of the line. But in that case, Candy and Karl, the two I'm talking about, they'd know him?"

"Nah. This guy's outta Vegas, just keeps a co-op here for when he visits. There's lots of them relocating. There's another good one in Santa Fe. He paints. I don't think he's working his day job no more, anyway . . ." Sammy grew reflective.

"I thought your business was kind of like the priesthood, Sam. You go where you're told."

Sammy laughed. "Priesthood, that's rich. Listen, I'll set up a meet with this guy. He lives in TriBeCa, I think. He likes to move around. I can tell you this: this one's such a good shadow sometimes I think he *is* one. You won't see him; they won't see him. You can meet him in one of them coffee places, maybe. I say that because he don't drink, not anymore. Only not Starbucks; Starbucks is gettin' to be worse than a spaghetti restaurant. Just last week another one of the Bransonis was blasted out of his chair in that Starbucks over on Eighth. It was all over the fucking tabloids. You read about that? Gettin' to be as bad as D.C. Anyway, he'll know what you look like even if you don't know him." Sammy described him—tall, thin, and blond. "But that won't help you much because he's like a fucking chameleon. He blends in. Never saw anyone who could blend as good as him."

"Right away, Sammy, if you can. I'm worried about this fellow Candy and Karl are, well, following, I guess."

"You got it. I'm makin' a note. So what are you doing, Paulie, you're messed up with Candy and Karl? You been seein' too many Francis Ford Coppola movies?" Sammy laughed at his own little joke.

" 'Fraid so. What's this fellow's name?"

"Arthur Mordred. And for God's sakes, don't call him 'Art.' He hates it people call him 'Art.' "

Paul wondered just how much Arthur hated it.

* * * * *

The meeting with Arthur Mordred was held in one of those crepe and cappuccino cafés in SoHo off Broome Street. Paul usually avoided such places, just as he avoided the center of Greenwich Village.

The coffeehouse was a yuppie hangout. Paul looked the room over. There were perhaps fifteen customers; he looked at each one of them. Finally, a man at a corner table whom Paul had passed over several times—somehow seeing and not seeing—raised his hand. Arthur Mordred looked like just another yuppie. Paul would never have picked him out. He had a narrow head, a thin mouth, seal-gray eyes, and flaxen hair so lightweight it looked ruffled by the air stirred up by the erratically circling fan overhead. His ears lay so flat against his head they looked cut and pasted there.

"I can't say how thrilled I am to meet you," said Arthur Mordred. "I've read every one of your books." Arthur fit his chin into his hand a little like a cupcake and looked volumes at Paul. Before him sat a big cup of cappuccino. Arthur tapped it. "Want one?"

Paul shook his head, pulled the brown envelope containing fifty thousand dollars out of an inside pocket of his raincoat, and handed it to Arthur, who took it with the same soigné manner in which he probably (Paul thought) did everything, including shooting people. Paul's notion of hit men was obviously antediluvian. Clearly your man didn't always run to muscles, no manners, and few words.

Because Arthur seemed only to want to talk, as if he'd been locked up for years—well, maybe he had—and was just getting his first taste of freedom. As he peeked into the envelope he asked, "Are you working on a new book?"

Paul didn't care for the way Arthur was eyeing him. He didn't want to get trapped in a Stephen King situation. *Misery.* "Not at the moment, Arthur. At the moment I'm sitting here with you." Perhaps one shouldn't be so free with the sarcasm around Arthur. So Paul flashed him an I'm-only-jesting smile.

But Arthur simply thought he was being droll. "Where am I to go, Paul?"

"Wherever this guy goes." From the same pocket the money had been in, Paul brought out the dust jacket for *Solace,* turned it to the back flap and the small picture. "Ned Isaly, another writer."

Arthur was impressed. "My goodness, this is what you might call the literary event of the year, not to mention the top ten hits."

He laughed at his little joke, his voice chirrupy. "Maybe we ought to put out a little magazine, you know—"

"Look, Arthur. Let's be sure we're on the same page here: what I want is for you to *keep* this person from getting shot. A couple of guys might be aiming to do that even as we speak. I can't believe they really are, but I don't want to take chances."

Arthur pursed his lips. "You mean you want a bodyguard."

"Well . . . yeah, I guess . . . yeah, exactly. A situation has simply gotten out of control. I'll summarize it for you: a publish—"

Arthur shut his eyes, squinched them shut, and fanned his hands palm out like a metronome. "No no no no! I don't want to hear the whys and wherefores, tell me nothing I don't absolutely have to know. Mention no names if you can help it." He looked at the dust jacket again. "Quite a handsome bloke, this Isaly. I never got around to reading that book. I'll certainly read it now."

Bloke? Did people still say that? It sounded like an old Terry-Thomas movie. "I guess you're really good when it comes to, uh, shadowing people?"

"Ordinarily, I don't have to. It's usually not necessary, is it?" Arthur beamed a smile at Paul.

The implication of which made Paul extranervous. "Here it is: there are two guys who always work together who are after him—" Paul tapped the photo with his forefinger. "Sammy said you'd know them. Names are Can—"

Again, Arthur shut his eyes, flapped his hands, made a little moue of distaste. "No names. Describe them."

"I can't. I've never seen them. Sammy knows them. Says everyone does. In the business, I mean." His voice even lower, Paul said, "Kar—"

But Arthur was adamant and even put his hands over his ears.

"Oh, for God's sakes! Wait a minute." Paul rose and walked

over to the glass-enclosed counter by the register. To the girl attending it, he said, "Give me one of those, will you?"

She plucked the Mars bar from a box and took the money.

Back at the table, Paul set it down before Arthur.

"How delicious! I love chocolate."

"Chocolate what?"

"With almonds and marshmallow."

Paul shut his eyes against such thickheadedness. "No, Arthur. I mean as a class of things."

Arthur raised his translucent brows in question.

"It's a clue, Arthur. The whole thing, not the separate ingredients."

Arthur bit his lip, then snapped his fingers. "*The Big Sleep.* Don't you love Hammett?"

"What in hell are you talking about?"

"The villain. Eddie Mars. Isn't that who you're talking about?"

Paul jumped up again and returned to the counter and came back with a Butterfinger and a Hershey bar. "Okay. Take all three together. What do you call them?" Paul glared.

Arthur shrugged, looking at Paul with an expression that begged Paul's forbearance. "Chocolate bars?"

Paul brought his fist down on the table, jumping the Butterfinger. This was harder than writing a fucking novel. The couple at the table next door jumped at the thud. Paul marched back to the counter and purchased a roll of Necco wafers.

This he slammed down on the table and waited.

After a moment or two of earnest thought, Arthur said, "I've got it! Can–"

Paul waved his hands this time. "You know the name of the second one?"

"I should say *so*. Those two. Somebody must really have wanted a button—you know. And had the money to get it. Those two do not come cheap." Arthur studied the photo. "What the devil's he— No, don't tell me. I'm just naturally curious, I guess. How long have they been, you know, on the job?"

"I don't know. A week?"

"Well, that's a good sign. At least they didn't hate him on sight."

Paul rolled his eyes ceilingward, studied the eccentric fan. "Praise be."

THE OLD
HOTEL

TWENTY-ONE

They headed for the Old Hotel whenever they got serious, or desperate (which amounted to the same thing). It was a place which, unlike Swill's, was a destination, not, like Swill's, a stop along the way. It was actually two different places, the bar and the swank restaurant above it, where the diners could look down and measure the success, or lack of it, of the various customers.

They could not afford the restaurant. That is, Ned and Sally couldn't. Saul had taken all four of them there several times to celebrate birthdays and holidays, and Jamie had taken them whenever one of her books was published, so they ate at the Old Hotel fairly frequently. It was odd, Sally sometimes thought, that these three were not jealous of one another. More than odd; it was extraordinary. They appeared to know and appreciate one another's worth.

What the four of them often mentioned, as if freshly surprised, was that none of this looked phony or faux hotel. It was a large prewar brownstone and they wondered if it had actually been a hotel once. That perhaps it was a hotel turned into a bar and restaurant, rather than a bar and restaurant called a hotel.

Ned liked to talk about what might have gone on here and make up stories about guests who might have come here. "Manhattan in the forties, the thirties."

The bar, the Lobby, had its name written on a small wooden sign above its doorway. It did resemble one. There were a lot of easy chairs and love seats covered in linen and faded cretonne, and gathered around small tables. The wallpaper was dark red and flocked, and a dozen or more Gibson Girl tinted drawings hung against it. And then there were the *Godey's Lady's* prints, women in wide hats, cosseted waists, rucked sleeves. Clouded light diffused from shell-like wall sconces. There was a fireplace and big, brass-knobbed andirons. The air was scented with mint, and they had attempted to track it to its source, but couldn't, until Ned, going up to the bar to get another drink, reported back that the bartender had a reputation for the best mint juleps just about anywhere, and customers from Kentucky, Georgia, and the Carolinas pronounced this to be true.

Then they had all ordered mint juleps and had gone to the bar to sit on stools and watch them being made. It was a prodigious undertaking, and no wonder they cost more than twice as much as any other drink.

The last one to be told of this place was Jamie. She had walked into the Lobby's minty environs, looked around with large, wide eyes, and had said she had never seen anyplace so much like her aunts' rooming house in Savannah. "It's awesome; it's uncanny. I mean, of course this is bigger and there's a lot more furniture and stuff, but it still looks just like Aunt Eloise and Aunt Jeb's."

Her eyes wide and wondering was a look rarely seen on Jamie's face, whose sense of wonder had been vastly depleted by the unwondering, squint-eyed, skimpily clothed worlds she inhabited every day.

(It was Saul who had talked about Jamie's writing worlds in this way: romance, mystery, science fiction. It was very strange, he'd said. Here was subject matter—murder, romance, altered reality—that should free up any writer's imagination, subjects to bring the muse to heel, and yet it didn't work that way.)

Ned had often said he bet Jamie worked harder than he did, possibly harder than any of them did. It infuriated him when some hack over a pint of Corona at Swill's said all Jamie had to do in her mystery series was toss the characters up in the air and record their descent. It was said, of course, with a contemptuous smile.

But Saul said, no, that's not what he was talking about. Far from enjoying the wide-open spaces of country where no rules applied, Jamie was stuck in a small airless room with the constant threat of the walls' closing in. "That's what makes it genre fiction, not the subject matter itself. It's writing in the service of nothing. The world is hedged and trimmed back until it fits whatever generic rules you're applying."

Saul had got wound up and drunk and harangued on this subject. His voice was rich and deep and soothing, even more so after he'd poured a good deal of single malt whiskey down his throat. Ned stopped listening, getting drowsy with bourbon and thinking about Nathalie. Thinking about what she was doing and feeling and realizing he didn't have to worry whether what she did would "fit." He opened his eyes, then, and said to Saul, "You're right."

Yes, they quarreled and occasionally ranted but it was different. Jamie might criticize Ned's revisionist theories about early days in Pittsburgh, but she didn't carry such criticism over into his work, into his plans for Nathalie. (She did not know this name because Ned never talked about what he was writing. Jamie had to refer to his "protagonist, or whatever.")

Tonight, there was a quarrel, and it was started by Sally. Ned (who, Sally noted, seemed to have entirely forgotten her bad news) said he was going to Pittsburgh. He was to take three or four days off from writing and do this. And they'd better not (he warned) lay on him a lot of sentimental or pseudocynical crap about not being able to go home again.

"That's not what Wolfe meant, anyway," said Jamie.

Saul took his cigar from his mouth as if that would make him see her better. "Don't be ridiculous. Of course that's what he meant. Wolfe was a sentimentalist. I don't mean that necessarily as being wrong."

"Oh, stop being such a pompous ass," exclaimed Jamie.

Saul blushed a little. He did tend to be pompous, he knew.

Jamie turned to Sally, sitting there stuffing cashews into her mouth. "Why are you so mad?" Jamie asked, snapping shut her old Ronson lighter.

Sally inclined her head toward Ned. "Something's going on at the house. I think they're going to try to get out of their contract with him." Sally told Jamie about what she had overheard in Bobby Mackenzie's office.

Jamie found it hard to believe. "That's crazy. Ned?"

He had been studying the Gibson Girl drawings, wondering if the one with the upswept red hair had been his model for Nathalie a long time ago and he'd forgotten.

"Ned!"

He lurched in his seat. "What?"

Sally put her head in her hands and moved it back and forth. "He won't listen; he won't take it seriously." This came muted from behind her hands.

"Sure, I do. I sure as hell do. Yes, I do."

"If you have to say it three times," observed Saul, "you probably don't."

Ned said, "There's nothing much I can do, is there? All I can do is ask Tom Kidd."

"Tom wouldn't know."

"How do you know that?"

"Because if he was supposed to"—Sally said this through gritted teeth—"he'd have been there."

"He'd have to know sometime."

Sally was about to respond when the waiter came over to take their order. He knew what they wanted; they always had the same thing, the same drinks, except for that fling with the mint juleps. Saul and Jamie martinis, Sally some icky-looking cordial, Ned bourbon. The waiter smiled and left. Saul always left him extravagant tips.

Perhaps one reason they liked to come here was that things seemed muted in the Old Hotel. It was not an "arty" hangout. It was on some lesser known street on the fringe of the Village, a half street that dead-ended at a whitewashed church. But the patrons only sometimes looked as if they came from Chelsea or the Village or SoHo. And as a group they changed nightly, or seemed to. Sometimes they looked like they came over from Queens, blue collar and conservative. And then there were the nights filled with the Uptown people: Central Park West, the East Sixties, Sutton Place. It was always switching. It looked tonight as if they'd all organized themselves in the lobby of the Dakota and come downtown en masse.

How had they found the Old Hotel, these Uptown emigrants? These thin and high-strung women in their filmy, flowing clothes; like butterflies, with their iridescent lips and nails? The dining room wasn't even—heavens above!—in *Zagat*. How it could have been missed was a mystery. Its food was good and not too expensive, but it was the ambience that was thrilling. Saul said it was because Nina and Tim Zagat had been turned away. That's what he'd heard.

They all thought that was screamingly funny.

Yet it was never crowded. People weren't stacked up around the bar on a Friday evening the way they were at Swill's (where they muscled one another out as if they were trying to put down a bet before the window slammed down).

They had tried, as had just about everybody, to get information about the Old Hotel. Each of them had at one time or another tried to talk to the owner-manager to get answers to these questions. But he always seemed to have "just stepped out" for a moment. They knew (or supposed they did) that there actually was a manager for he had once been pointed out by the bartender to them as he was walking through the Lobby. His name, the bartender had told them, was Duff. That'll be him, sir. I'm sure he'll be glad to answer your questions. I would do myself, but I haven't been here very long myself.

Duff fascinated Saul.

("He would," Jamie had said, inscrutably.)

Duff was a question mark; he was unfinished; he was pure potential.

So they stopped trying to track down the manager because they apparently weren't supposed to know. Oedipus didn't, did he? Sally had said. There was something that smacked of fatalism in the whole encounter—or rather the lack of one.

"Pittsburgh's changed a lot," said Ned, as if they'd been discussing this since he brought it up. He finished off the silver bowl of cashews.

"Why're you going, anyway?" Whenever Ned left Manhattan Sally got anxious.

"Research," he lied.

Jamie sighed heavily to let him know her estimation of this move. "Just for fuck's sake don't go to McKees Rocks and come back and run things by me. Do I remember this? Do I remember that? I'm warning you."

"Remember Duquesne Incline? And the steps up the side of Duquesne Heights? You know how long a trail of steps that was? I went up them."

Jamie looked as if she could spit. "No, you didn't! You *didn't* because they were torn down sometime in the sixties. The early sixties. You wouldn't have been more than a day-old baby, for God's sakes."

"Maybe my father carried me up." Paying no attention to Jamie's pained look, he said, "Order me another drink, will you? I'm going to the gents." Which was what it was actually labeled here. GENTS and LADIES. They thought that fit in perfectly with the Old Hotel's diverse styles.

Sally watched him walk away and turned to Jamie. "You shouldn't ride Ned all the time about Pittsburgh."

"Why not?" Jamie seemed genuinely surprised at Sally's criticism. She was used to criticism, but only in her professional life, where she got three or four bad reviews to every good one. "He's so stunningly sentimental about the place." She saw Saul looking at her. "Why are you looking daggers at me?"

"Because Pittsburgh's what he is; it's what he has."

Jamie felt abashed far more by Saul's tone than she had by Sally's. With her, Saul really counted. This only served to stoke her irritation.

Sally said, "You can be really arrogant sometimes, Jamie."

Jamie ignored this as she could think of nothing to say in her own defense. "Ned remembers things that weren't there and things that never happened!"

"How do you know that?"

"Because I looked them up!" Too late did she think of the depths of animosity and even jealousy that might be ascribed to such a thing. Quickly, she added, "I lived in McKees Rocks, remember. That's right by Pittsburgh."

Sally gave a little wondering laugh. "So what? Are you saying Ned's memories have to mirror yours?"

Jamie stuck the olive from her martini in her mouth, glad that the two couples at the next table provided distraction. They were clearly first timers. They looked around the room a little too much for customers who'd seen it before. They were too loud; they wanted to attract attention, which the women were doing anyway, given the waist-deep cleavage of their black and red dresses. They rose rather elaborately, collected purses and cigarette lighters, and moved off toward the stairs.

Saul watched them for a minute and then spoke again. "It really makes you mad as hell, doesn't it, Jamie?"

Jamie frowned. "What does?"

"Here you and Ned grew up in almost the same place and have many of the same memories—or should have, according to you—so why don't you have the same degree of talent? You feel you have to turn out two or three books a year, which you don't, to make up for your not having his talent, and even though you drown yourself in words, it still doesn't do it."

Jamie blushed. "Don't be ridiculous! I'm not jealous of Ned, for God's sakes!"

"You're not jealous of *me*. But you *are* jealous of Ned." Saul leaned closer to Jamie. "Let me ask you something: are your parents still there in McKees Rocks? Your brother and sisters? Aunts—no, you've got an aunt in Savannah, you said. But the rest? Are they in McKees Rocks?"

For a moment Jamie didn't answer; she wore the look of a person trying to stay clear of certain danger. "What if they are?"

"Ned's aren't. What he's got is Isaly's Ice Cream. His family are all gone."

Jamie looked around the room as if Saul weren't speaking at all.

Saul said, "You're so competitive; you're so competitive you even have to compete with yourself—which also might account in part for all of those different hats you wear—"

"Fuck you, Saul! You don't know what you're talking about. And I'm right about those steps. Ned couldn't have been more than a baby—"

"Then he remembers an image someone else supplied, his father or mother, maybe. Ned's a memoirist. Just because it's a memory, that doesn't mean it's sentimental."

"Well, it's sentimental to hang out on memory lane."

Saul laughed. "We all hang out there."

"Not me. I don't; I don't look back. I don't believe you do, either."

"I don't? Jamie, I live in a houseful of artifacts. It's drenched in the past. I never change anything, beyond turning a desk around so that it faces a window. I want it to stay the same."

"That's not the same thing. History is provenance when it comes to antiques; provenance belongs to them." Here she gave a self-satisfied little smile and polished off her martini. She tapped her glass. "Anyone want another?"

Sally said, "Are we having dinner here or what?" She felt vaguely dissatisfied and depressed and not able to pinpoint the cause of it. Then she thought: *Am I afraid he'll go to Pittsburgh and just—disappear?*

"*What a stupid question,*" she answered herself.

"What if he never comes back?"

"Oh, for God's sakes . . ."

"But what—"

The other voice turned away in disgust. Murmuring.

Sally spied Ned making his way back through the tables—the Lobby was crowded, even more than usual—and watched him as he crossed the room as if he might go up in a puff of smoke if she looked away.

"What's wrong?" asked Saul

Jamie had left the table to go to the bar and sulk for a while. This section of the Lobby was smoky. Saul always asked Sally and Ned if they minded sitting in the smoking section (which, oddly enough, seemed to hold the smoke to it, a phenomenon no one had been able to explain. But that was the Old Hotel). Saul always made a point of saying he didn't have to smoke. To which Jamie always retorted, "Well, I do." Saul just stomped all over her.

"Nothing," said Sally, answering his concern. "I just think maybe I'll go to—" She stopped.

Ned was there, taking his seat again. "Are we leaving or having dinner?"

"Sorry, I forgot your drink," said Sally. "Yes, we're having dinner."

Saul was watching two couples going up the staircase to the rarefied air of the mezzanine.

"Saul?"

"What?"

"You ready to eat?" said Ned.

"Sure." Saul took out his money clip, tossed a couple of bills on the table, all the while watching the two pick their way past the tables up there.

The two in the park, later in Swill's. And their female counter-parts, right here in the Old Hotel. Saul laughed.

"What?" asked Jamie.

"Those guys." Saul nodded upward. "In the park and in Swill's."

They all looked toward the mezzanine.

"The suits with books."

TWENTY-TWO

Clive arrived some ten minutes early, knowing Mort loved to keep people waiting and Clive was set to humor him tonight. Even so, Mort was already there, bellying up to the magnificent mahogany, marble, and jade bar when Clive walked into the Lobby. Mort was flanked by a black couple and two women, a redhead and a blonde. Flashy. Whatever Duff's criteria were, one's trade didn't enter into it. At a nearby table sat four scruffy-looking men, dark skinned, mustachioed like Zapata, and one turbaned like Lawrence of Arabia. This party was acceptable, apparently, but not on the mezzanine level. They kept raising their eyes and casting lovelorn looks at the balcony.

Clive was surprised Mort had gotten past the front door.

Mort cleared that up. "I gave them my name and for some reason that didn't get me to first base, so I gave them yours." Mort shrugged, witness to the Old Hotel's arbitrary standards. "What's your poison?"

Clive smiled at this arcane mode of expression. "Same as yours, martini, but on the rocks with two olives." He finished the description for the bartender, who said it would be there in half a minute. Clive took the half to look the place over. He knew he was a rubbernecker straight from the sticks. There was the usual people watching going on, though no one wanted to be caught doing it, so there were a lot of darting glances and head turnings on the pretext of lighting cigarettes. The Old Hotel had knuckled under to the nonsmoking movement to take in most of the Lobby and the rooms off the mezzanine, which was sensible since those were small, enclosed places.

The food here was very good, if not great; the prices were incredibly low for Manhattan; the service was impeccable. It was one reason its customers didn't merely like the place, but loved it. Nothing in Manhattan could beat it for service and surroundings and, of course, cachet. There was no other restaurant that gave its customers the kick of having been there when even their good friends hadn't.

Clive had his martini and downed half of it while Mort asked for another. Clive wondered what he was so edgy about.

A hostess came to take them to their table upstairs. They made their way up the beautiful staircase, which served as a focus for those left behind. Clive had often thought it was like watching a solemn procession, several men and women making their way up as if the diners were gathering for a state occasion.

They sat in armchairs so comfortable Clive thought he might never get up, ordered wine, ordered the Hotel's speciality, Chicken Paprikash with Spaetzle. It had been rumored that Duff was born in Budapest. It had been rumored he'd been born in at least a dozen other places, too.

All that taken care of, Mort drank the last of his martini and asked, "Okay, so what about Paul? And when are you going to sign the contract?"

Why was his tone so wary? Were there unexploded mines around Giverney's feet? He said, "What do you mean? It's your client who won't sign it until his demands are met." Mort, Clive now suspected, was in the dark as to what those demands were.

"Are you telling me the deal's changed or what?"

"Nothing's changed except in a small way." Clive was angry with himself for not having thought this through; he knew Mort would ask about the contract.

"Small? Ha! Where a contract's concerned there's no small, Clive."

Oh, for Christ's sake, take out the money and the delivery date and hardback/paperback split and everything left is small. "Come on, Mort, you go over contracts like you're picking out chiggers."

"I am. So tell me the small."

Clive lit on and discarded several possibilities, then settled on one. "Bobby'd like joint accounting."

"So would the elves; I don't see Santa giving it."

"You're not Santa Claus, Mort." The waiter had set before them their chicken and now Clive spent a few moments tasting the wine and nodding to the waiter, who poured it into both glasses. He had expected the subject of Paul Giverney, given that this was his agent, would arise in a perfectly easy, natural way. It was his fault, Clive's, for telling Mort that Giverney was what he wanted to talk about.

He drank his wine, ate his dinner, and listened to Mort talk about joint accounting and its implications for the writer (and the agent, obviously) and felt his attention wandering to the Lobby below them. Clive's eyes traveled over the tables and then back again. "I'll be damned. Hey, look: half the great writers in Manhattan are sitting down there."

Mort looked. "Isn't that Saul Prouil? Jesus, it's like a sighting of Elvis. The man's practically invisible."

"No, he isn't. Tom Kidd's assistant sees him all the time." Clive liked being in on things when Mort was out. "And Ned Isaly. You know him?"

"Jimmy McKinney just signed him," Mort said, unhappily. "Ned's got a book coming out soon and he didn't have an agent. Tom Kidd recommended Jimmy. Tom really likes Jimmy, who knows why? Jimmy's just too laconic to make a really top-drawer agent."

Unlike you, you charlatan, thought Clive, as the plates were cleared away. "But he's one of yours."

"Yeah, yeah. Well, people like Jimmy. Say he's soothing. Should an agent be soothing, I ask you?" Mort laughed. Then he went on. "Isaly's a good writer, no question. Do you think Prouil's going to have a book coming out? He's unagented. I would certainly like a piece of that. . . . Isn't that one of your girls there?" asked Mort.

"Sally. She's Tom's assistant."

"Cute kid."

"Where's Paul from?" Clive asked, casually. He wanted to get Mort to continue to talk about Giverney.

"Ummm." Mort seemed to be thinking, trying to remember, his eyes moving upward, following the trail of smoke from his cigarette. "Pittsburgh, I think."

Clive looked down at his place, now empty, waiting to be filled by the Chocolate Dome. He was also trying to remember a conversation with Tom Kidd about Ned. Pittsburgh? Wasn't Ned from Pittsburgh?

"Born there or went to school there or something, I dunno." Mort went on, still talking about Paul Giverney, his arm cocked atop the fancy balustrade, his eyes looking down at the Lobby. Mort lifted his chin and blew a strand of smoke upward that eddied away to fuse with the dappled light of the chandelier.

Clive smiled as their waiter set down the Chocolate Dome and poured the last of the wine. This dinner (which would set him back—set Mackenzie back, rather—two hundred or so) wasn't paying off. His fork came down on the dome, cracking the chocolate shell and revealing layers of chocolate mousse and sabayon, a paean to calories and cholesterol and worth every artery-clogging, waist-spreading bit. He decided the hell with it, and jumped right in: "What's this I hear about a feud between Ned and Paul?"

Mort frowned. "Feud? Don't know what you're talking about." It was clear he disliked not knowing about something as gossip-worthy as this about one of his own clients. "What?"

"Oh, just a rumor. Maybe Giverney just doesn't like Ned Isaly for some reason. Something I heard in passing, that's all."

"Well, it beats me. Never heard Paul mention him one way or the other. I can believe Paul would be feuding with just about any-body, though, he's such an arrogant bastard."

Clive laughed. "Arrogant bastard" was the sobriquet by which Paul Giverney was best known. And it occurred to Clive, then, that of course Paul wouldn't talk to Mort about it. Indeed, he was sur-prised with himself that he hadn't realized this earlier. Paul had lit-tle use for agents, including Mortimer Durban, even though Paul was a client. He wouldn't get into anything personal with Mort.

As the layers turned to a heavenly mixture in his mouth, Clive looked down at the Lobby, where he saw that the redhead and the platinum blonde who'd graced the bar beside Mort Durban earlier had found their dates, or had just made them, for now they sat with two men at a table near the writers'. He watched, frowning slightly, as they rose in concert and, drinks in hand, headed for the marble staircase, which they ascended, laughing.

My God, those two.

Candy and Karl.

Among the anointed.

TWENTY-THREE

Clive sat the next morning running a pencil across the tops of his fingers, trying to ignore the Dwight Staines novel piled high and untidy on his desk. Perhaps in time it would molder into dust and he'd be shut of it. Not that it was at the forefront of his consciousness; that particular spot was reserved for the twin psychos, Candy and Karl, and the assurance that they were on the job, given last night.

Clive frowned. How in hell had they got into the Old Hotel on the previous evening? If those two could get in . . . (But then hadn't he seen someone in there who looked like Danny Zito awhile back?)

Well, the two hoods had gotten in and they were sitting only a few tables away from Ned Isaly. What occupied Clive's mind this morning was finding a way to extricate himself from this plot. He glanced at the manuscript. What Bobby should have done was set the two of them onto Dwight Staines and save the best-seller list a dozen weeks of yawning popularity.

Maybe he could have another talk with Paul Giverney. No. Pure wishful thinking. Still, he didn't think Giverney meant he wanted Ned Isaly dead, for God's sakes. Just out of the publishing arena, that's all. But what in hell had Ned done to arouse such enmity?

Clive sat there rolling the pencil for another minute or two, then yanked out the Verizon, thumbed through its Yellow Pages wondering whether it was "Investigators" or "Private." He found it. There must be hundreds of them; why was he surprised? This was New York, wasn't it? He didn't much like the idea of picking a name out of the Yellow Pages; there was the randomness of it, the gamble. It was hardly any more of a gamble than what was already going on, though. He closed his eyes and thought of people he knew who'd used a private detective.

Helen Shearling. She could recommend one; she must know a dozen. She'd got out of marriages one, two, three, and four with all of the houses, the BMW, the Mercedes, the Porsche, the condo in Cancún, in addition to hefty alimony payments that should keep the ex-hubbies in hock for the rest of their lives. It was all owing to the PIs and their cameras, catching hubby (one, two, three, four) with his current inamorata. *Flash. Click.* "How sexually puerile," Helen had said on seeing the photos as she chose among them for two or three to present to her lawyer, who would in turn present them to the husband's lawyer. What Clive couldn't understand was why none of these husbands had turned the tables, given that Helen was no stranger herself to sexual puerility.

The trouble was he didn't want a private investigator whose work was largely finding the bedrooms of unfaithful husbands or wives. A recommendation— Clive sat up suddenly. Of course! There was always Danny Zito. He searched through his desk drawers, through layers of paper clips and rubber bands and then remembered he'd copied the number from Bobby's Rolodex card onto a scrap of paper that might still be in his overcoat pocket. He moved to the closet and went through every pocket. Right!

Clive picked up the receiver, dialed the number.

"What is it with you guys you spend half your time whacking people?" asked Danny, cheerfully. "How the hell do you get any books published? I sure hope you got a few minutes left over to read my manuscript when you're done with capping your authors." Danny fake laughed a *ho-ho-ho.*

Lowering his voice without actually whispering, Clive said, "Cut it out, Dan—I mean Johnny—"

"Jimmy, fuck's sake. You can't even get the fake name right?"

"Okay, okay, sorry. Anyway. I'm not trying to cap anybody. I just want someone, you know, followed."

"Yeah, sure, I bet, and I want the Pen/Faulkner Award." He paused, Clive assumed to turn up a name. "Yeah, I do know somebody. Just don't go thinking this person'll take out Candy and Karl, man. We don't gun down our own—I mean not unless it's war declared. But on a daily basis, no way. We got scruples, unlike you publishing wanks that don't give a shit as long as you can get some birdbrain on the best-sell—"

Clive broke into this building rave with, "Okay, okay, Danny. Spare me the lecture. You can get in touch with this person?"

"Have you forgotten I'm in the fucking witness protection—"

"Yes, yes. I mean should we handle it the same way? I meet you—"

"At the Chelsea Piers. Same place, same time. Tonight if you want. Listen, I got nearly a third of my book done."

"Danny, how could you have that much? It's only been a few days since we saw each other."

"I write all the time. Me, I'm another Trollope, who I've been reading—well, glossing over kind of. I do what he does. I set my clock beside me and write two hundred fifty words per fifteen minutes. Actually, I can even go faster. I'll bring along what I done."

The writing habits of Danny Zito. What the world is waiting to hear about. Clive cast a weary look at Dwight Staines's pages and shook his head. Nothing could be worse than Staines. "Why not, Danny? See you."

Rarely did Clive veer from their main corridor, the one hung with posters and framed Mackenzie-Haack book jackets, at the end of which was Bobby Mackenzie's office. But today he did turn a corner to a narrower passageway off which Tom Kidd sat in his book-swamped little room. Clive pulled up at Sally's desk, situated outside Kidd's open door.

"Is he in?"

"You're taller, you tell me."

Clive went up on his toes, looked over the stacks of books on Tom's desk, then came down again. "Nope." He was really here to see Sally, not Tom, hoping he could pry some information out of her, since he'd seen all of them in the Old Hotel last night. Isaly's last book, what was it called? Shit. It started with an *S*, he remembered that. It was one word, he also remembered: *Sadness? Sorrow?* No. Oh, let it go.

He sat down in the hard, uninviting chair placed to one side of Sally's desk. It occurred to him then that he had, for a change, a conversational opener. "Saw you last night in the Old Hotel." Just having been there should be enough to engage anyone, given how difficult it was to get into the place.

It didn't engage Sally, however, for she didn't respond. He thought she looked a little grim and not because he was there.

"I was eating upstairs"—Clive poked a finger toward the ceiling, toward which Sally raised her eyes. He had never noticed it before, but Sally had, at times, a medieval look with all that thick dark hair and those peasant dresses—"with Mort Durban."

Sally made a face, straightening up some manuscript pages. "I didn't see you."

"Great place, isn't it, the Old Hotel?" said Clive.

She smiled and looked now as if the memory of it were coming back.

"For some reason, it makes me feel—" Clive stopped. There it was again, the impossibility of putting it into words. "—I don't know. Kind of . . . homesick, or something."

Sally's expression changed again to the gloomier one of before. "It must make Ned feel that way because he's leaving."

Clive's spirit soared. Was it possible? Could it *be*? "You mean he's leaving Mackenzie-Haack?"

No, it couldn't. "Of course not. I only mean he's going home."

"Where's home?"

"Pittsburgh."

"Pittsburgh?"

She looked almost wounded, as if she'd defend this city to her dying day. "Well, people do live there, after all. And what's wrong with Pittsburgh?"

"Nothing, nothing at all." Oh, thank you, God, for this free information. "For how long?"

She shrugged as if a day or a year made no difference. He was going, that's all. "Three days, maybe."

Clive zipped his thumb along a stack of pages. "Huh. Does he have a house there? His parents still live there?"

"No. They're dead. They were the ice cream people, you know, the Isaly's Ice Cream people. It's that really famous ice cream in Pittsburgh, probably still is." If it weren't, wouldn't Ned have said so? It was his favorite topic after writing, Isaly's. "He's going to stay at some hotel." She pretended to have to dig for the name, which was branded into her brain. "The Hilton, I think that's what he said."

"I'll be damned." Clive rose, stuffed his hands in his trouser pockets. "I guess I won't wait for Tom. I'll come back. Uh, when's he going? I mean, you know, in case we need him for something."

Sally looked at him with suspicion. "What would you need him for? Tom's his editor. And Bobby probably wouldn't know Ned if he fell over him."

"Oh. Well, Ned's supposed to get his new manuscript to us in a couple of weeks. I think that's what the contract says." He wondered why Sally glowered at him.

"I've never known us to hold anyone to the exact *day*, or even *week* before. So what if the manuscript's late?"

"Oh, well, nothing, really. I only meant the book's due soon. Anyway, he'll probably be back by then." Clive thought that was quite smooth.

Her suspicion appeared to deepen. But she said, "Wednesday morning, I think he said that's when he's going." She *knew* he'd said. She just didn't want to tell Clive, who now took his leave looking considerably more pleased than when he had sat down.

As he walked back up the corridor, Clive said the name—Pittsburgh—as if, with it, he might call spirits from the vasty deep.

But will they come when you do call for them?

Who'd said that? He looked around. Not him, that was certain. And even more certain, not Dwight Staines.

Sally's sigh back there had been so heavy Clive wondered about her feelings for Ned Isaly, scion of the Isaly's Ice Cream family.

Now he'd have to call Paul Giverney again. Paul wanted to be kept informed of whatever was going on with Ned. Probably, Paul hadn't meant something like Ned taking off for Pittsburgh, but if Clive told him about it, then it would certainly make it appear he was bending over backward for Paul. Christ, it was as bad as Candy and Karl. You'd think Giverney would rather *not* know Ned Isaly's movements.

Paul Giverney was getting to be a royal pain in the ass. That's the way it was with these big-time writers; they thought they owned the publishing house lock, stock, and barrel. Probably, they did.

He picked up the receiver and wearily dialed the number.

TWENTY-FOUR

You're *what*?" Lily was close to a shout loud enough that it would push through the McKinney walls and windows across the ample lawn and into their nosy neighbors' house next door, the Thinpugs'. The Thinpugs were sure Jimmy was gay—married or not, children or not—because he wrote poetry. ("Poor Lily," they enjoyed saying.)

Lily did not wait for Jimmy's answer, not when she could easily supply her own: "Like hell you are!" She had been making brownies (which Jimmy hated because of their name, poets living under the iron hammer of language) and brought the dough-sticky spoon down on the dough-sticky pastry board.

The money that would come to him via Jimmy's commission on Paul Giverney's books hadn't, in the long run, made up for Jimmy's potential six-month absence, if it came to it.

"Yaddo. What the hell is Yaddo?"

"I told you. A place where you can have your own cottage and just write. They even deliver your lunch to your door." Jimmy tossed in that detail just to stir the pot of her anger. He couldn't help himself. He had grown that detached. "It's not absolutely certain yet."

"What isn't? That you'll be Giverney's agent?" A piece of news she'd met with martinis and merriment. "Or deserting me and Mikhail?"

"Mikhail" was actually Michael (or Mike), their son, who'd ostentatiously changed the spelling of his name to align it with some Russian polemicist, even though Mike didn't read, or at least Jimmy had never caught him doing it.

"Don't be ridiculous." Jimmy poured himself another martini, ice diluted. "We'll have enough money, as you were eager enough to acknowledge when I told you about the Giverney commission. A commission from a three-book contract would easily double what I'm getting now. All you have to do is continue your present lifestyle (a Barneys one, a Bergdorf one, he didn't add). You can keep on with your tennis lessons at the country club and Mike can continue his teenage-jerk lessons."

The spoon came down again, clattering among the aluminum mixing bowls. "That's terrible! That's a terrible thing to be calling your own son!"

Jimmy kicked himself, mentally. He had no desire to get derailed onto the subject of his teenage-jerk son. "Only kidding." Heh, heh. "You'd have all the money you needed, Lil, don't you see that? You'd want for nothing."

Nothing except the prospect of Jimmy's enjoying his life without her there to act as umpire.

With the back of her hand, she swept her red hair ("—*her famous hair*") back from her forehead in a cliché gesture of "little woman baking brownies." His entire life, Jimmy had decided, was a cliché. It made him shudder, comforted only by poetry, his or others'.

("Not even Lilith, with her famous hair.") How stupid of him to think the money he would get as an agent for Paul Giverney would overshadow, for Lily, Jimmy's leading his life out from under her control. Control was what she thrived on.

"You and your poetry," she said, as one might say to Robert De Niro, *"You and your movies."*

". . . Nothing . . . that you cannot walk out on in thirty seconds flat if you spot the heat around the corner." Was this, Jimmy wondered, going to be a line his mind tossed up as it did lines of Robinson and Frost?

Lilith was still complaining and all the while running knife lines through the pan of brownies. "You and your poetry are amateurs, the both of you."

His face burned at that, but he kept his voice level. "Actually, publication takes you out of the amateur league. Because you get money for it. It's like an athlete going with a national team. I'm a professional."

"Ha!" The door bounced shut on the oven. "So now you're Michael Jackson!"

"Jordan. You mean Mikhail Jordan."

"Six months in some cabin and a lot of other writers. You really think that's all it takes to improve your poetry?"

Before they had married seventeen years ago, she would have bit out her tongue before she'd said that. And even ten years ago she'd been excited when he'd published *Lapses*. Being utterly unaware of publishing—even though he was an agent—she'd assumed a lot of things would come their (her) way because he had become a published poet. Parties, fame, fortune. There had been one party; there had been little of the other two elements. That the book had brought in its wake respect, both Jimmy's own self-respect and that of a few others, meant nothing to Lily. That Jimmy had remained utterly thrilled by his book's being published for a long time afterward made her think he was a sap.

But he wasn't a sap and he knew that. It was the difference between himself and Mort Durban. Jimmy understood what the siren song of publication meant to a writer, what a writer felt when a book was bought and published and he held it in his hands. Even if writers appeared to have lost this naïve delight in their books, Jimmy knew they hadn't. Even if they appeared to be laboring for a big advance and bucking for a place on the list, Jimmy knew they weren't. No, it was something far more important; it was finding the right word, it was *knowing* what the right word was. It might even have made them God-fearing if God had been, in that moment when exactly the right word came, at that point, necessary.

Then having declared his poetry unworthy of discussion, she said, "I think we'll go to the Stuarts' this weekend." She tossed the bowl and spoon in the sink. "They invited us for dinner."

"You go. Me, I'm going away this weekend. To a writers' retreat upstate."

It was too much. "You mean you're going *now*?"

She would make it sound as if he were abandoning his homeland in the manner of Odysseus. "For the weekend, that's all." Jimmy laughed and scooped ice cubes out of the bucket, mostly water by now, and dropped them in a glass. "Can I say anything that doesn't astound you tonight?" He poured a couple of fingers of vodka in the glass.

"Most of what you say doesn't astound me." She held her hands in a floppy position as if they were broken at the wrists.

Good one, Lilith, he thought, sadly. He explained about places such as Yaddo and the MacDowell Colony. "This one, though, this particular retreat lets you come for a weekend, to see if you like it."

"Why would you want to see if you *liked* it?"

"To decide if one of these writers' colonies is what I want to do for six months or a year. That's what I've been saying: I want to take time off to write."

She quit her floppy-handed pose and crossed her arms beneath her breasts. She was wearing white cashmere and looked especially beautiful tonight. With that red hair.

Her beauty stung him, as if he had betrayed it in wanting to do anything that displeased her, in wanting anything but to go to the Stuarts' this weekend simply because she wanted to. He moved across what seemed limitless space and wrapped his arms around her, stroked her hair, kissed her on the cheek. "Lily, you once were—"

My girl. But she broke away before he could say it, not at all wanting to hear what she once was. "You're springing all sorts of things on me and don't expect me to be surprised?"

"Of course I do, except you're not only surprised, you're resentful—" This was going no place. "I'm sorry, but I *am* going."

She wheeled around and stomped out of the kitchen.

("I cannot hate you, for I loved you then.

The woods were golden then. There was a road . . .")

Jimmy sighed and went to the room he called his office.

TWENTY-FIVE

The Chelsea Piers. Same movie-fog, movie-fog-horn ambience. Danny Zito—writer, artist, bon vivant—would come trailing out of it like a movie-mob guy.

Clive wondered about all that while he waited in the wet and seeping cold: the Godfather, Don-who's-it—Corleone?—name like a kind of pasta. Gotti was real. But was it really like that? He wondered what, exactly, you had to do to be a made man. Did you get points for different things? So many for a body stuffed in a car trunk? Buried in the desert outside of Vegas? A gunning down in some spaghetti restaurant? (Extra points for the Four Seasons or Le Cirque?) Avoiding the slaughter of innocents? Not avoiding the slaughter of innocents? Drive-by shootings probably ranked really low—no panache, no style. Or was being "made" more to do with longevity? Was it loyalty that was important? Would he know the answers to all of these questions when Danny handed over the next hundred pages of opus number two? Probably not; probably it would be a treatise on ephemeral art.

Clive looked out over the Hudson, at the mist that clung to its surface like a river specter, ghosting across the water's surface. What he should have done when he was young was to catch a freighter. He could still do it . . . Oh, get real. Nothing kills you quicker than romancing things. The trouble with those romantic ideas is that your mind always shoots straight to the payoff—to the black sands and turquoise water, and you walking the beach; to the exotic and the beautiful. The mind skips right over the day-to-day stuff it takes to get to the good parts. Buy the castle in Scotland. The mind sees you moving through the baronial splendor of the big rooms, finger-ing the lush fabrics of draperies and sofas, conveniently omitting the hassle of moving the sofas in and hanging up the drapes, or the dreary cold from inadequate fires, the clanging pipes, the awful plumbing, the hook-nosed gardener, and the need for many ser-vants. In other words, the daily grind, the dreadful awareness of being You again, only now you're You again and cold as Scott of the Antarctic.

And for you who abscond to backwoods cabins in Minnesota and Saskatchewan so that you can write that edgy memoir—are you going to set down the days and weeks each following one another until you collapse from the boredom of it all?

"Mr. Editor, yo!"

Clive jumped.

"Man, you were orbiting. What the hell are you smoking?"

"Hello, Danny. Marlboro Lights, a carnival of sounds and col-ors. I started again." Clive dropped the cigarette, ground it with his heel, nodding at the white Dean & DeLuca bag Danny carried. "That where you do your grocery shopping?"

"Absolutely. Best produce in town."

"Most expensive, that's for sure." The man had to be kidding. "You're in the witness protection program, remember?"

Danny winced. "Oh, come on. Who'd expect one of them to turn up in Dean and DeLuca?"

"Well, hell, then, why don't we meet in produce at Dean and DeLuca instead of this godforsaken pier?"

"Dean and DeLuca ain't a place for a meet, Clive. That's what you got piers for. Come on. And what's so 'godforsaken' about it?" Danny swept his arm out. "You got your skateboarding, your hoops down there"—he pointed into the darkness—"and there's two more galleries opening in that warehouse." He nodded to a place over Clive's shoulder.

Clive did not bother looking around. "Spare me Chelsea art. What about the, uh, contact, Danny?"

"Yeah, yeah. I got a name for you. Did you get those details worked out? What we talked about?" Danny folded a stick of gum into his mouth.

"Details?"

"What we talked about."

Clive tried to call this up, which was hard with Danny's damp brown eyes wide on him as eager as a Derby entrant a furlong from the finish. Then he remembered. "The hard-soft deal, the split? Sure. Fifty-five, forty-five, just what you asked for."

Danny kept looking at him. "And—?"

"'And'?"

"Jacket art."

"Oh, yeah. Jacket approval. No problem. It's yours."

"*And*—?"

Clive searched his mind but did he need one for this? "And . . . copy. You write your own copy?" That would be a break for Clive or a copy editor.

"Good. Here." Danny smiled as he handed over the white bag. "I think you're gonna like it if I do say so. It's set in Vegas."

"In Vegas? My, my. De Niro will be all over it. Come on, Danny, do you think that's wise?" Wise? What in hell did wisdom have to do with any of this? "I mean, there was *Casino,* there was *Bugsy*—every mob story's set in Vegas or New York."

Danny shut his eyes, pained by such obtuseness. He shook his head slowly. "No, no. This is way different. This is totally different."

Clive hated himself for asking, but he did. "How?"

"Well, for one thing, it's like a comparison with the Romans. All of them Caesars. Julius is only one—"

"How does Julius get to Vegas?"

Danny snorted. "You never heard of Caesars Palace? The old world and the new. Just read it, you'll get it. It's myths. That Bellagio place, you know, with the fountains out front, hell, that's a myth run wild. I got another hundred pages done."

Myths. "I can hardly wait." In some insane way, this was true.

"And when it comes to movie rights, I get cast approval. And director. That's important. Lynch would be right for it. Maybe Christopher Nolan. As me I see Pacino or maybe Ray Liotta. Joe Pesci, I don't think so. But that newer guy, what the hell's his name . . . ?" Danny was chewing gum furiously now, thinking of who he wanted to play him.

"Good." Clive smiled. "The name, Danny?"

Danny snapped his fingers. "Vince Vaughn."

"Not the actor, Danny, the investigator."

"Oh, yeah. You got a pencil? Oh, a Montblanc, excuse me."

Clive had his pen out and gave Danny a sour look.

"Blasé Pascal, that's P-a-s-c-a-l. Phone number—"

For a moment Clive was struck dumb. "Hold it. That's a philosopher."

"What philosopher?" Danny frowned.

"Blaise Pascal. He was a philosopher. You've heard of that famous wager—"

"He's Vegas, too?"

Jesus! "This name. What is it, a pseudonym?"

Danny shrugged, chewed his gum. "Fuck do I know? B-l-a-s-é P-a-s-c-a-l."

"Danny, that's 'blah-*zay*' you're spelling. Meaning, 'apathetic,' 'bored.'"

"Don't blame me. Anyway, here's the number." He watched Clive write it down, then said, "So how's Karl and Candy doing? They're good, right?"

"I don't know. They're certainly on the job. But would you please explain something?" He was feeling pretty damned edgy. "Why do these guys insist on getting to know the target? Or mark or whatever you call him?"

Danny shrugged. "That's how they operate."

But Danny, Clive felt, was not attending to his answers; his mind was all on the Dean & DeLuca bag and Vince Vaughn and his hundred pages. Clive said, "I can't imagine wanting to know anything about the person I was hired to gun down."

"Me neither, but that's us." Danny shrugged his dark peacoat up around his shoulders. "You'll get back to me on that"—a nod toward the manuscript—"real soon, okay?"

Clive nodded. Blah-zay Pascal.

TWENTY-SIX

Arthur Mordred was eating a lemon crepe when Paul sat down at the table in the same espresso-cappuccino café. Paul had nearly missed him again, even though he'd seen him in here before. What was it with this guy? How did he manage to blend to the point of evaporation, like the steam coming off the espresso machine?

"So, Paul," Arthur said, "we meet again."

"I'm curious. Sammy says you can't stand the telephone for, ah, business arrangements."

"True. They're too easy to tap. I assume mine is."

"But isn't it more dangerous to be meeting in public places?"

"No."

Paul waited. No explanation. He sighed. "I wanted to tell you that Ned Isaly is going to Pittsburgh tomorrow." Paul consulted a page of his small notebook. "In the morning on American Airlines."

"I know, 204. I got myself on the same flight."

Paul's mouth dropped open. "How'd you—"

A labored sigh was Arthur's response. "Because I was in the

travel agent's at the same time. I *am* supposed to be following him. Though why anybody needs a travel agent to get to Pittsburgh, I ask myself. This guy's the head-in-the-clouds type."

"Just keep him in view, that's all."

His chin resting in his hand, Arthur made an *ummm* sound, as if he'd tasted something rich and sweet. "I love Pittsburgh, always have. My mother was born there. A gem of a woman, dead now, God rest her." He polished off another bit of the crepe. "I can do this quickly if you're in a hurry."

Paul waved both his hands as if clearing the space between them of smoke. "You don't remember what I *said* last time? Listen to me: remember that you're not supposed to shoot him; you're supposed to keep anyone *else* from shooting him."

Arthur looked at him for a blank moment, then squinched his eyes shut. "Oh, yeah. Sorry, sorry, I must've been thinking about someone else." He forked up a piece of his lemon crepe.

"Wait a minute!" Paul was beginning to panic. "You're saying you *forgot*? You *forgot* what you're supposed to do?"

Arthur pulled a paper napkin from the aluminum holder and touched his mouth with it. "Paul, you're much too excitable. But then I guess that's because you're a writer. You artistic people do seem to be high strung."

Paul glared. Then whispered, "Look, how do I know you won't forget again? Jesus Christ, if you can forget *once*—"

"Because I won't." Arthur grinned. "Never lost a client yet!" Arthur laughed, appreciating the double entendre.

Paul realized he couldn't pull Arthur off the job at this point.

The white heat of Pittsburgh was coming up like the sun over the horizon.

TWENTY-SEVEN

Clive sat behind his desk, hands tented before his face, waiting for Pascal. He was afraid he was starting something he couldn't stop, like a runaway train. Correction: he had *already* started something. What he was trying to do now was slow it down.

Pascal's secretary—he hadn't talked to Pascal himself—hadn't sounded smart, exactly, but she'd been perfectly polite. "Yessir, I was to tell you Tuesday at three P.M. if it suits your convenience." The voice grew even more nasal when she got off phrases like "suits your convenience." Clive pictured a soft·pillowy-breasted blonde wearing something that showed her cleavage. She'd be chewing gum that she cracked or blew bubbles with.

He shook his head to clear it. Had he fallen victim to such stereotyping because of this fucking Dwight Staines manuscript? *StandOff*. Clive wished Mr. Staines had been as parsimonious with the content as he had been with the title. The title promised all sorts of brevity, conciseness, and crisp prose. But no, the damned thing was six hundred pages long (a number that would be mercifully shortened in print) and the prose as turgid as ever. *StandOff* still sat in the same place atop his desk. Seventy-five pages was as far as he'd gotten. What he'd probably do would be to skip a couple of hundred pages and find something in the middle to comment on and editorialize over to keep Staines thinking he was really being edited. He'd already forgotten what was in the seventy-five pages he'd read. He actually did the exercise of setting his mind to remembering. All he could dredge up was that female on the train—Blanche? Belle?— and the only reason he remembered her was because she was irrelevant, even at that early stage of the character's appearance.

The trouble was that Dwight Staines had a way of asking, What do you think of this character or of that twist in the plot? Did you like the scene where—? That's what Mercy Morganstein, Dwight's former editor at Quagmire, had told Clive when she was chirruping away about Dwight. Mercy Morganstein was moving to another house. Hard to believe that the woman had actually liked these books. What she'd—what *they'd*—minded so much at Quagmire (she'd told him) was their not being able to work with "our Dwight."

"Mercy," Clive had asked her, "did you ever talk to Staines about going with you?"

No, she hadn't. It had never occurred to her to do that. She'd sounded offended, as if this practice were unheard of and underhanded. It might have been underhanded, but it was hardly unheard of. An editor would be some kind of chump if he didn't cart off as many writers as he could. It happened all the time when editors changed houses. The writers themselves would initiate this move if they had developed a tight relationship with their editors. But there was no convincing Mercy of this, and since Dwight

Staines must be aware she was leaving, well, maybe he didn't care or didn't want her as an editor. Or, rather, he knew on which side his bread was buttered, for Mackenzie-Haack's image was that of a "literary" publisher, whereas Quagmire's was almost completely commercial. "Our Dwight" seemed to want to move up a rung. "Our Dwight" was an idiot if he really thought a more literary publisher would turn his sow's ear into a silk purse. Oh, well. Dwight (Clive had heard) was doing one of his book tours, which would keep him out of the Mackenzie-Haack offices for three weeks.

It was all a fucking mirage as far as Clive was concerned. But it was a mirage a lot of people swore was really that shining patch of water they took it for. All of these editors' assistants and associate editors working at salaries so low you'd call it slavery, they wanted nothing but to become full-blown editors. The image they packed around was of Peter Genero and his dogs, or else Tom Kidd and his genius. You couldn't dissuade them. *You'll never be Tom Kidd,* he'd told the ones who had voiced this hope. *Never. You'll be like the rest of us.*

Us. When had he started devaluing his own work? That wasn't hard to pin down: when he'd gone along with Bobby Mackenzie in this whole outrageous charade. Up to then, he hadn't really given his work all that much thought.

Amy's voice: "There's a Blase Pascal here to see you?"

Pronounced by Amy to rhyme with "place." Clive told Amy to send him in.

Only "he" was a "she." Clive, who prided himself on his cool head, gaped. Ms. Blaze Pascal (Danny Zito was hardly spelling bee champ) was a very good-looking woman with red hair. Fiery red hair, actually. He'd never seen any red like this red. When the light hit its copper surface, it spat sparks.

He adjusted his expression as he rose to shake her hand and to indicate a comfortable leather chair for her. "You'll have to pardon me; Danny didn't tell me you were a woman."

"Mind if I smoke?" When he made a forgiving gesture, she drew out a silver case, offered him one. He said no, but picked up the table lighter—his nostalgic look back at a pack a day—and lit her cigarette. "Incidentally"—he paused, feeling a bit stupid, but his curiosity was killing him—"your first name, just what is it? How do you pronounce it?"

"Oh? It's Blaze. B-l-a-z-e, you know, as in fire." She drew out a strand of hair, raised her eyebrows. "I got the nickname when I was in school and I couldn't ever get rid of it."

"I see. Well, I suppose it does suit you."

She wasn't listening to him; she was peering around the room. "Some office!" she said. Her glance seemed actually to light on this or that object admiringly—the Chinese vase, the cut-glass whiskey decanter (that Clive used only for visitors; he preferring the gin in the bottom drawer). "It beats mine all to hell, I'll tell you. Mine's the stereotype. Sam Spade, Philip Marlowe. The dank and dreary cell with the beige paint. Clients like that, surprisingly. You'd think they'd want some indication of success, palpable images—you know, like the real estate agent who drives a Jag. A visible show of riches. Uh-uh—" She pulled over an ashtray. "Once, I put in an espresso machine, but that kind of threw people off stride. What was I, anyway? A private eye or a Starbucks franchise? No, in this game you gotta stay with the stereotype. It's hard enough being a woman in the trade, much less one who's into a lot of yuppie shit. But I'll tell you, it'll be nice working for someone who knows the difference between Woolworth's and Waterford"—here she tapped the cut-glass ashtray with a long fingernail—"and it's gonna be my last job. Actually, I only said yes because Danny recommended you. Good publisher, he said. I read his book. Not bad. A writer's life, that sounds like the best–"

He stomped on it. "Ms. Pascal–"

"Blaze." She held out a strand of hair again, winked at him.

"–you're not thinking of writing a book, are you?"

"Who, *moi?*" She pressed her hands against the green silk shirt that did much for her breasts. "You're kidding. It never entered my mind."

Clive relaxed a little.

"I should tell you, though, I'm particular about the kind of case I take. I don't do divorces. I don't bust into crumby hotel rooms with a flash and start snapping pictures. Which I never do; I don't do stuff in the tits and dick department. I don't do wires . . ."

As she rambled on, Clive stared. What was going on in the underbelly of New York City, anyway? Where had they come from, these boutique killers who wouldn't commit to a contract until they got to know their subject? Private eyes with more reservations than Danielle's on a Thursday night? It was all so damned genteel anymore. He hoped he'd never have to hire a stalker only to be told: *"I don't do nasty messages; I don't do telephone calls at three A.M.; I don't go uptown if they move, which they usually do. I'm strictly TriBeCa, Village, SoHo, Chelsea. I might stretch a point and stalk the East Thirties, on occasion, if it's absolutely necessary."*

What in hell was New York City coming to?

"Don't worry. There's nothing in this job that requires any of that. All I want you to do is follow this person." (Should he come clean about Candy and Karl?) Clive shoved Ned's book across the desk, back jacket open.

She picked it up, looked at the photo. "An author! What's he been up to?"

"Nothing."

"You just want to know where he goes, what he does. Authors are pretty boring." She raised the book. "Can I have this?"

"Yes, of course." Clive felt his feathers slightly ruffled. "I wouldn't say authors are boring. Not the successful ones, anyway." Why was he defending them?

"I only mean, whatever goes on, goes on up here." She tapped a Chinese-red lacquered fingernail against her temple. "Their minds are so juiced up they don't have any energy left over. Except maybe to go to a movie. See, I went with one once. The guy was so into his thoughts he'd walk straight out in front of a fleet of yellow cabs when the light was changing. Or he'd stand on a corner and gape. Or he'd get on the subway, forget his stop—if he ever had one to begin with—and wander around wherever he did get off. His name was Sam Devene." The slightly raised eyebrow she turned on Clive suggested that possibly Clive knew him.

"Has it occurred to you that your friend Sam might have had some malady unassociated with writing? I don't think Mr. Isaly has a problem with traffic and subway stops." Why was he engaging in this talk? "All you need to do is fly to Pittsburgh tomorrow—"

"Pittsburgh!" She hurtled forward in her chair as if she'd been shot in the back.

Clive shut his eyes. She was going to tell him she only "did" Manhattan (and not all of that).

"I lived there when I was married. Not right in the city. In Sewickley. It was so beautiful, Sewickley. Any chance he'd be going there?"

"I've no idea. He was born in Pittsburgh. As you can see from the flap copy." Clive nodded toward the book in her hands. That's all he needed, for someone to stroll down memory lane with Ned Isaly. Maybe neither one of them would ever come back, which would solve his problem. "Ned will be going to Pittsburgh tomorrow for a couple of days, perhaps three or four at most."

"Why's he going?"

"He's doing research— Look: does it matter?"

"Just curious. So what do I have to look out for, since you're not interested in where he goes?"

"Nothing in particular to look out for. I imagine it's just walking around." Clive fiddled with his letter opener. "I should tell you: he's being tailed."

"What? So what you want me to do is tail the tail? Who's doing the tailing?"

As she was looking over the top of his desk, probably for another book jacket photo of the tail, he said, in as acid a tone as he could manage, "I'm sorry I don't have a picture of them."

"Them? More than one?"

"Yes."

"So let me get this straight: What you really want is a bodyguard?"

"You could say so, yes. Except in this case the person you follow won't know he has one."

She held up her hands, palms toward him. "Just let's get one thing clear: I don't do wet work."

Now, if Dwight Staines (and Danny Zito) had taught him anything, he had taught him this term. "That only applies to hit men. Contract killers." Clive felt a chill and shivered. "You'd only be acting defensively. And there'll be no need for anything like that anyway." He said this with more conviction than he felt.

She appeared to be turning this over in her mind. "Okay, but this'll cost you double my usual fee. And I'd want some now."

Clive pulled his checkbook out of a drawer. It hardly seemed right that he couldn't put this on an expense account. Maybe he could if he called it something else. Wet work. That'd be good. That'd go down in the old expenses column really well. He snickered as he wrote the check, tore it out. "Five thousand. That enough?"

She took it, blew on it. "That should do it. What's his flight number?"

Clive smiled because he had managed to get this information. There weren't all that many daily flights to Pittsburgh. "American 204. Leaving Kennedy nine o'clock, Wednesday morning. It's ticketed electronically."

"I'll be going, then." She rose, book in one hand, purse in the other. "Nice talking to you. Expenses, of course, are added on. Hotels, food, et cetera."

Clive nodded his understanding, rose, and showed her to the office door. "Enjoy Pittsburgh."

He shoved a wad of *StandOff* into his briefcase, thinking first he'd go to Le Cirque, his usual restaurant, then go home and read it. Home was his co-op on Sutton Place, which he'd first rented, then bought at a considerably lower price than was being offered to strangers off the street.

If Candy and Karl were going to move on Ned, somewhere out of New York would be a golden opportunity, wouldn't it? When Ned was alone and hadn't much chance of hooking up with friends, wasn't as sure of himself or of his surroundings? Maybe as disoriented as Pascal's boyfriend, Sam?

Clive closed up his briefcase and turned to look out of his window at Manhattan, darkening even as he looked. And as he looked the Chrysler Building's lights switched on, then the Empire State and MetLife. What a triangle of light it was! No other city in the world had it, that configuration of light. Not London, not even Paris.

And God only knew, not Pittsburgh.

TWENTY-EIGHT

Saul sat in the living room of his house in the wing chair his great-grandfather had brought from Paris; he knew even more specifically that it had come from the house of a good friend who lived in the Marais. In all of this time, the chair had never needed reupholstering. Perhaps this was because his family, his grandfather and then his father, had not used it much, out of respect for the old friend. The family wanted to keep it in as perfect condition as possible. It was upholstered in tapestry with a dull gold background upon which unlikely birds embroidered in blues and greens spread their wings.

Saul knew the provenance of every piece of furniture in this room—a hand-painted table belonging to his great-aunt Laura; the butler's desk his grandfather had chosen to place at the window where he could write letters and do his accounts. Saul also used this table for writing. He had turned it around, though, so he was facing the window rather than the interior; he liked to look out and see the passersby: the au pairs and child tenders pushing baby carriages;

joggers; cyclists; old men bent over walking sticks. Their movements did not distract him; he could see them and yet they did not register on his mind as separate beings, but seemed all of one with his writing, though they made no appearances in it.

He wrote at this table every morning and some afternoons, despite Jamie's thinking he'd "retired." He felt ashamed that she had drawn this conclusion, but then he reminded himself that this was Jamie, whose output was like a rabbit's, two and sometimes three books a year, year in, year out.

He read all of her books; he couldn't imagine not doing so; he was her friend. And he was delighted to find in them glimmers of truly fine writing, though not one taken as a whole was finely written. He didn't see how it could be, not with the weighty superstructure of one or another genre in whose confines she had to fight her way around. He would have liked to talk to her about this, but who was he, with his monumental problem and minimal output, who seemed never able to get to the end to give advice to someone who could cross the finish line twice yearly?

Rising to get the cigarette box, he walked over to the desk and peered down at the manuscript lying there, pages neatly stacked beside an elderly Olivetti typewriter. Upstairs in a small room off his bedroom was the computer that he used only to type the final draft. When there was a final draft. This manuscript here didn't look like it would ever become one.

"No ending" could mean the manuscript lacked a chapter, or one page, or even one paragraph. A longish paragraph it would have been, too. But it had never gotten written. In the deep drawers of a dresser upstairs were manuscripts. There were other manuscripts, each with some fatal flaw (Saul thought). He was vague about them with his friends.

He looked at the manuscript pages sitting beside the typewriter, anchored by a paperweight of cobalt blue Murano glass he'd bought in Venice. He liked the color and egg shape. It held down the top pages that otherwise might have blown away in a breeze through the window. The growing stack of pages was a comfort to Saul. The stack was substantial, a good two or three inches. There would be only one more chapter, possibly long, but probably short. How he knew this without knowing the substance of that chapter, he couldn't say. Except that he knew its nature; he knew its ethos. He just didn't know its form in words. There was a chance that the end would become clear in the course of that chapter. The end, he believed, was always there, there since he'd written the first chapter. The problem was something within himself that prevented him seeing the end.

He removed the last page and read it:

"The square was empty of everything but the two cats slinking around the base of the fountain. The woman walked out of the mist and across the cobblestones that looked wet in the moonlight. She did not hurry; her walk was slow even in this lonely hour of the night. She was dressed in black and white, an eerie echo of the two cats, one white, one black, as if a photographer had arranged both cats and model to create a dramatic view of Venice. The Venetian moonlight ebbed and flowed in little waves, so that the woman, moving slowly, appeared to be wading through a river of light, an aqua alta of light. Where, then, was she going? She asked herself this question. And why–?"

And why–? And why–? Saul looked at this, shook his head, returned the page to the stack and the paperweight to the pages. It was harrowing. The form he had used for the entire story was harrowing, and difficult. Its movement was backward, last to first. He had started at the end, that is, at what one would normally suppose to be the end. This character who had traveled to that most ambiguous city, Venice, and who was uncertain of her destination had begun—or had appeared to, rather—at the beginning as a woman strongly grounded, rooted in small-town life, marriage, kids. A reversal had occurred.

He looked out of the window and poured himself a brandy. The bottle was on the desk. He thought about Ned. He wondered, not for the first time, how their friends could attribute qualities to Saul that were much more clearly Ned's. The reclusiveness, the vulnerability, the confidence, the almost naïve disdain of reviewers—all of these were Ned's virtues (for Saul saw them as virtues) and not his own. No, it wasn't he who would occupy the high room in the ivory tower; it was Ned. Of course, if he said this to Ned, Ned would tell him he was nuts.

And then there was all of this business at the publisher's. He wondered about what Sally said she'd overheard. There were probably a dozen different explanations. But Saul knew Bobby Mackenzie was ruthless. He'd do anything to get a book or a writer. It was the reason Saul had refused to go with Mackenzie-Haack, though his then-agent had pushed to move him there. She had defended this by saying it was because Mackenzie-Haack was "a better house, more literary, more prestigious. It wasn't (she'd said) the money."

"You're an agent; they're a publisher. It's always the money." Had she even felt the sting of that rebuke? Probably not; agents didn't appear to think they ever got rebuked. She continued to press for Mackenzie-Haack. He dropped her.

He returned to the wing chair. He pulled a crumpled pack of cigarettes from his pocket, remembered he'd smoked the last one, and pulled over the silver cigarette box. He didn't really use it and thought the cigarettes in it now must be stale. There were a number of articles in this room he would never have chosen for himself—that embroidered fire screen, for one—but he kept everything in the same place as his mother had done, and she had done it for the same reason, he was sure, for he could remember her admonishing him sometimes after he'd picked something up and returned it to another place ("That's your aunt Livvy's special pillow, so put it back in her chair, dear.").

The sense of loss made him wince. Don't go there, he told himself, then realized the expression was the title of Paul Giverney's new book. He'd seen it that morning on Tenth Street when he'd stopped by the Barnes & Noble near the square. More power to him, Saul thought. Fame and money. He wondered how much the lack of money shaped what a writer did, how good his books turned out to be. There had to be some effect. He was lucky to have as much as he needed. But, then, one could argue he'd have been better off without money; that might have pushed him to finish the book.

Don't go there. He thought about Pittsburgh. He picked up the phone at his elbow and then put it back. Saul went to the bookcase across the room, pulled out a Pennsylvania travel guide. (Rarely did he travel, but he had guides to everywhere.) He thumbed up Pittsburgh accommodations and found the Pittsburgh Hilton, which he then called. Yes, a Mr. Isaly was due in tomorrow and did he want to leave a message? No, no message. He hung up. When he read the description of the Hilton, it didn't surprise Saul that Ned had chosen it; it was located on the Point where the rivers come together.

Saul took the guidebook to the wing chair, pausing to pour himself another small measure of brandy. He sat down and thought about the men in suits, the "two suits," as he came to know them. Why did they keep turning up?

And would they, he wondered, turn up in Pittsburgh?

Saul looked at the book, got the number again, called the Hilton a second time, and made a reservation.

Like the woman in his story, Saul wasn't sure precisely where he was going, or why.

PITTSBURGH

TWENTY-NINE

When he was a boy, there was one snowless winter when he dreamed all of the time about snow—daydreams and night dreams. He saw himself crouched on the window seat in the living room of their house, staring out at a hill that fell away at a perfect angle for sledding or else those round aluminum dish things a kid could position himself on to go twirling downhill, or even on the old rubber tires that served the same purpose. He would crouch in the window seat and imagine the hill with its fine icy crust that cracked under the first bit of pressure. He did not remember the house so well as the hill and the steps up to the house, a few more than the neighboring house on one side and a few fewer than the one on the other for the houses also flowed uphill. Pittsburgh was a city of hills. Snow mounded on these steps and they lost their sharp outlines. He would wake up in the early morning, only the rim of the sun risen and casting a cold bluish light across the snow. He could look out of his bedroom window, right over the porch. From up there he

227

could see the steps better, the tantalizing smoothness of the mounds he would be the first to disturb.

As he sat there, in his mind's eye, from the dark behind him he heard a voice, probably his mother's. *"What are you doing, Ned?"*

The only answer if you didn't want what was in your head to blow away with words was "Nothing." If you went ahead and said, "I'm sledding," you'd have her in there right away saying, *"There's no snow, how can you?"* It was hard enough to do it in your head without somebody's coming along and saying you couldn't. That was him; that was winter.

All of this went through Ned's mind as he waited for a cab on the concrete island of the Pittsburgh International Airport. He was so taken up in this dream of snow that he didn't think that the two men behind him should have looked familiar.

* * * * *

"Christ! It's dropped ten degrees just standing here," said Karl.

"Where's the fucking cabs? They got a hundred lines of them at Kennedy."

"It's not New York. Pittsburgh's a pretty small city as cities go. Philly, that's three, maybe four times as big as Pittsburgh."

"Philly is? I never knew that." Candy gave Karl an appreciative look. "Hey, you're wound, K. You must have been researching."

"Nah. It's just stuff you pick up. Here's a cab, thank God– Hey! Hey! You see that? That bitch muscled right into our cab." As her cab drew away, she gave them a tiny smile and a shrug. Candy and Karl gave the cab a slap.

The next cab was taken almost before they could register the fact it was their turn. "Get that! Did you see that guy take our cab?" said Candy.

"What guy?"

* * * * *

Sally didn't care; she'd seen worse than those two in New York. If it had been New York, those two would probably have shot her. But where had she seen them before?

The black-and-white cab behind her was now pulling abreast of this cab and going on ahead. When the driver asked her where to, she said, "Just follow that black-and-white cab up there."

"Follow it?"

He was trying to meet her eyes in the mirror as if they would prove or disprove Sally's intentions toward the black-and-white cab were honorable. "Yes, that's what I said." Why was she bothering to explain to a cabbie? "It's my friend and I got separated from him in the airport."

The driver was still trying to engage eye contact. "Your friend?"

Sally felt like taking a swing at him with her carryall. He was, at least, following the cab as he was attempting to wrest the story out of her about her relationship with that cab ahead. "My fiancé."

The driver laughed. "And he just takes off and leaves you standing there? Jesus God. You sure you want to marry the guy? You had a fight on the plane, I bet. I bet you and him—" and he went on, making up a story for his own amusement.

Was everybody on God's green earth a fledgling writer?

* * * * *

When the next cab pulled out of the line and stopped, Candy gently shoved an old lady out of the way, said excuse me ma'am, we got this emergency, and the two of them climbed in.

"Pittsburgh Hilton." They'd got it right away when they started phoning up hotels. This was not sheer coincidence; Candy and Karl worked on the supposition that anyone would choose the hotel the two of them would choose.

* * * * *

Twenty minutes later, another flight landed at Pittsburgh International nonstop from New York City.

As Clive waited for a cab, he wondered if Ned Isaly would recognize him, provided he even saw him. When Ned appeared in the Mackenzie-Haack offices, he came to see Tom Kidd and nobody else. The only contact Clive had had with Ned was when they'd passed a few times in the hallways, and Clive doubted that the absentminded smile or nod Ned gave him was proof that he'd even seen him. Anyway, what difference would it make if Ned did recognize him? They were both in Pittsburgh at the same time. So what?

Clive just wasn't used to following people.

When he checked into the Pittsburgh Hilton, he scanned the lobby looking for Pascal. There was no sign of her; there was only a couple sitting in a section marked off for morning coffee, the couple and a blond woman whose face was bent over a newspaper. How could she see the print through those dark glasses?

The desk clerk returned his credit card to him along with a key card. Clive refused help from the bell captain, having only one small bag. He walked over to the bank of elevators. Two elevators arrived simultaneously and as he was about to step into one, he saw Ned coming out of another one on the other side. Ned didn't even look at him. Clive thought he was probably wandering around in writer daze. He watched and saw him going up to the bar. So Clive would have time to leave his suitcase and wash up. Just as he pushed the up button, he saw a woman entering the glass door of the hotel.

It was Pascal.

At first glance he didn't recognize her. It was her hair; it was pulled back and wound into a bun. He assumed she had done this the better to follow Ned. The hair loose and abundant would have called attention to her. He thought the makeup less liberally applied, too, not so heavy on the eye shadow. He thought how unnerving it was to think that a woman could so easily create a wholly new persona with nothing but a hairbrush and—sweet Christ! The guy in the boots with the beard coming through the automatic doors! Clive dived into the elevator as the door was closing. What was Dwight Staines doing here?

*　*　*　*　*

When Ned threaded his way through the tables, heading for the bar, Sally dropped the *Pittsburgh Press* on the floor and bent down to retrieve it, hitting her head on the edge of the table. He had come so close. But he hadn't seen her. She pulled a bit on the blond wig to make sure the bump hadn't dislodged it.

As she righted herself she caught a glimpse of a man who'd just boarded one of the elevators and thought surely she must be wrong. Why for God's sakes would Clive Esterhaus be in Pittsburgh?

*　*　*　*　*

Ned had checked into his room, dumped his duffel bag, and gone down for a cup of coffee before setting out to look at Pittsburgh. He hadn't been back since he was in high school, just the first year before they'd moved to Scranton.

Scranton was a sepia blur in his mind, but his Pittsburgh past, those days he could recall of it, were sharp and bright. He remembered "downtown," those few city blocks that had seemed spectacularly bright—the movie theaters, the department stores. Horne's, Kaufmann's. He was surprised to see Joseph Horne's all boarded up as if it had been a crack house, a broken-down haven for weepyeyed druggies. He found that none of the downtown was as he remembered it; all of it looked condemned, or, he supposed, downtown had moved; it had relocated, and part of it was now the handsomely built-up area of the Point. That Golden Triangle Pittsburgh was so proud of. Deservedly so, he thought. It was a city that had rein-vented itself.

*   *   *   *   *

They had been walking for more than an hour when Candy ex-claimed, "Fuck's sake! Don't this guy eat or anything?" All Candy had eaten for breakfast *and* lunch had been the mingy bagel and so-called cream cheese.

"Don't worry. Even if he doesn't, one of us can grab something to go."

"I don't feel much like eatin' on my feet, K."

"There she is again," said Karl. He had called Candy's attention to the redheaded woman originally because he thought that under the shapeless raincoat she had a great body; then he called Karl's at-tention to the fact that the great body had been with them for an hour—sometimes walking behind, sometimes walking ahead. She was good, Karl said. If the two of them hadn't been even better, they'd never have spotted her.

"There's another thing. You see that guy go by in a cab? Well, he's done it twice. I didn't get a good look at him, but something about him's familiar. Now why would he be going around and around?"

*   *   *   *   *

Saul decided he would have to forget this waving down of cabs and instead hire a car. Cabs were just too purposeful and too hard to di-rect if what you wanted to do was start and stop and circle back all the time.

He had seen the two men on the pavement stare after him; it was them all right, the same two men who'd appeared in the little park, later in Swill's—Paulie and Larry-something?—to sit down at his and Ned's table. Had they said they were from Pittsburgh? They'd talked about Pittsburgh somehow, only he'd tuned them out, thinking about his book (the last fifty pages of which he had brought with him, the way Ned always did, because you never know when something will hit, do you?).

And Saul wondered, as he had many times before, about convergences, confluences, sudden meetings of things you had never thought of as coming together. The rivers, for instance: the Monongahela and the Allegheny.

It would be easier if he knew just what he was looking for when it came to Ned. He didn't know; it was just this general feeling of something's being out of whack, skewed, even ominous.

The cab drove by a huge billboard advertising Porsche, Mercedes, and BMW. Ned, he saw, was coming back this way. It was nearly six P.M. Saul told the driver to drop him off at the Porsche dealership.

THIRTY

Ned crossed the street to look at the river. It was wide and gray and not especially pretty, but he thought he could remember himself standing at some point along the river where it passed through the city; he saw himself looking over the barrier, perhaps being picked up and his feet squarely planted there by his father. He was fantasizing. He did not know if that had ever happened, but it could have. Over there, on the North Side he thought an aunt had lived, rather poorer than the other relatives. He was not sure about the aunt; he could not picture her, not her face not her voice not her mannerisms.

*   *   *   *   *

Sally walked on past him. She was getting pretty good at shadowing people, she thought. The trick, or one of them, was not to be taken by surprise, not to alter one's course because the person you were following did. Sally considered this useful training because she lived most of her life startled. People could get a reaction out of her even if they weren't looking for one. So Sally moved with great purpose past Ned, eyes looking straight ahead, her blond wig curls bouncing. A little farther along she would stop and take out her compact and look in the mirror to see when he started walking again.

* * * * *

"You like it? I don't. As rivers go, this one sucks," said Candy. "He still standing there?"

"Hasn't moved. Probably caught up in some childhood dream." Karl seemed to ponder what he'd said.

Candy made a face. "Ever since you been reading that book, you come out with shit like that. So what's he looking at?"

"The other side of the river, looks like."

"I sure hope he's not thinking of going there. This ain't a bad city, is it? Stuff to look at. That stadium over there."

"If you're from New York, it's not much."

"So no place is if you compare it with New York, fuck's sake." Candy looked across the wide water. "Paris, maybe. Rome." But his tone was dismissive, suggesting he was convinced Paris could not go head to head with New York. Neither could Rome.

They stood looking across the river.

Karl pulled the guidebook out of his coat pocket, thumbed a few pages. "Heinz Field." Helpfully, he explained: "Three Rivers Stadium—called that because these rivers meet there—it got torn down couple years ago."

"How come?"

"Who knows?"

"Bummer."

"The one before that, that was Forbes Field. Tore that down, too."

"This city's got nothin' better to do, it tears down its stadiums? The history of a city's in its teams, not its buildings. Willie Mays caught a line drive in Forbes Field that's like nothing no one ever saw before. And what was that guy's name was so great played with the Pirates? Even before my time? Clemente, that was it, Roger—no, Roberto Clemente. And Sandy Koufax. He pitched a string of no-hitters. Broke the record. Remember Sandy Koufax? We were kids, but remember?"

"Everybody remembers Sandy Koufax, even the ones that don't. We were what—? Six, seven? But he was the Dodgers, not the Pirates."

"Yeah, of course. I didn't mean he was a Pirate. But the Dodgers played here. The Pirates were hot, really hot. They played them all. Koufax pitched there." Candy inclined his head in the direction of a stadium long gone. "Jackie Robinson ran the bases there. Stan Musial—" Candy broke off and shook his head sadly. "If you're a baseball fan, it could bring you to tears."

Karl returned the book to his pocket. "Chrissakes, C, you remember all that stuff? What a memory."

"Yeah, well, you know—you don't remember, then you forget."

The two of them turned their heads and looked down toward Ned. Still there. "Wonder why he came here anyway?"

"He's from here. It says so right in my book. So's the other one."

"Givenchy? My guy?"

"Giverney. Can't you keep his name straight? 'Givenchy'—that's that mineral water from France."

Candy frowned. "You sure about that? We don't drink nothin' but Pellegrino."

"I told you—" Karl gave Candy a severe look. "It's that water. Anyway, both these guys are from here. So that might be it. Like Ned did something to Paul Giverney when they were in school together. Paul's never got over it. I blame myself for not probing into their backgrounds more. Find out what school they went to, you know, stuff like that."

"Yeah but you can't be sure they went to school together."

"Didn't I say? No, I'm not sure. It's just possible."

"Do you really think a grown-up would carry a fucking *grudge* from his school days? Jesus. He must be real childish to do that." Candy's back was bothering him—it always did when he had to do a lot of walking. He turned to rest it against the stone wall. Here came a couple of black kids on skateboards, arms out and going at a good clip. It was cold, and they weren't even wearing jackets. Candy thought about when he was young and how he didn't like coats. He nodded toward the street where a few cars, like the kids, seemed to float by in the river mist. "That cab's been sittin' over there for as long as we've been standin' here."

Karl turned. "Who's in it, can you see?"

Candy squinted. "Can't see, except it's some guy."

Karl was looking down the street, in the opposite direction from Ned, laughing. "Kids nearly ran into old Clive. He's standing down there. Beats me, really beats me why he's here."

"Dipshit," said Candy, looking, too. Then in the other direction, where Ned was standing. Had been standing. "Yo! Our quarry is moving!"

Karl chuckled. "'Our quarry'—you been reading too many CIA spy novels, C."

*   *   *   *   *

". . . a real departure, right? Literary, mainstream, whatever. But I figure, since it'll be literary, well, Tom Kidd could edit me."

Clive was looking up the sidewalk at Candy and Karl and rubbing the shin that the skateboard had bumped into. "No, Dwight,

Tom Kidd would not edit you. You cannot get Tom Kidd." It was the only thing Clive had heard clearly in Staines's monumentally long monologue that made *Moby-Dick* look infinitely beguiling in its brevity, or *A la recherche du temps perdu* recited by a stammerer simply fetching.

"I'm not saying you're not an editor par excellence, Clive, far be it from me to say that." Dwight gunned his rented motorcycle.

Clive was gearing up to grab this jerk by the strap of his helmet when he saw Candy and Karl move off. On the other side of the street, Pascal was going into the store whose window she'd been looking into. Clive could not see Ned; he was too far away or obscured by passersby. "Where's your signing?"

"It's an independent, not one of your big chains. It's over on"– Dwight took the Pittsburgh *FastMap* from his back pocket and scanned it–"Fifth Street."

"Why didn't they hire you a limousine?"

Dwight flapped his hand. "Hell, you know me, Clive. Just a kid from the sticks." He gunned the engine again.

If that was the case, "the sticks" was a warren of clichés, trite phrases, jargon, and neologisms. Yes, those were "the sticks" and Clive saw himself in the role of director of one of those summer blockbusters blowing the sticks all to smithereens and taking Dwight Staines with it. Clive suppressed a scream. Then he suddenly asked, "Who in hell is Blanche?"

Dwight stopped revving the engine and looked mystified. "Who's what?"

"Blanche. The woman on the–oh, never mind." Clive tried to laugh it off with a sickly little laugh, sickly because he had almost spoken honestly (a rare treat when dealing with one of their authors) for he had been about to say, "You know: the stick-figure woman in your latest. Blanche, the irrelevant little tart riding the train and thinking, thinking in your Molly Bloom-like excretions of consciousness—something you, Dwight, handle with as much subtlety as an elephant on ice skates—" He had almost said it before he remembered that robbing Queeg and Hyde of Dwight Staines was a rear-end run by Bobby that was an even more outstanding coup than the usual sneaky publishing coup. There were so many publishing coups in any one day that one publisher—it might have been Dreck—had ended up buying back one of its own authors. And he wondered why those few seconds before he'd veered off into unholy editorial scamming, why those seconds had been so liberating. He felt a yearning for those few seconds, something like homesickness. Clive could not understand this; he was not given to sentimental attachments. What he said instead was, "Have a good book signing, Dwight."

"Right. You're reading *StandOff*, yes? This one's really complex. I'd give you a capsule treatment of it—"

(And I'd hide it under my tongue until I could spit it out.)

"—only I veer off here. See you in the funny papers."

Clive hadn't heard that expression since his dad had paused by the front door and said it to his mother before he walked out of their lives. Where in God's name was he from that he'd be using that expression? Ah, but Clive knew where: the sticks, where "See you in the funny papers" was on everyone's lips.

Across the street Dwight flowed, *whirr-whirring* the cycle until he'd nearly jumped the curb and rammed the black beast into Pascal, who'd walked out of the store. Suddenly, she bent at the waist, and Clive saw her arms come up and hands flash out like a character in a John Woo film, and for one thrilling moment (almost as thrilling as the near approach of honesty a minute before), he thought Pascal was going to toss Dwight Staines back into the street. It didn't happen, of course; her reaction was no doubt automatic when danger threatened. Dwight was running at the mouth over there, no doubt apologizing for being one of the world's most popular writers, telling her to come to the book signing. Jesus.

He zoomed off.

A bus drove by and stopped a couple of blocks up ahead. He saw Candy and Karl board it. Clive hailed a cab. Its driver looked as if he'd fall asleep in the middle of the next intersection and didn't look too keen on following anything, but he pulled away from the curb and followed the bus.

* * * * *

Ned stood in Schenley Park watching a small group of boys playing kickball. Now he supposed it was soccer, but back then, it had been kickball. He must have played it. He thought again of that deep winter, the sky like slate, opaque and impenetrable; pools of water with ice skins; frosted glass, rime on sills . . . what winter was it? Was it even here?

* * * * *

They were sitting on a bench beneath a huge oak.

Candy complained. "Christ, I never knew a guy could stand around and look so much."

"Sing it again, C. And what's to look at anyway?" Karl's eyes scanned the park, stopped to watch the little group of kids playing soccer and a little girl on her own squatting down, digging in the ground at the base of a tree with a stick, then transferring the mound of earth to a pale yellow bucket. "They shouldn't let her do that."

"What?" When Karl pointed, Candy said, "The kid?" He shrugged. "Probably she's with one of the other kids."

"Yeah? Well, is any one of them watching her?"

"Don't be so fuckin' paranoid."

240

"Paranoid? *We're* the guys she needs protecting from."

"Hey! No fuckin' way, man," said Candy. "We were never into that stuff."

"Remember years back when that dickhead Robanoff hired us?"

"Yeah, the pedophile? Come on, we didn't whack no kid, did we? Can we help it if you got moral degenerates out there? We're real careful who we whack, who we don't. Any other way, why are we here? We're fuckin' fastidious, man. I don't know anyone in this game takes more care than we do. Gave back his deposit, didn't we, I mean just before we capped him? Asshole."

"Yeah, you're right." Karl sighed as if he were missing the experience and took out a cigar.

Candy took out his Juicy Fruit gum, folded two sticks into his mouth. They sat in silence for a few minutes, watching the boys kicking the ball around.

Karl said, "You play kickball when you were a kid?"

"Me? Sure. They call it soccer now."

"Probably he did, too." Karl nodded toward Ned.

They went on smoking and chewing.

* * * * *

Why was he so headstrong? Sally asked herself this, trying to convince herself, probably, that she knew him. Which, after watching him all afternoon, she felt she didn't.

It did not surprise her that Clive had turned up here also. That is not to say that it didn't worry her. He must be spying on Ned, but for what reason? To see he didn't hop a freighter to Europe? He must be watching him for Bobby Mackenzie, acting out some plan they had set in motion that must involve more than simply breaking Ned's contract with Mackenzie-Haack.

The woman with the red hair: she was leaning against a tree,

smoking. Had she been sent by Bobby, too? Was she part of the sur-
veillance team? Sally was tempted to go over and ask her what she
was doing; instead, she opened her purse and took out a sandwich
she'd bought at a concession stand. It was cheese and it was dry. She
ate two bites and then wrapped it back up and tossed it into one of
the trash cans. Ned had been standing there for a good half hour,
watching the boys play and the little girl dig.

What was he doing this for? What was he after? Sally sighed
and leaned forward, her elbow resting on her knee, her chin on her
fist.

* * * * *

If they intended to do something to Ned, here was ample opportunity for the park was nearly empty of people. Saul wondered if Ned
had played here as a boy, like the ones over there kicking the ball
around without any serious intention of playing a soccer game, just
back and forth, killing time (they who still had time to kill).

As for Saul, he remembered books, remembered only that window seat in his home, the window where the butler's table sat, and
looking out when dusk came on at four o'clock, and snow drifted
slowly past the window, illuminated by the corner street lamp, and
his mother bringing cocoa.

Had it happened, or was his version his revisionist childhood?
No, it had happened. Snow in winter, leaves in autumn. His mother
with a tray of cocoa. As if in coming here and sharing Ned's childhood, his own began to press upon him.

* * * * *

Clive felt like diving in among them and giving the ball a hell of a
kick, two kicks, three, four, messing up their game just to mess it up.
Kick the ball to kingdom come. Or else go over there where that

child was digging in the dirt and take her pail away from her, just to watch her cry.

Where was Blaze, where was his bloody gumshoe? Oh, there she was, by that tree. It was strange how she managed to melt into the autumn colors, as if she were a drift of leaves herself. But didn't melt nearly so much as what Clive thought was a tall figure looking around a tree—no, he supposed it must have been a branch moving in the wind. Christ, but it was cold!

* * * * *

Ned closed his eyes and rocked on his heels. He was watching a woman with light hair watching the little girl, who, with great care, was transferring earth from ground to pail. It was one of those childhood activities that adults can never understand because it's pointless. But then that was its attraction—to be doing something where the point lay simply in the doing of it.

He had heard this somewhere: that by simply observing (or was it simple?) one might master a landscape. Ned was not sure what "master" implied here. He tried to let it sink in—the dry brownness of leaves and branches, the kids playing kickball (wasn't that what they used to call it?), the pine-scented air—tried to let this settle over him like a mantle.

One had to look at the landscape from every conceivable angle. Who had said this about landscapes? Saul, probably. Or perhaps not. It was probably Tom Kidd.

* * * * *

"How long's he staying?" Karl asked.

"Coupla days. Going back to NYC day after tomorrow." Candy reached down and picked up a leaf from the path. He had gotten the last sugary taste from his gum, and he took the wad out of his mouth, delicately rolled it up in a leaf, and flicked it toward a wire trash can. It went in. "Are we takin' this job?"

"I don't know. What do you think, anyway?"

"I don't know."

His hands in his pockets jiggling change, Karl settled his spine down farther on the bench and gazed around, as if the answer to Candy's question might be written somewhere in Schenley Park. "It's too early to decide that, C. You know, we always give it at least a week. Right?" When Candy nodded, Karl went on: "That's why we don't make mistakes."

"Like that turd Robanoff. If ever anyone deserved to get whacked." Candy removed his baseball cap, rubbed his hair back, and replaced the cap. "We'd have been—you know—derelict in our duty we hadn't capped him. Guy like that goes after little kids." He waved his hand in a dismissive gesture.

They sat in silence for a moment or two, contemplating this.

Karl asked, "You finished your book?"

"Me? No. You?"

"No."

"You think we should switch? You know, I read the second half of yours, you read the second half of mine, and then we tell each other what's in it?"

Karl thought about this, shook his head. "That's another thing: why this Giverney guy wants our guy out of the way." He nodded in Ned's direction. "I think we ought to know."

"Yeah, except Bobby Mackenzie and old Clive over there—they don't know, or say they don't."

"So the only one does know is Giverney himself," said Karl.

"You think we need to go around, have a little talk with him?"

"No, not a chance. We don't need one more witness. But, I think, maybe old Clive there knows something we don't. I mean, why in hell is he here? Not only him, why the fuck is Ned's buddy over there"—Karl gestured toward Saul, standing a distance away, nearly hidden in the low branches of one of the trees—"Mr. Charcoal-gray-cashmere-coat, why hasn't he tried to talk to him? Matter of fact, I'm surprised he hasn't tried to talk to us, seeing as how we were all hanging out in Swill's."

"Okay, maybe when we get back to the hotel, have a drink—hey, our boy's leavin'."

They watched Ned turn and walk back down the path, in the direction from which he had entered the park.

* * * * *

Ned stopped for a moment, thinking that the light-haired woman sitting over there on that bench looked somehow familiar. Then he realized who she reminded him of: Nathalie. Why? Nathalie had dark hair. He shook his head.

For one crazy moment he thought he saw Saul, at least the back of him, disappearing down the path through the trees. It was probably only because of the cashmere coat.

Ned remembered Shadyside.

This was the part of Pittsburgh where he'd lived. There should be landmarks, places where he'd gone as a boy and whose names, seen now, would spring a lock in his mind and memories sluice from a mental reservoir.

He knew if he looked long enough, he would find an Isaly's, and here it was in Shadyside, as if no time at all had passed between his sledding self and his grown-up self, his writing self. Time lapses. Why couldn't there be these errant stops in what we thought was a continuum?

Ned looked at the plate-glass window with the name written in white paint and the little tents of snow shuddering down from the trees. It had stopped falling from the sky. Ned liked to think it was an ice cream cone, melting as one watched.

He didn't know if this was the Isaly's his dad had taken him to when he was small or, later, if it was one that he'd worked at. He had worked at several, he thought. But his memory was terrible, so probably it was not.

Inside he was glad to find a few customers besides himself. That made it clear that this Isaly's wasn't some ghostly visitation he had conjured up because he wanted it still to be here—an ice cream parlor materializing out of the snowy afternoon.

Two adults were looking over the ice cream, probably the parents of the little girl who peered at him from under the lattice of her pale gold, windblown hair, as she held on to the man's leg. She treated the leg as if it were a tree trunk she could peek around or hide behind, in case she didn't like what she saw, or else engage who she saw in a game.

Ned could have smiled one of those concocted smiles grown-ups reserve for children, but he didn't. She responded to him by clutching her father's trouser leg with small fingers Ned bet could nip like pincers.

He was not sentimental about children. It wasn't that he disliked them, for he usually found their rascally ways to be rather charming. He felt a pang of remorse that they would have to change or be forced to change into something else, something more socially acceptable. The child with the tangled golden hair would still be looking through its strands, but the look would be coquettish, tartish even. A thirteen-year-old tart. Then the twenty-year-old sorority girl. Then the thirty-year-old mother with just such a child as this one, the one trying to get Ned's attention.

Her father put a chocolate cone into her hands and she jumped once, twice for joy.

Ned was almost jealous. To be back at a time in your life when all it had taken to make you happy was an ice cream cone. *His* ice cream, he wanted to tell her. Isaly's! He ran his eyes over the tubs and when the kid behind the counter (which could have been him) had finished up with the family of three, Ned asked for pistachio. He asked if they still had the cone-shaped ice cream dippers, and the boy said, yes, sure, and reached round to a counter behind him and got it. It's kind of an Isaly trademark, Ned told him. Then he took his cone-shaped pistachio ice cream and paid and left.

* * * * *

The cabdriver went on incessantly about this part of the city, the nice part, Shadyside and East Liberty, at least they used to be, used to be where the well-to-do lived, the driver laughingly not including himself among them. He went on, worse than a tour guide.

Candy and Karl were ready to pop the guy if he didn't shut up. They had followed Ned's cab to this place and had found a coffee shop whose window gave them a clear view of Isaly's, the ice cream parlor. They had participated in a brief argument as to whether this was Ned's family or what. It could have been, maybe that's why he wanted to come here.

In the café, they had cups of plain coffee with cream and sugar. Candy was trying to cut back on that because he thought he was getting a little paunchy. Karl said to forget about it. Karl had binoculars around his neck and every once in a while trained them on the building Ned had gone into, the Isaly's place.

Candy was carrying his book, that is, Paul Giverney's book, and continuing the story. "So now it seems she's got a little kid who's supposed to be home but isn't."

Karl had raised the binoculars. "I thought I saw him come out. I guess not." He set the binoculars back on the table, took a drink of coffee. "Look. The redhead over there, isn't that the same one we saw before—"

Candy took the binoculars from him and looked. "Down by the river, yeah."

"Is she following him? You know it doesn't seem to register on him somebody's shadowing him."

"Maybe she's good at what she does."

"Well, but you'd know; *I'd* know. You can tell if eyes are boring into your back. *You'd* know if there were footsteps behind you. *You* could tell a figure around a corner—"

"K, come on. That's *us*. We're trained professionals. We're attuned, yeah, we're *attuned* to all that. So we ain't, you know, your typicals."

"It's a point."

Candy thought for a moment, riffling the pages of the book. "I remember when I was a real little kid my mom taking me to one of those old-time pharmacies. You could get sodas, a chocolate soda like I got, for fifty cents."

"Fifty cents? When could you ever get an ice cream soda for fifty cents? Dream on, Giverney." Karl shook his head.

"Well, you used to be able. And that's part of the whole mystery. When is this happening? But I'm telling you about the writing."

Karl had picked up the binoculars again and was fiddling with the focus. "What writing?"

"For Chrissakes, pay attention."

"Sorry." He put down the binoculars but still fiddled with the focus a little.

"On the check, I mean on Laura's—did I tell you she had a soda in the pharmacy?—the soda jerk's written 'Choc soda'—"

"Fifty cents, I know."

"Beneath it is written 'Don't go there.'" Candy tilted back his chair. "So naturally she shows it to the soda jerk—a kid, sixteen, maybe seventeen. He looks as puzzled as she does. He tells her he never wrote it. He wrote 'Choc soda' and that's all."

"Fifty cents, he wrote that too."

"Yeah, yeah. But what about 'Don't go there'? Is that weird or is that weird?"

"He's lying. Of course he must have written it."

"That's what she thinks, yeah. Had to be him because there's nobody in the place but the two of them."

"What about this pharmacist, though? Where's he? He was talking to her earlier," said Karl.

"Good question. I don't know where he is. He's not mentioned in the soda scene."

"Right, but where is he?"

"I just said, I don't know."

"I'm just speculating," said Karl.

"It's pretty spooky, the way he wrote it."

"Maybe I'll read it when you finish so maybe you don't tell me any more of the story."

Candy frowned, looking through the window. "What in hell's he been doin'? It ain't gonna take a half hour just to get ice cream."

Karl snickered. "Maybe he's getting a chocolate soda. But not for any fifty cents. That's him—" Karl snatched up the binoculars. "Yeah, he's come out and he's got an ice cream cone it looks like. It's green. It's a funny shape, too." He handed the binoculars to Candy.

"Huh. It's cone shaped. Like a clown hat."

"It's green. What kind of ice cream is green?"

Candy shook his head.

* * * * *

Ned stood outside on the pavement, watching the street and eating his cone. He wondered why people thought he was an idealist. Was it because he appeared to be blind to what was going on around him a lot of the time? Or because he didn't much care for anything except his writing? He cared for his friends, yes, but not for much else. None of this struck him as characteristic of the idealist. He was a cynic. Witness his response to the little girl with the golden locks–Goldilocks. Witness Nathalie; witness Ben Strum in *Solace*. That, thought Ned, was the most that life could offer: solace. And you were lucky to get that.

Nathalie wasn't going to find it.

All of this sounded, of course, extremely sentimental, and he was no more a sentimentalist than he was an idealist–but maybe he was both. Maybe he didn't understand himself.

And maybe it made no difference, not as long as he understood Nathalie. But he wasn't even sure he did.

He ate his ice cream and felt, without his manuscript pages, orphaned. It wasn't because he was afraid of fire or flood or some disaster that he carried the book around. He carried it for company. He carried it because of Nathalie; he wanted to keep her close. He was, in fact, afraid that Nathalie would grow sick of being locked into Patric's half-life and would gather herself and her old records together and leave. Run away, and Ned would never see her again.

It could happen, and if the only way to hold on to her was to secure Patric for her–perhaps get him to leave his wife–no, it wouldn't happen. It wouldn't work. People like Nathalie and Patric never worked in the long run. They didn't work because there was no distance between them, the sort of distance that inevitably arises between husband and wife. The distance saves them.

He'd reached the end, or not far from the end of the story. It could happen.

* * * * *

When Ned moved, so did they. Karl dashed some bills on the table and they hurried out. They kept Ned in sight as he walked up the street in the blue afternoon.

"Kind of a coincidence."

"What?"

"Ned. Ned in that ice cream place. Us."

Candy was thinking. "Pistachio?"

THIRTY-ONE

Candy and Karl sat down at the bar, bookending Clive, who was in the process of draining his second Scotch and ordering another.

"So, Clive, what brings you to Pittsburgh, man?" As he said this, Candy waved the bartender over. "You got a local brew?" The bartender told them Rolling Rock. "Sounds okay to me." He turned back to Clive. "So. Like I said, why are you here?"

Clive didn't know why he should feel it necessary to fabricate, but he did. "Author tour. Dwight Staines." He hoped Dwight wouldn't appear and renounce him for this lie.

"Oh, yeah, we saw that book," said Karl. "Big stack of it in Barnes and Noble—right, C?"

Candy nodded.

Clive was surprised they could even say it, much less go in it. "Doing research, were you?" They just looked at him. He looked away as the bartender set the beers on the bar.

Karl said, "In Schenley Park, that was where this book signing was?"

"What? No, of course not." Clive signaled the bartender, making a bar of air between thumb and forefinger. "I was taking a walk."

"That's a hell of a coincidence," said Karl, "since that's just where our Ned was taking his walk."

"Really? I didn't see him."

Karl took a pull from his bottle of Rolling Rock, and said, "Clive, what we want to know is why you hired us."

"You mean why the publisher hired you." Clive's voice, already low, went down a notch after he looked around to see if anyone was listening. "Paul Giverney won't publish with us as long as Ned Isaly's on our list."

"You told us that. Excuse us if we say that don't make any sense. Why's Giverney doing this?"

"I don't know why. He wouldn't tell us."

"You mean," said Karl, "you'd toss Ned off a cliff without even knowing why? That's pretty harsh."

Clive just flicked a glance at him and said, "I don't think you should be questioning our ethics, considering."

"That's shitty to do that to a writer. Wouldn't you say it's shitty, C?"

"Real shitty." Candy belched and hit his chest lightly with his fist. He belched again.

"Sorry to offend your delicate sensibilities, but that is, indeed, the case. Shitty or not. Publishing is quite shitty. Publishing is about money, my friends. Beneath all the crap about Pen/Faulkner awards, National Book awards, the Booker Prize; beneath the jacket crap of 'brilliantly orchestrated,' 'mesmerizing debut novel,' 'shattering climax,' et cetera—" Clive was really beginning to feel the end of the third Scotch, which was okey-dokey with him. "I've watched good writers with five or six published novels get dropped because they weren't making a bundle for the house. It's best-sellers and no sellers. Money. Of course, there are exceptions to this publishing rule, I mean people who don't bow down before money, but I'm not one of them and I can guarantee neither is Bobby Mackenzie."

"When you know Isaly's a better writer?"

Clive looked at him. "How the hell would you know?"

"We're reading their books."

Clive blinked. "Why?" It was all he could think of.

"To see what gives with them, what kind of guys they are."

Clive stared from Karl to Candy and back again. Candy's position, his head propped in his hand so that he could see Clive even when Clive was looking down, put him nearly as close as the glass of Scotch. "For a couple of—you know—you guys have a strange way of looking at a, uh, contract."

"Yeah, well for a couple of you-know's we don't mess up."

"Hah! The way you've been showing your faces all day doesn't say much for your tailing expertise."

Candy made a dismissive gesture. "You watch too much TV. It don't make a shitload of difference he sees us. If he does. I get the impression our Ned is so wrapped up in Pittsburgh and writing, we don't even register."

"I ought to just fire your sorry asses—" Boy, was he ever drunk.

Far from taking offense, Karl and Candy laughed as if Clive had just told them a side-splitting joke.

Then Candy tugged at Clive's sleeve and, in a stagy whisper, one hand to the side of his mouth, said, "Not so loud; there's a lady sat down a minute ago."

Clive looked to his right. Two seats away sat Blaze. He hadn't even seen her come in. How could he have missed her? How could anyone, seeing her hair released from the imprisonment of that schoolmarm bun? She smoked a cigarette and thanked the bartender for the martini ("Straight up, twist") he set before her. She gave all three of them a glancing look a little like sun striking a cold surface before slipping behind a cloud. She had a book. She opened it and proceeded to read.

"And here comes our Ned." Candy righted himself and turned his back.

*   *   *   *   *

At the far end of the lobby, Sally watched Ned walk from the elevator to the bar. She'd been watching the bar over the top of a magazine. What was Clive talking to those two men about? They were the two who'd lately started coming to Swill's. Who in hell were they? They were turning up everywhere. All of this was so confusing. On top of this, she could have sworn she'd seen Saul in Schenley Park.

*   *   *   *   *

In the mirror over the bar, Clive saw Ned sit down in a booth in the corner. There were three small tables embraced by the shadows for people who didn't care to sit at the bar. Guests occupied the other two tables also. No, just one table. He could have sworn there was a man sitting at the third table when he'd first looked . . . but it must have been just a mess of shadows he had seen.

And wasn't this just like Ned Isaly? Sit in this gray area, be only half there, which was nearer the truth than not. Fugue state. Writer's coma. Or whatever the hell it was that had writers legging it out of this sorry old world alone, yes, but aloneness had never before looked so tempting. Maybe there was a parallel world where characters were like the several of them in Schenley Park, more or less exposed "to a divining eye." Clive shook his head. Christ, he must be drunk if he was quoting Emily Dickinson. With his fourth

Scotch sitting sunnily before him—Bobby's contract goons must have bought a round—Clive settled in to imagine a writer's day and found he couldn't. He couldn't get any further than a cup of coffee by the notebook or typewriter. He couldn't get past the blank page. He felt his shoulder gripped and an unwelcome voice exclaiming, "Clive, man!"

Dwight Staines. Oh, hell. Since Candy and Karl both greeted Dwight he would now have to introduce them since Dwight could not get through an encounter unless everyone present knew he was a best-selling author.

"Monumentally best-selling author," said Clive, while Dwight pretended a humility he neither felt nor could stick to.

"Hey, we read your book—"

Clive seriously doubted it. He turned away as Dwight droned on. He must be the writer laymen imagined: talking constantly about what you wrote, and why, and how (pen and ink? typewriter? computer?), talking constantly of your experiences, admonishing your rapt pupils to write write write.

God! Don't tell them that! Tell them their chances of getting published were less than zero; tell them getting an agent was almost as impossible, since agents wouldn't take on unpublished writers (a catch-22 dilemma that had always delighted Clive). Clive was always being cornered at cocktail parties by round young people who seemed to think one word from him would be the open sesame to publishing. "Where," they would ask, "should I send it?" To which Clive would reply, "Into the great beyond and the sweet hereafter." He loved the uncertain looks this reply called up. The unconvinced would keep it up: "No, but where?" "Nowhere, not a chance, nil, nix, zero." They were greatly offended, either because he hadn't offered to read what they'd written (or had an idea to write) or because they'd been caught out in their fantasy: editor likes it, publisher buys it, reviewers love it, fame and fortune follow.

The total lack of understanding of what writing was about never ceased to astonish Clive. No one would have expected a plumber, an electrician, a mechanic to proceed along the lines these wannabe writers did. Imagine a mechanic saying, "Hey, I'm gonna take this Porsche apart" without knowing the difference between a steering column and a brake pad.

A person like Ned Isaly (Clive surprised himself by thinking). Ned, who sat over there in the shadows with his notebook, whose thoughts were anywhere but here in the bar of the Hilton, who did not think of best-seller lists or six-figure advances, who was lucky enough—good enough, that is—to have an editor like Tom Kidd, who himself didn't think of these things, who didn't press notions of money and fame on his writers and who didn't encourage them to seek them, who never spoke of promotion or publicity. These things were not Tom's job.

Unlike Clive, who acquired books—an "acquisitions editor" (an appellation that should shame him into speechlessness). Some of the books he acquired, he edited "lightly." He did not edit with ease; he hardly edited at all other than to speak in relatively safe generalities. The trouble was (and he could not recall ever admitting this) his belief in himself was very frail; he was simply not good enough to take a manuscript and improve it. That's why he'd assigned himself to best-selling drivel, Dwight Staines drivel. He was at least bright enough to know what was wrong with Dwight Staines.

Clive took another sip of his drink. Behind him Dwight was still going at it, hammer and tongs, talking about his new book. Candy and Karl were both talking about collaborating on a book and Staines was giving his pithy advice on that subject.

At the same time, on the other side of Dwight, Blaze Pascal was getting up with her book and her cigarettes. She walked over to Ned's table.

("Dust hath closed Helen's eye." What was all of this poetry about? And who was Helen? Helen of Troy? Or someone who had simply wandered in off the street to sit in his mind? An enormous, empty room, except for the one chair—Queen Anne?—she sat in. She simply sat.)

What was Blaze doing? He could not hear what she said, but he did know she was offering Ned a book—that is, Clive assumed it was Ned's book *Solace* that she was asking him to autograph. Ned reached over with his pen and signed it and smiled. She kept on standing there talking to him. Good manners must have dictated that he ask her to sit down, which she did. Another round of drinks was ordered.

She refused to meet Clive's eye. "Refusal" was what he wanted to think. Actually, she probably wasn't aware that he was staring at her. What was she up to? What was she doing? What she was doing was, apparently, picking Ned up.

*   *   *   *   *

Sally looked up from her magazine and saw Ned and the woman with red hair walking through the lobby, moving in her direction. Quickly, she raised the magazine to cover her face. She'd been sitting here ever since Ned had gone into the bar. She'd been sitting here for what felt like hours. Bored, she had gotten careless of anyone's recognizing her.

As they passed, Sally could see the redhead was carrying a copy of *Solace*. Ned, Ned! Surely you didn't fall for that cheap trick! That "would-you-please-autograph-this?" ploy! But they were standing by the bank of elevators, both of them, obviously going somewhere together and the somewhere that the elevators could take you was up. Sally did not know what to do. Probably she would just go upstairs and order through room service.

* * * * *

Clive had left the three sitting at the bar just after he'd watched Ned and Blaze walk out. He had no idea why Blaze thought this particular approach was needed by way of "keeping an eye on him," but it certainly met the criteria, he supposed. He got off the elevator and walked down the corridor lit by tiny lights that made it look almost as if dusk were settling in. Clive caught a flash of blond curls when a head poked out of a door as if checking on the cause of some disturbance. Down farther, a hand adjusted the DO NOT DISTURB sign and he thought he saw a flash of red hair. At the far end of the hall (which gave onto another corridor), the man in the cashmere coat came out of a room and disappeared around the corner.

Sweet Christ! Were they all on the same floor? Even the same corridor? Had the clerk, in her madcap way, kept them all together?

His watch told him it was nearly ten. How could that possibly be? How in the world had he spent all of that time in the bar, and not happily, either? He ordered coffee and a *croque monsieur* from room service, undressed, and fell into bed. The waiter came and left as in a dream. Dipping into sleep and coming out again and dozing off again, he wondered if he could stay awake long enough to eat the sandwich.

He heard singing.

It wasn't that the voices were loud; rather that the voices were the cutting kind that slid as easily through doors and walls as a knife through butter. Clive was glad he'd left before the fraternity party began. The voices drew closer, nearing his door. So Dwight, Candy, and Karl must be up here, too.

"Waltzing Matilda,
Waaaaaltz-ing Matilda,
You'll come a-waaaltzing Matilda with meeeee."

As they passed Clive's door they even threw in a little harmony, as if to say to him, What the crap difference does it make if we can't write? We can *sing*!

THIRTY-TWO

Ned stood outside of another Isaly's, the small store set within a line of other small stores—a bookshop, a Tru-Value hardware store, two little dress shops—wondering if he wanted another pistachio ice cream cone and then wondering if that's what he ate when he was eight years old. Probably not. His taste probably wasn't adventuresome then; probably he stuck to chocolate or maybe cherry. But he didn't remember.

He wished he hadn't been so careless of the past. You always started too late saving things, collecting things, keeping a journal. His parents had died within a year of each other and he was orphaned. Everyone made sure he was aware of this particular disgrace, as if he'd been careless with his parents as well as with the past and now look what happened. Beneath the arrangements of sad expression, he had felt their disapproval.

What Ned remembered of his childhood was not love, but solace for the lack of it and solace had come in many forms. Even though he couldn't have seen them, there were Forbes Field and Jackie Robinson and Stan Musial, his bat unwinding like a snake; there was Panther Hollow and East Liberty; there was dawn smog, afternoon smog that darkened the whole city at noon—no, this could not possibly have been his own memory but memory in a picture in a book. But still there had been wonderful, unbreathable Pittsburgh!

And there was the occasional visit to his well-to-do relations in Sewickley. They were very proud and very severe and they kept servants. They were the Broadwaters and were referred to in that way as if "Broadwater" were a fiefdom. Ned remembered the dining-room table and the buzzer beneath it by which Isabel Broadwater would summon the maid, who would appear with the next course. He especially recalled that dinnertime when the buzzer had been pushed following the soup, but no one had come with the lamb. Isabel Broadwater's thundery demeanor refused any of the diners' going out to fetch it. Suddenly the cook appeared wringing her hands to tell her mistress the dire news that the maid had died: as she had been carrying the lamb she had slipped down to the floor. "And the lamb?" Isabel Broadwater had asked with a raised eyebrow.

Mary-Anne, the dreadful ten-year-old daughter, had reacted with much excitement at this news. Mary-Anne was always excited by others' misfortunes. The servants milled, the doctor arrived, the poor maid was pronounced dead at the scene. Heart, probably. The body had been carted off to some morgue where there would be an autopsy. But Mary-Anne later insisted, in Ned's attic room, that the maid had been murdered and everyone suspected him, Ned.

Mary-Anne liked these visits of Ned's as it gave her the opportunity to lord it over him, to drag out her latest new toy—a Barbie doll or badminton set. Ned brought along his baseball cards, wanting so much to share the wondrous crack of Jackie Robinson's bat or that time Willie Mays caught a fly ball with his bare hand or that incredible home run of Maz in the 1960 series. Oh, to have seen this! To have been alive then and in Forbes Field! Mary-Anne only made fun of him and his cards. She always reminded him that he was orphaned. The only thing she was sorry about in his history of dead parents and being orphaned was that she hadn't been the one to tell him first they had died.

He said it didn't make any difference for he was an Isaly and he could get free ice cream whenever he wanted. Wasn't it too bad there wasn't an Isaly's in Sewickley? Then he could get her a free ice cream cone. This infuriated Mary-Anne, but she couldn't think how to rid him of this belief.

Despite Mary-Anne and her stuck-up friends with their superior smiles, there was solace in Sewickley, for it was beautiful. There were the chestnut and oak trees with their flame- and copper-colored leaves lining the wide streets; the huge Victorian and Colonial-style houses set within brilliant emerald lawns and immense laurel bushes; the pool at the country club; the little movie house they visited on Saturday afternoons; the games around the fireplace. Yes, there was solace in Sewickley.

Ned stood there thinking of solace.

* * * * *

Snow was coming down now, soft and dreamy, in big flakes you could catch on your tongue. That's what Sally was doing while she stood at the bus stop. Snow stuck to her synthetic yellow hair. She was across the street and down a little way from where Ned was looking at that building. What was it? She was bored with standing there, pretending to be waiting for a bus. This would fool no one (if anyone was watching her) since four buses had already come and gone without her boarding one.

*　*　*　*　*

"Don't this nut know it's snowin' for fuck's sake?" Candy gathered the top of his down jacket more firmly around his neck and pulled the hood forward.

It was not really cold; snow just made it feel that way. The sun was still out, having made its late-afternoon arrival in glorious form. Sun spilled across the buildings on the other side of the road. Candy and Karl sat at a green metal table in another coffeehouse watching Ned gaze at the Isaly's Ice Cream store. Candy and Karl were drinking cappuccinos, Candy doing his summary of *Don't Go There*.

"It's a noir-type thing."

"I don't follow. You mean like that 'film-noir' stuff? Kind of thing Al Pacino's always in?"

"Not all of his stuff is noir." Candy wanted accuracy here.

"That's not the point. Anyway, your book doesn't sound like noir to me. All that stuff about drugstores and boutiques. That, my friend, ain't noir."

"So what about Ned's book? You finished it?"

"I'm maybe two thirds through."

"And?"

"It's about a man and woman who keep passing each other. They never get together."

"And . . . ? What happens?"

"That's pretty much it, I guess." Karl was feeling almost apologetic, as if there should be more to his critique than what he'd just said.

"That's it? In a nutshell, that's it? What do these writers do for excitement, anyway?"

Karl pondered. "I guess they don't need much."

"Jesus." Candy shook his head.

"So maybe Ned thinks, you know, that less is more."

"Ha! Well, that sure won't get him off the hook." Candy shook his head. "Sounds like *Sleepless in Seattle*. You know, where they never get together till the very end? It's got what's her name in it?"

"Meg Ryan." Karl shook his head. "No, it's not like that at all. These two come across each other several times."

"They did in *Sleepless in Seattle,* too. Remember, she saw him by the water—"

"Look, it's not the same. You just know how that movie is going to end. With them together and happy. This *Solace* you don't know, except I have a feeling they don't."

"Don't what?"

"Meet, get together. It's not going to have one of your happy endings."

"So?" Candy raised his palms and his shoulders. "Who wants to read it if it's a downer?" He scooped up a handful of peanuts, popped one at a time into his mouth with his fist. After all, Karl had found nothing but fault with *Don't Go There*. "Right? Reading's for escape, ain't it?"

Karl was impatient. "That's crazy, C. Look at your ancient writers, your great writers, your Shakespeare, your Russians. Those aren't for escape. I bet you none of them ends happy, not one."

Candy flapped his hand as if shooing away misery, and said, "Ah, come on. Sure they do. How about that one where this girl Laura Doone has all this trouble at the beginning, but in the end it works out to be happy? Now, that's one of your classics. It starts out bad, but it ends up good. At least, that's what I heard."

"Life's not like that. Something goes bad in life, it stays bad."

"So where's the solace come in?"

Karl frowned and put his hand on top of his head, as if literally adjusting his thinking cap. "It hasn't come in yet." He dropped his hand and looked disappointed.

Candy was delighted to have something else to attack. "Two thirds through and you still ain't got to the solace? That's the *title*, man."

"Well . . . maybe it's in there and I'm not getting it."

"I sure as hell ain't getting it, either." Candy spooned up some foam. "Bummer."

They watched Ned looking at the building. Then Candy said, "I never seen anyone for standing around like this guy. He can stand so fucking long you'd think he'd turn stiff. What the hell's he staring at, anyway?"

"The ice cream place. Isaly's," said Karl, binoculars raised to his eyes.

"You ought to be careful with those things, K; it makes you look pretty obvious, I mean like you're staring at something."

"I *am* staring at something. That's what they're for." Karl adjusted the focus. Then he pulled out a pocket diary in which he'd been recording Ned's movements. There was not much written down. He wrote "Isaly's" again. After that, he couldn't think what to set down. Zero, zilch. Then he got worried he, Karl, might be missing something important and so wrote the name of the street and the names of a couple of business, such as that bookstore over there and this café where they sat. He even wrote "1 cap (C) 1 espresso (K)" and noted down the time.

Candy asked, "You seen the redhead anywhere?"

"She's here; she's around."

"Over there. Look."

"What?"

Candy squinted, shading his eyes with his hand. "Looks like the guy jumped into our cab at the airport."

"Nobody jumped in our cab—"

"No, I mean the one that muscled in and grabbed our cab—"

Karl shook his head. "I don't see anyone—your eyes giving you trouble, C?"

Candy laughed. "If I didn't know better—I mean if we wasn't doin' it ourselves—I'd almost think our Ned's got another tail." Candy looked in all directions. "Have you noticed we keep seeing the same fuckin' faces all the time? I mean faces from the hotel. That cute little babe that was sitting around the lobby last night. That's her at the bus stop across the street."

Karl narrowed his eyes against the sharp sunlight flooding through the café's window. "You're right."

Candy picked up the binoculars and was training them on the end of the street. "Lookie who's here."

"Who?"

"Old Clive. See that bookstore? It's got books outside in those carts. Don't the owner know it's snowing?"

"It's stopping. Put down the binoculars, Christ's sake. You want another coffee?"

"Uh-huh. Maybe a latte this time."

"It's hard getting just plain coffee anymore. It's coffee with an attitude." Karl stood with the cups in his hand, shaking his head. "What I want to know, where's our Ned get his ideas? I mean he never goes anyplace or does anything. Relatively speaking, I mean. How can he think up stuff to write about?"

Candy picked up the binoculars. "He came to Pitts-fucking-burgh, didn't he?"

Karl said, "Yeah, lucky us." He turned to go to the counter for refills, but stopped. He was looking again at the tall fellow across the street who had stopped to look in the window of a florist's. "C? You don't really suppose that crazy Mackenzie put out more than one contract?"

This truly startled Candy, who looked up, wide eyed. "What the fuck, K, why would he do that?"

"Because he's an arrogant son of a bitch and a publisher. And remember we were very clear about the way we worked."

"So he goes and hires somebody *else* to cap him? Some *slob* without any fastidiousness or principles—"

"If so, it means Ned could get smeared all over the pavement anytime now. Maybe we ought to forget the coffee and get out of here."

*   *   *   *   *

Clive had never realized how few transactions good writers made with the physical world. The bad ones, like Dwight Staines, were in constant contact with the world outside because they lacked boundaries, like babies. Everything was theirs. They were the world and everything in it.

What was it that made the crucial difference? He would have to ask Tom Kidd—wait a minute! He never spoke to Tom Kidd beyond an unenthusiastic "hello" if he passed Tom in the hall; it was further evidence of his psyche's crumbling if he could say almost automatically "Ask Tom Kidd."

Clive shuddered and looked up the street. Ned had been standing there in front of that ice cream store for nearly twenty minutes, halfway between Clive and the two goons down there at the other end of the pavement. He didn't have to get any closer to know they were Candy and Karl.

There were the usual people going about their business: a tall man walking out of the florist's a few doors up, a woman into a laundromat; a blonde hanging in the doorway of a beauty shop; and the token beggar sitting near the bookstalls.

Where the hell was Pascal? What was he paying her for? To play fuckall with Ned Isaly in her free time? Clive was feeling put upon as he wandered into the used-book store, comforting in its smell of old bindings and page rot. Clive fussed around in the fiction shelves looking for Mackenzie-Haack authors, found a couple of Dwight Staines and a copy of Ned's *Solace.* He had never read it, but he had certainly never advertised that fact at his workplace. One by Dwight Staines he took up to the cash register to a waif of a clerk who looked as if putting in the energy to read one book would fell her where she stood. He paid for the book, returned to hide among the shelves, where he took out a penknife and cut a square in the center pages big enough to deposit the handgun he'd been carrying in his pocket. It was small, a .22, and fit nicely.

He had a vague and shifting scene in his mind of police trolling by after somebody had shot somebody and Clive didn't want them to know he was carrying a .22. *Good thinking, Clive.* (His addresses to himself had grown increasingly sarcastic ever since Bobby's "plan" had been put into operation.) *Good thinking. You hold the book the wrong way and the gun falls out at their feet.*

So nobody's perfect, big deal.

He ran a finger along the row of *P*s, looking for that book of Saul Prouil's that had received so much praise. Here it was in the first edition and it was expensive. That didn't surprise Clive, given the landslide of awards it had won, that and the fact that Saul Prouil had up to now not published another book. It probably took him decades to write one, and no wonder.

Clive walked up to the cash register where now a beetle-browed old man was taking money from a woman with a coil of dark red hair. He was about to tap her on the shoulder and ask her how she could keep her eye on her mark when she turned and looked at him blankly, as if he were indeed not worth the change the old man returned to her. He had been so certain that she was Pascal.

He paid for his Prouil book, the old man fussing over the AmEx card and finally putting the books in a worn paper bag and handing them over.

Clive took them and left, glancing at the beggar woman and taking out some coins—even this act of mild kindness surprised him. He thought of a line of Yeats—"the rag and bone-shop of the heart"—and dropped the coins in a little metal box. The clothes fairly swarmed on the old woman, layers and layers of cloaks and scarves. There were additional garments in a baby carriage nearby.

"Seventy-seven cents, geez, thanks a lot."

Sarcasm? Clive was about to say "Ungrateful wretch!" when he realized it was Pascal who'd said it. "Ah, Pascal. This is truly a marvel of disguise; who'd ever have thought of a beggar?"

"Fuck you. A cigarette? I'm all out." She held out her mittened hand, and he handed her the pack that he carried for emergencies (though hard to explain to himself what constituted a smoking emergency). She took one from the tight pack and wiggled it for a light. "Thanks. Nice talking to you."

Clive walked on by, shaking his head. He should write a book.

* * * * *

Purchasing a red Porsche was not one of his better ideas, but Saul had gotten tired of standing in the snow and trying to hail a cab, so the WHITE GLOVE SERVICE sign over the Porsche showroom had seduced him. Lord, but weren't those beautiful cars! He had entered the showroom with a view toward renting a car for the day and had become more and more enamored of them.

Put it this way: he might need to yank Ned from the sidewalk where he was so determinedly standing but that would be difficult in a cab, even if he could find one. One needed one's own vehicle if one were rescuing somebody. That still didn't explain buying one.

Out of the corner of his eye he caught a figure moving in Ned's direction. But when Saul turned his head, the person was gone. It had looked almost as if he were shadowing Ned.

* * * * *

Ned was at the end of *Separation* and didn't know what to do about it. He was walking around Shadyside, stalling. All of Pittsburgh was a stall. Or maybe not, maybe not. Maybe Nathalie was thinking what to do as he stood staring at the ice cream store before going in. He had found another Isaly's.

* * * * *

Sally watched from the doorway of a hairstylist's, fingering her wig as if the stylist had misplaced the curls.

In the bookstore down the block she had bought *Pittsburgh: Little Known Facts*. She was hoping a knowledge of arcane facts would make her appear more interesting to Ned, if not more lovable. Another red sports car—was everybody in Pittsburgh driving one?—came out of an alleyway up ahead and turned onto this street. Where did all these Porsches come from? It could be the same one—she couldn't see the driver—but she didn't think so; no Porsche owner would drive about aimlessly at 25 mph. He wouldn't be caught dead.

* * * * *

Personally, Clive disliked ice cream but it served as rather a good cover, he thought. He was licking a cone of vanilla, that being the blandest of all in those tubs at the Isaly place. He was clutching the book. It made him snigger when he thought of asking Dwight Staines to autograph it, and Staines opening it and finding the center cut out (minus the gun, of course).

He was keeping a good way back from Ned, thinking he must be wrong, that Candy and Karl had had several opportunities to plug Ned and if they hadn't done it by now, they probably wouldn't. They must have decided Ned was okay and they'd let him live. God, he hoped so. Never having handled a gun in his life, the idea of having to shoot one made his adrenaline pump.

* * * * *

"K, is there something about all this that strikes you as awful peculiar?" Candy was looking up and down the street.

Karl was looking, too, but he was watching through the binoculars. "What do you mean?" Funny that there weren't more people around, but that's the only thing he thought at all peculiar. There was Clive over there doing God knows what, in and out of that bookstore, then the ice cream place (another one of those!), now carrying a cone and a book. The blonde they'd seen in Schenley Park leaving a hairdresser's where he didn't think they'd done much of a job on her. A woman in dark glasses, pushing a baby carriage along their side of the street, and now here came that goddamned red Porsche again. He sighed. "Sweet ride," he said.

"What?"

"That Porsche."

"Again? Uh."

Candy was reaching beneath his jacket to one of his rear trouser pockets to get his Juicy Fruit gum when he felt something sting him. He slapped his face. "Goddamned mosquitoes this cold—?"

Karl stared. Had the binoculars not been on a strap around his neck, he would have dropped them to the ground. There was a red streak, a blood streak across Candy's face. "No mosquito, C. Look."

Candy pulled his hand from his face and saw blood. "Wha—"

Their hands went for their guns, Karl's to his shoulder holster, Candy's hand dove to the belt at his back. They didn't fire because they weren't sure what they should be firing at.

Then their mouths fell open.

The woman several yards away sent the baby carriage flying toward them, just after she'd pulled a gun from beneath the blanket and rags. The blonde on the other side was pointing a small gun in their direction; even old Clive had pulled a gun out of the book he was carrying, and in the course of doing so shot the book, which made a wide spiral in the air before landing.

Candy's voice was just flirting with hysteria. "What kinda city *is* this, Chrissakes, everybody's packin' heat?"

The red Porsche, as if it had lost both driver and direction, was coming straight at them, its erratic path from street to pavement to street again forcing everyone to drop back into doorways and press against walls.

Guns went back into purses, holsters, baby carriages, and books.

Ned came out of Isaly's with his ice cream cone (pistachio again). He stood there licking it and meditating on the end of *Separation*. He was walking along the street, away from this block of businesses when he heard what sounded like a shot, but turned too late to see (it was over in five seconds) anything but the aftermath of this brief melee. He did see the fleeing Porsche, however, and thought he'd seen it before. Whoever was driving had to be drunk or crazy or both.

There were Candy and Karl, and there was the woman he'd spent a blissful hour with last night—Rhoda? Rhonda? She was righting a baby carriage that must have fallen on the pavement. My God, had a *baby* been killed?

THIRTY-THREE

Back in his room, Ned packed his duffel bag. He disliked leaving the packing until the morning as it made him feel rushed, even though all he'd brought along was an extra shirt, shorts, socks, and an electric razor. He never packed more than would take five minutes to repack, yet he always felt pressured. No matter whether he liked the place or not, knew it well or not at all, there was the same sense of loss.

Finished with the packing, he sat on the edge of the bed thinking about Pittsburgh, the usual signs of anxiety creeping over him. It was anxiety about something left undone, unfinished; something attempted but not, in the end, accomplished, as if he had failed to do what he had come to do.

Maybe he should stay another day.

Solace, Ned had thought, would be somehow cathartic and would relieve him of such feelings. It had done, while he was writing it. It was a story of a man and a woman who, by all the rules of life, should have fallen in love, married, had children. Yet they kept touching and slipping away, passing and not stopping. They were kept apart both by their failure to see how important it was that they meet and by an inability to rise above conventions. One day the brown paper bag of groceries she was carrying broke, spilling cans and boxes. He was there; he helped her pick up the groceries. They smiled at each other; she thanked him sincerely. It was a situation wherein the next thing said could easily have been, "Let's have coffee," but he didn't. She didn't. They recognized in each other's glance something familiar, something they had lost, although neither could have put it that way because each was self-involved, no more than the average person, perhaps, but then the average person is much too caught up in himself. They did not recognize signs and portents. They could literally have fallen over each other and still wouldn't have figured it out. Their solace was forgetting.

* * * * *

Saul was wondering if people had epiphanies in Pittsburgh. Pittsburgh seemed such an unlikely place for them.

He was standing at his bedroom window, which overlooked the Point. He was watching the water, the confluence of the Monongahela and the Allegheny, where they became the Ohio River. The Ohio flowed into the Mississippi. Never ending but becoming something else.

This was, Saul told himself, hardly a novel idea. But in a way it was, too. It set off a train of thought that was not unpleasant, that was, for him, rather startling. He thought of the woman in his book, his protagonist. *"And why—?"*

"Where then was she going? She asked herself this question. And why—?"

This *was* the end: *"And why—?"*

* * * * *

In his room, washing up, Clive thought about writing. All editors felt it now and again, that creepy feeling one was already ghosting for a writer, was already writing rather than rewriting. The thought *I ought to write a book:* he wondered if Tom Kidd ever had this compulsion—for it was beginning to feel like that—compulsion and just a few steps away from obsession.

No, Tom Kidd was too happy doing just what he was doing. But if he had ever had to edit a book by Dwight Staines, he wouldn't be so smug about writing!

Clive had stopped his electric razor to look in the mirror. That was definitely a middle-aged face, and not early middle age, either. The best he could do was middle middle age.

He felt a spikelike pain in the area of his stomach, which split apart and moved upward, that he could take for a heart attack except he knew it wasn't. Perhaps gas, perhaps loss.

* * * * *

In spite of her having read *Solace* every year since its publication, this was the first time she had looked up wonderingly from the page and thought that if, at that moment while she was sitting here in the lobby, Ned had appeared, Sally knew she'd be bold enough to do what his protagonist, Ruthie, had failed to do: she would ask him, "Is she me?"

THIRTY-FOUR

Candy and Karl had their elbows on the Hilton bar and their hands tight around double shots of Kentucky bourbon.

"Never have I seen anything like it," said Karl. It wasn't the first time he'd said it, more like the fifteenth. Candy just shook and shook his head in silent agreement. "I mean," Karl went on, "in our checkered—you could say—careers we've seen some weird things, but never a bunch of strangers on the sidewalk suddenly go for guns."

"Maybe it's the area. I mean, maybe it's a high crime rate area."

"What? Did it look like one? No bars on the windows, no grates on the doors." Karl shook his head, disbelievingly. "A mother with a little *baby* packing heat? Some dumb blonde just got her hair done with a .22 stashed in her bag? That maniac running his car up on the *sidewalk*? Come on, stuff like that? You don't see stuff like that in your high crime areas. In the movies maybe, but not in a real high crime rate area."

"And who the fuck were they gonna *shoot*, K? One another? Not even *I* could say where that shot came from, so how could any of *them*?" Candy delicately touched the two Band-Aids on his cheek. It had been a purely surface wound, but they still wondered, Who the hell?

"Us?"

"What? Shoot *us*? We weren't doin' nothin'."

"I'm just saying"—Karl tilted his glass to drain it—"it looked to me like one or two of those guns were pointing in our direction. Didn't it you?"

"It makes no sense. This whole fucking city makes no sense."

"Well, gentlemen!"

A new voice came from behind and both of them had a hand placed on a shoulder. They whirled around, going instinctively for their guns, but stopping the movement just in time.

"Arthur!" said Candy.

"Mordred!" said Karl, at the same time.

"What in fuck you doing in Pitts-bloody-burgh?" asked Candy.

They gave each other a slap-hand handshake and Arthur said, "Visiting. Another round," he said to the bartender, circling his finger above the two glasses. "I'll have a Perrier." He turned back to them. "What about yourselves? What brought you here?"

Karl shrugged. "Same thing."

"Hell," said Candy, "we haven't seen you in ten, fifteen years."

Arthur hitched a stool out from under the counter. "I'm in Vegas now."

"You're fucking kidding me," said Candy.

"What? You don't like Vegas?"

"You get enough action there?"

"Christ, yes. You know it."

"Used to," said Karl. "Used to have a lot of grit, Vegas. Then people with too much money and no sense, these financiers, started building all of these 'theme' hotels and the place went to hell. It's all families now. Hell, you couldn't get off a round there without hitting six kids under twelve." Karl said thanks to Arthur and raised his fresh drink and clicked glasses with the other two.

"It's not so bad, I mean you get used to stumbling over babies and so forth. But what brings you two here?"

"Work." Candy shrugged.

"It went okay?" asked Arthur.

"Sure, except this is one fucking crazy city." Candy was about to recap the afternoon for Arthur when Clive came up to the bar.

He was introduced to Arthur Mordred. Clive gave him a curt nod and asked of the three, "Do you think you can tell me what in God's name *happened* this afternoon?"—Clive nodded in the general direction of where they'd been—"out there?"

Candy pressed his hands to his chest, his eyebrows bolting to his hairline. "You asking *us*? *Us*? What about *you*? It sure looked to me like you had that piece aimed at me."

Karl said, "It couldn't've been him, C. The shot didn't come from that direction."

"What shot?"

Candy leaned toward Clive, tapping the Band-Aids with his finger. "This shot."

"That's a scratch."

"Okay, so a bullet scratched me. What were you doing with a gun, Clive-O?"

"I've always carried a gun. I live in New York; you almost have to." Clive pawed the little dish of nuts, taking out the cashews, which he popped in his mouth one after the other.

"In a book? You always shoot the book, too?"

Clive found two more cashews and held on to them, thinking. He said, "I was just copying Robert De Niro. In that movie with Eddie Murphy? De Niro's a cop. In this one scene he's gotten himself a twenty-four-ounce paper cup of soda at a Seven-Eleven and walks into the dope dealers' place holding it. Only what he's really done is pushed a gun up the bottom. He sips through the straw; I guess the straw's there to lend it greater verisimilitude."

"You're full of shit, Clive," said Candy.

Arthur plucked a peanut from the dish. "You all seem to lead such interesting lives." He ate the peanut, and asked Clive, "What line of work are you in?"

"I'm an editor. Senior book editor at Mackenzie-Haack. If you're writing a book, please keep it to yourself."

Arthur's laugh was a little on the trill side of hearty. "Not to worry on that score."

Clive looked at him. "Why not? Everybody else is doing it."

"But it must be fascinating, working with all kinds of writers."

"Oh, it's all kinds all right. *All* kinds. Here comes one of the kinds now, lucky us."

Dwight Staines bade them a hearty hello and shouldered his way in between Clive and Karl. "Terrific book signing," he said, "as per usual, right?" and he cuffed Clive on the shoulder. "Line stretched all the way into the street."

Clive cuffed him back, as hard as he could, and Dwight nearly fell over.

*   *   *   *   *

In the lobby, Ned cast a glance at the attractive blonde in the Buddy Holly glasses, wondering why she looked familiar. That was it: he'd seen her in Schenley Park that morning. Or had she been one of the people on the pavement that afternoon, part of that queer scene that had dissolved just as Ned had turned to look at what sounded like some kind of shootout, or what he'd first thought was possibly a TV show being filmed? Maybe a movie.

But then in the next ten minutes the police had come and the fire trucks *and* the omnipresent TV news teams (as if they'd all been stationed behind bushes and down alleys). Their anchors or field reporters were being brushed and brightened by their on-the-run makeup artists before the newscasters faced the cameras. Customers came out of shops, cafés, and bookstores, restlessly milling and watching as police looked for the place to cordon off the crime scene. Unfortunately for their purposes there wasn't one.

Watching all of this, Ned doubled back on the pavement, licking his ice cream cone. He stood where one of the cops was listening to a group who swore there'd been shots.

"How many?"

"Oh a lot," said a fat woman with incandescent orange hair who'd hurried out of a beauty parlor.

The officer looked dubious.

"And farther along the pavement," another woman said, pointing at the place imagination selected as the crime scene, "some woman was abducting a baby—right out of its carriage!"

The group more or less swept the officer along to the dark blue carriage. "Look, see, it's empty! This baby's been kidnapped!" She was close to tears.

Ned had gone along with them, all in a bunch with a single mind, from what would now be a crime scene (police spooling out their yellow tape) to where one television crew was ensconced before an antiquarian bookstore. You could tell Miss Channel 5 was bursting with a news-nugget "exclusive" (which is how she put it), the one concrete piece of evidence found. The field reporter was very pretty in her powder blue suit. (Why did all women TV presenters look like Nicole Kidman? wondered Ned.)

She had a man in tow, apparently the owner or manager of the bookshop. "What has been found, and Mr. Stooley will confirm this, is a book sold by him to a customer that was later discovered in the street with a bullet hole through it!"

This was probably the single piece of evidence police would choose to withhold. Ned had read enough of Jamie's novels to know that. Too late now.

The disaster scene—though short a documented disaster—was in fact becoming a block party, with the café owner distributing coffee and bottled water to whoever wanted it.

"A red Porsche was seen speeding away from the scene; there is speculation as to whether it was a failed drive-by shooting or if the Porsche transported the missing child, whose mother, described as a redhead in her midthirties, has not come forward."

Ned wandered on to another clutch of people, the onlookers dying to be interviewed, claiming to have witnessed one thing or another. Here was another newscaster (Nicole in sea green with a frothy collar) from another channel, this one Channel 13, according to the print on the big white van stationed near her.

"—blonde in dark glasses and a trench coat who appeared to have shoved this carriage—" Here she gave the empty baby carriage a poignant look before returning to her brisk manner.

Ned moved around with his pistachio ice cream cone and made his way to a police officer to tell him he, too, had seen the red Porsche, which struck him as acting suspiciously. "It was at Schenley Park, driving around slowly, you know, circling around more than once."

"You didn't see the driver?" The officer had his small notebook out, taking down what Ned said.

"No."

"Nothing else you can tell me?"

Ned shook his head. "No. Nothing. Are you sure there was a baby in that carriage?"

The policeman frowned. "Why wouldn't there be? It was a baby carriage."

Ned shrugged. "Just a thought. I mean did anyone actually *see* the baby?"

The officer studied Ned for five seconds and then said, "What kind of ice cream is that? I've never seen green before."

"Pistachio. Isaly's."

"Oh."

"You want some, there's a store just three doors down."

The policeman nodded and returned his notebook to his pocket.

"That's my name, Ned Isaly."

"No kidding?"

"It's my family. I'm from here, from Pittsburgh."

The officer nodded, not terribly interested in this personal history. He looked toward the ice cream shop. "Did they have any Rocky Road?"

"Oh, they must have."

"You're visiting your family, then?"

"Not really. My mother and father are dead."

"But there must be a lot of other Isalys."

"Well, yes. I don't know any I'm directly related to, though."

"Oh." The policeman looked puzzled by this obscure relationship. "Well, I guess I'll go check, see if they have any Rocky Road."

"Probably, they do."

"Nice talking to you."

Ned pondered the scene that had taken place that afternoon and which he had a hard time believing was an honest to God crime scene. It struck him as an event—no, a nonevent—he might want to write into his novel. He stopped halfway to the bar and thought of the possible implications of such a thing happening to Nathalie in the Jardin des Plantes. In the hands of a Camus or a Kafka, the blackness of the comedy would shine like ink.

But think (he walked on, giving the blonde on the lobby sofa an absentminded smile): Nathalie . . . couldn't it be used to show her self-delusion? Why not? Certainly not in the last part of the story, but in the first part? Nathalie with an ice cream cone. What was that famous ice cream you used to be able to get only on the Ile St.-Louis? He remembered that ice cream vividly—Bertelsmann's? No, that was the German conglomerate that was eating up publishing houses. This ice cream—Berthillon, that was it!—had the most nuanced selection he had ever tasted, far more subtle than Isaly's. It was the fine print of ice cream, the slow sunrise of ice cream: "Maron glacé," "Grand Marnier," "Amandine." Stuff like that.

He was leaning against the bar and registered some conversational buzz before he realized the talk was directed at him. "What? Sorry. I was thinking." He was being introduced to Clive.

Ned gave Clive a sort of smiling frown. "Aren't you with Mackenzie-Haack?"

"I am. I've never had a chance to talk with you, though. You're always jammed up (Clive was getting somewhere with the argot) with Tom Kidd."

Ned asked the bartender for a beer. "Yes. Well, he's my editor."

As if everybody at Mackenzie-Haack, indeed of all of New York publishing, didn't know. "I admire your work. I really do."

"Thanks. What are you doing in Pittsburgh? Bobby trying to nab some writer?"

Clive was surprised that Ned had any consciousness at all of the underground (not to mention underhanded) workings of his publishing house. "Nab" didn't necessarily mean "steal." Except where Bobby was concerned, it did.

Clive smiled; since he couldn't use the Dwight Staines excuse for being here, he'd have to find another reason, but let it go for the moment, saying, "Do you know Dwight Staines?"

Dwight turned toward Ned, eager to meet anyone famous, or, rather, eager to have the anyone meet him. Dwight knew that Ned Isaly wasn't in the same ballpark—hell, wasn't in the same hemisphere—when it came to royalties. "Me, I'm here on a book tour. This is my first stop. Tomorrow it's Chicago."

Having nothing to say about book tours, Ned simply nodded. Clive was sure you couldn't get Ned on a book tour at gunpoint. Well, he didn't care much for that analogy. Clive always thought there were two kinds of writers: public and private. He preferred the private ones. On the other hand, didn't readers deserve to see a writer they were paying out a good bit of money to read over the years?

"It's already on the *TBR*," said Dwight.

"No," said Clive, "it isn't. It can't be because the pub date was only four days ago." Why was he arguing with this idiot?

Dwight brushed that aside. "I meant it *will* be. Have you read it?"

The question was addressed to Candy and Karl.

"No. I'm reading Ned's." Karl held up *Solace*.

Dwight brushed that aside as he had the *TBR*. "Hell, that's five years old." He said this as if quality could rub off the book like dust from a butterfly's wing. "My new one is a megamonster! Creepy as hell!"

Arthur said, "I can believe it," and drank his bourbon.

While Dwight was monopolizing the conversation, Blaze appeared at Clive's elbow, burnished hair glowing like cognac. "Oh,

Bla—" Wait. Was he supposed to know her? "Uh, sorry, have you met—?" Clive waved his hand around.

Blaze said, "It's Betty. Betty Bunting. People call me Baby." She moved over to Ned's part of the bar, laid her hand on his arm, and ordered herself a martini.

* * * * *

Sally squinted toward the people at the bar. These drugstore glasses were killing her, the magnification was so strong. But she certainly knew the woman with the fiery hair. "Bloody hell," she said, slapping down her copy of *Architectural Digest*. She rose, flounced across the lobby to the elevator bank, and fairly threw herself into one.

* * * * *

Ned turned to Candy and Karl. "What're you guys doing here?" He laughed as if their presence were outlandishly amusing.

"Remember?" said Karl. "We're from here."

"Yeah," said Candy, "the both of us. Funny running into you. And here's another pal of ours—" He introduced Arthur.

Ned started to shake hands at the same time he felt a hand on his shoulder. "What the hell—? *Saul!* Where in hell did *you* pop up from?"

Saul shrugged, smiled. "Manhattan. I got bored."

"You could've gone to the Bahamas for *that*."

Saul ordered a Dewar's for himself and another round for everyone else, tossing a hundred-dollar bill on the bar.

Clive was simply stunned. "You're Saul Prouil. I'm an editor at Mackenzie-Haack. I'm a great admirer of your work. I feel honored."

Saul thanked him. "There's no honor in it, believe me."

Ned shook his head. "The only person missing is—*Sally*?"

Saul turned and stared for here she came walking across the lobby as if she were perfectly at home in it, even wigless and minus her dark-rimmed glasses.

"Sally!"

"Well," she said, "aren't you going to introduce me to your friends?" It was the one friend, Blaze, she had her eye trained on.

"Betty," said Blaze. "My friends call me Baby."

Sally nodded at the half circle of people around the bar, realizing too late she hadn't made up an excuse for being there. "For God's sakes," she said with a little laugh. "We might as well be in Swill's."

"Yeah," said Candy, snickering. "When are you leaving?"

"Tomorrow," Sally answered.

"Tomorrow," said Saul.

"Tomorrow," said Clive.

"Tomorrow," said Blaze.

"Tomorrow," Candy, Karl, and Arthur said in unison.

"Tomorrow," said Ned, "or maybe the next day."

Seven pairs of glazed eyes glared at him.

THIRTY-FIVE

Paul returned, he hoped for the last time, to the steamy environs of the crepe and cappuccino café. Since he'd hired Arthur Mordred, Paul had been in a highly agitated state during which he'd watched several different newscasts, hoping not to hear a report of a dead writer in Pittsburgh. Pittsburgh, it seemed, was far less enamored of dead writers than New York City. Here you might find a dead writer at the bottom of any subway stair.

There was nothing. He could not help supplying Channel 4 with the details they weren't reporting: *"Police say the shooting is a complete mystery. Whoever fired the fatal shot that killed writer Ned Isaly—"* No, it would be more like *"Award-winning novelist Ned Isaly has disappeared and—"*

At several points in his newscast, Hannah had appeared, clutching one of her stuffed Dalmatians, in order to change the channel to *The Simpsons* or some other cartoon. To get her away from the TV, Paul would tell her one lie after another: *"Wile E. Coyote finally*

*got the roadrunner so it's not on anymore; the Simpsons have been kid-
napped—the whole family—and the producers are waiting to see what happens . . ."*

(Hannah did go away on these occasions; he heard her telling
her mother that Daddy was acting really weird, even for a writer,
and her mother would find some alternative activity to absorb Hannah, better than watching television, but not necessarily better than
watching Daddy.)

Back to supplying his own details: *"—the fatal shot. The body was
discovered in a dark alley by a child with her dog . . . with her Dalmatian—"*
And in the middle of this, the phone rang. It was Jimmy McKinney.

A welcome interruption. "Jimmy! You're back! How was the
weekend? . . . No? . . . Sure, I can meet you. Tomorrow, how about
that coffee shop? . . . Can I take it this Birches colony wasn't a
howling success . . . ? For some people, maybe . . . Okay. Tomorrow
around three. Good. See you then."

Paul went back to haunting the TV.

When last night there had still been nothing reported from
Pittsburgh except for an incident in Shadyside that involved a red
Porsche and people with guns, none of whom had yet been tracked
down, Paul found that he could breathe a little easier. At eleven P.M.
Molly asked him if anything was wrong. Would he like a drink? *"Do
you think there might be a mention of* Don't Go There *on* Larry King
Live? *It wouldn't surprise me; you remember how much he liked the last
book."*

Paul smiled and took the drink she brought, knowing that
Molly knew not even Larry King could stand himself for three or
four hours two nights running. It was her way of making up a story
to let him know she didn't find his watching television all of this
time peculiar. She just wanted to give Paul an excuse for gluing himself to the TV and not insisting she know why. *What a wife!* It would

have been impossible, even given his fertile imagination, to make up Molly.

She sat down on the chair arm and massaged his neck while they watched Andrea Thompson give the performance that hadn't gone over very well with *N.Y.P.D. Blue.* Paul leaned back, feeling much more relaxed after Molly's massage. CNN's anchor mentioned again the extremely queer incident in Pittsburgh (Shadyside section), a name that in the last two days made Paul tense up like a harp string no matter what its context. "*. . . including a wildly driven red Porsche and people with guns.*"

Molly, her cheek resting on the top of Paul's head, said she liked that. " 'People with guns.' Sounds like a John Sayles movie."

*   *   *   *   *

Arthur was eating a crepe, this time with strawberries. Paul sat down, telling Arthur he'd brought the additional "fifty large." (Paul couldn't stop writing dialogue sometimes.) "So what happened in Pittsburgh?"

"It went fine," said Arthur, spearing a strawberry.

While Paul waited for Mr. Assassin to comment further, to enlarge upon the "It went fine," he looked around the café: rickety tables and mismatched chairs (chosen just for those reasons) and a lot of people with beads and facial jewelry sitting in and at them. It was *so* Village. They were reading or writing or talking about reading and writing. Paul would have much preferred a real bar, but Arthur nixed that idea because he was an alcoholic.

"Recovering," Arthur had told Paul when he wedged into the booth in the steamed-milk environs of the café. He said it with a snicker, as if he didn't value his recovered status, at the same time looking impossibly smug as if he did. "Two years now. My liver was on its last legs, let me tell you—"

Let you not, thought Paul.

"—and so I always carry my chip." As if to prove it, Arthur brought this bauble out of his pocket into the café's lemony light. It looked like a poker chip.

"Good name," said Paul, fearing he was about to hear Arthur's drinking history. He was.

"See, they give these out for a lot of your nondrinking anniversaries: a month, a year, five years, and so on."

"A month? Sounds like you don't have to work very hard. Now, about Pitts—"

"What? Don't have to *work* hard?" Arthur threw up his hands, looking up, enjoining the malingering ceiling fans to witness. "Listen to the man! Just listen to him. Nonalkies just don't realize. What one of us has to go through—"

Impatiently, Paul shifted into another gear by bringing out the envelope and saying, "Here's the rest of it." He plunked it down on the table caring not a jot for whatever FBI agents might be in the café drinking cappuccino. "Now, tell me what happened."

Forgetting all about his spent liver, Arthur snatched up the envelope, took a look inside, apparently counting the bills with his eyes, then stuffed the money in an inside pocket. "Okay, you heard right. These two, Candy and Karl, they were there, sticking out like a sore thumb—"

"Only because you knew who they were, Arthur."

"Well, yes, that's possible." He looked toward the espresso machine, which seemed continually to be spitting out steamed milk. "I'd like another latte. You want something? Cappuccino? Latte? Coffee? I'm treating," Arthur said, prissily.

Paul sighed. "Sure, why not?"

Arthur picked up his cup and went over to the bar.

At least, thought Paul, he had tried to protect Isaly. But that didn't do much to lessen the guilt about putting Ned Isaly in jeopardy in the first place. And still was in danger, even if these two goons hadn't made a try in Pittsburgh. What in hell were they waiting for? When Arthur came back with the cups, Paul asked him.

"Sam didn't tell you about them?"

"No. I didn't want to know, either, why should I? Now I do." Paul paused, dredging up the phone call to Sammy. "Yeah, he did say something about them taking their time."

Arthur set down his fresh cup with an *Ummm* and lowered his voice. "They have to scout things first. They get to know the mark, you know, his or her routine, friends, stuff like that. They watch him. They eventually draw their conclusions and decide whether the mark deserves it or not."

"*Deserves* it? What in hell do you mean *they* decide? But what—who?" Paul realized he was near to shouting and dropped his voice. "Who the hell would hire guys like that? I may be old-fashioned, but I always thought it was the person laying out the money who got to decide."

Arthur shrugged. "They don't do the job, they give back the money. That's what I heard. I guess they got principles, same as you and me. Well, you, anyway." He patted the pocket in which he'd deposited the money. "I feel almost guilty. I mean, I didn't do all that much."

For a brief moment, Paul panicked. "Ned Isaly is still alive, isn't he?"

"Oh, yes. Yes. Unless his plane crashed. I couldn't get a seat on the same plane, but I stayed with him, meaning behind him, until I saw him go through the checkpoints."

"You don't think he's still in danger?" Paul said, his voice brimming with hope.

"Probably not. If Candy and Karl were going to take a shot at him, they'd certainly have done it in Pittsburgh. As a matter of fact, maybe they did. I *might* have aborted one attempt by Candy–"

"What, what?" Paul leaned across the table, arms crossed.

"I thought he was going for his gun, you know, he likes to keep the holster strapped to his belt in back–?"

"Actually, I don't know where this guy keeps his gun."

"Heh, heh. I was sure he was going for it, but–" Arthur shrugged. "I guess not. That's why–" Again he patted the pocket, this time making a frowny face worthy of Hannah.

Paul made an equally frowny face. "Tell me I'm wrong, but isn't the bottom line here simply that the vic lives on? I mean, it makes no difference whether you do or do not shoot the man who's after him." Paul wanted to get the protocol straight here in case he decided to write a book about it. The actual meaning of services *truly* rendered had never come up in the fictionalized version of Sammy Giancarlo's career since Sammy always assumed he deserved the money.

Arthur took a sip of his latte and nodded. "Theoretically, yes."

Paul held his palm flat out as if pushing that answer back into Arthur's mouth. "Wait a minute, wait a minute. *Theory* isn't involved here. You were hired as a bodyguard, not as"–Paul lowered his voice–"a button man" (still that dialogue).

"You're saying, then, the one is not contingent upon the other?"

Paul tried to ticker-tape this question through his addled brain. "Yes."

Arthur nodded. "I see."

Paul really wanted to pop him. He wasn't giving this hired hit man fucking *lessons*.

Arthur said it again: "I see, yes. Yes, so *theoretically*–"

Paul slammed his fist on the table, making Arthur jump as well as the people sitting at the nearest rickety table. He gave them a lopsided smile and mumbled an apology. Then he turned again to Arthur. "Look. We'll compromise on the money: if Ned Isaly gets killed by the end of the week, you can give back the fifty large (he couldn't help himself). Is that fair?" Paul assumed Arthur would agree with alacrity since he was the one to question the morality of taking Paul's money.

He didn't. After another thoughtful pause, he said, "Thing is, he could meet with an accident and that doesn't come into the arrangement." He took a bite of strawberry crepe and chewed thoughtfully.

Paul stared at him, then leaned across the table, resisting the temptation to pull him forward by his collar. "If the 'accident'–like getting in front of a car–were *arranged*–wink wink, nod nod–then it most certainly *would* come into the 'arrangement.'"

Arthur considered and nodded. "But there's always the possibility it might really be a total accident, like, for instance falling on the subway tracks–"

Paul laughed a trifle hysterically. "Arthur, when has that ever been an accident? People get pushed, that's what happens."

Arthur looked around the room blindly. "Okay, so do you want to include the type of accident that would be covered? Like, if it's the subway, then he was clearly pushed?"

Paul blinked. "I'm not Metropolitan Life, for God's sakes." His head sank into his hands. He shook it. "What in hell are we talking about?" He'd forgotten.

"What?"

"What are we *talking* about?"

Arthur whispered. "My fee. Why don't we split the difference and say twenty-five thousand goes back to you if *anything* happens to him."

Paul just looked at him.

Arthur shook his head. "I don't know how you manage to write books. You can't keep your mind on a thing for more than ten minutes. Right now you look blank as a plate."

Blank as a plate. Paul liked that. He made a mental note.

THIRTY-SIX

The coffee shop near the entrance to the Durban Agency's building was virtually empty, something worth noting in Manhattan, where nothing was ever empty except in the event of a bomb scare or Memorial Day weekend.

Jimmy was sitting at the same table they'd shared before, with the same waitress hovering with her coffeepot. She set down another thick white mug, filled it, and walked off.

"I feel as if I never left," said Paul, sliding into the booth.

"Just be glad you never left for Upstate New York."

"So what happened?"

"Ah! What happened—"

"Incidentally, you look like shit." Paul smiled as if to say shit didn't bother him at all. "You've got a John Grisham beard going, purplish circles under your eyes, and your whole being seems, well, unruly. Twitchy."

"Have you actually been to any of these writers' colonies?"

"No. But I have friends who swear by them. They say Yaddo is better than Paris. Better than Rome, even."

Jimmy's hand crawled across the table to grab Paul's forearm. His eyes would have crawled, too, if they hadn't been totally spent. "How in the fuck do Paris and Rome come into it?"

Paul shrugged. "Beats me. That's just what they said."

"Okay." Jimmy pushed his spoon, napkin, and water glass closer to one another as if trying to gather himself in. "I'm given this cabin—one room, bathroom, a coffeemaker, and a little refrigerator. It's very nice. No telephone, thank the Lord. No television, ditto. It's in the woods, a really gorgeous woodland—"

"That's how I pictured it, kind of."

"For an hour I just lay on the bed listening to nothing. Nothing. When was the last time you ever listened to nothing?"

Paul shrugged. "Last time I talked to my agent?"

Jimmy glared. "That question was rhetorical, for God's sakes. Stop interrupting. Then I get out my notebook, the one I write my poems in, you know—"

Paul grunted as an answer, in case the notebook business was rhetorical, too.

"This was Friday, after dinner—"

"What was for dinner?"

Jimmy squeezed his eyes shut. "I don't damned well *know* what was for dinner; I got there after dinner was over, didn't I?"

Paul bit back any comment.

"So I lay there thinking of a poem I was working on—"

"Excuse me for interrupting, but is this accounting going to be your basic summary or is it a blow by blow? I only ask because if it's the latter, maybe I should get a piece of pie—"

"Just hold on. Now I was lying there watching the trees turn dark, thinking about this poem, when suddenly there was a pounding on the door that nearly knocked me off my bed." Here Jimmy raised his fist, pounding on air. "I open the door and there's these three guys totally drunk or stoned out of their minds, smoking cigars and one holding a fifth of Montecristo rum—"

"Great stuff. It's old Guatemalan rum, really rich. Good with cigars."

Jimmy blinked. "I get the feeling you're missing the point here."

"Go on."

"They introduce themselves. Two of them are Irish and they're all poets. They gibber on about how the IRA spelled death to poetry in Northern Ireland and all sorts of shit like that. Two of them think they're fucking Dylan Thomas—"

"Ha! It'd take at least two to make one of him."

"They're still standing outside, the woods apparently being their Harry's Bar while in residence, while one of them starts reading some long involved blank verse and the other two are blowing smoke in my face and offering me the Montecristo bottle. I say, 'No thanks, see I'm really trying to write.'"

"'Write? *Write*? Hell, you can do that anywhere, boyo. Why waste a perfectly good weekend in the woods doing it?'"

Paul laughed. "That's good, that's really good." He raised a finger to the waitress. When she appeared he asked her what kind of pie they had here.

"Oh." She put on her pie-thinking cap. "Well, there's berry, that's blueberry and strawberry, apple, lemon meringue—"

When Paul saw Jimmy drop his head in his hands, he ordered him a piece, too. "Make it two apples. Thanks. And more coffee. Thanks."

"There must've been a dozen of these little cabins; when I was being shown to mine, one of the managers or whoever she was pointed them out, each one buried in among the trees. It was an idyll, really. I mean, it should have been. Mine, for some fucking reason, became the hub. And where were these writers getting their booze? There wasn't supposed to be any drinking, I mean except at the main house just before dinner when they served cocktails." Jimmy drew in breath as if he'd just surfaced and went on.

"Finally, these three left and I thought I might as well go to bed. Saturday morning I decide to skip breakfast in the main house and just write. So I make this sign on a piece of notebook paper: DO NOT DISTURB! PLEASE!! and scotch-tape it to the door—"

The apple pie arrived with more coffee. Jimmy shoved his pie aside and, with burning eyes, continued his tale:

"I'm finally getting close to four lines I've been grappling with—see, this poem is really hard because of its form; it's analyzed rhyme—you know what that is."

Around a big bite of pie, Paul said, "Sure." No, he didn't, nor did he want to. "I should have ordered this à la mode. Do you want a scoop of ice cream?"

Jimmy went on as if Paul were merely a recording device. "Around lunchtime, I hear this tapping on my windowpane, finger-nails *rat-tat-tatting*, and I open the door, thinking it's my lunch de-livery. I'm *really* hungry because of no dinner, no breakfast. I open the door and here's this girl—more of woman, she's got to be in her thirties, trying to look like thirteen, you know, like gypsy clothes, head wrapped in a polka-dot scarf, big gold earrings—"

"You're really good on details. You should write some fiction—oh, sorry." Paul ducked his head toward his pie when Jimmy made a movement with his fist.

"She comes in as if my cabin is her cabin and plops down on my bed. She says, 'Kee-*rist*, what a night! I keep reminding myself not to drink Eddie's martinis. They're lethal. Hi, my name's Marie—'

" '—and I'm an alcoholic,' I say."

Paul's laugh sputtered around piecrust.

"Well, that surprised her. She chirps, 'Oh, are you in the program, too?'

"'*Too?*' I manage to get some acid into my tone. 'You're saying *you* are? Ha. No, I'm not in the fucking program, what do you want?'"

"'My, aren't we tetchy this morning?' As if I'd been drinking with her or fucking her the night before.

"'I came here to *write,* that's why I came.'"

"'So did I, so did we all. But you gotta take a break sometime.'"

"'This place is break heaven. That's all you guys do here.'"

"'*Um,*' she says; a lot she cares. 'Can I bum a ciggy?' I tossed her the pack. She lights up and starts rattling on about her awful life, which is why she's here because she's writing a memoir about how she was abused as a child by her father, her brother, her uncle, her cousin—you know, your typical memoir—and what a great book it's going to be—'If you ever get around to writing it,' I say. And she says, 'Oh, I do. My self-discipline is legendary.' *Legendary!*" Even Jimmy had to stop being mad and laugh at that.

"She goes on. 'So I guess you don't want to fuck? Right?'"

Paul snorted out another laugh.

"'You guess right. Actually, *leave,* will you?'"

"'Awright! Awright!' She hands me back the Winstons and I tell her to keep the pack. By now, it's got to be two, three in the afternoon and I'm starving. I look outside and my lunch isn't there, so I figure the DO NOT DISTURB! sign made them hesitate about even leaving it. Didn't Hemingway say you could only write on an empty stomach?"

Paul didn't know, nor had he any intention of finding out. "Are you going to eat that pie?"

Frowning over his cabin in the woods, Jimmy shoved it toward him.

"Thanks. Then what?"

"Finally, I get this stanza written, the analyzed rhyme. Do you know—?"

"Absolutely. Go on."

"Seven or eight writers, so-called, including Marie and the Irish jerks—without the Montecristo because they know they'll get drinks at the main house—come along and veritably herd me out of the door to go to dinner. I knew there was no way of avoiding all this because I *had* to get some food inside me even though I wasn't particularly looking forward to a whole bloody woodsful of writers like these. Off we troop to the main house, where I'm pleasantly surprised—for all of five minutes—to see that the other fifteen or twenty people there are reasonably quiet and reasonably sober. I'm hanging around the drinks table and this really tall fellow who looks like your paradigmatic poet—long scarf, black hair, sleepy eyes as if he can hardly bear to listen to one more person not himself—and I ask him what he's working on. Turns out he's not a poet, he's a sculptor. That pretty much stopped me cold, knowing as much as I do about sculpture, which is zilch. I say to him, 'I'm surprised this place has, uh, sculpting materials.' Brilliant, yes? He says, 'Well, they *don't*, do they? One brings one's own, doesn't one?' and walks away.

"I tried a few more opening ploys with a woman with huge hair, so damned thick it looked as if she'd borrowed other people's; it stuck out on both sides of her head like wings, and after a banal conversation, me providing the principal banality, I decided I was better off with the rum drinkers and Dylan sayers than the others who were either insufferably snotty or insufferably boring or both. There was another orgy that night to which I just succumbed and Sunday morning, I was out of there. I started back to New York and checked into a Red Roof Inn along the way and slept."

Paul, finishing up Jimmy's apple pie, wondered where the silence had come from. The air had fairly crackled all around him in Jimmy's flow of talk—ah! He'd stopped! That was it. Paul, having grown unused to the sound of his own voice, then said: "So, I guess the six months at Yaddo won't work for you."

"You've got that right, boyo." Jimmy drank his cold coffee, signaled to the waitress.

"I guess you're thinking you've learned to appreciate your home more." Paul was disappointed.

"Are you kidding? Hell, no. I appreciate it even *less*. It's all part of the same thing. What I realized was how much I appreciated being *alone*. For those few hours right after I got there, I felt weightless. Privacy may be the fucking greatest gift you can find for yourself." Jimmy moved his head backward. "Behind this booth I've got my suitcase and my typewriter. I moved out of the house. I told Lily—that's my wife—I thought we should do a trial separation. All hell broke loose, which is one of the reasons I wanted a trial separation, come to think of it. You know what I'm going to do? I'm going to stay in a hotel while I look for an apartment. All I need is a studio; probably I can find something in lower Manhattan or TriBeCa. My son's fifteen. Mike. This way I won't feel like I'm abandoning him because he loves Manhattan and can come to my new digs and sulk instead of just sulking at home. The only danger there is he might want to move in. At any rate, he'll think he's got enough to send me on a major guilt trip. Leaving his mother and the homestead, why, that'll give him more ammunition to resent the hell out of me than he could ever hope for if I stayed. Lily, ditto. Imagine all the lunches and cocktail parties where she can run me down." Jimmy grinned. "It's a good move all around. Then I'm going to tell Mort I'll work three and a half days, no more, so I can be your agent and agent for a few others I respect. If he doesn't like that"—Jimmy shrugged—"then screw it, I'll leave. I'll leave and open my own agency with you as top client. I hope you'll agree to that, but even if you don't, I'll manage with the few writers I think will go along with me."

Paul shook and shook his head. "Wow."

"So, have you seen it?"

Paul frowned. "Seen what?"

"How far I'd go."

Paul grinned. "Far enough. *Way* far."

THIRTY-SEVEN

Paul Giverney sat down in Clive's office without removing his coat. Just to let me know he's hardly got time for me, Clive thought.

"So?" said Paul.

Clive surprised himself by saying, "Look, I just had a very rough weekend. Take it up with Bobby."

"I'd sooner take it up with a turnip. Bobby's always had a very rough weekend. Bobby lives for rough weekends."

Clive frowned, thinking Paul Giverney more familiar with the Mackenzie-Haack mode of operation than would be expected of a writer not yet one of Mack-Hack's own. But of course Bobby's love affair with Glenlivet and the wines of Puligny-Montrachet was no secret in publishing circles.

Giverney was waiting for an answer. Clive could hardly tell him about the weekend followers, so they sat for endless seconds, silence soaked.

Clive broke it; he had never mastered the art of silence as a tool or a weapon. "Paul—" He paused. Were they on a first name basis? "Clive?"

Apparently they were, though Clive seriously doubted they shared wavelengths. If only the arrogant bastard would take his shielding hand away from his mouth. The bastard did so.

Paul asked, "How long can it take to nullify a fucking contract, Clive?" He mimed the act of tearing up a sheet of paper and tossing the invisible pieces over his shoulder. That done, he took up a pugilistic position with his arms crossed over his chest. He stationed the sole of his shoe against the edge of Clive's desk. That was *really* taking liberties!

Relieved he could at least speak to this point, Clive said, "It's not that simple. You know his editor is Tom Kidd. We can't afford to lose Tom—not just for himself alone, but for the writers he edits. You know they'd follow him to kingdom come, and that means another publisher. I've told you all this before. Look"—Clive spoke in his best conciliatory tone—"why do you want this?"

"I told you, you don't need to know. Anyway, Tom Kidd's a throwback, a 'literary' editor. There aren't that many left. Replace him with a sharp young acquisitions guy, someone who can pull in commercial writers like me."

"We don't want that many commercial writers. Mackenzie-Haack has always been known for its literary books. We have more NBA's, Pen/Faulkner, Critics Circle awards than any other publisher."

Paul Giverney looked pained. "Stow it, Clive. Your reputation rests on Bobby Mackenzie's uncanny gift for turning dreck into spun gold on his say-so."

"That's a gross exaggeration."

"So is the truth. Take, for one example, Rita-fucking-Aristedes. Black hair, olive eyes, white skin, Greek. The Greeks are in. It used to be Latinos, Central Americans, Portuguese, et cetera. Rita's been spreading this offal around for years and the one you published isn't any better than the others—"

Clive frowned. "How do you know—?"

"I know it all, Clive. You forget how often I'm asked to spill a little cat sick for the back of the jacket. Rita's agent sends me this tome for a blurb. Rita's agent couldn't sell emeralds in Oz. Now why does this drivel get snapped up by Mackenzie-Haack? Because the man foretold forsooth that *Greece* is *in*. Greece hasn't been in since Larry Durrell."

"That wasn't Greece, was it? The Alexandria Quartet?" Wasn't it Egypt? Paul Giverney made him uncertain of everything.

"There's no question but what Bobby's a fucking genius, a reader of everything under the sun, and a double-dealing cunt. The only writers this man respects are dead. Shakespeare, Aristophanes, Joseph Conrad." Paul spouted a few more names that had been included in a classic line they'd just started publishing.

"That's why you want us to—"

"No, that's not why. I don't need a fucking genius."

Clive's smile was a sliver, a remnant of moon. "But you want to align yourself with a literary—"

"No, I don't. I shouldn't have got off on this literary tangent."

Clive toyed with a knifelike letter opener, beating back the desire to plunge it through Giverney's heart or at least to torture him until he talked. Then, suddenly, he was startled to hear Paul say, "Okay, get the contract together and I'll sign. You can tell Mort."

Clive dropped the letter opener, stunned. "What? But you just—"

"Oh, just *do* it, Clive. Never mind my reasons. Don't try to understand it."

"All right, all right. I'm absolutely—"

"Thrilled." Paul rose and bade him good-bye. But at the door, he smiled and asked, "Has Bobby ever gotten into the Old Hotel?"

"No." Clive stood behind his desk with that slivered-moon smile. He remembered Bobby's white-hot rage when he couldn't make a reservation. He'd tried a dozen times, tried giving a different name and address. Still no. The twelfth time he'd gone there in a little pool of hopeful people, watching a few admitted, a few turned away, including himself and a woman in pavement-touching sable. (They were red in the face, they were outraged, they swore they were going to call the mayor—who, it was rumored, hadn't got in, either. But no one knew this for a fact.)

Paul Giverney said, "Me neither."

"I have." Clive felt smug. "I could get you in." It would be chancy. Clive would be compromised if it was discovered his guest was someone who had tried repeatedly to get in on his own. He had taken a chance with Mort Durban. But he certainly wasn't going to take another with Bobby.

"Thanks, but that's one of those things you gotta do on your own or it doesn't count."

Clive was a bit taken aback by Paul Giverney's modest admission he had never gotten into the Old Hotel. People had tried to circumvent the Old Hotel's rules, which was difficult because no one knew what they were.

The two of them, Clive and Paul, stood silent for a few moments turning this over. What were the rules? It might have been the only time they did share a wavelength. It wasn't wealth or social position; it wasn't who your ancestors were. Politics? No. There was sometimes a prominent politician, sometimes a sleazy one, sometimes both. The burning question during Clinton's siege was not, Should the Big Creep be impeached, but had the B.C. ever got into the Old Hotel. It was rumored that he hadn't.

"Maybe," said Paul, "it's a working out of chaos theory."

Clive, before the Giverney business, had never been introspective; if the surface looked good enough, he'd skate on it. But now he speculated: was the Old Hotel the working out of chaos theory? "How very strange."

"Strange indeed," said Paul Giverney, and he was out the door.

THIRTY-EIGHT

He really wants you to edit him."

Even Tom Kidd liked Jimmy McKinney, but not so much he'd consent to becoming Paul Giverney's editor. "Come on, Jimmy. You might as well ask me to edit Dwight Staines or Rita Aristedes."

Rita was a writer so sorely in need of an editor to bash her head in that the only person Bobby could get to do it was Peter Genero, champion of lost causes. It wasn't because Peter Genero agreed for humanitarian reasons, but because he was convinced he could do anything, including editing Rita.

"Oh, *you* come on, Tom. You know there's no comparison."

"But there is, there is; all three of these writers are at the top in sales. You think Bobby would keep Rita if her books didn't sell in the zillions?"

Jimmy nodded. "Okay, I grant you that. But you know Paul Giverney's a much better writer."

Tom gave a cut-off laugh. "That's not saying much."

"Have you read his latest book?"

"Does it sound as if I've read his latest book?"

"No." Jimmy laughed.

"Anyway, what the hell happened that Mort handed Giverney over to you?"

Jimmy wasn't sure how much of what had gone on between Paul and him should be bruited about. He looked around at the books Tom had stacked everywhere. Covering two walls were floor-to-ceiling bookshelves and even that was inadequate. Books were stacked on the floor, on the desk, on the wide windowsill. He thought of his own neat office at home, kept that way by Lily. Neat, orderly, compressed. (*Think not, because I wonder where you fled—*")

"What are you smiling about? You're the only person I've ever known who could actually 'crack a smile.'"

Jimmy cracked another one. "I was thinking of poetry. Not mine, though. Edwin Arlington Robinson's. Oh, would it were mine . . ." Jimmy sighed.

Tom's eyes widened. "I didn't know you were a poet. You published? Not"—he held up a restraining palm—"that publication is any measure of a work."

Jimmy edged closer to Tom's desk, picked up what looked like a fossil, and studied the ridges. "But it is, Tom; it is a measure. Emily Dickinson thought so despite all that garbage about her not caring, not wanting to see her poems published, at least in her lifetime. When I got my book published it was as if I'd been released from solitary; now, at least, I could mix with the other prisoners."

"The 'other prisoners' being us, I take it?"

Jimmy nodded. "I could communicate." Keeping his eyes on the fossil, still in the palm of his hand, he sat back.

"That's fossil bark, in case you're wondering."

"Where's it from?"

Tom shrugged. "No idea. I like to rub it around. That's why it's so smooth."

Jimmy thought of the wood behind his house. (*"The woods were golden then. There was a road–"*) He loved the suspension of those four words, "road" hanging at the end of the sentence as if it might go on forever. And that was the way he had felt; that was the way Lily had felt, he was sure, a long time ago. "In another year, I'll probably quit."

"Quit writing poetry?"

"No. Quit being an agent."

"Oh, Christ, *Jimmy!* Don't tell me that! You're the only fucking agent around who has the least idea of what it's all about. You're the only one who can see the skull beneath the skin."

(*"Webster was much obsessed by death–"*) " 'And saw the skull beneath the skin.' "

"Eliot, T.S." said Tom. "I know my quotations, if not my poets. When do I get to read some of yours?"

"Anytime you want. I'll bring you the book next time I come."

"Good." Tom scooted down in his chair, looked up at the ceiling, in the manner of one who expected to find cracks and loosening plaster. "You know, being unselfish about it in one weak moment, I'd say maybe you should get out of this business. *I'm* happy in it because I do what I want." He gave Jimmy an earnest look. "I'm considered to be a fairly valuable commodity, see." He said this earnestly, as if he'd only recently made the discovery.

"As if everyone didn't know that, Tom."

"The thing is, if you're seen to be valuable, people–people here being Bobby–don't try to mess with you. Because if he did, I could just go elsewhere. And probably take a writer or two with me."

"They'd *all* go with you, Tom. Some of the best writers in New York. Bobby would go nuts." Jimmy rose. "I'd better go."

"Okay, okay, okay." Looking as if he were about to be given lye to drink, Tom said, "I'll dig up the Giverney book, but I'm only reading a little of it. That's all it'll take, probably."

"You're a good sport, Tom."

"No, I just think it would be insulting to you if I didn't at least try."

Jimmy smiled. "Oh, it would be."

At the door he turned. "Tom, is Bobby trying to screw up Ned Isaly?"

Tom got up, frowning. "Why do you say that?"

"Pau–" Jimmy stopped short of naming him. "Someone warned me I should be looking out for Ned's interests. That's all he said, no explanation."

"What do you think he meant?"

Jimmy shrugged. "I don't know. Ned has a manuscript due pretty soon, hasn't he?"

Tom levered up the top bunch of papers on his desk. "I've got it here somewhere. Next week, I think."

"Has Bobby ever invoked the clause about failure to deliver?"

"He better not start now."

"You know Bobby enough to know he can do anything he wants. At times I wonder if he's even got a reason for what he does. Or if he simply does things because he can." Jimmy nodded. "See you, Tom. Thanks for recommending me as an agent."

Tom shrugged. "Who the hell else would I trust?"

THIRTY-NINE

Ned had spent the entire morning and some of the afternoon in bed. He couldn't understand what had made him so tired. He felt as if he were being watched. He felt hounded. Paranoid, that's what he was.

It had begun in Pittsburgh, but he was too busy observing things himself to pay much attention to it. It was like ignoring signs of a cold until the cold or flu hit you in earnest. He sat up and took two more Motrin and lay back down again.

Ghosts. That would explain the sensation, the air hovering around him.

He thought back; he pictured the places he had been—Schenley Park, watching the kids play kickball. The Isaly's Ice Cream stores. Shadyside. The stadium across the river. But his problem was that most of what he saw happened inside his mind. He was shamefully unobservant. He didn't know how he managed. He wondered if the Jardin des Plantes and the Luxembourg Gardens were anything like the way he described them. Which took him back to Nathalie again and the very odd sensation she was gone. He should never have gone to Pittsburgh; it was like walking out on her. He should have stayed here and spent his time trying to right the miserable state he had left her in.

A knock at his door startled him, especially since it was a sound he rarely heard. Maybe a package, UPS or Fed Ex. As he was getting out of bed he imagined a man whose only contact with the world beyond his door was a courier service. He stood thinking about this and forgot to go the door. Knuckles rapped again, louder, and he went to the door.

It was Saul.

Ned was flabbergasted. They were friends of long standing, of more than a decade, but Saul hardly ever came here. "Saul!"

"Ned. Will you do me a favor?"

"Sure. Of course. Come on in. What's wrong? You look like hell. It's the first time I ever saw you look like hell. What's this?"

Saul was reaching out a package wrapped in brown paper and tied with string, some three or even four inches thick. "A manuscript. The one I've been working on."

Ned's eyes widened. He was almost alarmed.

Saul went on. "In Pittsburgh it came to me suddenly that maybe the reason I couldn't write the ending was because I'd already written it. Maybe what I had down was the ending."

Ned was hefting the manuscript as if weighing it. "I'll be more than glad to read it, Saul." An understatement if there ever was one.

Now Saul looked genuinely pained. "Well . . . I was thinking of Tom Kidd. Do you think he would? Since I don't have an editor."

"Are you kidding? Of course he would. My God." Ned started to laugh. "God . . . a new book from Saul Prouil. I can guarantee he'd read it. I can take it over there right now." Ned had never seen Saul in what one might call "a state." Saul was always the epitome of cool. He was disappointed that Saul was not giving the manuscript to him for a reading, but he himself would have done the same thing. Or would he? Probably he would have felt a manuscript was getting a far better reading if in Saul's hands than in the hands of an editor. Except, of course, Tom Kidd. "I'll get dressed."

Saul called after him, "Are you sick? You were still in bed."

"I was just tired. That trip seemed to wear me out." In five minutes he was out of the bedroom, barefoot, pulling a sweatshirt over his head. "I don't know what the hell it was. Did you ever get the feeling you were being watched?"

"Watched? No. You going paranoid on us?" Saul smiled.

Ned stuffed his feet into shoes. "Yeah. Right. Who'd want to watch me? Let's go."

He gave Saul a push through the door, locked it, and they left.

FORTY

Candy and Karl were standing in front of a travel agency in Chelsea looking at a flock of cardboard flamingos whose shocking pinkness advertised two weeks in South Beach and Key West. That poster sat against a hodgepodge of smaller pictures and travel ornamentation: a bucket of sand, a bikini, an exotic drink with a stirrer featuring a naked girl.

Ruminatively, both were chewing gum. They were not talking about Key West, but about Ned Isaly.

Candy said, as he studied the bikini, "So how do we proceed here? I mean, the only other time this happened was with that little kid? Remember that little kid, K?"

"Do I remember? How could I forget. Six years old, cute as Christmas."

"Heir—or is it heiress—to twenty million smackers," said Candy.

"Well that was a no-brainer. We just gave the jerk his money back."

"Before we put him on a plane to Australia," said Candy.

"Dumb fuck went, too." Karl sniggered. "Without so much as a complaint."

"Easy to do with a Walther in your ear." Now they both sniggered.

"Tell you one thing, C. If it was this Mackenzie creep, it'd be no trouble for me taking him out in the middle of Lincoln Center. I mean it."

They stood for another silent minute thinking about that and looking at the window, Candy tilting his head nearly to his shoulder to look at a picture of a couple of women playing with a huge beach ball.

Karl said, "Listen, let's go in."

"We want to go to Key West? You kidding? That's where all the faggots live."

"Not all a them. A lot are in Provincetown, the ones not in Chelsea." Karl said this out of the corner of his mouth so the travel agent wouldn't hear them as he bent his glossy strawberry blond head over some brochures.

Karl got the agent's attention and made his inquiry. Candy laughed. "You thinkin' what I think you're thinkin'?"

"Wouldn't be surprised." Karl laughed, too.

The agent sighed with all the pleasure of one who'd finished either a good meal or good sex. "Now, gentlemen, I think I've got everything in order here," at which point he shoved over a ticket, an itinerary, and several brochures. And a glossy magazine advertising one of the cruises. "In case you decide later."

Candy pocketed the ticket, Karl the glossy stuff. They thanked him and left.

Fresh sticks of gum in their mouths, they stood on the sidewalk as the swell of gypsy-looking women and kids with nose rings on skateboards swept around them.

"I could use a beer, C, how about you?"

"Swill's?"

"Yeah, why not?"

*   *   *   *   *

They had come to think of themselves as regulars and the table midway down the room as theirs and were offended when they found others occupying it, Candy fantasizing bringing in his sawed-off shotgun and gunning them down as would, he claimed, have happened in Depression years.

Swill's was, as usual, dusk dark; one seemed to be looking through the gray haze of time, which was kind of restful. Almost like watching one of those black-and-white movies they didn't make anymore, except when some director wanted to make one over again.

Candy had got their beers at the bar and said hello to Ned, who was standing there talking to that fag poet. He returned to the table to hear Karl talk about this black-and-white movie thing. "One of these days some asshole producer is going to do *Casablanca* in color."

"Assholes," said Karl, pulling his beer over. "*Casablanca*'s got to be in black and white." Karl had lit a cigar and sucked in on it and was inspecting the coals at the end. "Trouble is, everyone wants something for nothing. Make a movie already been made once, you can do it with your head up your ass. I ask, where's the imagination in that?"

"It's only foreign movies show any imagination. That and indies." Candy had heard this observation made more than once in Swill's. "You got your Fellinis, your Kurosawas—"

319

"He's dead."

"Did I say he wasn't? You got your David Lynch, your John Sayles."

"You're right, one hundred percent. Think of the guy who re-made *Psycho*. What he was doing was just playing on people's nostalgia. You know, the Hitchcock one."

Candy gave a moment's thought to this and said, "Well, but wait a minute, K. You can't feel nostalgia for *Psycho*. You never been to the Bates Motel."

"I know I haven't. But I could think I was when I was watching that movie."

Candy was dismissive. "Come on, K. You can't feel nostalgia for someplace you never been."

Ned was still standing at the bar, talking now to the bartender and owner, Jimmy Longjeans.

Karl pointed toward Ned and said, "Let's get him over."

One on each side, they got him.

"I would have gone peacefully, for God's sakes," said Ned. "Something on your mind?"

Karl said, "We're having a kind of argument."

"About what?"

Karl said, "I'm saying you can feel nostalgia for a place or time you've never been to."

Ned still stood, drinking Bud from a bottle. "Well, yes, you can. I mean I think so." Why had these two been in Pittsburgh, really? Ned wondered. There was something wonderfully old-fashioned about them, like Kennedy fifty-cent coins.

Karl kicked back a chair in a way that suggested he was used to kicking back chairs and said, "Sit down," in a way he was used to telling people to sit down. But he did not mean to give offense, which was pretty much what he said, together with "Please (sit down)."

So Ned sat.

Candy said, "You were saying?"

"About nostalgia? That it might not have to do with a particular time and place."

They squinted at him as if compressing the field of vision might leave another faculty free to play around.

"I don't get it," Candy said. "You?" He turned to Karl, who was thinking and didn't answer.

Ned said, "You might be attaching a feeling to somewhere that wasn't ever the source of it. Maybe you don't recall the source because remembering it's too painful."

They cocked their heads like big birds, listening carefully.

"Anyway, it's what the book I'm writing is about."

Was it? It gave Ned a jolt. He thought of Nathalie and thought she had been sorely used and not just by Patric but by Ned himself. He saw her there in the Jardin des Plantes, waiting for Patric, who wasn't going to come. He'd left Paris for his house in l'Hérault. Why was she waiting if she knew he wasn't coming? Hope against hope, a strange way, thought Ned, of denoting hopelessness. She thought:

He will walk toward me, turning in from the Rue Linne, carrying roses. He will not have gone, after all; he will have sent his wife and children off without him to Beaulieu-sur-Mer. Now they could be together for two weeks, two weeks uninterrupted. They would sit in cafés along the Boulevard St.-Germain, in Deux Magots, or along the Rue de la Paix, the café jammed with Americans who remembered it from the old song.

Nathalie imagined Patric with the same ferocious intensity with which he, Ned, imagined Nathalie.

She watched the path with such an intensity that Patric might actually materialize there, holding flowers . . .

He only half heard the question asked of him and looked up. "Sorry, you said—"

The taller one nodded, then asked, "What's your book called?"

"*Separation.*" Ned said, "Why were you guys in Pittsburgh anyway?"

"Oh . . . yeah . . . we got business in Pittsburgh. Accounts, you know."

"No kidding?"

"Coincidence. Listen, we're just on our way over to Mackenzie-Haack. We want to see Mackenzie before he leaves town. He's one of our accounts."

"Yeah," said Candy. "Before he leaves town." He grinned.

FORTY-ONE

Candy and Karl walked into the enormous lobby of the Mackenzie-Haack Building. The lobby looked like a marble sepulchre with its black floor tiles reflecting upward and white Doric columns on either side. The floor looked slippery slick and icy black enough to skate on.

They walked up to a black marble half-moon structure with RE-CEPTION on a small brass plaque. Behind the counter sat a guard. Another guard stood by him. Both looked bored. On the wall behind them were the huge intertwined initials *MH*.

"Bobby Mackenzie," said Candy, rolling his wad of gum from the left side of his mouth to the right. He had worn his black fedora.

Karl had worn his, too. Both of them also wore their mirror Ray-Bans.

The guard looked them slowly up and down, obviously not caring much for what he saw. "Names?"

"Mr. Black and Mr. White."

The second guard stopped yawning, narrowed his eyes at them, and adjusted his Sam Brown gun belt.

The first one scoured a big book of names, dates, and times, looked almost happy that he didn't find Mr. Black and Mr. White. "You got an appointment? Because here it says you don't."

Karl reached over the marble surface of the desk, picked up the phone, and held it out. "Call him and say we're friends of Mr. Zito's. Danny Zito's."

The guard looked increasingly unhappy and, now, fearful. He buzzed a number, spoke into the phone, waited a few seconds, and was given an instruction. He hung up and wrote "Black" and "White" on two identification tags. He handed these over to them. "S'posed to keep this on at all times you're in the building."

The tags had little metal clips that they used to fasten them to their lapels; they were directed to a bank of elevators that would whisk them to the twentieth floor. Nonstop. As soon as they entered the elevator, Candy and Karl jerked off the tags. They didn't think much of wearing identification.

Out of the elevator, past another receptionist, down a carpeted hall, blowups of book jackets lining the walls right and left.

"These guys are really into books," said Candy.

* * * * *

Bobby Mackenzie was seated at his desk, feet planted on top of it. He appeared to be editing some pages. Clive was standing by the window that gave out on a panoramic view of Manhattan. Bobby did not rise. He did not invite them to sit down in the two leather chairs on the other side of the desk.

Clive did.

"Clive, my man!" Candy gave him a high five.

Clive rather enjoyed returning it. He offered them chairs on the other side of the desk.

Bobby looked displeased. After all, he hadn't arranged this meeting and he didn't want them sitting down. "So why are you here? There wasn't supposed to be any further meeting until the job was done. Far as I know, it isn't. I saw Ned Isaly this morning walking into Tom Kidd's office, unmistakably alive."

"Don't be testy, Bobby. This ain't as public as Michael's. Nice office." Candy looked around.

"The job is finished, as far as we're concerned." Karl drew an envelope from an inside pocket; he was sitting near enough to the desk that he could skid it across the polished mahogany. "The advance. It's all there except expenses incurred. Pittsburgh Hilton, that kind of thing."

Bobby looked at the envelope as if it were a package of vipers that he'd dearly love to toss back. "So you can't do it? That's what you're saying?" Bobby sneered, or at least tried to; a sneer in this company wasn't easy. "Clive?" He turned then to Clive as if offering him the job.

Clive shrugged. If a shrug could look happy, this was it.

"But that ain't all, Bobby," said Karl. "We got a couple things to take up with you, things we want done."

Bobby stared at them in genuine disbelief. "Things *you* want— done?" He laughed abruptly and turned to Clive again.

The happy shrug returned, even happier.

"Things *you* want done," Bobby said it again, shaking his head. "I don't think so. Now why don't you just get out of here. Fuck off." He fluttered his fingers toward the office door.

Clive looked from Bobby to Karl and Candy, this time a trifle nervously. Was Bobby so totally unaware of life going on outside of himself and his little publishing fiefdom that he thought he controlled everything? Including these two? Hadn't he, for God's sakes, read Danny Zito's book while leafing through it?

Karl and Candy looked at each other as if questioning the wisdom of the term: " 'Fuck off.' Bobby says 'Fuck off,' K. Does he really mean us?"

"Yeah, I heard him, C. You talking to us, Bobby?"

Clive thought this sounded exactly like Robert De Niro in *Taxi Driver*. Karl even looked like him. Clive had never noticed this before.

Bobby looked up from the pages he was marking up, pretending to think the two of them had already gone. "Get lost."

Clive squirmed. But he was enjoying it.

Karl looked at Candy in mock surprise. " 'Get lost.' That's in case we didn't understand 'Fuck off.' " His expression settled in a little. "Now, Bobby, listen up: all we want is for you to ensure Ned Isaly's book, his new book, makes it to the *TBR* best-seller list. (Their time spent in Swill's had definitely not been in vain.) No no, hear me out—" He held up his hand to stave off whatever reply might be coming from Bobby's dropped-down mouth. "It don't have to *begin* in the top ten; it don't have to suddenly *appear* there in a hail of bullets—"

(Clive liked that analogy a lot.)

"—it's okay if it's on that 'extended' list for a couple weeks. After all, Ned's stuff is a far cry from Dwight Staines—which is a relief— and since Ned's literary, and, well, it's hard getting that on the list at all. But we insist it's in the top ten for the rest of the time, say, five or six weeks. At least five or six, maybe seven's better. And maybe it ought to crawl up to the top five, now we're talking about it—"

Candy shook his head, "Top ten, K. We ain't asking for miracles. If Ned's never been on the list before, then top ten's a real victory, right?"

Karl brooded. "It should be top five, a good writer like him. He should be in the top five."

"You're both nuts." Bobby's hand shot to the telephone.

Synchronized as the Rockettes, choreographed by Bob Fosse, liquid as Twyla Tharp, in one fluid motion they thrust their hands inside their Armani jackets (deconstructed for just this relaxed effect) and pulled out guns.

Frozen silence. They shoved the slides up and back. In that still room, they made a noise like Niagara.

Clive felt a jolt of electricity, a rush of adrenaline putting his senses on red alert. It was not an unpleasant feeling. How often did he ever have it? But were these the amiable "Waltzing Matilda" boys of the Pittsburgh group? Even hit men had their lighter side, he supposed.

Karl continued. "That's the first thing—the list. Understood?"

Bobby slammed himself farther back in his chair. "You're—" (He wanted to say "crazy" but looked again at the black muzzles pointed his way.) "—kidding. I don't control the best-seller lists. Nobody does. Nobody but the public, the reading public, the ones who buy the books."

Candy and Karl both laughed richly and shook their heads.

Karl tipped his hat back on his head and said, "Bobby, the *public* doesn't control anything. They are controlled by whoever or whatever blows the strongest wind their way. And in addition, Bobby, there's one thing our line of work has taught us and that is nothing, *nothing,* is impossible if you want it done *enough.* You'd be surprised." Karl raised the gun a fraction.

Bobby made a dismissive noise that brought Candy to his feet, gun hand propped in his other hand. "Shit, K. This guy don't know any more about marketing than my aunt Fanny. Lemme cork him up."

Bobby's eyes grew several sizes rounder before Karl motioned Candy down. "It's okay, C. Bobby here'll see reason."

"Reason—" Bobby's voice was a rasp. "You walk in here with guns and that's *reasonable*?"

"Kindly remember who brought us to this ugly pass in the first place," said Candy as he raised the gun fractionally.

"Impasse," said Karl.

"Impasse. You seemed to think then we were being real reasonable. So 'be reasonable' really means 'Do what I want, sucker, just don't do it to me.'"

Bobby opened his mouth.

"Stop interrupting, Christ's sake, we'll be here all day. Clive"—Karl's head made a little motion toward the door—"see what the girl's doing and tell her to do it someplace else."

Clive felt a fresh wave of self-respect wash over him. They considered him to be one of them; they were treating him as an ally. He walked over and opened the door just enough to get his head through and told Amy to go down to the café off the lobby and bring back whatever everybody wanted. To take someone else with her so she didn't have to make several trips. Then Clive withdrew, gave Candy and Karl the thumb's-up, and went back to his perch by the window.

"So, Bobby, we're agreed on the *TBR* list."

"Goddamnit, I told you, I can't—"

Karl shut his eyes, pained. "Haven't you been listening, asshole? Say I walk into a bookstore looking for something to read. Now, what am I likely to pick up? A book that's buried in the back or a book that's in my face everywhere I turn? A book that's *all over* the fucking place. Get real, man. You *pay* for what you want in this world, as you sure ought to know." He pointed the gun barrel at the envelope that still lay where it had been tossed on the desk.

Bobby leaned back, stuck his hands behind his head, and put his feet back up on the desk.

Apparently, thought Clive, Bobby couldn't see that he was not the puppeteer in this situation, wasn't plying the strings, or that this was not an occasion for pomposity, for he said, pompously, "We don't control the middleman—"

Whereupon, Candy was up. "I'm gonna clip the little fucker, K."

Bobby went white and quickly returned to his victim's position, arms and legs down.

Karl motioned to Candy, who sat down, reluctantly.

"Thing is, you know you're lying. Lying or plain stupid and we don't think you're stupid."

Clive saw Bobby actually smile. His ego was so huge he didn't consider it to be any less of a compliment that it came from a guy with a gun in his hand.

Karl went on. "As I was trying to say before, but apparently you weren't listening, you control whatever you pay to control. Tell the bookstores you're putting out a mil to promote this book, they buy more copies. They sell more copies. You buy space up front, you hawk dumps. Then they put the book up front. You do this for bestselling authors; it's nothing new. You pay the chains to do this; it's what you might call a hostile collaboration. In the case of Ned's book, you just pay even more. Maybe a mil and a half, even two. I'll say it clearer: you can buy *anything* and you, of course, goddamned well know it. Bottom line is, we see Ned Isaly's book on the *TBR* next year"—he raised the barrel slightly to point at Bobby's forehead and added—"or we come back."

"Yeah," said Candy with an evil grin, his pupils glittering like sequins. "We come back."

"There's another thing we want to remind you. And this you better believe: Ned Isaly better not meet up with an accident. So pray he's careful crossing streets and turning off the gas. You better pray he don't get mugged—"

"You can't hold me responsible for something like that. Christ, every other person in New York gets mugged."

"Really? Then hope he only meets up with the other fifty percent."

Candy said, "Now, Paul Giverney, how about him?"

"Yeah. Paul Giverney, the writer you're trying to sign. What we want to know is, was hiring us done at his suggestion? Was murder his idea?"

No one said anything, letting "murder" swing slowly from a noose of air.

"Yes," said Bobby. His eyes traveled the room, lit behind him on Clive. "Yes, it was Giverney's idea. And Clive's."

"Wha—?"

"It was you Giverney talked to, not me." Bobby tossed this over his shoulder at Clive, not bothering to look at him.

"So, it was Clive's idea?"

"Yes."

"Which means no," said Candy.

Bobby got up in a sudden burst of bravado but was quickly waved back to his chair by two guns in motion.

Karl said, "We know old Clive here. In this business you get you can read character. Clive would never have thought this up."

Candy put in, "But you would, you little dipshit."

"So had Giverney signed a contract?"

"No." "Yes." Both Bobby and Clive spoke together.

Bobby stared at Clive. "What? When, for Christ's sake? And you didn't tell me?"

"That's what I came in here to tell you. We got—sidetracked."

"So you can die happy," said Candy. "Just a figure of speech, Bobby." He snickered.

"One last thing," said Karl. He pulled another envelope from his pocket, tossed it on the desk.

"What's this?" asked Bobby.

"Ticket."

"What the fuck are you talking about?"

"To Australia. Didn't you always want to see Australia? Melbourne? The Outback? Sydney Opera House? Kangaroos? We're sending you."

"I can't—"

"Bobby, you're always saying that. Sure, you can. For a while, six months maybe. You get back in time to take over the marketing of Ned's book. To convince everybody on your staff that no holds'll be barred. You can leave ol' Clive here in charge."

Bobby gave Clive a lethal look.

"Look," said Candy, "it coulda been worse."

Bobby moved the lethal look from Clive to Karl. "How?"

"We coulda written a book."

Candy and Karl howled.

FORTY-TWO

Sally sat at her desk reading the book about Pittsburgh she had brought back. What she supposed she meant to accomplish by doing this was to be able to talk to Ned about the city. The one she was looking at now was heavy with illustrations and old newspaper photos.

Was he interested in the actual history of the place? Or was he interested only in its symbolic history? He did not know about the Pirates' wins and losses over the years, or who the team's coach was, or how many people had filled Forbes Field. What he wanted to think about was the rush the spectators must have felt when Roberto Clemente slammed the ball out of the park; the way the clouds looked massed in the gray . . .

Maybe that's not the history that draws me. He had said that a long time ago, arguing with Jamie. *Maybe that's not the real history.*

Tom Kidd came to stand in the door of his office. He'd been closeted or barricaded behind his stacks of books for twenty-four hours. She bet he hadn't gone home and probably hadn't eaten since that coffee cake Amy had brought around. Bobby's treat. Tom had been reading Saul's manuscript for a whole day and night and part of another day. He looked goggle eyed.

"Tom?"

He turned the empty eyes on her. Who're you?

He went back into his office.

When she looked out into the busy room—not as bad as a newspaper, perhaps, but not far behind—she saw Clive wandering in and out and around the cubicles like a bum with an empty cup. He looked slightly delirious. A few people called after him, rising to look over the cubicle walls, calling their congratulations, or perhaps they were hectoring him.

Sally hoped he'd pass her by (but here he came) because she had too much on her mind to deal with Clive.

But of course he didn't pass; he stopped by her desk, lit a cigar (Bobby's Cuban) and dropped into the wooden chair. "Sally."

"What's going on? Did you finally sign up Paul Giverney?"

For everyone was waiting for this.

"Yep."

"That's wonderful, Clive! I'm really happy for you." It surprised her that she was. But he looked so happy himself that it was hard to feel her usual antipathy toward him. And then she thought, but he's changed in the couple of weeks. He'd certainly changed since Pittsburgh. What a strange experience that had been.

Sunken cheeked, he sucked in on his cigar, turned it in his mouth, withdrew it, exhaled, and said, "That ain't all, Sal–"

Ain't? *Sal?*

"–Bobby's taking a holiday. Six months, maybe longer. I'm taking over for him."

What was going on? "Clive–?"

"Cheap thrills." Tom must have picked up on something going

on for he was standing in the door again. But he said this in a sporting, kidding way.

Sally was again surprised by her reaction to Clive's news. As though she'd been heavy with a weight that now lifted. If Bobby was leaving, if the contract was signed, then he'd have no reason to get rid of Ned.

Clive left and Tom went back inside his office, to leave Sally wondering about Paul Giverney. What was he like? Really like? From what she had gathered, he was bossy, arrogant, self-indulgent, a writer who commanded several million per book. Yet he had seemed pleasant enough when he stopped by her desk.

Sally was mooning over Giverney when Tom came to the door a third time, this time with Saul's manuscript in his hands. "I'm dead and gone to the sweet hereafter. Go make a copy of this and don't leave the copy machine until it's finished. And don't tell anybody what it is. But first, get me Jimmy McKinney on the line."

But of course it got around like wildfire. The buzz over Saul's book was exceeded only by the furor over Paul Giverney. To have cornered either of these writers was a coup; to get both of them was nothing short of miraculous. The parade could commence down Fifth, filled with ticker tape and confetti. All the other publishers could lay down their books; it was war's end.

Though Mackenzie-Haack hadn't actually signed up Saul, they would. He didn't have a publisher or even an agent—which might have been the reason for calling Jimmy McKinney, whom Tom probably meant to recommend.

To have both Ned and Saul under this roof, and Tom Kidd as their editor, made Sally happier than she'd been at any time in the last year. She returned to the Pittsburgh book, grinning at every line, and in this frame of mind her eyes skipped over the text, barely touching.

Thus, she would have missed it had there not been a picture of an Isaly's Ice Cream parlor, taken back in the forties, with several employees out front, smiling and squinting into the sun and holding the ever-popular ice cream scoop, like the one Ned kept on the shelf beside the picture of himself and three others, in front of the shop they worked in.

It wasn't the caption, but something in the picture that made her draw in her breath.

Oh, no, she thought. *Oh, dear.*

The caption read: *"Outside one of Pittsburgh's famous ice cream parlors."*

One of the people in the row, a teenage boy smiling beamishly, was holding a small sign, printed with the Isaly name, and more than the name.

"Isaly" wasn't a family name—or at least, it looked as if it wasn't the family name of the ice cream kingdom. Here, it was an acronym: *I.S.A.L.Y.*

I Shall Always Love You.

Ned wasn't an ice cream Isaly. Sally leaned her head in her hands. She just couldn't help it; she wept.

I SHALL
ALWAYS
LOVE
YOU

FORTY-THREE

He was standing by his window, the one that looked down at the Luxembourg Gardens (or so Ned liked to imagine the little park), where Nathalie still sat on the green bench where he had left her. No, she was holding a letter and that meant she would have had to go back to the Ile St.-Louis to her apartment.

When had she done that?

Ned waited. He thought. He knew the source of the letter. Should she just hold it? Or should she read it?

"My dearest Nathalie, we both knew this had to end sometime—"

She wanted to tear the paper to shreds. It was that "we both knew" that made her furious, the furor nearly blocking out the sadness like the cloud that had just moved over the sun. We both knew. Patric had never shown such cowardice before; but when, she asked herself, had he ever been called upon for a show of valor? Or even backbone? Had she ever made any demand on him or tried to force

him to choose? No, because she'd known how he'd choose. So per-
haps it was she who was the coward.

"We both knew . . ." Yes, but had she? She had always feared
it, but had she actually known the end would come? And the letter
went on in its base and fainthearted way about this trip to Roque-
brun, how it would be the occasion of his parting from Nathalie.
He could not do it in person . . .

Ned thought he saw her turn on the bench and look up at his
window, at him. And she said,

Why have you done this? Why couldn't this story have ended a lit-
tle more happily? Or at least in a more sanguine state—?

Because I didn't know it was ending, Ned thought.

Then I'm to sit here forever?

No.

Then what? What, then? I can't move by myself. That's always
been the problem. I must sit here because you've left me here, hold-
ing this letter and very likely weeping forever because you've had a
failure of nerve. You think it would be sentimental—

No, that isn't it. Nathalie and Patric don't belong together.

Don't talk about me as if I'm not in the room, damn you!

All right: you and Patric don't belong together. You couldn't
have made a life together.

Because of his wife and children? You mean they would always be on his mind? What a cliché!

No, that's not why. It's because you don't really love each other.

What? What? Those nights in my flat, those long weekends in Provence—?

You're talking about passion. That's a strange way of describing love, if you stop to think about it. Love is much more the breathing in of everyday air. Look: you don't have to take the blame for all of this. It's not all down to you. There's Patric. He's been far more self-ish than you.

And he's not here to defend himself, is he?

He doesn't need to be. You'll defend him.
She started to say something, and stopped. She tried to leave the bench, and couldn't.

Ned, look: you've brought me all this way; you've watched me over four hundred pages; we've wandered—with not much happening, I might add—

Your tone is unnecessarily acidic, isn't it?

—through the Jardin des Plantes and the Luxembourg Gardens—oh! How much time we've spent there! All of those cafés on the Right Bank (the Gold Coast, you called that), the Rue de Rivoli, the Boulevard Haussman; we walked around the Ile de la Cité and Notre Dame—

Unavoidable, in any book about Paris, you'll agree.

—the Boulevard St.-Germain, Florian's and the Deux Magots, Hemingway's haunts (used entirely too much in fiction, you'll agree?).

And now you're going to end this with my sitting here on this bench in the Luxembourg Gardens—in the rain, incidentally; it's started to rain—with this letter in my hand and Patric gone and nothing to show for this four-year affair—that's how long it's taken you to have me wind up with nothing. Four years wasted—

But I don't think—

You could at least let me get hold of a gun and go to Roquebrun and shoot him. It's nothing to you; it wouldn't hurt you and it would allow me to repay him—not to mention it would make a sensational ending that would sell far more copies of this novel than what you've got planned. Which is nothing.

An ending like that could easily come back to haunt me.

It's always about you, isn't it? You! You never think of anybody but yourself! So I'm to be left with this (she held up the letter) and Patric gets off scotfree, that's to be the end!

But he doesn't get off. He really suffers.

Oh, really? And how is it I don't seem to see anything about that here?

(Ned could almost hear her shuffling through today's manuscript pages.) He said, it's not written down; the thing is, you should know he suffers because of the sort of man Patric is—

No. That was a lie. Patric doesn't suffer much, the bastard. But he could hardly tell Nathalie this.

You know this was hard for him. You know he was torn. You know he loves you. You know all . . . Lies, again. Patric was never torn. His jealousy—and certainly he'd been jealous—was not a mark of love but of ego. He couldn't stand the idea of another man with Nathalie, even though he wasn't, most of the time, with her himself. But Ned couldn't say that to her, either. So he said again to her: You know how he'll suffer.

There was a long silence.

I'll think about it, she said, and turned her face away.

The shadows were turning into night. She tried to see her future; it was full of blank pages. They fluttered away like the pages of a calendar in a film, dated but empty.

Nathalie did not know why she was here, or where she would go after here, or even who she was. There was nothing to hold her to the gardens or the page.

Ned recapped his pen and looked at these few lines. If it had been worth saying at all, he'd said it. There was just nothing else to say. He put these pages with the others and sat for a moment staring at them. Then he put a rubber band around the manuscript. And sat looking down at it, wondering why he'd done this, why he'd ended it this way.

He didn't have that sense of exhilaration he'd felt after the last book, after finishing any piece of writing. He was not really very proud of himself.

He had wanted to see how far she'd go, and so he'd cut her loose. She had not spread her wings, she had not broken away even though there was nothing to hold her to the gardens or the page.

FORTY-FOUR

They had gone to the Old Hotel for dinner to celebrate the fact that both Ned and Saul had finished their novels. Sally insisted this was a cause for celebration. Saul had added, "Or cause for alarm."

"Saul, Saul, Saul, don't be ridiculous."

"Sally, Sally, Sally, you haven't read the manuscript."

"You look about as hopeful as my last romance," said Jamie, stabbing the tiny fork toward Sally that she'd received with her clams and refused to surrender to the waiter when he'd cleared the plates away.

Jamie meant, of course, her last Mardi Gras Publications romance, but Sally thought the phrase quite lovely. "My Last Romance." Had it been a popular song at some point? Then Sally started thinking about Jamie's books and felt the alarm Saul had hardly been serious about. Sally didn't feel up to being the only person at the table who wasn't even working on a book, much less finishing one, much less about to publish one.

"Haven't you finished another book?" Sally asked.

Jamie answered, "No. God, but I only wish I had. It's one of the mysteries. I can't solve it."

Sally frowned. "Don't you know the solution when you start, though?"

"You mean, how it ends? Christ, no. It's boring enough as it is, but at least I have the advantage of not knowing what's going to happen so I can surprise myself."

"But . . . how's that an advantage? I'd think you'd be on tenterhooks." For some reason, Jamie's not knowing worried Sally. "And what about all those loose ends?"

Jamie shrugged. "Life's full of loose ends. Every day looks like it's been through a paper shredder. And not knowing what's going to happen is an advantage because you don't have to do all that thinking and making up family charts—you know, who belongs where and when; and you don't have to make up character descriptions and that sort of junk."

"But, Jamie, you've got to do all that *sometime.*"

"Yes, but you can keep putting it off. You look shocked," Jamie said and laughed. "Look: you should write a book and see where it goes. You just keep writing and writing and try not to think too much. Half the writers in Manhattan have writer's block because they don't hew to that simple rule."

"*What* rule? The way you put it there *is* no rule."

"Well, not if you're looking at it in some Henry Jamesian way."

Sally looked at her, utterly perplexed.

Ned came out of the stupor brought on by Nathalie, a stupor augmented by two bourbons and two bottles of wine, not to mention the grilled clams, the duck, and now this dessert of baked figs Grand Marnier, asking, "Why Henry James? What Jamesian way?"

Jamie said, "Don't you think he had his books all plotted out and drowning in detail before he started? All of those perfectly carved paragraphs, all of those sentences as taut as piano wire. Pluck one and it resonates, right?"

"Yes, but that doesn't necessarily mean his plot was set before he started." Ned took a bite of fig lathered in whipped cream and thought what a comfort food was, and why all of those diet books failed.

"Anyway, Sally," Jamie went on, "you've been around writers long enough you surely can't think there's some mysterious something about book writing. Some trick, some trick to it that maybe Saul or Ned could tell you and then you could do it, too?"

Sally's face flamed up. She had to admit to herself that that's exactly what she'd been thinking. Of course, she got defensive. "Talent. You have to have talent."

"Whatever the hell *that* is. This dessert—wow!" Jamie went on, "You take out your yellow legal pad and pen and just start." Her hand scribbled in air.

"Oh, come on, Jamie." Anxiety was building in Sally. "A person has at least to have some *idea*."

Jamie chewed her figs Grand Marnier while she looked at Sally, swallowed, and said, "About what? I never started a book with an idea in my life. If you want to write a mystery, just start with a body draped over a gate. If it's set in England, make it a dry stone wall."

"You make it sound so damned easy."

"I didn't say it was easy, for God's sakes. Try describing a body thrown over a dry stone wall and you'll see it isn't easy. My new one begins with a dismembered body in a rowboat. Only I'm afraid I might have stolen that from P. D. James. That would be a bummer."

"What's up with you? Or down?" Saul said to Ned, who'd slipped back into his fugue state.

"Nothing."

346

"Ned can't stand ending a book. Unlike you—" Jamie pointed the little devil's fork toward Saul.

Saul just gave her a look and turned to look down into the Lobby. His chair was closest to the railing. "I'll be damned," he said. "Guess who's here?"

"Who?"

"Who?"

"The two suits. Well, I guess that description doesn't fit anymore. They were here the other night, too. Maybe they come every night, who knows? The moving business must be lucrative."

Ned got out of his chair to have a look at the Lobby. "You know you live your entire life without seeing a person, and then he's everywhere. What the hell were they doing in Pittsburgh? And there's that other guy, too. What was his name? Alfred?"

"Arthur," said Saul, who was leaning farther over the black iron railing. "Yeah, that's him. He's a friend, isn't he?"

Now Sally and Jamie were out of their chairs, leaning over the railing.

Jamie frowned. "Do I know them?"

"You weren't in Pittsburgh or you would."

"Thank God I wasn't."

"You saw them in Swill's. In the last couple of weeks they seem always to be there."

Now, Candy and Karl looked up, and then Arthur did. The three of them waved to the ones on the mezzanine.

"Oh, yeah," said Jamie. "The two goons."

Three pairs of eyes stared at her. "You know, hit men."

The other three burst out laughing. Saul said, "In the Old Hotel? Hit men? Somehow I don't think that exactly meets the Duffian criteria, do you?"

Ned sat down and ate his dessert. "I told you yesterday, didn't I tell you, I had this feeling I was being watched, I mean all the while in Shadyside and Schenley Park. And that whole business going on in the street, the guns, the red Porsche?"

Sally and Saul had returned to their figs.

Jamie asked, "What whole business? Wait! Are you talking about what's been on the news? Are you talking about the missing baby? You mean you were actually *there*?"

Irritated by this whole idea, Saul tossed down his napkin. "There's no missing baby, for God's sakes." He exhaled cigar smoke. A veil of it hid his eyes.

"How do you know? Were you there, too?"

"No. I was in the Hilton. Having a nap," said Saul.

"Well, then, you wouldn't know. They think the baby was kidnapped by someone in a red Ferrari."

"Porsche," said Saul. When she gave him another look, he added, "Well, that's what these idiot TV newspeople are saying."

Jamie turned again to Ned. "You saw it all go down?"

"Not really. By the time I'd turned back and wondered what was going on, it had all happened."

"But you'd still be considered a material—my latest is a police procedural—witness."

"They did question me, or at least one cop. But I couldn't give him any information except for seeing the red car driving away."

"Didn't you get the plate number?"

Ned was getting irritated. "Of course not. Why would I? How was I to know the car would be important?"

"How do we know it actually *was* important?" said Saul.

"Because they're saying the baby was probably handed over to the driver of the Porsche."

Saul dropped his demitasse spoon on his saucer. "Do you know how insane that sounds, Jamie?"

Jamie gave him a look. "It's not *my*—"

"Very, very, very insane. I mean we might be able to conceive of the baby's being snatched from the carriage, but from there to the Porsche is just too much of a stretch."

"But then what happened to the baby? And what about the mother? Where was she?" Jamie turned to Ned.

Who shrugged. "Gone. Vanished."

"The ten o'clock news had an interview with a behavioral psychologist who said he thought the mother's disappearance was more shocking than the baby's kidnapping, that it was just one more example—"

"Who knows if there *was* a fucking kidnapping?" Saul said.

"—of the sort of throwaway lives we continue to lead. But wait a minute! If the mum disappeared and the baby did, *too,* why wouldn't they have gone together?"

"Why would she leave without the carriage?" said Sally.

"Maybe there was evidence—exculpatory evidence."

"What?"

"My book's a courtroom drama, too. Maybe the baby carriage was filled with cocaine? Maybe Saul's right and there wasn't any baby! Cocaine and heroin stashed under the baby blanket."

"Remind me," said Ned, "not to read this book."

Saul dropped his head in his hands, washed them down over his face, and brought them to rest in a prayerful position over his mouth. "This conversation is crazy." He tilted his chair back, motioned to the waiter several tables over, then mimed the signing of the check.

The waiter came toward the table, scribbling on a check, which he presented in its dark blue holder to Saul. Was there anything else? There wasn't.

Jamie snatched the blue holder away, saying Saul was one of the celebrants and he couldn't pay for this dinner.

Saul thanked her and asked, "Are we all through?" in a tone that suggested they'd better be, especially Jamie. "Let's go to Swill's."

The four rose and trailed down the vast staircase, at the bottom of which stood Candy and Karl and Arthur. They all said hello, Candy and Karl being especially effusive at their chance meeting here.

Saul said, "You guys seem to be turning up everywhere. It doesn't look exactly like chance anymore, you know?"

Candy laughed. "That's just what Larry here was saying about you. He said he wondered if maybe you were following us." The three laughed heartily.

Arthur frowned. "Larry? Who the hell's Lar—"

Karl shut him up by stepping on his foot and introducing him to Jamie. And reintroducing him to the others. "You know Art—"

"Arthur." Arthur scowled.

"Sorry, *Arthur.* Anyway, you remember him from Pittsburgh?"

"I feel," said Ned, "I've known him all my life."

The four of them—or was it the seven of them?—left the Old Hotel and headed for Swill's.

FORTY-FIVE

Five minutes after they got there, Johnnie Ray was belting out "Please, Mr. Sun," which meant that Jamie had made a beeline for the jukebox and that "Please, Mr. Sun" would be followed by "Cry" with, possibly, a lettuce-leaf palate cleansing of an old Bobby Darin speciality, something slow, like "What a Difference a Day Makes."

"Your Johnnie is the only singer I know who can spread a word like 'please' over the course of four syllables," said Saul. "No? Just listen."

And Johnnie sang: "Pul-ul-ul-eeeez Mi-is-ter-uh Sun . . ."

"Oh," said Jamie, "stop exaggerating."

"I'm not exaggerating; Johnnie is. Not even Elvis stretched a syllable that far, and he could really beat up on a syllable. It's a kind of tuneful stutter," Saul added.

They were standing at the bar, politely waiting for a group of strangers to surrender their table in the window. That is, Saul and Sally were politely waiting. Candy and Karl were about to remove the little group of four and were deciding on the best way to do it.

"Come on, leave 'em alone," said Saul.

"You kiddin'? They got our table!"

Swill's was more crowded than usual, as if everyone downtown had come to celebrate what would be the publishing event of the year.

"Where's Ned?" asked Sally, turning as if she had expected to see him when she turned, but didn't. She was anxious. She'd been anxious all evening about Ned, partly because she was always anxious about Ned, partly because of that I.S.A.L.Y. acronym. She didn't know whether to tell him or not. She was not going to tell anybody else, for sure. It would end up being her secret alone, she supposed. This depressed her.

" . . . *and tuh-ake her under your bur-ur-ran-ches, Mi-is-ter-uh Tu-ree-ree.*"

Ned was standing at the window behind their table, not trying to hurry the group of four away but just standing and looking out of the window. He was looking out into what would have been darkness and rain to any other observer. To Ned, it was also darkness and rain, but he thought he could see through it; indeed, he did see through it, he could see across the street and into the park where a single lamp illuminated its small patch of ground—the bench, the walk, the tree.

He was afraid it would be empty, that bench, those gardens, the Jardin des Plantes, the Luxembourg Gardens. He was afraid he'd seen Nathalie for the last time and this was what had depressed him the entire evening. But now he made out a figure, dark haired, dark coated, her face as white as the letter she still held. She was waiting for something, for him to do something. And he remembered her crying that she couldn't leave on her own.

When Ned set his beer down on the occupied table ("their" table), the people sitting there looked at him, puzzled. He said nothing, just pulled on his anorak and made his way through the crowd to the door. Sally's voice followed him, asking where he was going and sounding anxious; Johnnie Ray's voice followed him with "Cry" and sounded even more anxious:

"Whe-en you-r-r-r Su-WEET-ha-art sends a lu-ET-ter-r of good-by-uh-eye-eye—"

He stood on the pavement across the dark, rain-slicked street, looking into the park. Was she going to argue with him again? Demand a rewrite? Tell him this scene and that scene with Patric was a total wreck, a waste, a pack of lies? That Ned did not deserve a character such as she?

But what she did do was move. She rose from the bench (no help from Ned), shoved the letter in her black pocket, and walked away down the path. Turned after a few feet, gave him a little wave and a little smile.

"Nathalie!"

He started across the street, too distracted to see the car that had pulled away from the curb bearing down on him.

Sally screamed.

Sally had been waiting all day to scream, and the people behind her, Saul, Karl, Candy, and most of the Swill's population swarmed out onto the sidewalk.

Someone yelled, "Call 911!"

A dozen cell phones were already in hand and in operation. The ones who had reached the pavement first had tried, but had failed to see the plate of the car that, though it had been going quite slow when it rammed Ned, immediately picked up speed and was now careening around a corner three blocks up the street.

Saul and Sally bent over Ned. She was crying.

Ned looked up, blinked as he opened his mouth and started to say something, but Saul cut him off. "Don't talk."

Ned paid no attention to him. He blinked, slow as a cat and said weakly, breathily, "That no-good fucker, Patric . . . that jealous son of a bitch . . . why did I—?" Then his head lolled to one side and rested on the pavement.

"Oh, *shit!*" said Saul.

"He ain't dead," said Candy. "He just passed out. Believe me, we know the difference."

Karl said, "Where's the fuckin' ambulance? Why can't you ever get an ambulance in this fuckin' town?" He asked this of the night in general, just as the ambulance came sliding around the same corner the car had taken a few moments before.

After Ned had been loaded in and Sally gone, too, to sit with him, and the ambulance bulleted off, siren screaming, the crowd dispersed with a lot of head shakings and sad murmurings.

Candy said, "I don't bloody believe this, K."

"Me either. I'm thinking . . . who do we like for this?"

"Who in-fucking-deed do we like for this? That son of a bitch, Mackenzie, that's who."

"Yeah, except"—Arthur passed his finger around the inside of his collar as if it were too tight and asked—"who the fuck's Patrick?"

FORTY-SIX

When Paul opened the door of his apartment to the two men, he was instantly glad that Molly had gone to that foreign film with her friends. He was also glad that Hannah was asleep in her bed at the far end of the hall.

"Paul Giverney?" asked the shorter one.

"I am. But how did you get up here? Clarence is supposed to announce anyone who comes in." Paul's antennae were jittering around.

"Clarence? Oh, you mean the guy at the front desk? Well, we didn't exactly come in that way."

"No," said Karl. "Being announced kind of takes away the element of surprise." He smiled broadly.

"Oh, I don't know," said Paul. "The gun would probably keep the surprise fairly undiluted."

Candy and Karl looked at each other and, having worked out "undiluted surprise," both laughed. "He's Candy, I'm Karl, Mr. Giverney. We have a mutual acquaintance?"

Arthur. Who else? Paul hadn't been as circumspect as Arthur in divulging his address. Not that it would have been hard for these two goons to find him, anyway. "Well, look. I've never been good making small talk in the hallway with a gun in my face. You know?" He managed a bitter little smile; he was scared witless.

"Oh. All right." Candy said this a little sadly, as if playtime were over, and stuck the gun between his back and his belt.

(Paul noted that for the next conversation he had with Sammy Giancarlo.)

Candy was smiling. "All we want to do is have a little talk with you, Mr. Giverney. Actually, we just have a couple of questions. Could we come in, do you think?"

"By all means," said Paul, bowing fractionally and extending his arm. "My study's just down the hall, there."

They followed him. The room was small, but there were two chairs in addition to Paul's own swivel chair—a club chair and a chair with fancy scrolled woodwork that had always struck Paul as vaguely Oriental. They all sat down and, for a moment, made a study of one another.

Candy said, "Listen, before we have that little talk, I just want to say I think your book's terrific. *Don't Go There?*" Candy added, as if Paul might have forgotten what book Candy was talking about.

Paul was so surprised he lurched back in his chair as if the gun had gone off near his head. "I'm . . . uh . . . glad you liked it."

"Maybe you'd sign my copy?" Candy held up the book he'd been carrying.

Paul wanted to laugh out loud, but didn't know how safe that would be. "How about I sign it after you tell me what it is you want?" It was nice to have a bargaining chip, even one so slight as an autograph.

Candy tucked the book between himself and the chair arm. He

had taken the club chair, Karl the Oriental-looking one whose woodwork he kept inspecting as if he were valuing it. "This is one fuckin' chair, Mr. G."

"Mr. G."? Was this to be the sobriquet he was hence to be known by? And after he was dead? He said, "Late Fung dynasty. A good example."

Karl frowned and looked at Paul almost with suspicion, as if Paul were pushing baby powder and calling it cocaine. "I never heard of that period."

I know you idiot; that's because I made it up.

"Karl reads a lot. And he likes antiques. You should see his place."

"Well, that's what I was told," said Paul. "I'm no expert on Chinese artifacts. Or periods."

Karl said, "I just hope you didn't get ripped off."

"Me too." Paul was beyond irritated. "Look, *why* are you here?"

"Oh, yeah," said Candy. "That."

"That"?

"We wanted to talk about Ned Isaly. Ned had an accident. He's in the hospital—"

Paul cut in. "Yes, I know about that. We have the same agent and the agent called me right away. It's too bad, but I don't think it's life threatening." Like you two are.

"Why'd he have this 'accident'?"

"Why? Am I supposed to know?"

Karl said, "We thought you might know something. It was a hit-and-run."

Suddenly, Paul's adrenaline shot through him like a bolt of lightning. "I know it was, but what's that have to do with me?"

"Could be a lot, Paul. See, here's Ned, who just managed to escape getting shot in Pittsburgh by assailant or assailants unknown—"

Paul was shaking his head and clearing the air with his hands, "Hold it, hold it. This Arthur Mordred is a friend of yours, right?"

"Right, but what's that got to do with the price of eggs?"

"Well, for Christ's sake, didn't he tell you?"

"Tell us what?"

"That I hired him to watch Ned Isaly. As a *bodyguard,* not an assassin!"

Candy looked at Karl and Karl at Candy as if neither of them could believe his ears. "No, he didn't tell us. You think we go around discussing our work?" said Candy.

"You think we meet up and high-five each other and say, 'Yo! I just took on a job to whack Ned Isaly. So how's *your* day?'" Karl put in. "What we do, what we take on is done in the strictest confidence. We can't go around comparing dicks, for God's sakes."

Paul shot his hands out, scrubbing at air again. "Okay, okay, I get the idea. Nevertheless, I hired Arthur to see no harm came to Ned. That's the truth. You can certainly ask Arthur. If you want we can all meet and he'll back me up."

They were both silent, studying Paul.

Then Karl said, "Thing is, we don't like coincidences. Don't it seem to you that a hit-and-run coming right on top of the Pittsburgh thing—"

"'The Pittsburgh *thing*'? You think I forced Ned to go to Pittsburgh?"

"No, no. But don't you think it's a hell of a coincidence we're hired to cap Ned and don't do it and then he's hit by a car?"

Paul leaned forward; indeed he rolled his swivel chair toward them as if they might see sense if he sat closer. "Now, listen: first of all, it was not my idea to hire you two—('goons' was bitten off just in time) guys to kill off Ned. Of *course,* I didn't! You two were hired by crazy Bobby Mackenzie because he couldn't figure out any other way to get me to sign a contract with Mackenzie-Haack."

"Yeah, we figured that had something to do with it," said Karl, wagging his finger at Paul. "But it's still your fault; you're the one started this whole thing. What in hell do you have against Ned Isaly?"

Paul started to reply, but Karl enjoyed being in a speculative mood and continued: "We thought maybe, seeing both of you come from Pittsburgh, that maybe you and Ned were in school together? And he did something to you when you were kids? Something real horrible?"

It was clear Karl wanted the something real horrible to have happened, not just to clear up the mystery, but horrible for its own sake. Paul sighed. We're all such sentimentalists, even these men with guns shoved down into their belts, even they go for the easy explanation, the quick fix, the uncomplicated motive, with no ambiguity, no play of light and darkness, no shading, no nuance.

Paul smiled. "Like maybe I ratted him out for something? Made him take a blame he didn't deserve? Got him kicked off the team? Stole his girl or fucked his mother?"

They liked that last alternative, Paul thought, as their lips pursed and their eyes narrowed. Yes, that would really be an act demanding retribution. Paul was almost disappointed that he couldn't give them the easy out, the clear and undiluted reason he'd done what he'd done. One problem was that he was no longer sure of the motive himself.

He said, "Let me show you something." And he rolled himself and the chair back and left it bouncing as he opened a desk drawer. He had kept the page on which he'd set down his shortlist of publishers and authors. Now he handed it to Karl, saying, "On that you've got a list of three publishers and three writers. Now, you know I could go to any of those houses—"

Candy nodded, rather proud of himself for having picked up a lot of publishing arcana. "Sure, because you're a guarantee of a million-copy sell-through."

Paul looked at him oddly, shrugged. "So given I think publishers these days are so full of shit—not all of them, mind you; there are still one or two good ones—but I think most of them greedy, grasping, immoral, and vicious. Certainly those three. I was curious—no, more than curious: I wanted to see how far they'd go to get me into their stable. What a ghastly expression. Now, come the three writers, all of them very good and with real integrity that keeps their heads above the publishing swamp. Those three very good writers—"

"But Ned's the best," Karl put in, wanting their candidate to win.

"Yes, he is. But the question remained: which of those three, if any of them, could be threatened with a terrible blow to his career, could be having his contract canceled, or rumors spread his wife really wrote his books, or people in the trade otherwise firing away at his reputation? Which of them wouldn't panic? Which wouldn't hire a brace of lawyers and sue? And which—in some very real sense—just wouldn't give a good goddamn?"

Paul went on. "That's a quality I think all of us might have had once, but a quality that went south when the first book got published." Paul rocked himself in his chair, back and forth, back and forth, looking out of the little window at a skinny tree branch as if he were comforting himself. "After that first book which we were deliriously happy to see published, and the hell with whatever the 'publication process' was, after that there was an almost constant nattering away about how much publicity and promotion do I get.

How much money up front–? What? I'm not getting as much as King or Grisham? Go screw yourself. I'm not getting a book tour? Screw yourself twice. What about that snotty review in *Kirkus*? That starred review in *Publishers Weekly*? Reviews, reviews, reviews– tearing our hair out, plagued by jealousy over *that one's* or *this one's* reception, arguments over screen rights, reprint rights, foreign rights, electronic rights, and on and on.

"It used to be writing we cared about; now it's whether we get our own dumps, what kind of placement at Barnes and Noble. Now it's the two-day laydown. Now it's the *TBR* list." Paul had picked up a pencil and was rolling it back and forth over his chair arm, still rocking. "Writers rail against the trash that turns up regularly on the best-seller lists and keeps on hanging around for weeks, months, effectively blocking the appearance of *their* books. But you know what amazes me? Not that dreck appears on the list, *but*–think of it–only fifteen books hit that list on any given Sunday out of thousands. Tens of thousands–so what gets me is the pure arrogance of *any* writer's thinking his book should be on that list."

Candy and Karl listened with interest. They nodded right along, as if Paul were recounting their own history.

Karl said, "Man, it's a cutthroat business. You know, it's disillusioning, isn't it, that all that would creep into the book world? At least the book world, you'd think they'd be more, I dunno, idealistic."

Paul looked at him. He supposed he'd better not tack on that *they'd* crept into the book world. Instead, he sighed. *Say good-bye,* he thought, sadly.

Candy said, "So you're sayin' what you wanted to find out was how bad a publisher could be?"

Paul nodded. "That, and how good a writer can be."

"Like Ned Isaly. Some guy that's like what you were talking about before all of the shit publishing splatters around happens. Maybe you miss it, the old days of writing; maybe you wanted to see them again." Candy cocked his head. "Maybe instead of the bastard we think you are, you're like leading a charge. Something like that. Know what I mean?"

Paul tilted back in his chair, eyes on the ceiling because the eyes seemed to be filling up and if they did too much, the tears could run backward. "Yeah. Not leading a charge; I never did anything courageous in my life. But the old days of writing? I know what you mean."

There was a silence almost sepulchral in its heaviness as if they were gathered around a grave.

"On a cheerier note," said Candy, "we had a little talk with Bobby this morning. Hell, K"–Candy turned to his partner–"and we kind of wonder if it ain't Bobby involved in that hit-and-run." He and Karl, finding this idea humorous, started to laugh.

Paul leaned forward, scarcely able to contain his joy. "You 'had a little talk with' Bobby?"

"We just wanted to get a few things straight about how Ned's book was going to be published. You know, the stuff you were just talking about. To guarantee Ned'll be in the top ten. Starting in the top fifteen then moving up."

Paul laughed. "That's hysterical. But how could he guarantee it?"

Candy raised his eyebrows. "Ain't that being a tad *naïve*, Paul? I mean you're the first person I'd think would figure a publisher can guarantee just about anything, as long as he spends the money, and we just wanted to make sure Bobby's going to spend a *lot* of money. Yeah, Bobby's going to see to that book's being a huge success."

Paul laughed again.

"And Bobby's taking a six-month leave of absence. He's having a vacation in Australia."

"Oh, *Christ! Yes!*" Paul shot his fists in the air.

"We got these friends in Australia," said Karl.

Candy nodded.

" 'Friends'?" Paul grinned like the very devil.

Karl tipped his head. "Like good friends. Like friends'll do whatever we tell 'em to do. You know, like escort him to the Sydney Opera House, escort him to the Outback. Whatever works for them."

Paul went on laughing. These two guys were a real tonic. "So who takes over at Mackenzie-Haack?"

"Old Clive. Old Clive surprised us both. He actually went up against Bobby Mackenzie and that could be a real career cooler, right?"

"That's the truth."

Karl got up, stretched; Candy followed suit.

"We gotta be goin'," said Candy.

"Yeah. Well, as long as Ned's okay, we don't have a beef with you, Paul. It's been very interesting, this talk."

Remembering his book, Candy pulled it away from the chair and held it out. "Now, will you sign?"

"My pleasure." Paul got a pen from an old cup and signed the book. "There." He snapped it shut.

Paul walked them to the door where they shook hands.

"A very interesting conversation," said Candy.

Karl said, "Ditto that. Only listen, Paul, you just got to stop fucking around with other people's lives. You're a controlling son of a bitch, you know that?"

Paul blushed. He knew it.

They were walking down the hall when Karl turned and asked, "You don't happen to know some guy connected with Ned named Patrick?"

Paul shook his head.

"Huh. Just a thought."

They said good-bye again.

FORTY-SEVEN

In the publishing industry, news travels fast. Very fast. Especially bad news, which is the good news of the publishing industry. Night, day, dusk, dawn—makes no difference. It's on the street.

When Bobby Mackenzie heard, a couple of hours after Ned had been hit and a couple of hours before any word was given out on his condition, that Ned Isaly was the victim of a *hit-and-run! Sweet Jesus!* he grabbed his ticket to Australia, ordered a car be sent round, wrote a note to his wife (which he considerately pinned to his pillow) in which he told her he was trying to sign up a writer in Australia and he had to get there fast. "Good-bye. Don't let anyone into the wine cellar."

FORTY-EIGHT

What a peculiar question to end up with. Patrick? Paul stood in the open doorway, gnawing at a small callus near his thumbnail and thought about it after they left.

He closed the door and went back to his office and sat slumped in his chair as ashamed of himself as he had ever been in his life. Poor Ned Isaly, for God's sakes. He didn't believe the accident had been anything but your average New York City hit-and-run, but, still . . . He had signed the contract; Candy and Karl hadn't done it; Arthur certainly hadn't done it—anyway, those three were at the scene. And God knows Bobby Mackenzie hadn't been involved. Not only was there no reason now to get Ned out of the way, but also Bobby was scared shitless of the pair he had so insouciantly hired himself.

What a jerk.

What a business.

"What's a casque?"

Paul thought he had asked this in his mind until he turned around and saw Hannah, materialized in the office doorway, wearing her nightgown and clutching one of her pages. How long had she stood there, ghosting around?

"Honey, how long have you been there? What are you doing out of bed? Where—" He stopped when he realized he was asking one question after another and not waiting for the answer. "A casque? Isn't that a headpiece? Like in armor?"

"I don't know. That's why I was asking. I need a weapon to put in the hunted gardens for the Dragonnier. I think he's having a lot of trouble."

"Well, a sword would do. But does he need one?"

The Hunted Gardens evolved at some point—and Paul assumed at the same point as the manuscript did for just about every novel: that is, the point of clammy fear that it wasn't any good, that it wasn't working, and even if it was, the writer couldn't think of one damned more thing to say—into becoming the near-exclusive domain of the Dragonnier, a character whose main hold on life (and fame and a story) was his ability to get along with dragons. So he wasn't a dragon slayer, but a dragon tamer, or something like that.

He held his arms out and Hannah whisked across the room to sit in his lap.

Paul said, "I wonder if maybe you're making your story kind of melodramatic because you think this garden hunting isn't exciting enough to hold your reader's attention."

Her little forehead creased into furrows. "Mela-what?"

"Dramatic." As she channeled her anxiety into rolling and rerolling the page she held, he said, "It's what's called unearned emotion."

Oh, yes, that cleared the whole thing up, her squiggly little eyebrows told him.

"You're afraid that maybe people won't want to read any more about your gardens—"

"No, I'm not. I just think they'll want to read more about the Dragonnier. And, anyway, I didn't stop writing about the hunted gardens. I can't because that's where the Dragonnier lives. And the dragons are. See, they've always been there. I just haven't told anyone until lately." Her sly look said *Gotcha!*

Lord knows he had to give her credit for pulling that particular rabbit out of the hat. Still, as a reader, he felt a bit cheated. "But, listen, you've gone for ninety-some chapters without ever mentioning the dragons. I mean, do you think that's playing fair?"

"They were hidden, see. It's not my fault if they were hiding. The Dragonnier should have said."

"Said what?"

"That the *dra*-gons were there." She pinched up the sleeve of his shirt and started to hum.

"But, Hannah, it's your story so it's *your* responsibility."

"Maybe we should send her to Bread Loaf this summer."

Molly's voice. Molly stood in the doorway, leaning slightly against the doorjamb, one foot tucked over the other and her arms folded across her breasts. "Bread Loaf might help. She'd probably get some editorial advice, have an opportunity to get a lot of feedback, maybe snag an agent."

Hannah slipped off his lap and went to swing on her mother's hand.

"I didn't hear you come in, Moll. I was only trying to help Hannah with her story."

Molly rolled her eyes. "Some dads read stories to their little girls; other dads tell their little girls how the story should have been written in the first place. Cinderella, your feets' too big, that kind of thing."

Hannah laughed and ran down the hall.

Molly said, "Listen, I like your friends."

Paul felt a little frisson of anxiety. "Friends? What friends?"

"The ones downstairs. In the lobby. They said they were really happy to meet me and that I should tell Paul—that's you—to keep out of other people's business. They said it wasn't healthy to mess around." She shifted to the other side of the door, leaning again. "I really liked that 'healthy' bit. We chatted for some time about your book. What have you been up to?"

Paul clamped his hands flat against his chest. "Who, me? Nothing. Absolutely nothing!"

"Yes, you have. I know you." She turned and walked down the hall. She turned back and blew him a kiss.

Ah, Molly!

Could he really leave her in thirty seconds flat if he spotted the heat around the corner? Paul grinned.

Maybe not.

After Molly left, Paul looked at the telephone on his desk. He thought for a moment, and then picked it up and punched in the number. At the other end, a voice floating on a sea of calm said, "The Old Hotel, good evening."

"I wanted to make a reservation. Tomorrow night?"

"For how many, sir?"

"Two, my wife and me." He didn't know why he was moved to tell the Hotel's personnel who the other person was; it could as easily be "my girlfriend/mistress/trainer." Was it the Old Hotel's business? He thought perhaps it might be.

"If you'll wait a moment, sir, until I check."

Paul closed his eyes. It was at this point the Old Hotel would say, Sorry.

"Your name?"

"Giverney. Paul." No, it was at *this* point. He squeezed his eyes shut, waiting for rejection: "*Sorry, Mr. Giverney, but we're fully booked until Christmas/New Year's Day/Easter, whatever.*"

"Yes, sir. Would nine o'clock be too late?"

What was going on? He shook the receiver as if to dislodge this false response, this clear lie.

"Uh, yes. Absolutely. Nine o'clock."

The voice thanked him, told him the Old Hotel would look forward to seeing him.

Slowly, Paul replaced the receiver.

Why? Why was he all of a sudden on the Old Hotel's anointed list?

"Molly! Come in here for a minute, will you?"

In a little while, Molly appeared in her old, ratty-looking dressing gown. "What's up?"

"You're not going to believe this."

"It pertains to you? Try me."

Paul thought maybe it was Molly they were really admitting. But he'd tried to make reservations for the two of them before and failed. He told her about the Old Hotel. "We're in! Tomorrow night!"

Molly just gave him a patient shake of her pillow-tousled head, turned, and waved his news away. "Oh, that old place."

He stared after her, mouth open. Then he called after her, "'That old *place*'? What? What?"

Her voice floated back to him. "They're all crazy there. 'Nighty-night."

Paul sat, staring through his open door down the hall where she'd gone. Then he yelled, "They are not!" And he wondered why he didn't want to believe they were all crazy at the Old Hotel. The idea disturbed him greatly. He mumbled something even he didn't get.

Then Paul swiveled around and looked at his computer screen

with the haunted house screen saver. He also had an old Royal portable that he used to type up rough copy because he liked the sound of the keys and because he felt as if he were working harder and more like a real writer. When he made a mistake he would *X* it out. The page would eventually look like nothing but cross-hatching.

There was a file on casters in which he kept manuscripts and parts of manuscripts. He rolled it over and pulled from it the thick copy of the novel he'd written before *Don't Go There*. This was *Half a Life* and it had sold upward of two million copies. What had been returned to him was the original manuscript he had given to Queeg and Hyde. It had been returned some time after the book had been published, which was standard practice. What he wanted to look at now was the note that had come with it. Here it was, clipped to the manuscript. Paul recognized the handwriting—he had seen it often enough—of that officious little squirt, DeeDee Sunup, who had pompously written:

> Dear Paul,
> We are herewith returning the foul matter of *Half a Life*.

The first time he had seen this phrase he had laughed until he choked (and Hannah had run in to pound him on the back). But DeeDee Sunup (and others like her) failed to see any sort of humor, irony, or even anything cabalistic in the phrase. "Foul matter": this was what publishers called all of those original manuscripts, frozen in time, before they had been blue-penciled, red-penciled, edited, reedited, chicken pecked to death. This was the first look at the book, the manuscript out of which they'd tried to suck the marrow, drain the blood, leach the life, while they hammered the book into fame or obscurity, it hardly mattered which.

What had been returned to him was his foul matter. The gunk,

the sludge, the muck that preceded all the placement, the sales figures, the ads, the reviews. Yet the original had been the writer's best
effort, the work he was willing to send out into the world and be
judged by.

Paul grinned his devilish grin and fed a sheet of paper into the
old Royal. He typed:

```
                F O U L   M A T T E R


                       by

                Paul Giverney
```

Damned book would write itself.